Play It Safe

Kristen Ashley

PLAY IT *Safe*

A ROMANCE NOVEL BY

KRISTEN ASHLEY

NEW YORK TIMES BESTSELLING AUTHOR

Cover Image: Pixel Mischief Design

Acknowledgments

A shout out to my Facebook posse for kicking in yet again when I was stuck. Lindsey Tong came up with the idea for the bar name "The Alibi," and I loved it so I used it. But my crew on FB shouted out so many ideas, I have a huge file and I'll never have to worry about naming a bar again. Thanks, you guys. You don't know how many times I go on there and you make me giggle or say things that keep me going. You're awesome!

Another big thank you to my dear, beloved friend, Jody Briles, who gave me the names Shim and Ronan. Through our friendship over the years, Jody has given a lot...it's just this time she gave me a couple kickass names.

Love you, Jody.

And last, for the original cover of this book (long since retired), the beautiful cover photo of gorgeous wild ponies was taken on the Crow Indian Reservation in Montana by my wonderful friend, Joe Vedovati. Joe has been my friend for a long time. He has made me laugh. He has no problems telling me I mean something to him. He is an accomplished photographer and he let me use his image, an image that part-inspired the book you're about to read, for free. And he calls me dollface.

As he was so kind to do that, and he was mentioned in the original acknowledgements because he was, even though that photo is no longer in use, the acknowledgement doesn't fade away.

Love you, Joe and *thank you.*

Chapter 1

No Connections. Play It Safe

It was time to get back to the hotel, I knew it.

But I didn't want to go.

Because he was still sitting at the bar, drinking beer from a bottle, chatting and smiling at the bartender, nice, friendly. She was very pretty but older than him, five years, maybe ten. They knew each other, they liked each other, both well. But not like that. Just friends. Maybe good friends. He came in a lot or in this small town they ran into each other a lot.

Whatever.

It was just friends.

Which was good.

Not that I was going to do anything about it. I couldn't.

No connections.

Play it safe.

Still, if I could connect, if I could let go, if I could take a risk, I'd do it with him. In all my wandering, all I'd seen, all the people I'd met, he would be the one I'd smile at and do it without a guard up.

He'd be the one I'd want to smile back at me.

Time to go.

I sucked back the last of my beer, set it on the table in front of me, shrugged on my jacket, buttoned it up and wound my scarf around my neck. Then I pulled the long strap of my bag over my head, hooking it around my neck so it slanted across the front of me. Then, eyes to the door, I slid out of the booth and left.

I didn't look at him.

Couldn't.

So out I went without even a glance.

The cold hit me like a slap. It was late January. We should be in the south. What we were doing up here, I didn't know. But Casey led and I followed. That was always the way.

Always.

Half a block down, cross the street, two blocks up, I went through the parking lot to the cement walkway, then down to our door.

I stopped at it and stared.

I didn't need the Do Not Disturb sign to tell me not to disturb. I heard the giggling moans, the chuckling grunts.

Hells bells.

I sighed, lifted my hand and looked at my wrist.

It was eleven oh two. Nothing open in this burg except that bar.

And he was there.

I couldn't go back.

It was also cold.

I sucked in breath, lifted a fist and pounded on the door.

The giggling, moaning, grunting and chuckling stopped abruptly and I shouted, "Fifteen minutes to wrap it up!"

Then I turned and walked through the parking lot, checked both ways even though in this tiny town at this hour, traffic was light as in, non-existent.

Still, I hadn't survived my life to get run over on a deserted road in a nowhere town at twenty-two years old.

I crossed the street and headed into the park I'd spied there. Even in this weather, I'd noticed kids playing in the playground, folks walking their dogs, men jogging, women jog-walking. Active community. Safe community.

If I let myself think about it, I knew I'd like it. It would intrigue me. It would make me feel things I couldn't feel, want things I couldn't want.

So I didn't think about it.

I headed to the playground, sat down in a swing, wrapped my hands around the cold chains and started swinging.

I needed gloves.

We didn't have the money and I didn't spend a lot of time outside. So I didn't really *need* them except right now.

So no gloves.

I was lucky I had a scarf.

I kicked my feet out then shoved them back and again until I was swinging, not high, just back and forth, gentle, soothing. Something to keep my mind on while I waited. Something to keep my mind off other stuff while I waited.

Surprisingly, I heard the rattle of a car and not a good one. My eyes went down the street and I saw a beat-up pickup truck heading my way. It kept going. Streetlights showed it was light blue. Lots of rust. Not just old, *old*. It looked it and it sounded it. I kept swinging as it passed right on by.

I stopped watching and kept swinging.

Then, my heart beating a little faster, I kept swinging as it came back in my eyesight, this time reversing.

Not good.

It stopped opposite the park, opposite me and it idled.

I counted. One, two, three...I got to twelve and it shut down, the lights going out.

Really not good.

I heard the creaking, loud squeak of a door that seriously needed some WD-40 then the same sound ending with a slam.

But I saw him over the roof of the car and my heart beat even faster. I kept swinging slow and gentle as the man from the bar rounded the hood of his truck and walked toward me.

Faded jeans. Leather jacket. Scarf. Hands shoved in the pockets of his leather jacket. But I knew he had gloves.

I saw all that hours earlier when he walked into the bar. Scarf and gloves said he had someone who cared about him or he worked outside. Men like him didn't buy scarves, women bought them for them. The leather jacket was a nice one, expensive, but it wasn't new. It hung down over his hips, had flannel lining I'd noticed when he swung it off in the bar. It was beat up but not worn out. Fit him well.

Too well.

Like the jeans.

He headed my way, and in the dark without streetlights close I couldn't see his eyes on me.

I could feel them.

I dropped my feet and my heels thudded into the frozen dirt mixed with packed snow under them. My body kept swaying and my feet brought me to a halt about a half a second before he came to a halt six feet away.

"Park's closed at nine."

That wasn't good. Not that I was in the park well past closing hours but that he had a nice voice, deep, resonant, rich. It was attractive. Very much so.

Also not good.

My guess, he was in his twenties, not as young as me but not much older. Still, his voice and manner—both held authority, confidence. Lots of it. More than his age would give him in normal circumstances. Men that age, they were still boys.

Unless life made them men.

"Just waiting for the all clear," I told him quietly. "I won't be here long."

"It's after eleven, it's dark, it's cold and there's no one around. Not safe for a woman to be sittin', swingin' in a park all alone. Wherever you need to get, you need to get there," he told me.

Okay, well, that was interesting. He wasn't a local who didn't like a stranger breaking the rules in his town. He was a man who didn't like to see a woman alone in a relatively safe, nevertheless-there-was-always-danger-anywhere situation.

And he acted on it.

And he did it late on a cold, dark, winter night.

That said a lot about him.

What he'd say next said more.

"Walk you where you need to go," he offered.

"I'm staying at the hotel. I can see my door. Thanks but I'm good."

His torso twisted and he looked to the hotel.

My eyes didn't leave him.

He was tall. He was lean. His shoulders were broad and they were that even without the leather jacket. Very long legs. Power in them. Power in his shoulders. Power in his veined hands. Power in his wide chest. I'd seen it all across the bar. Even at his age, he was not a man you messed with. This was half to do with the way he held himself, the way he moved. The other half had to do with how he was built. He had a beautiful frame, silhouetted now in the streetlamps. But it was unmistakable that he knew what he could do with it. I figured he was fast. I figured he was strong. I figured he was smart.

And I was never wrong, so what I figured I knew to be true.

Only a stupid man would underestimate this man, regardless of his age.

He turned back to me and asked, "Reason you can't get in?"

"My uh...friend is enjoying himself. I gave him fifteen minutes. Reckon he's got about five left."

He made no response and his silence lasted awhile. Then he lifted his chin and made to move back.

"Have a good night," he muttered, turned and walked back through the park.

I shouldn't have watched, I shouldn't have.

But I did.

I couldn't tear my eyes away.

I liked the way he moved. Just walking. I liked it.

A lot.

Too much.

So I watched him move, round the hood of his beat-up, light blue, rusted-out pickup. And I watched him swing in. And I watched him start it up. Then I watched him rattle away.

I closed my eyes tight, sucked in a breath and wished, not for the first time, but with a burn I'd never felt before that hurt and it hurt badly, that I didn't have to play it safe.

Then I opened my eyes, looked at my watch, pushed off the swing and headed to the hotel.

Chapter 2

I Would Love That

T*hirty-four hours later...*

I LOOKED out the window of the diner trying not to see what I saw.

But I saw it.

I'd been to a lot of towns in a lot of states and I'd even seen this.

County seat but the county seat of a sleepy county. Courthouse square. A red brick and ivory mortar and stone courthouse-slash-police department smack in the middle. Attractive. Sweeping staircases up two sides with big urns at the bottoms of the balustrades that, no doubt, would be filled with flowers if it wasn't January. Down staircases at the two other sides that didn't attract attention. This was because lockup was down there. Offices and courtrooms on the upper three floors. Big American flag flying from a flagpole at the top.

The square had large, what would be green patches of undoubtedly well-tended grass in spring and summer but it was now covered in snow. Huge trees that had been there decades, maybe even longer, that were now barren but in fertile months would throw a lot of shade. Benches for folks to sit on. Even bigger but matching urns that were now empty but in summer months would be filled with flowers dotted around. A cross of sidewalks leading to the four sides of the courthouse, crisscrosses too, all now cleared of snow in a way that it almost looked like someone had edged it right up to the turf, the removal was so precise. Curlicue wrought iron, handsome street-lamps that had been cleared of their Christmas decorations.

This town didn't have Christmas decorations in late January. This town took care of itself. The Christmas decorations went up in a town lighting ceremony that everyone showed up at on the day after Thanksgiving then were quietly taken down and stowed away as soon as possible after New Year's. I had been there three days, it was late January so I did not know this for a fact. But still, I knew it for a fact.

My eyes moved to the buildings around the square. Most of them, like the one the diner was in, were two storied red brick. Some had creamy mortar plates close to the top stamped with dates. One said 1899, which surprised me. That was old especially for here. Another said 1907. Shops, restaurants and sandwich places on the bottom floors, offices with signs in their windows (mostly attorneys and bail bondsmen) on the top.

One whole side, though, was taken up by a large department store. The stamp at the top of that building declared it was built in 1912. How the hell that thing survived, I would never know seeing as it was clearly locally owned and had not been gobbled up by a conglomerate. That said a lot about the town. If they needed whatever that store sold, they didn't go to some other store where they could probably get it for less. They took care of their own. That department store had probably been there and owned by the same family for four, five generations, maybe all the way back to 1912. And the town wasn't letting it go anywhere.

Same with the butcher across the square from the diner. No town had a butcher anymore. That meat probably cost twice as much as grocery store meat and even if it was probably better meat than you could buy in any grocery store, twice was always twice and money was always money. Still, it was there and it was bustling.

So were the sidewalks. Folks out and about, smiling, calling greetings.

The whole place might be creepy if a third of a block of the two-story red brick buildings that were across the street behind the courthouse hadn't been torn down. In their place was a modern (for the time, I was guessing at least two decades ago), glass fronted, somewhat glitzy (now tarnished with age, it was dated and not in a good way, it would need at least another decade or two to come back into retro style) restaurant. Someone had sway with the city council to build that monstrosity. It marked the space, was totally out of place and didn't look good. Someone thought their shit didn't stink, thought it was cool then and would be cool forever. They were wrong. Still, its presence said this place wasn't perfection. This place wasn't a creepy, weird town lost in time that Casey and I somehow found ourselves in and we'd never get out because we'd eventually either be captured, deprogrammed and reprogrammed as perfect, small town dwellers. Me in my apron, Casey bringing home the bacon in a manly way. Or we'd be eaten by or become zombies.

So that restaurant was good.

To me, the blight of that restaurant made me like this town even more.

To me, that restaurant made the town with the unbelievably cool name of Mustang, imperfect perfection.

"Hey."

At this word said in a man's deep voice, I blinked at the window and turned my head.

Then I froze.

This was because opposite me in the booth sat the man from the bar, the man from that night, the man from the playground.

How did my guard go down so much I didn't sense him even approach much less make it so his behind was sitting in the booth across from me, his eyes on me, his attractive hand unwinding his scarf?

"Uh...hey," I replied quietly.

This was not good.

It was sunny. The diner had big, plate-glass windows and my booth was right up next to one. It was not a darkened bar or an even more darkened playground.

And he was not attractive.

He was beautiful.

His hair wasn't dark brown, I was shocked to see. It was actually blond but a blond I'd never seen before. Very dark blond with a hint of red burnish that was nowhere near making him a redhead, just enriching the color of his thick, longish hair so it wasn't just fantastic, it was astonishing.

His bone structure wasn't strong, defined and interesting. It was striking.

And I could see the color of his eyes surrounded by thick, long, dark lashes with the same rusty burnish as his hair.

They were a deep, dark blue.

And as he unveiled his throat, I saw its corded, supremely masculine length and my palms got sweaty.

Hells bells.

I pulled it together.

"Can I help you?" I asked.

He opened his mouth to speak as he dropped the scarf next to him on the seat but I heard shouted, "Gray! Breakfast or coffee?"

He turned his head and my eyes followed to see my waitress across the way. She was wearing faded jeans that were too tight, definitely bought before she'd put on the extra fifteen pounds she wore and that extra fifteen had been added to an extra thirty. Same with her sweater. An apron was tied around her disappearing waist and it did her no favors, unfortunately.

"Had breakfast, Ang. Coffee," he called back then turned to me.

Finishing shrugging off his jacket, he swung it out from behind him and dropped it on his scarf. "I'm Gray," he announced as he settled.

"Hi, Gray," I replied then repeated, "Can I help you?"

He grinned and he really shouldn't have done that. He really shouldn't have.

Because he had a dimple in his left cheek, it made him go from strikingly handsome to strikingly handsome with a hint of cute thrown in for good measure. And if that wasn't enough, it brought my attention to his lips, which I did not know how but I hadn't noticed until then were full and inviting.

My mouth got dry.

"I'm Gray," he repeated. I tore my eyes from his now moving, beautiful lips to his equally beautiful eyes and he went on, "You are?"

I pulled it together again.

"I'm wondering how I can help you."

His eyes went funny, assessing, watchful as his head tipped slightly to the side.

Then he untipped his head and noted, "You're still in town."

I looked down at myself then at him and agreed, "Yep."

He grinned again.

Hells bells!

"You get warm the other night?" he asked.

"Yep," I repeated.

"Good," he muttered and Ang, our waitress, hit the table with a mug of coffee for Gray.

We both looked up at her. She was looking at Gray.

"How's Mirry?" she asked.

"She's good," Gray answered on another dimpled smile.

Jeez oh Pete, that smile.

I had to get out of there.

"Been a while since I been out to see her. She want some company?" Ang asked Gray.

"Always," Gray answered.

"Can she take a visit from the brood?" Ang went on and Gray's smile got bigger.

Yep. Oh yes. I had to get the heck out of there.

"You know she can, Ang," he replied.

"All right then, I'll pack up my monsters and swing by this afternoon after school," Ang declared, dipped her head at Gray, looked at me, gave me a head to chest then she looked back at Gray. Her head tilted to the side, she grinned a knowing grin then waddled (it had to be said, it was definitely a waddle) away.

Gray's fantastic blue eyes came back to me.

"That's Ang," he told me.

"Got that," I murmured.

He grinned again.

God. I had to *get out of there.*

"She's got one boy, three girls, the boy..." he shook his head, still grinning. "Not sure which way that kid's gonna swing but I had to guess, I reckon my guess would be accurate. The girls, all tomboys. It's wild. Never seen anything like it. They're more boy than most boys and her boy is more girl than *any* girl."

"That's fascinating," I stated. It was and more, it felt good him sharing that with me. I didn't know why. It could be the casual way he did it, like we were having a conversation, like we were getting to know each other, like this would be one of many such situations we would find ourselves in, together, just like we were then. Conversing. Sharing. Getting to know each other until we knew each other. Therefore I had to shut it down. "But you still haven't answered my question."

His smile faded and his eyes went watchful again. He also didn't speak.

He studied me for a while as I assessed my options, deciding to get some money out, throw it on the table in order to pay for my already-eaten-and-plate-cleared breakfast and mostly-drunk-not-cleared third cup of coffee, get my stuff, say a farewell that wasn't rude but was final and get the heck out of there.

Before I could put this plan into action Gray spoke again.

"Man you're with, not old enough to be your dad, looks enough like you, gotta be kin. He your brother?"

That had my attention.

When had he seen Casey?

I didn't ask this question.

Instead I made a point.

"You the sheriff or something?"

He shook his head, his eyes never leaving mine.

"Then can't say I'm real comfortable with that kind of attention," I told him.

"Bet not," he replied quietly.

"I—" I started but stopped when he leaned in.

"Can't say I wanna say this but I'm gonna say it. You're not here to look into the waitressing gig at Jenkins, you and your guy best be moving on."

Not good.

"Sorry?" I asked even more quietly than he was speaking.

"Don't know the game, don't care, don't 'spect you'll share since you won't even tell me your name. Do know what he's doin' and I'm not the only one. Don't know when he calls you in to do your part. What I'll tell you is, you move forward on whatever mark he thinks he's found, you will find trouble. They're expecting it. They've clocked him. You need to move on."

I was right. Not good.

Casey had been made. And Gray, knowing I was laying low, made me.

Gray was right. Time for us to move on.

I was about to do that when he kept talking.

"That said, Jenkins's girls get good tips. Food is top-notch, top dollar, always has been. Tips are big. Shelly, head waitress there, pulled down nearly forty grand last year. Nothin' to sneeze at. She gets extra due to hirin' and trainin' but all the girls there been there awhile, they like it. It's only that Diane left 'cause her man got that job in Oklahoma so she had to go. Be a good place to be, you're lookin' for that kind of place."

I stared at him and now my mouth *and* throat were dry. Not because he was handsome and all the other things he was. Just because he was sitting there calmly offering me a dream.

I was probably the only girl in the world who wanted to be a waitress.

And it wasn't being the waitress I wanted to be.

But that would work for me.

In this town.

With him in it.

Roots.

Connections.

Wake up every day and know where you are and go to bed every night knowing you'll wake up that way.

I would love that.

And just thinking about it made me want to cry.

So I had to get the heck out of there.

I set about doing that, getting money and suiting up against the cold while muttering, "Appreciated, Gray. Your time. Your honesty."

I didn't button my jacket or wrap my scarf around, barely had my wallet back in my purse as I slid out of the booth, scarf in hand, bag scrunched with it, still shrugging on one side of my coat.

But I gave it to myself, one last thing. Foolish. But I wanted it. Badly. And I didn't get anything I wanted so I took it.

I looked back in his beautiful eyes surrounded by his striking face, his fantastic lips, his thick, unusual hair all on top of broad shoulders and a wide chest covered in a Western-style denim shirt with pearl snap buttons, and I whispered, "Take care."

Then I got the heck out of there.

Chapter 3

I Owed Him Everything

F*ifteen minutes later...*

"That works for me," Casey stated and I stared.

"What?" I asked.

He grinned and I knew that grin.

My brother.

Darn.

"Had a hot one the other night, gonna take another dip in that. Good to have the time and not have to be on the job."

I told him about what Gray told me, he was made, Gray made me. The situation was hot. We couldn't proceed.

We had to get out of there.

"Casey, I don't think I have to remind you but we have five hundred twelve dollars and thirteen cents. We gotta get on the road."

His grin didn't fade even a little.

"Just one night," he replied.

I shook my head. "No, we gotta go."

"Ivey," his voice turned cajoling as he moved towards me, "we got a night."

"We don't. We have five hundred twelve dollars and thirteen cents without a play to make. We gotta get on the road, find a new burg, find a new payday. That takes time. We have a week before we got nothing."

"Honey," definitely cajoling, the grin getting bigger, "it's only one night."

"One night means one more night's hotel stay and one day we're not on the road, a day we lose. We don't have a night."

Casey stepped back and his face got hard.

This was not good either.

My life was filled with not good. It happened a lot. And a lot of when it happened was when Casey got this way.

"Jesus, Ivey, what the fuck? It's just one night!" he clipped loudly.

"Casey—"

"No," he shook his head. "Fuck that. I liked her. She made me laugh. Spendin' time with you, love you, sis, you know it." He thumped his chest. "Bottom of my heart, *you know it*." He said the last three words leaning in, emphasis made in his tone, his body, his face. Emphasis he made often. "But you aren't about shits and grins, honey. She made me laugh. I had fun. I don't get that a lot. I'm not askin' for a week, I'm askin' for one night. The least you could give me."

Over the last ten years there were a lot of, "the least I could give Casey."

And just like then, I gave them.

"One night."

He wasn't done being angry.

"Jesus," he muttered, moving away. "Why you make me jump through these hoops..." he trailed off and I closed my eyes.

I did it because I learned a long time ago. I kept our bank. I paid attention. I kept us on target. Casey wasn't good at that.

Casey wasn't good at a lot of things.

Except taking care of me.

In his way.

And I knew exactly how far five hundred twelve dollars and thirteen cents would get us in food, gas and hotels.

We had a week.

We didn't have a day to blow.

But I'd blow it for Casey. I owed him that. I owed him everything.

"Tonight, need you to make yourself scarce," he declared, lifting the phone out of its cradle.

Oh no.

I was giving him his night, he didn't get the room.

"No way," I replied, turning to face him fully.

His still angry eyes came to me. "What?"

"No way," I said. "You had the room last night. Not again. I was sitting in a bar for three hours and then I was out in the cold. You need a visit with your hot one, you get creative but I get the room."

He put the phone back in the cradle and returned, "I can hardly bang her in the car. She's a class piece."

Right. She was a class piece.

I didn't believe that for a second.

My brother nailed his fair share of pieces and none of them had been class.

"Then, like I said, get creative," I replied.

"That is uncool," he bit out.

"What?" I asked. "We should not be staying an extra day and you know it. You want to have a little fun, laugh a little, enjoy her company, you got it. I gave in. We can't afford it but it's yours. You also got the hotel room last night. Tonight, it's mine. I know you can be creative, Casey. So be creative."

He scowled at me.

I let him.

I gave in a lot, most of the time I let him walk all over me. I owed him so I gave it to him.

But I wasn't going to sit in that bar, not tonight, not when Gray could walk in. A Gray who knew what Casey was, what I was. No way. No stinking way.

Casey waited, hoping I'd melt. I did this a lot so he had a lot of hope.

I held his scowl and didn't melt.

"Fuck," he hissed, snatched the hotel phone out of the receiver, dug into his back pocket and took out a wisp of paper. Then he looked at it and started punching buttons.

"I'll give you a second to talk to your girl," I muttered and his eyes cut to me.

"Thanks, big of you," he said sarcastically.

I sighed.

His eyes went to his feet and his face split in a grin. "Hey beautiful, it's Casey," he said into the phone.

I got out of there.

Chapter 4

Never Been Kissed

"Kitchen still open?" I asked the bartender.

I was back at the bar. It was a stupid place to be. It was the last place I should be. The last place I wanted to be. But there I was.

And I knew why.

Because I was lying to myself.

It wasn't the last place I wanted to be. It was the only place I knew he might be.

Stupid.

She was the same bartender. Lots of thick, dark hair that flowed over her shoulders and down her back, nearly as long as mine. Even though it was January, she was wearing a skintight tank and skintight jeans. Better tips that way, I'd guess. She was long and strangely very trim, no meat on her yet she had large breasts. They didn't appear fake though obviously I wouldn't know. Either someone did a phenomenal job or God liked her a whole lot.

I figured God liked her a whole lot. Up close and closely inspecting, she wasn't five years older than Gray, seven to ten years older than me. She was ten years older than Gray but wore it well. Didn't hide it well. Wore it well.

Comfortable in her skin. Comfortable in her place.

She either owned the bar or was sleeping with the person who owned it. It was her space and she liked to be there.

"Five minutes, hon," she told me on a genuine welcoming grin. "You're in luck."

I nodded and grinned back, mine probably not genuine or welcoming but I wanted it to be.

"Then can I have a cold one, bottle, and whatever is easiest for them seeing as I'm not picky and they'll be closing the kitchen after making it?"

Her grin turned to a smile. "Pulled pork sandwich," she replied. "I don't know whether it's easiest or not but you can't leave Mustang without eating one of The Rambler's pulled pork sandwiches. And we got those curly fries, can't be beat."

My grin got bigger too and I nodded again. "Sounds perfect."

She tipped her head to the side, "No preference, like last night?"

Yep. Her tips were huge. She paid attention. It was midweek but there were two bars in this burg and only this one in walking distance or close to the courthouse square and residential areas, so I had no doubt there were nights and even days when it got busy. In fact it was *on* the courthouse square. The other bar was where Casey and I were going to do our business. Still in the town limits but removed. When we'd made our first pass, I'd told Casey I was not going to work in The Rambler. The other bar was seedier, not as welcoming, not nearly as nice and the people in it were the same way. I didn't mind taking that money. Anyone who came into The Rambler, though, different story.

But she remembered me from last night even if there weren't a load of folks in. It was a nice thing to do, remembering me, letting me know it.

She was nice.

She liked Gray.

Gray liked her.

Her smiles were genuine.

And again I found myself wishing my life was different.

"No preference," I confirmed. "Whatever beer is closest at hand."

"Wish all my customers were like you," she said through her perpetual grin.

But she didn't. She didn't know me. If she knew me, she'd probably kick me out.

She pulled out a Corona, popped the top and placed it in front of me. "I'll go put in your order. Lucky for you, it's late, they won't mess around."

I nodded yet again then muttered, "Thanks."

She took off to the middle of the bar and then through some swinging half doors to the kitchen.

My eyes slid around the room.

It was five to nine. Our hotel room had cable but not many channels. I didn't want to be bored but I was.

Casey and I traveled light. I'd read the three books I kept with me at least a dozen times. We didn't have money for me to hit the bookstore I saw on the square and buy another one. Casey had stormed out in a huff after his call and told me not to wait up for him. I suspected this meant he wouldn't be home until dawn. This also meant I got the first shift on driving the next day.

This was not unusual.

I should have stayed in, stayed warm, just stayed.

I didn't. I moved. I did stupid stuff like refreshing my makeup. Fluffing out my hair. Spritzing on perfume. Putting on my slightly nicer cowboy boots.

Then I did even more stupid stuff like walking down to the bar.

I didn't do stupid stuff. Careful. Played it safe. Always.

I didn't know what came over me.

But I was hungry and I was bored and I'd been in that hotel room all day and nothing was on TV and the bar was warm, I'd smelled and seen the food last night and it looked good.

And Gray could be there.

He wasn't.

I told myself I was relieved.

I wasn't.

The crowd was lighter tonight than last night. Dinner crowd (if there was one) gone, people home in front of their TVs.

Two men sitting at a square table, not across from each other, beside each other. Slumped over the table, shoulders curved in, bottles of beer on the table held between both hands. Their conversation was quiet and probably not interesting. They either had women at home they didn't want to be home with or, by the looks of them, they had no women and no prospects. Both heads of hair needed to be cut. Both sets of clothes needed to be tended better, cleaned more. Both bodies were not temples. The shoulders curved in meant they didn't want attention and/or they were trying to detract it away from the unhealthy bulk on their frames. They were there last night. They were probably pretty, trim, big-boobed, genuinely friendly, happy bartender's best customers. They were probably there every night mostly because they had nothing good to go home to and didn't want to be reminded of that fact.

My eyes moved and I saw her at the bar. I didn't want to see her, didn't want to look at her but I did. I'd seen a lot of her kind in my life, what with my profession. A shade too much makeup. Not put on well mainly because she was drunk when she put it on and this was because, in some way, she was always drunk. Decent clothes also not well-taken care of but she tried. She had a cardigan on now, a tight skirt. Later that cardigan would come off, she'd show skin. She'd try for attention or spend some time when she was relatively sober telling herself she wasn't going to go for it, wasn't going to do that to herself again. Then she'd get drunker and she'd want company. She'd want to talk. She'd want someone to convince her that her life wasn't in the toilet and swirling. She'd want someone, even if for an hour, to make her think she was pretty. She'd give him a blowjob for it. She'd do anything. She'd do more if he bought her a couple of drinks.

Barfly.

I saw that in my future like I had a crystal ball and the gift.

I saw it and it terrified me.

I looked down at my beer. Then I lifted it as if to extend a big middle finger to my life and my future and took a drag.

Happy bartender came back then leaned into me. "Order's in."

"Cool," I said quietly. "Thanks but sorry. They probably weren't happy getting a last minute order."

Her twinkling, hazel eyes left me and scanned the bar then came back to me. "Thursday. They haven't exactly been run off their feet and they need me to have the extra five bucks in my cash register."

Her cash register. As usual, I was right. She owned the joint.

"Right," I said and took a sip of beer.

Her brows drew slightly together. "You the new waitress at Jenkins?"

I shook my head and dropped my hand.

"The new teacher?" she went on.

I wish.

I didn't even have a high school diploma. I could hardly be a teacher.

"Nope," I answered.

"I'm Janie," she introduced herself, stretching out a hand I took and squeezed while she kept talking. "Good place to settle, Mustang." I let go of her hand and she dropped it but kept going. "Followed a man here, got shot of that man, he got shot of Mustang, thank God. I got the town in the breakup."

"So you came out on top," I noted and she grinned again.

"Definitely. Also got me a Mustang man. He's *way* better."

I again grinned back. I liked that for her.

"You got a man?" she asked curiously but still friendly. I was in her bar the night before, came in alone, left alone. The same tonight. I was young. She thought I was new in town. She probably wanted to fix me up with someone.

But I didn't have a man. I didn't have anything. I had three pairs of jeans, four t-shirts, five long-sleeved shirts, two of those being Henleys like what I had on now, a heavy sweater, a lighter cardigan, two tank tops, half a dozen pairs of undies, three bras, two nightshirts, seven pairs of socks, two pairs of cowboy boots, one pair of flip-flops, three pairs of shorts, a bikini, three books, a watch, a jean jacket, a scarf, seven bottles of perfume (my only splurge, I loved scent), some makeup, assorted cheap jewelry (and not much of it) and a brother.

That's all I had in this world. All of it.

I had nothing else except my life, my health and a special talent that made enough money to eat, keep ceilings of cheap hotel rooms over our heads and gas in Casey's tank.

I lifted the bottle to my lips, my eyes slid away and I murmured, "Nope."

"Pretty girl like you?" she asked and my eyes slid back to her as I took a sip.

I didn't answer.

I dropped the beer.

Then, as much as I wanted to talk to a pretty, friendly, happy bartender I knew the drill.

So she had to know it too.

I turned and dug in my purse at my side, pulled out a bill and slid it on the bar. The tip was decent, more than I could afford, as much as she deserved.

"Keep it. Gonna shoot some pool," I told her, not meeting her eyes. "Nice to meet you, Janie."

I grabbed my bag, jacket and scarf, slid off my stool, tagged the bottle of beer and wandered along the bar, through the scattering of tables and up two steps to the platform that held two pool tables, their felt red.

I liked the red. It gave a warm feel to the space.

I also liked that the tables were freebies. No sign that said you had to get the balls from the bar. No slot to insert coins or bills. Balls available. Cues on the wall. Proof Janie was friendly. She wanted people to come to her bar and stay awhile. It was just a bonus that when they did, they had to buy beer.

I set up the balls and chose my cue.

I'd broke and downed half a dozen of them by the time Janie came up the platform with my red, oval basket, its white waxed paper, my sandwich and fries with matching, plastic squeezy bottles of ketchup and mustard, red and yellow, these in one hand with fingers expertly wrapped around.

"You're good at that," she noted, putting my basket on the high table by the wall in between the two pool tables, three stools around.

"Thanks for delivering the food," I told the table, lined up, pulled my hand back and let fly.

Down went the six.

She hesitated, I felt it, then she moved.

I glanced and I knew she wouldn't see. I could watch for hours and people wouldn't know I was watching them. I'd perfected the art. I didn't, I wouldn't get paid.

Her face had changed. Slightly disappointed, slightly miffed. I wasn't as friendly as I'd seemed. It was a slow night and slow could be boring. But mostly, she liked friendly in her bar. She thought she'd like me. She was wrong. So she didn't like me in her bar.

But she'd take my money.

I shook it off. It hurt, always did, but I was used to it. Then I played pool alternately eating.

One could not say I'd had the finer things in life, any of them. Not once. But I'd been on the road long enough to eat in enough diners and bars to have some really good food.

That pulled pork sandwich, at bite one, hit my top five—maybe top three.

It wasn't excellent.

It was superb.

I finished it, finished my beer and went down to Janie to buy another one. She didn't make another attempt at friendly. This was when I knew she'd worked that bar awhile. She got me.

I bought it, no tab, and wandered back to the table.

I was executing a difficult shot with no problem when they showed, moving up the platform with their beers toward the other table.

My eyes slid through them and I read them in an instant.

They were Gray's age, maybe a bit older. They were the bullies in school. Athletes, undoubtedly. Not out of school long enough for their bodies to go to pot but at least for one of them, it was starting. He was likely married or had a steady girl he knew would never leave. The other two were still looking for "the one" or just the one who would get them off for a night. Therefore, they felt the need to keep in top form, wanted attention, wanted to get laid and often. Made an effort. Clothes, haircuts, bodies. It said it all.

But their eyes were eyes I never liked to see in anyone. Entitled. I couldn't say they weren't good-looking. They did not have the looks or manner of Gray, nowhere near. But they weren't hard to look at and knew it. They either came from money or made it. They went to college. They'd had the finer things in life. They were looking forward to having a life filled with finer things. Maybe not daily but they'd have their toys. They'd have their hot pieces. They'd marry one. She might go to pot after the second or third kid but she'd do her damnedest to keep herself together so she'd keep hold. She'd fail mostly because they'd cheat. They were used to having what they wanted and they'd take it. She'd know it then she'd lose it one way or another then lose them.

Divorce in their thirties or forties. Replacement hot piece who would also go to pot eventually either when they finally let go of the glory days or she did.

Kids bounced around.

Ending life in Arizona or Florida close to a golf course.

I didn't want them playing pool by me.

I'd been playing pool for ten years, lots of it. Boris Becker could play tennis and won Wimbledon at seventeen. I could play pool and wipe the floor with absolutely anyone by fifteen. It was a gift. I couldn't explain it. It wasn't even practice. I just saw the table, saw the shots, felt them, knew how to take them and did. I'd pocketed balls in shots world-class players couldn't execute.

And it was lucky I could. It kept my brother and me fed, clothed and in gas and hotels.

I was a pool hustler and that was likely all I'd ever be.

But not that night. That night, I had a good sandwich in my belly and a cue in my hand.

I was playing just for me.

I cleared the table, set it up then cleared it again, in my zone, ignoring them. Ignoring everybody.

But it wasn't a surprise when a male presence hit the end of the table as I was bending over it to break yet again and I heard, "Honey, you got a way with a stick."

My eyes went up but not my head. It was a pickup line and a rude one. A different kind of girl, he'd lead in another way. But he saw the scuffs on my boots. He saw the quality of my Henley. He knew my jeans were faded because I'd had them for years not because I bought them that way.

And he watched me play pool.

He thought I was the woman at the bar, younger, less rough around the edges, able to hide that I was used to being rode hard and put up wet.

I hated him on sight.

I looked back at the table, muttered, "Yup," and let fly.

Balls scattered, two went in pockets.

I searched for my shot, lined it up, took it and the ball went down.

I shifted, moving the opposite direction as him as he stated, "Hundred dollars says I can take you."

He was rude, entitled *and* cocky. He'd seen me play.

Stupid schmuck.

I opened my senses. It was getting later. There were more people in the bar. I felt them. There was a slight hum, not much. Not busy. But more populated. I'd garnered some attention. I felt eyes on me and not just the eyes of the four men at the table next to mine.

"Thanks, but no," I murmured, bent, lined up my shot, took the tap and it went in.

"Seems easy money for you," he noted.

He was right. And I needed it. Badly. A hundred dollars I could stretch a long way.

The answer was still no.

He had trouble written all over him. Trouble I didn't need.

"Just want a little private time, me and a table," I told the table, shifting around it, eyes to it, not giving him anything.

"Two hundred, one game," he pushed.

Darn.

Two hundred I could stretch a *long* way.

"Thanks, but no," I repeated, found the ball I wanted to take, leaned over the table, took it and it went down.

"Five hundred, best of three," he went on and my eyes went to him.

Five hundred was another week. Five hundred was a lot of money. Five hundred wasn't breathing easy but it was breathing easier.

I still wasn't going to buy his kind of trouble.

"Seriously, no offense, but I'm looking for a quiet night. Just me, a beer and the table."

He grinned. Short-cropped dark hair. Plaid shirt that wasn't bought at a western wear store but in the designer section of some posh department store, and not the one across from the front of the courthouse. Jeans not faded. Soft hands.

He worked a desk. Daddy was probably in the manager's office.

"All right, gorgeous. I'll buy your beers, five hundred, best of three."

I sighed. Then I stated the obvious, "I'm really good."

He grinned.

Totally cocky. His grin was nothing like Gray's. It didn't warm his eyes. He had no dimple to make his male beauty cute. I wanted to curl my lip but I didn't.

"You haven't seen me."

Double entendre.

He kept talking. "Got a pool table at home, have since I was a kid."

Well la-de-da.

And he wasn't done. "I'll give you a run for your money."

I studied him then my eyes went through his friends. Two were watching. One was bent over their pool table pretending he wasn't listening. Cocky Guy was the best looking of the lot, knew it and so did they. They were his sidekicks and probably had been since junior high.

Five hundred dollars.

We'd wasted three days with nothing to show for it.

It would be easy and it would double our bank.

Tomorrow, we'd be gone.

Hells bells.

"Best of three, you buy my beers," I agreed.

He smiled and his eyes got lazy. He thought he was in there. He wanted to watch me leaning over a table. Then he thought he was going to take my money. Then he thought he'd likely get me drunk then take *me* and he also thought I'd remember it happily for the rest of my life.

Idiot.

"Janie! My girl here needs a beer!" he shouted and I looked toward the bar.

Then my chest seized.

Gray was sitting on a stool at the bar on the side closest to the pool platform. Janie was at the bar opposite him but his back was to her, his boots to the rungs, his eyes on me.

Darn.

I turned my attention to the table.

"Got a name?" Mustang's resident playboy asked and my eyes went back to him to see he was pulling balls out of the pockets.

"Yup," I answered and said no more.

He waited and his face grew confused. He didn't get me and what he didn't get was that I seemed immune to his charms. He thought a girl like me took one look at a boy-man like him, his looks, his clothes, his obvious money and my dreams would soar even though he had no intention of giving me anything other than a couple of beers and a little attention.

Yep. Idiot.

I went to the chalk and put it to the tip of my cue.

He kept trying as he racked the balls, "Been in town long?"

"Nope," I answered, putting down the chalk.

He looked at me. "Staying in town long?"

"Nope," I repeated and Janie came up with my beer. I looked at her, took it, smiled and muttered, "Thanks."

"You bet," she replied then got closer in that way girls can do, that was to say without looking like she was, and she whispered, "Careful."

I caught her eyes as she moved away and slightly tipped up my chin.

I took a sip of my Corona.

Then I looked at Cocky Guy. "Flip to break?"

"Ladies first."

Total idiot.

"Seriously, flip to break," I said again.

He pulled the rack off the balls and grinned. "You go, honey."

I studied him and tried not to think of Gray watching me. But I knew he was. In fact, I knew everyone was.

As usual, I didn't disappoint. I broke and then approximately seven minutes later, I pocketed the eight ball and there were three extremely difficult shots where I knew Cocky Guy thought he had me but I made without hesitation.

I went back to my beer and took a sip, put it down on the shelf on the wall and stated, "This time, you break."

He wasn't looking cocky anymore. He was looking pissed. Not only did I clear the table in seven minutes, I didn't look at him once.

I moved around the table, pulling out the balls. He made me rack them this time. He moved to the head of the table, watched me and waited. I set them up, pulled the rack away and went to my beer.

He executed a solid break. Then he downed three balls. He wasn't bad but his options dried up and he flubbed the fourth ball.

I took a sip of beer, stepped to the table and in approximately seven minutes, cleared my stripes and pocketed the eight ball.

"Fucking hell," he muttered.

I lifted up, put the butt of my cue to the floor and said, "Best of three. Five hundred dollars."

His eyes came to me. "Best of five, a thousand."

Darn!

I shook my head. "That wasn't the deal."

"I barely got a shot in," he returned swiftly.

"You saw me play. I offered you the flip. That's the breaks." I lifted a hand, palm up. "Five hundred dollars."

His eyes narrowed and he accused, "You're a hustler."

He did not lie.

Still, I didn't hustle him.

"I'm good at pool, you knew it and you made the bet," I replied, hand still lifted. "Five hundred dollars."

"This is stupid," he hissed.

"Five hundred dollars, Bud." I heard from behind me. I twisted my neck to look over my shoulder and saw that Gray was three feet away at the top edge of the platform.

"Stay out of this, Cody," Cocky Guy warned.

"You made the bet, you lost, you pay. Five hundred dollars," Gray stated, taking another step forward on the platform.

Cocky Guy glared at him as his brethren closed ranks.

This was not good.

Hells bells.

I felt Gray close in on my back.

Hells bells!

"Bud, five hundred dollars. Now," he said low, his voice almost a growl, his patience clearly waning.

I wanted to look at him to assess and compare. I knew he knew this guy. They probably went to school together. But somehow his maturity and masculinity had eclipsed Cocky Guy's about seven thousand times. He was all man. He was losing patience, this vibe filled the space and not only Cocky Guy but his buddies were all taking it seriously. They didn't like it but they were taking it seriously.

Maybe they weren't total idiots.

Finally, Cocky Guy muttered, "I don't have it on me."

"Then get it. Cash machine on the corner. We'll wait. You're not back in ten minutes, I'll be collecting," Gray returned.

Wow. That was nice.

Cocky Guy continued glaring over my shoulder at Gray then his eyes flicked back and forth between him and me.

"You two know each other?" he asked.

"Yeah, she's a friend," Gray answered instantly. "And I take care of my friends. Now, cash machine. Corner. Five hundred dollars. Ten minutes. You should be back in five."

Cocky Guy kept up the glare to save face before he stomped away. I let out the breath I was holding. His friends drifted back to the other table. Gray took my elbow in his grip and led me to the opposite end of the platform.

When we got there, he didn't let me go and used my elbow to position me in front of him.

I looked up.

He was still beautiful and now he looked slightly pissed, definitely impatient and that meant, as close as he was, he was even more beautiful. He was also the perfect height, well taller than me but I knew, just tipping up on my toes, I could round his shoulders with my arms. A slight bend of his neck, he could kiss me.

My palms started sweating again.

"Coat, scarf, purse, get them, get them on. Take the money, stow it and get outta here," he ordered. "Do not delay. Walk fast, get to the hotel, chain and lock the door."

That didn't sound good.

"This guy trouble?" I asked.

"You know he is, dollface," he answered quietly.

He called me dollface.

I liked that.

I swallowed.

"Okay, is this guy more trouble than I thought he was?"

"Yeah," he answered instantly.

"Right then since I knew he was definitely trouble and not the good kind, how much more is he?"

"On the trouble scale of one to ten?" Gray asked and I nodded. "A hundred and fifty."

That surprised me. I rarely underestimated anybody and especially not trouble.

I felt my brows go up. "Seriously?"

His face underlined his one word answer, "Seriously."

Wow.

"You're not getting your stuff," he prompted, letting my elbow go.

I held his eyes then walked to the stool where I put my stuff. I pulled on and buttoned up my jean jacket, wrapped my scarf around my neck and pulled the strap of my purse over my head.

Once I'd done this, my eyes went back to Gray who hadn't moved. The minute they hit him, he lifted a hand, index finger extended and he moved it back and forth, indicating I should go there.

And when he did that, I knew I was definitely stupid. Not the game of pool with Cocky Guy stupid. Coming to the bar stupid.

Coming to the bar to get exactly what I got. Another eyeful (and then some) of Gray.

And I knew this because him wagging a long, handsome finger at me in that self-assured, manly way of his made things happen to me I'd never felt in my life. Not once. They happened on the inside in a way that I wasn't certain I could hide on the outside. And I also wasn't certain if my suddenly trembling legs would keep me standing.

I went there.

When I got there, again his hand came to my elbow but this time I felt it, every centimeter. The touch was light. He wasn't manhandling me. He wasn't making a point. But I felt every centimeter of his fingers that were touching me.

Every centimeter.

"You and your partner didn't leave town," he remarked.

"Uh...he had something he wanted to do. We're gone first thing in the morning."

"He at your hotel room now?"

I didn't want to share this.

I had to share this.

"Doubtfully."

Gray studied me. Then he nodded.

Then he ordered, "Don't leave your hotel room unless he's with you. No visit to the diner for breakfast. Nothing. Yeah?"

Wow.

"Is he *really* that serious of a problem?" I asked.

"Absolutely," Gray answered.

Hells bells.

I looked away and whispered, "Darn."

"Dollface," he called, my belly shifted in a way that felt really nice and I looked back to him. "I didn't think you'd make the bet."

I stared before I asked, "Sorry?"

"You were blowin' him off. Then suddenly you made the bet. I didn't think you'd make the bet."

He was saying he would have stepped in if he knew I was going to give in.

This was nice too.

He was just nice.

I liked that.

Stupid, stupid me.

I nodded.

Cocky Guy showed and wasted no time glaring at us and shoving bills at me.

Gray let me go and took them.

"Good you're just passin' through," he said to me and his meaning was clear. I wasn't welcome in his town.

I didn't reply.

I noted out of the corner of my eye that Gray was counting the money.

"It's all there, darlin'," he said softly.

I looked at him, nodded, looked down, took the money, looked to my purse and used both hands to stow it in my wallet without taking my wallet out of my bag.

Then I looked at Cocky Guy. "Nice to meet you."

"Bite me," he muttered and moved away.

Well there it was. Rude.

I looked to Gray.

"Thanks again," I whispered.

"Get gone," he whispered back.

Not two words I wanted him to say to me but now, essentially, he'd said them twice.

I wished I was the kind of girl who had the gumption to lean in and kiss him. Even if it was just his cheek to say thanks.

I wasn't that kind of girl. I'd never kissed a man, never been kissed.

So I didn't.

I just took in a deep breath and then I got out of there.

Chapter 5

Scoop Up All the Pretty Ones

E*ighteen minutes later...*

"Bud, not good."

Lying on my back in my bed in my darkened hotel room, I sighed.

That didn't take long. I was in my hotel room maybe, at most, fifteen minutes.

And those words, said by who I knew was Gray, came from outside my closed and locked door.

"Fuck you, Cody. Go home. You don't know this bitch. Don't get involved."

That was Cocky Guy.

I had the lights out. Boots on. Coat on. Baseball bat in my hand.

Casey had a gun. I didn't do guns.

I did baseball bats.

I lifted up, throwing my legs to the side and twisting my hips. My cowboy boots hit floor silently. My hand gripped the handle of the bat tightly.

"Not movin', you know it, you want in there you gotta go through me."

That was Gray.

"Honest to God, you're one mean fucker but you can't take four of us."

That wasn't Cocky Guy. That was a sidekick.

They'd all come.

Gray was right, not good.

"Not sure you want to find out."

That was Gray.

I pushed to my feet.

Then I heard the grunt of pain.

Hells *bells*!

I rushed to the door and looked through the peephole.

There they were, all four of them on Gray.

Gray.

Gray, a man who had seen me three times, looked out for me three times and on the fourth was being beat up in the parking lot of a small town hotel to protect me.

I shouldn't get involved. I should call the front office. I should tell them to call the cops. Or I should just call the cops.

I didn't.

I pulled back the chain, turned the lock and charged out.

I advanced swinging.

I aimed low and caught one of the sidekicks on the side of the knee. He yowled and scuttled sideways. I left him, swung back and connected with sidekick two's back. Another howl, he jerked around and advanced *with* the other guy I'd nailed who'd recovered.

I got another lick in, smashing into sidekick two's hip. Another grunt of pain but a quick recovery. I jabbed the top of the bat in sidekick one's stomach twice, hard. He went back at the same time trying to snatch the bat away from me.

I kept hold then swung, also hard, this time higher. He lifted cocked forearms and one of them deflected the blow but he emitted a grunt of pain and fell slightly back.

My attention turned to sidekick two who I was instinctively shifting from. Sidekick one wasn't the threat, sidekick two's eyes were mean. On swing five, moving fast, sidekick two caught the bat. He twisted, I held on. He twisted harder, angry eyes never leaving me. Taller, stronger, I was no match. He wrenched it out of my hands then tossed it aside.

Not good.

They advanced. I backed up, caught my heel on the curb up to the walkway outside the hotel rooms and fell right to my ass. Hard. And it hurt. No time to feel the pain, they kept coming and I scampered back on hands and feet.

Sidekick two grinned.

Yep. Mean.

I kept scampering and my head and shoulders hit brick.

That hurt too.

I heard the ratchet of a shotgun just as I heard the quick start and stop of a police siren.

My body froze but my eyes flew to the side and I saw a man in a wife beater, a beat-up, dark-colored, terrycloth robe, a pair of slacks that led into a pair of bedroom slippers and he was holding a shotgun.

My eyes then moved to the entrance of the parking lot where a squad car, no flashing lights, was pulling in.

Peering around the two sidekicks in front of me, I saw Gray had dispatched one guy. He was groaning and kind of rolling but mostly he seemed to be fighting for consciousness. He had Cocky Guy down on his knees in front of him, bent back, his fist was wrapped in Cocky Guy's collar and his other arm was cocked back ready to deliver a blow. He had blood streaming down his face from a cut over his left eye, but Cocky Guy appeared to be bleeding profusely from his nose, a cut lip and a gash on his cheekbone.

Jeez, the whole thing lasted maybe five minutes. How could he inflict that much damage in five minutes?

"Buddy, what the hell?" the guy in the wife beater asked loudly. "Christ, by now, don't you know better? How many times does Gray gotta teach you this lesson?"

I found this comment interesting.

The hotel guy got no further and therefore, alas, didn't explain this because the cop had stopped the car and was folding out.

I found this alarming.

I was not a big fan of being in the presence of cops. At first, long ago—health hazard. Now it was an occupational hazard.

The cop rested his arms on the top of his open door, leaned into them and demanded of the parking lot as a whole, "Tell me my eyes are deceiving me."

My two sidekicks moved cautiously back while one of them muttered, "Uncle Lenny."

Uncle Lenny?

Suddenly, the cop straightened like a shot and he did this when the boy-men had moved out of his line of sight and his eyes hit me.

"Oh no." I heard him say softly. "*Hell* no."

He moved out of his door, slammed it viciously and advanced on the sidekick I caught on the knee. He advanced fast, aggressive and very angry until that particular sidekick was pressed against the side of a car with his angry, cop uncle leaning over him threateningly.

"Convince me not to rip your dick off," he growled.

Wow.

"Uncle Lenny—" the sidekick started, his voice trembling.

"That a girl I see on her ass?" the cop asked.

"We were—" the sidekick began again but his uncle leaned even closer and I held my breath.

"Is that...a girl...I see...*on her ass?*"

"She hustled Bud at pool," the sidekick said quickly.

"I did not!" I snapped at the same time I heard Gray's deep voice state, "That's a fuckin' lie."

I looked to him to see he'd tossed Cocky Guy aside, Cocky Guy was pulling himself up but Gray was walking to me. He got to me, hand extended and I put mine in his. He instantly pulled me up and close, his hand firm in mine and not letting go.

He was also bleeding from that cut over his eye and he was bleeding a lot. It was running down his temple, cheek and dripping off his jaw onto his leather jacket.

Through this, the cop didn't move.

Instead, he spoke and what he said was, "I don't care if she hustled him, mugged him, drugged him or bit his dick off givin' him a blowjob. Bud got fucked in some way, he's a man, he takes it like a man. He's got a legal problem, he takes it to the law. *Whatever* happens to Bud Sharp *you* do not get involved. *Especially* if he's got a beef with a slip of a girl. And *I never* drive up in my cruiser seein' you loomin' over a slip of a girl who fucked you, who fucked Bud or who fucked the fuckin' Pope. You get me?"

"I get you, Uncle Lenny," the sidekick whispered.

"Jesus, fuck, it's like nothing grew between your fuckin' ears," the cop muttered, moved away and turned to face the assemblage, his eyes honing in on me. "You makin' a complaint?"

"They leave me and Gray alone, no," I answered instantly and he nodded just as quickly before his eyes cut to the guy in the wife beater. "You makin' a complaint, Manny?"

"They leave my customers alone and I don't got fights in my parkin' lot for, say, the rest of all eternity, no."

I thought Manny was kind of funny.

I thought this but I sure as heck didn't laugh.

The cop's eyes sliced through Cocky Guy and his sidekicks. "This girl, Gray or Manny got any problems with you boys?"

"No sir," his nephew said immediately.

"No," sidekick two answered at the same time.

The third shook his head. He was the one who'd been fighting for consciousness. He was up now and swaying a bit so I wasn't sure he had words in him.

Cocky Guy was glaring at Gray.

"Bud?" the cop called and Cocky Guy tore his eyes from Gray

and looked at the cop. When he did, the cop went on in a quiet voice filled with warning. "Don't mess with me, son. You know you don't mess with me. You're smart, you'll go home, clean up the cuts Gray's opened up on you and think on those. My count, this is the third time Gray's drawn your blood. Learn and don't let there be a fourth."

It seemed to me that Gray and Cocky Guy had a long history.

"She hustled me out of five hundred dollars," Cocky Guy spat to the cop.

"Len, I was there and that's not fuckin' true," Gray said low, clearly pissed and the cop looked to him.

Then he looked to me and his eyes moved up and down.

I could read people. I had to. Survival.

Cops could read people too. I knew he sized me up the second he looked at me.

Not good.

Gray spoke again.

"She's the shit at a table. He and his boys watched her wipe it clean, he knew she had talent. The whole bar did. He offered the bet, she declined. He pushed the bet. She took it. He lost. What he says is bullshit. Ask Janie."

The cop held my eyes and I held his. His dropped to my hand, which Gray still held firm in his. Then he looked to Gray only briefly. Finally he turned back to Cocky Guy.

"Do you not think I see what this is?" the cop asked Cocky Guy softly and I didn't get that, but I did see in the parking lot lights Cocky Guy's face go pale even as it went hard. "Go home, Buddy," he finished on a near to whisper.

His sidekicks immediately shuffled to exit the scene. With no other choice, Cocky Guy aimed a laser sharp scowl at Gray and me, cleared his throat and hocked a loogie in our direction.

"Got shitloads of money, not an ounce of class," Gray muttered, his eyes locked on Cocky Guy as he followed his boys.

Manny, the cop, Gray and I watched him go.

Then Manny turned to the cop. "Thanks for bein' quick, Len."

"My job, Man," he muttered and Manny looked at me.

"You okay, miss?"

I nodded and said softly, "Thanks."

He nodded back then looked to Gray.

"Would say good to see you, son, but be better seein' you without blood on your face."

"Right," Gray replied and he sounded amused.

"Catch ya at The Rambler for a drink sometime," Manny went on.

"You got it, Man," Gray muttered.

Then Manny turned and walked toward the office.

The cop looked at Gray and me and when he did, his eyes again dropped to our hands, mine *still* held in Gray's.

He looked to Gray and grinned. "Bud would probably stop bein' such a jackass if you didn't scoop up all the pretty ones."

I liked that and I didn't. I liked it because it was a compliment. I didn't because that meant Gray had a lot of girlfriends and even though this was by no means a surprise and it made no nevermind to me, I didn't like knowing it.

"Wrong way around, Len. He wasn't such a jackass, he might get a shot," Gray returned.

This was true.

Len agreed with me and I knew this because he kept grinning and also nodding. His eyes flicked up to Gray's forehead before going back to his.

"I got any shot you'll go to the clinic and get that stitched?"

"I'll be all right," Gray answered.

That meant no.

Len looked back down at our hands, to me,then to Gray, all quickly.

His grin turned to a smile but he did this right before he looked to his boots and said, "'Spect so." He looked back to me. "You sure you'll be all right, miss?"

I nodded. "I'm just fine. Thank you for intervening."

"Like I said. My job," he replied, jerked up his chin and moved toward his cruiser.

Gray's hand around mine squeezed and I looked to him to see him looking down at me.

"No lie, you all right?" he asked.

And right then, without me even trying to stop it, I did something stupid. Something unsafe. Something I'd never done and something I never expected I'd do.

I answered, "I will be, you let me see to that cut."

And that was when I got it, probably what I was looking for, definitely what I wanted.

He smiled at me and I saw his dimple.

Chapter 6

Feels Good Though

"You think, you're cleanin' blood off my face and all, you might give me your name?"

That was Gray, sitting on the end of my bed in the hotel room as I stood over him doing exactly what he said, cleaning blood off his face.

Blood he shed for me.

Hells bells.

My eyes went from the short but deep and gaping cut to his.

He was close, really close. I'd turned on most the lights in the room so I could see what I was doing and I saw that his eyelashes weren't russet. They were dark brown.

The *tips* were russet.

Oh my.

"Dollface?" he called and I blinked as my body started.

I needed to pull myself together.

"Ivey," I muttered, looking back at the cut.

"Ivey," he muttered back and I could swear, him saying my name gave me goosebumps.

"Yeah," I whispered then ran the damp cloth down his face, wiping off the blood.

"What we got?" he asked and my eyes flicked to his but I'd learned.

Don't look long. Don't get captivated.

I looked back to the blood, kept gently wiping and asked back, "What we got?"

"The cut," he explained. "How bad is it?"

My attention went to his cut then I went back to cleaning his face while answering, "Short but deep. You should get stitches."

"No stitches," he murmured and I looked to him but I braced myself beforehand.

Nope. Bracing myself didn't work, so I tried to look at him while not so I ended up mostly looking at his nose.

"No stitches?" I asked.

"Nope."

"It's deep."

"It'll heal."

"You'll have a scar."

"Yeah, but it'll heal."

I looked back to his eyes. "Gray, really, you should have it seen to. If you don't get stitches you should have plasters and it should be disinfected."

"You got a first aid kit?"

I did but it was in Casey's car.

"It's in my brother's car."

"So he's your brother."

Darn!

This was why you didn't connect. This was why you played it safe. You played with fire, you were going to get burned.

But he'd bled for me so what could I do?

"Yeah, Casey. He's my brother," I whispered.

Gray grinned at me with dimple, and that made it worth it.

I moved away from him to the bathroom.

"When's he gonna be back?" Gray asked my back and I turned to him.

"Sorry?"

"Your brother. When's he due back?"

I couldn't tell him this.

I told him this.

"Late, very late and that's the earliest. Probably not until morning."

Gray's face changed and it wasn't a good change. He looked mildly angry.

"Not until morning?"

"He...uh...well, he's busy doing something so no, not until very late or morning."

That was when Gray stood and announced, "You're comin' home with me."

My body froze and I stared at him.

Then I forced my mouth to whisper, "Sorry?"

"You're comin' home with me."

"I—"

He interrupted me, "First, I got a first aid kit. You can disinfect and put shit on the cut. Second, I got a grandma who lives with me. She's not ancient, she's not young, but she could be three hundred years old and still she'd have the hearing of a German shepherd. She goes to church every Sunday and she'd lose her mind if I brought a girl home with any intent other than to make her dinner or study the Bible."

I couldn't help it. That was so funny, it made my mouth twitch.

Gray watched my mouth move and flat out smiled.

Then he started speaking again.

"And last, got an extra bed. Manny takes pride in his place." His arm moved, indicating the space around us that was clean and to my practiced eye I knew it had been renovated sometime in the last five years. Although the cable was basic and I wouldn't want to live the rest of my life there, it was pretty nice for what it was and a whole lot nicer than many places I'd laid my head. "But I bet the bed at my house is more comfortable and I can guarantee a thousand other people haven't slept in it. So, what I'm sayin' is, you're safe, you'll be comfortable and last, and most important, you're *safe*."

I read him and my eyes locked to his.

"You think they'll come back," I said quietly.

"No tellin'. Jim, Ted and Pete, no way. 'Specially Pete. Buddy is an asshole and he was pissed. You were immune to his charms then you bested him then he got bested by me. That shit doesn't lay well with him so..." he trailed off and shrugged.

This wasn't good.

Another trickle of blood slid down his face. It wasn't much but the cut was still bleeding.

That wasn't good either.

Darn it all to heck.

I closed my eyes.

"Ivey, swear to God, you'll be safe with me." I heard him say softly.

I opened my eyes mostly because him talking soft was nice and with my eyes closed it seemed a heck of a lot nicer.

"Get what you need and write your brother a note. I'll bring you back in the morning."

I wanted to bite my lip.

I didn't.

I went to the bathroom, did my best to rinse his blood from the washcloth, I wet another one then took it out to him.

Stopping as far away as I could, I held it to him and said quietly, "It's still bleeding. Maybe I should drive."

He took the cloth from me but he did it grinning.

Hells bells.

"Go on through to the kitchen, I'll take this upstairs and get the first aid kit," Gray ordered on a mutter, his fingers flipping a light switch, which illuminated the hall.

He'd already illuminated the entryway.

At the end of the hall was a kitchen.

He turned and went to the foot of the stairs and jogged up, carrying my bag.

I stood in the hall and allowed myself to bite my lip.

He didn't live in town.

He lived out of town and not close to anyone. I couldn't tell in the dark if it was a ranch or an orchard. There were a lot of shadowy trees close to his house. There were also outbuildings and some fenced but empty pens. One of the outbuildings was a barn.

But it was his house I liked.

It was old. It wasn't a ranch house, it was a farmhouse. Not big. Compact. Two stories. From what I could tell, white outside but the woodwork was painted something else. A rectangular porch out front with a porch swing, the family room jutting out so the porch only had two open sides.

Stained glass in the door.

I didn't have to peruse the rest of the house, the entryway said it all.

People lived here, the same people for generations. When I say that I mean the same family. The furniture was old and pretty. The pictures on the wall faded and pretty. The décor the same. This house had been lived in, maybe stuff had been added but nothing had been taken away. Still, instead of full and suffocating, it seemed warm and welcoming.

I sucked in breath and moved down the hall to the shadowed kitchen. Feeling around the opened, doorless doorway, I found the switch and the kitchen was bathed in light.

I closed my eyes but I still saw it.

No renovation, not for years. This house might have been built before modern appliances but it was modernized shortly after and left to be.

I opened my eyes.

Cupboards painted bright red. Little white ceramic knobs to

open them looking like polka dots in that sea of bright. Soffits papered in wallpaper that had a white background, green vines and leaves, white and yellow flowers and big fat strawberries. Cream fridge, the old kind with the bulging front, huge handles and curved edges. Big, old gas burner stove.

Someone had cut out some cupboards to insert a cream fronted dishwasher next to the sink. Butcher block countertops that had seen so much use they didn't have grooves, they had waves and their edges were rounded.

A big, beat-up farm table in the middle of the room with six chairs around it, only three matching, all of their seats sporting big, red poofy cushions tied to their backs. A huge bowl filled with apples, oranges and bananas in the middle.

The countertops covered with appliances and crocks holding utensils. A back door that led now to darkness, but its window was covered in wispy white curtains held back with red sashes.

A huge window over the double-bowled, cream ceramic sink with the same wispy white, red-sashed curtains hanging. Another window at the side, under which there was a low, wood-framed cabinet, its doors inlaid with punched tin, its top holding a vase of slightly wilting flowers, some greeting cards turned on their sides and a bowl full of keys, change and other life detritus.

My eyes swept the space.

Many Thanksgiving dinners had been cooked there. Christmases. Birthdays. And just because you had to eat.

I loved it.

Every inch.

Every stinking inch.

"First aid kit." I heard, jumped and turned to see Gray sauntering down the hall toward me carrying a big box, the bottom blue, the top white, the size of the tackle box of a very serious fisherman. If that was his first aid kit, I had a feeling he had a history with more than just Cocky Guy Buddy.

"That's a big first aid kit," I blurted and again he rewarded me with a grin.

"Man now, Ivey, but used to be a boy," he muttered intriguingly, deposited the box on the table then flicked the latches and flipped it open.

It was stuffed full.

He grew up here.

This wasn't his house, it was his grandmother's.

I wondered if that was a fib or something else.

I wondered a lot of things.

None of which I would ask.

"Alcohol wipes, plasters, scissors," he murmured, digging and pulling the stuff out as I dumped my purse on the table, unwrapped my scarf and shrugged off my coat, tossing them over the back of a chair. His neck twisted and his eyes hit me. "We're good."

I nodded, my head dropping, my experienced eyes scanning the stuff then I looked up at him and ordered, "Sit."

One side of his mouth hitched up a bit before he shrugged off his leather jacket, hooked it on the back of a chair, unwrapped his scarf, tossed that on top and he sat, tipping his face up to me.

I put out of my mind how handsome he was. How, if I just bent at the waist, I could kiss his mouth. When I managed that, I got busy.

I tore open the wipe, tossed the packet on the table and cautiously dabbed at the cut.

He drew in air on a hiss and his head jerked.

"Sorry," I whispered, for some reason affected by his reaction deeply. Too deeply. Hating that I hurt him. Actually hating it.

It wasn't like I hadn't done this before. Before (and after) we'd instigated the pool hustle, made it an art, Casey saw a lot of action that wasn't so good, ended up in cuts and bruises, which meant I was in this same spot, clean up and resident untrained nurse.

I didn't like it when I hurt Casey while tending to him but I *really* didn't like to make Gray feel more pain for me.

So I did something crazy. I did something stupid. I totally lost who I was, where I was, who I was with and I did exactly what I did when I worked on Casey.

I leaned close, dabbed light and after each dab, I leaned closer and I blew air gently between my lips against the cut.

I did this three times before Gray said in a voice I would never forget in my whole life. Never. Not if I lived like he said earlier, to be three hundred. It was soft, it was quiet and it was gentle to the point of tender.

"Dollface, you blowin' on me defeats the purpose of the antiseptic."

My body shot straight and my gaze shot to his.

He grinned and kept speaking.

"Feels good though."

"Sorry," I whispered.

His eyes changed. Those beautiful blue eyes with their russet tipped lashes. They changed in a way I also wouldn't forget. Not ever. I'd remember them every day, dozens of times a day, for the rest of my life.

And they changed to become just like his voice had been. Gentle to the point of tender.

"Don't be," he whispered back.

My heart started slamming in my chest.

What was *with* me?

I had to pull myself together.

So I pulled myself together and kept gently dabbing, cleaned the cut, cleaned away the blood then expertly cut the plasters, pressed together the opened flesh and laid the three, thin, precisely cut strips to keep it closed.

I took a step back and declared, "Done."

His eyes captured mine.

"Made fast work of that."

I made no response.

His eyes held mine.

"Practice," he guessed accurately.

I turned to the first aid kit and started tidying.

I felt Gray come to his feet beside me. He tagged the used wipes and their packages and took them to the sink. He opened the cupboard under it, tossed them in the bin there, closed it and turned to me.

"Bed," he stated.

I nodded.

"I'll show you your room."

"Okay," I replied.

He led, I followed and he turned off lights as he did. He moved up the stairs, me trailing.

Upstairs, same as downstairs, settled, warm, welcome and everything had been there awhile.

He turned left at the top and took me to a room where the lights were on, shining softly and invitingly into the hall. He disappeared through the door and I followed him to see he'd stopped.

"Bathroom other end of the hall, last door on your right," he told me then he invited, "Make yourself at home."

I tore my eyes from the room with its white-painted, curlicue iron bed (tall head and tall, but still shorter than the head, foot) covered in an unbelievably beautiful wedding ring quilt, a folded soft looking blanket at the bottom and big fluffy pillows with ruffly edges. The room's floors warm, honeyed wood covered in a big, thick, pastel-colored rug with tangled fringe at two sides, its colors faded but it had started pastel too, I could tell. Jumbled mismatched furniture, some painted white but there were chips, some gleaming wood, all charming, and one dresser had a big, oval mirror affixed to the top. On the nightstands, both turned on and glowing, tall, thin lamps with dotted glass balls as lampshades, crystals dangling from the bottom. And on the walls, prints of flowers in frames distressed from age, not meant to be that way.

It was countrified beauty at its finest. A room you'd expect in a farmhouse. A room you'd pay big money to rent in some B&B

because the owners had paid big money to make it that way. A room that was just that enchanting naturally.

"Sleep well, Ivey," Gray muttered.

I nodded.

He lifted a hand, curled his long fingers on my upper arm, gave me a squeeze and walked out the door.

I sucked in another breath.

I pulled it together, moved to the door and closed it.

Then I decided to get ready for bed fast, get in bed, turn off the lights, close my eyes and try to erase this from my mind.

Tomorrow, he'd take me back to the hotel. Tomorrow, I'd pack our stuff. Tomorrow, Casey would come back, we'd load up the car and we'd be away.

Mustang would be in our rearview mirrors.

Mustang would be a memory.

And so would Gray.

I moved directly to the bag Gray left sitting on top of the bed and did just that.

In my nightshirt with my face wash, toothbrush, toothpaste and a hair clip, I shot out the door and moved quickly down the hall, eyes to my feet. I didn't want to take anymore in. *Couldn't* take anymore in.

And you know what stunk?

Looking at my feet, I still saw the carpet runner that ran down the hall, attractively worn and frayed in the middle where feet had trod a million times but near-to new looking at the edge, and beyond, more of that warm, honey-colored wood floor.

Yes, even the floor was warm and welcoming.

Hells bells.

I made it to the end of the hallway, the door to the bathroom slightly closed, light on. I pushed in, stepped in, lifted my head and stopped dead.

Gray, wearing nothing (nothing!) but a pair of light blue cotton, drawstring pajama bottoms, toothbrush in mouth turned to me.

Oh my.

Oh *my*.

His shoulders *were* broad. His chest *was* wide.

And...and...

Did real men actually look like that?

I mean, my brother Casey was relatively fit. He was lean. He did pushups and sit-ups a lot. He thought of himself as a ladies' man and he got enough action, he probably was.

But he didn't have all those planes and contours. Especially not across his belly.

And he didn't have those veins running down his arms.

Oh my.

"Big enough to share." I heard Gray say and my body jolted. My eyes shot from his chest to his face and I saw he had his toothbrush out, foam in his mouth and he'd shifted to the side of the sink.

How on earth could a man have toothbrush foam in his mouth and look just...that...*beautiful*?

"Ivey?" he called and I blinked but didn't move. "Dollface, you okay?"

No. I was not.

But I had to pretend to be.

"Just a weird night," I murmured, trying to decide if it was rude if I said I'd come back and left him to it.

I hadn't been a guest in someone's house. Not ever.

What was protocol?

As for me, if someone barged in on me brushing my teeth, I would expect them to slink away.

He kept brushing, eyes on me, and kept to his side of the sink. He didn't seem to have a problem with it and his behavior seemed to be inviting me in.

Maybe it was rude.

Darn.

I moved in and went to the sink.

I put the stuff down on the side of the basin, keeping my body to my side as far from his as I could. I lifted my hands and gathered my hair, twisted it then sunk the clip in to hold it back. I felt it flopping all around the clip but it was away from my face so I could wash it.

I carefully shifted to the front of the sink (thus closer to Gray), bent over the basin and turned it on.

"Jesus, honest to God, I've never seen that much hair," a still with foam in his mouth Gray noted and my neck twisted, my eyes lifting to his face.

"Sorry?"

"You got a lot of hair, darlin'," he said through the foam.

"Well...yeah."

He grinned through the foam and my heart skipped a beat because bare-chested, toothpaste foamed, grinning with dimple Gray would make any woman's heart skip a beat.

I turned back to the water.

Then I made short work of washing my face.

This, I did not want to do.

I did not wear a lot of makeup but at least it was something—a mask, a guard. I needed those.

No one but Casey ever saw the real me.

And now, so would Gray.

I turned off the water, reached for the towel and wiped my face bent over the sink.

"Shift, honey, gotta spit," Gray muttered and I did my best not to jump out of his way while getting out of his way and succeeded.

He bent at the waist, spit, rinsed, grabbed another towel and wiped.

Okay, good. This was done. It was done. He'd leave.

He opened the medicine cabinet and came out with floss.

Well, it couldn't be said I didn't notice that he had great teeth. Still, I had to admit that I kind of wished tonight he didn't choose to keep up all the good work he'd clearly been doing since he could wield a toothbrush.

He cut off a string, put it back and stepped aside.

I got down to the business of my teeth.

Gray stepped into the sink to rinse again before I finished and I felt relief.

Now he would go.

He didn't go.

He leaned into the basin and crossed his arms on his amazing chest.

I kept brushing and looked up at him.

I forced myself to keep brushing as my heart skipped another beat and this was because he was grinning while looking at me.

And he kept grinning while looking at me as I kept brushing.

This went on awhile.

I pulled the brush out of my mouth and said through foam, "What?"

"Never, in my life, in this bathroom have I shared a sink with a woman. Now, I'm doin' it and I don't even know her last name."

"I don't know your last name," I pointed out through foam.

"Cody."

I stared at him. Then, still through foam, I asked, "Your name is Gray Cody?"

"Grayson Cody," he corrected.

Jeez. That was like the Wild West rancher cowboy name to beat all Wild West rancher cowboy names. That kicked the name "John Wayne" right up the backside. It beat the heck out of "Roy Rogers." Totally slaughtered even "Wyatt Earp" who wasn't a Wild West rancher cowboy, he was a bad boy lawman famously known for his participation in a gunfight, so clearly more badass than your most badass Wild West rancher cowboy and still Gray's name kicked Earp's name's ass.

It was the best Wild West rancher cowboy name in history.

"Pay a mint to know what's goin' on in your head right now," he muttered, still grinning, still looking at me, still with his fabulous arms crossed on his wide, beautiful chest.

"You have the best Wild West rancher cowboy name in history," I told him.

He burst out laughing.

My heart stopped.

Then I bent over the sink, spit, rinsed, rinsed my toothbrush, wiped and grabbed my stuff.

I got the heck out of there, muttering, "'Night, Gray."

And I did it fast.

And I did it because I had to get smart fast.

Because I could handle his beauty. I could handle his smile. I could handle his dimple. I could handle that he looked out for me. I could even handle the gentle, tenderness of his voice and look earlier.

But I could not handle his laughter.

Definitely not me giving it to him.

It was the most beautiful thing about him in a long line of beautiful things. It was deep, it was rich, it was warm, it was engaging and it was the kind of thing you wanted to hear every day, a hundred times a day for the rest of your life. So much so, you'd work at it, you'd tie yourself in knots, you'd live and breathe to make it happen, giving him humor so he'd give that beauty to you.

So I had to get smart.

Fast.

Chapter 7

Preserves

S*ix hours later…*

I HEARD the movement and murmur of voices downstairs and I got out of bed.

Gray was right, it was far more comfortable than Manny's bed at the hotel. The quilt was thin but it was heavy and warm. The sheets were old and therefore washed frequently so they were soft.

I still had around two hours of sleep.

I had to get up, get back to town and get out of Mustang.

I dressed in the room then hustled down the hall. This time, I paid attention even though I still heard the murmur of voices from downstairs, the sounds of something happening in the kitchen, the smell of bacon so I guessed no one was upstairs.

The bathroom door was open, the light out. I hurried in, closed the door and saw it didn't have a lock.

Of course not.

Family knew, the door was closed, the room was occupied.

It was just me who didn't know stuff like that.

I did my business, washed my face, brushed my teeth. Without Gray in there, I now saw that the bathroom was countrified charm just like everything else. Claw-footed tub. Ceramic pedestal sink but it was very wide bowled, the bowl square, deep ledges at the top and sides to hold stuff. A bathroom mirror with frilly, beveled edges and scrolled etching at the top. Gray (or his grandma) didn't mess around with towels, I was surprised to see. They were not old, worn and soft like everything else. They were newish, thick and soft. There was a shelf with some old-fashioned, chrome boxes on it but also a little vase with more slightly wilted flowers.

Gray's grandma liked flowers, clearly.

It would be nice if I had the money to pop by the flower shop in town to order flowers delivered as a thank you to her for having such a wonderful grandson.

Unfortunately, I didn't have the money.

I got out of there, hustled back down the hall, made the bed carefully, fluffing the pillows, smoothing out the sheets then smoothing out the quilt and straightening the blanket at the end. I swiftly packed my small bag, zipped up and walked out. Down the stairs, the voices were stronger, the smell of bacon frying weaker, the sounds of cutlery on plates could now be heard.

Making my point, I dropped my bag by the front door, turned and started to head down the hall to the kitchen.

My step nearly stuttered when I saw her.

Long, attractive gray hair, top and sides pulled back in a clip at the nape of her neck, granny nightgown on, pristine white, buttoned all the way up to the frilled, high collar. Wrapped around her upper arms and shoulders was a fluffy, loosely-knit, gray wool shawl. She was a grandma straight from a TV show, but that TV show was set on a farm on the plains in the 1800s. I half expected Michael Landon to walk in the back door sporting suspenders and sweeping off his hat.

I didn't even know they made nightgowns like that anymore and I'd never, not once, seen anyone wrapped in a shawl.

Her eyes were aimed down the hall at me.

Her bottom was settled in a wheelchair.

Now I knew why Gray lived with Grandma.

Yes. He was a good man. Down to his bones.

When I got close, I forced a smile and said quietly, "Hi."

Her blue eyes shrewd, she took me in top to toe on a quick, experienced sweep, her gaze coming back to me giving nothing away and she replied, "Good morning, Ivey."

Gray had told her about me.

I entered the kitchen to see Gray seated across the table from me, back to the sink, a plate of half eaten eggs and bacon in front of him (as Grandma had in front of her), another plate with a stack of toast between them. Coffee cups, sugar bowl, small jug of milk, butter dish, jar of strawberry jam that was not purchased from a grocery store, silver spoon in it.

His eyes were on me and they were twinkling.

"Mornin', Ivey," he greeted.

I stopped a foot in the doorway. "Good morning, Gray."

"Sleep okay?" he asked.

"Yes," I lied.

The twinkle in his eyes went south, a grin hit his lips and the dimple came out.

My belly curled.

Stay smart, my brain reminded me.

"Want some breakfast?" he asked, tipping his head down to his plate.

I shook my head. "Thanks, but no. I appreciate it but I have to get back into town. Can I use your phone? I'll call a taxi so I don't put you out."

The twinkle faded and he opened his mouth to say something but Grandma got there before him.

"Everyone needs breakfast."

I looked at her. "I'm not usually up this early. I'll get something on the road."

She studied me a moment before she stated, "I'm Miriam Cody."

Darn. I'd been rude. I should have introduced myself.

I moved to her, not close, not too far she couldn't reach me and I stretched out a hand.

"It's lovely to meet you. As I think you know, I'm Ivey."

She took my hand, gave me a light squeeze then let it go, all of that not taking her eyes from me.

She tipped her head to a chair with its back to the door and invited, "Sit down. I'll make you some eggs."

She'd make me some eggs?

How would she do that in a wheelchair?

I didn't ask even though I wanted to know.

"Really," I shook my head, "thank you but no. Gray has been very kind, I've taken a lot of his time already and I'm really not a breakfast person. Especially not this early. But again, thank you."

I wondered if I was laying on the gratitude too thick. I could tell by her assessing eyes, her blank face and her aloof manner that she didn't like what she saw in me. I was used to this, especially from women and that especially was most especially from older women. They had experience. They saw things other people didn't see. She didn't like what she saw in me. She didn't like that her grandson hit the breakfast table with an angry cut over his eye that had to be closed by plasters. She didn't like that her grandson hit the breakfast table with a cut over his eye and the news he had a girl in their guest room.

She didn't like her grandson with me.

"At least have coffee, some toast," she encouraged.

Hells bells.

I had never been a guest in anyone's home but I suspected it would be rude to say no three times.

"Thanks," I whispered, moved to the chair she indicated as Gray scooted his back.

"I'll get it," he muttered.

"No," I said quickly and sharply, though I didn't know why and I shouldn't have done it.

Gray's gaze cut to me and I felt his grandmother's on me. His brows were slightly drawn. He was confused at my tone.

"Please," I said quietly. "Don't interrupt your breakfast for me. I can pour a cup of coffee."

He studied me a second, jerked his chin up slightly, settled back in his chair and pushed himself to the table.

I went to the coffeemaker that had a half-full pot and had also been pulled too close to the edge of the counter, likely so Grandma could get to it should she want to wheel herself over there to refresh her cup. Beside it was a stand with a bunch of mismatched but all interesting cups (and all *big*, apparently ranchers or orchard people liked their coffee) hanging from hooks.

I nabbed a cup, turned it on its bottom on the butcher block counter and grabbed the pot. It hit me and I turned to the table.

"Does anyone need a warm up?" I asked, lifting the pot.

Gray looked at me and answered, "Thanks, I'm good, Ivey."

"I could use a warm up," Grandma Miriam said.

I nodded, moved to her, warmed up her cup then moved back and got my own.

I barely had my bottom planted in the seat by Grandma Miriam before Gray offered, "Least have some toast. You gotta try Gran's preserves."

I looked to the pot of jam.

She cooked eggs.

She made jam.

In a wheelchair.

I thought this was very interesting.

"That sounds great," I murmured, and before I could protest Gray was out of his seat, in a cupboard and he came back with a small plate that had frilly edges and flowers printed on it, leaning across the table to put it in front of me.

The toast was already buttered, perfectly toasted, light and golden. I grabbed a slice, tagged the jam and prepared it. Then I splashed milk in my coffee, spooned in a sugar. Silently I went about eating and sipping.

Great coffee. I was right about the toast, perfect. And the jam was amazing. Jam, I thought, was jam. But I was wrong.

Granny nightgown. Homemade preserves. Strawberry wallpaper. Wilted flowers here and there.

I loved Grandma Miriam and it was just my life that she would never love me.

"So, how old are you, Ivey?" Grandma Miriam asked and my eyes slid to her.

This was not good. If she wanted to effect a third degree, I was sitting at her table. I was drinking her coffee. I'd slept in one of her beds. I was eating her preserves. And her grandson had bled for me.

I couldn't avoid it.

Darn.

"Twenty-two," I answered.

Her eyes moved over my face before coming back to mine to compliment, "You have very pretty hair."

"Thanks," I whispered.

"And unusual eyes," she went on. "Lovely."

"Thanks," I repeated on a whisper.

"Did you get those from your mother or your father?"

Steel slid down my spine and I had to do the impossible, give in at the same time fight it.

"My mother with the eyes. I don't know where I got my hair."

She held my gaze, unwavering.

I pulled mine away and ate my toast.

I didn't look back at her when she asked, "Where do you hail from?"

"We moved around a lot," I evaded.

Silence then, "I see."

Yep. I was sure she did.

I finished the toast, sat back, eyes to the table and sipped coffee.

Moments slid by then again from Grandma but not to me, "Best get Ivey into town, sweetheart. I'll do the dishes."

I didn't eat breakfast but I figured I should at least offer so I chanced looking at her again. "Why don't you let me do that? My way to say thanks for toast and preserves, coffee," my eyes slid through Gray to the window as I finished, "and everything."

"That isn't necessary, Ivey," Grandma Miriam said and I looked at her.

She wanted me in town, out of her house and hopefully, as soon as I could manage it, out of her grandson's life.

"It isn't any trouble. I'm sure I could have it done in a few minutes and be out of your hair."

"Got nothing else to do, child," she replied quietly. "Now, you get on into town with Gray."

In other words, get on wherever, just get on.

I nodded and stood.

In short order I had my jacket on, my scarf on, my purse strapped on, Gray had my bag in the back of his truck and we were on our way to town.

It was very early morning and still dark so I still couldn't figure out what it was, where he lived. Ranch or orchard. But it didn't smell like ranch though I couldn't say I knew what that smelled like. Still, if there was livestock close, it had to smell like *something*.

What I did see was that his truck was not only beat-up, it seriously needed a cleanup. Someone had a sweet tooth if the plethora of candy bar wrappers were anything to go by. They also had a taste for salty if the big, empty chip bags were any indication. There were also crunched pop cans, wadded what looked like receipts and gum wrappers, the car mats were caked with mud and there was a thin layer of dust everywhere.

I took my mind off what, I was certain in a weird but fascinating way, would be cleaning up his truck and the fact that I really, *really* wanted to do it and I pulled myself together.

"How's the cut?" I asked.

"Not the first. In this town, probably not the last. I'll survive," Gray replied, again intriguingly and again I wanted to ask and again I wouldn't.

"You stick around, she'll come around," he said quietly and I looked from the road to him.

He looked good in profile.

I already knew this. Still, it hit me and in a way I knew instinctively it always would hit me. If I lived a life that was the kind of life I was free to make connections and we connected, we held strong, I knew his beauty, no matter how time wore on it, would always hit me. It might eventually come as a surprise, still, there would be times it would hit me.

"Sorry?"

He glanced at me then back at the road. "You stick around awhile, Gran, she'll come around."

Oh my.

He wanted me to stick around. He wanted his gran to have a chance to come around. He actually thought that would happen.

I looked back at the road too, but when I did it I did it fighting tears.

Gray kept talking.

"She's had six men in her life, three of them good. Her daddy, her husband and my father. All three of those men are dead."

I closed my eyes.

His father was good, probably like him.

His father was also dead.

I did not like that.

Gray kept going and I opened my eyes.

"Leaves three sons who are no good. Part of how they're no good, including my dad, they got shit taste in women. Their choices but still, she bore the brunt of that. She's cautious, trained that way by a mean momma and then a lifetime of puttin' up with bad women. But, you stick around, she'll come around."

His grandmother read me like a book. She'd never come around.

And he was clearly like the men in his family. If he was attracted to me, he had shit taste in women.

He'd also said "including my dad," which meant his mom was a bad woman.

I didn't like that either.

I said nothing.

Gray kept driving.

We made it to town and he pulled into the parking spot outside my hotel door. I already had my key out.

Casey's car was nowhere to be seen. He was having a very good night.

Lucky him.

Hand on the handle, I turned to Gray, opening my mouth to say a firm farewell and tell him he didn't need to help me with my bag.

He was already turned to me and he got there before me.

"You stick around, VFW steaks tonight."

I stared, confused at his strange words.

Then I asked, "Sorry?"

"You stay another day, I'll pick you up, five thirty. VFW, every Friday night, they do steaks." He grinned. "This is meat country, darlin', best beef you'll find near anywhere and VFW steaks are the best I've had, bar none. You don't wanna miss that."

Was he asking me out on a date?

Definitely shit taste in women.

"We're leaving today," I told him.

"You stay, you get steak," he told me.

"I like steak, Gray," I said softly. "But we're leaving today."

His face changed, got that look, that gentle near to tender look and I braced.

"Ivey—" he started, leaning toward me but I shook my head and interrupted him.

"You know me," I whispered.

He leaned closer. "Dollface—"

I shook my head again. "You know, Gray. Don't be your daddy.

Be smart. Find a nice girl to take home to your gran. You know I'm not that."

His face changed again and the "near to" part evaporated. It was all tender.

God. Beautiful.

I could take no more.

I whipped around, opened the door and it creaked loud. I hopped out, shut it on another creak, hearing his creaking because he opened it. I ran around the back of the truck, leaned in, reached, grabbed my bag while I heard his door creak closed. I dashed around him, head down, hair hiding my face and went to the hotel room door.

I had my key in the lock when I felt his body close to my back and, lips at my ear, he whispered, "Don't, Ivey."

I closed my eyes but still turned the key.

Then I opened my eyes, opened the door and shot inside.

I closed the door on him without looking back.

Chapter 8

Lived My Life for You

F*our hours later…*

"I'M IN LOVE!"

That was Casey.

He had his arm around me, my feet off the ground and he was swinging me around.

This was new.

Brand new.

And this was not good.

Really not good.

As for me, I had both our bags packed and waiting by the door.

Casey slammed me down on my feet, let me go, stepped back and I looked up at his face.

He was beaming.

I wanted to cry.

"God, sis, *God*, wait 'til you meet her. She's *the shit*. I mean, never met a woman like her. *Never*. Funny. Sweet. Funny. *Hot*. Did I say funny?"

"Casey—" I started and he jerked away, moving to the bags.

"Need some money, babe. Nice dinner for my girl tonight."

My heart clenched.

"Casey, we gotta go," I told him.

He had my bag and was walking toward the bed.

He knew better. Our money was not in my bag. It was also not in my purse. He was due back. I'd put it in a safe place. It was tucked in my bra.

"We're not goin'," he declared, dropped my bag and zipped it open. "Hundred dollars. Good wine. Juicy steak. For my girl," he muttered, pawing through my bag.

"I had trouble last night," I announced and his head jerked back, his eyes cutting to me.

"What?"

"Got bored, went to the bar, was shooting some pool. Local guy thought he could best me. He bet me. He lost. He didn't like it."

Casey grinned and straightened.

"He lost?"

Of course he lost. Casey knew better than to ask that.

"Yeah, and he didn't like it."

"How much he lose?"

"Casey, it doesn't matter. He didn't like it. Things were hot here before. Now they're hotter."

Casey rounded the bed and approached me. "How much he lose, sis?"

"Like I said," I leaned in, "*it doesn't matter*. He came around last night, another local guy saw it go down, knew this guy was trouble, took my back. There was a commotion in the parking lot, the owner of the hotel got involved and so did a cop. He sized me up. We have to *go*."

Casey was now close but he leaned back. "A cop?"

I nodded. "A cop."

"He say shit to you?"

I shook my head. "No, but he took one look at me outside my hotel room and the guy accused me of hustling. I didn't, the local guy who stepped up for me confirmed this but this cop is not dumb. We gotta go."

Casey studied me.

Then he asked, "How much you win, Ivey?"

I sighed, then started, "Casey—"

"How much..." he leaned in this time, "*did you win*?"

"Five hundred dollars."

He grinned and leaned back, muttering, "Fuckin' awesome."

"Casey, really—"

"Give me a hundred," he lifted a hand, palm up. "No, hundred and fifty. I'm gonna buy my girl flowers."

I stared.

I needed gloves.

While Casey was carousing, to stop from being bored, I needed books.

A man bled for me and if I was going to spend any of the money *I* won, it would be buying him another warm scarf. Or a hat. Or, I didn't know, fifty candy bars. Or maybe, sending some flowers to his grandma who hated me then getting out of town which was what she wanted most out of me.

Casey spending a hundred and fifty dollars on some woman, absolutely not.

"Are you nuts?" I asked softly.

"Yep, I'm in love." He shook his hand at me. "Lay it on me, Ivey."

I shook my head. "No, Casey. Honestly, we have *to go*."

"You didn't hustle him, cop didn't hassle you. We're cool and we're solid. You got more money. We can stay another day, two."

God!

My brother!

"Casey!" I snapped, his face twisted, he took a step closer, bent and got in my face.

"She's special, Ivey. No shittin' you, this one is different. I like her. You're always whinin' about findin' somewhere safe, somewhere we can settle, somewhere we can take root. Maybe, you think, she's the one, this might be it?"

That was it. That was my brother, Casey.

I *was* always whining about that, or I used to. I quit. Waste of breath.

But I used to do it all the time.

Stop the hustle. Stop driving here and there and everywhere. Stop keeping track of where we'd been so we could make sure to avoid going back. Stop living out of a hotel room, a suitcase. Have more than some clothes, a few books, some makeup and jewelry. Have a coffeemaker. Eat food you cooked, not food cooked for you.

He never gave in. He never wanted to settle. He disallowed connection, especially for me, with a fervor that many would think was unhealthy but, what we went through, what *I* went through, then what he went through for me, was definitely not.

Now, because *he* had found something *he* liked, it was a possibility.

As for me, Mustang was exactly where I wanted to be. I knew it. It was Gray but it was more than Gray. It was Janie. It was knowing the cops in town were good cops, or at least one of them was. It was that crazy restaurant blighting the perfection of the town square.

It was Gray.

And, for Gray, I had to get the heck out of there.

"Casey, I don't want this to be it," I lied.

"I don't care. Lived my life for you. Minute Mom squirted you out, Ivey, I've *lived my whole fuckin' life for you*. Now, you give me a goddamned day or two, a coupla hundred dollars and *you* let *me* live my life *for me*."

I sucked in breath and held his angry eyes.

He was not right.

And he was also absolutely not wrong.

I closed my eyes.

"I'm fallin' in love with her, sis. I feel it." I heard him whisper.

I opened my eyes.

Darn.

"I cannot give you a hundred a fifty dollars, Casey and you know it."

He grinned.

"You get sixty, no more," I said softly.

His hand darted out, curled around my neck, he pulled me in and kissed my forehead.

Then he let me go and smiled huge at me. "I'll make that work."

Darn.

Chapter 9

You Didn't Leave

T*hree and a half hours later…*

I WAS IN MUSTANG LIBRARY, which was diagonal to the square opposite our hotel. It was a narrow, brick, freestanding building, attractive, the number in the cream mortar declaring it was built in 1928. Walk in, half flight of steps down to a basement full of shelves, half flight of steps up to the first floor full of shelves and more steps to another floor full of shelves.

As with the department store, I didn't think Mustang could sustain a library, not one like this. But on the basement level, I heard a bunch of kids, young ones, so obviously the school did field trips there. And it couldn't be said, perusing the shelves, there weren't a variety of old folks obviously on fixed incomes looking for free entertainment, same with a few housewives whose husbands clearly had trouble making ends meet so the romance novel addiction couldn't be assuaged by purchases but instead borrowing.

I was there to borrow but I didn't have a library card. My book would make it to my purse. I read fast and I had all night. I'd return it in the outside return tray I saw when I walked in. I wasn't a thief, I was a hustler. But even if I was a thief, I'd never steal from a library.

With love blooming for Casey and an indeterminate stay in Mustang, we had to be even more careful with money. This meant I couldn't buy a book, definitely, or even any magazines, which were really just throwing money away. I was not going back to the bar, no way. And if there was nothing on TV, which from experience there really never was, I'd need something to keep me from being bored.

I found my book, slid it into my purse and smiled brightly and openly at the librarian as I walked out. I might not be a thief but, as mentioned, I was a hustler. To hustle, you learned what to hide and what not to hide. Game face. If you acted flakey and secretive, the jig would be up.

I figured the same thing for illegally borrowing library books and I figured right. The librarian smiled brightly back and I took off.

Down the block, across the street and in the square, I saw Casey heading my way, big smile on his face with a huge bouquet of flowers in his hand. More than a twenty dollar bouquet, which meant it was probably thirty or even, looking at it, forty. I had no clue. I'd never bought flowers or received them. But that looked like a lot of flowers.

This meant he was going to hit me up for more money.

Again.

I was considering asking him for the car so I could drive a couple of towns over (maybe three), find a bar and do a flash hustle. One-nighter, no Casey casing the joint, setting up the mark then calling me in. Just lots of bending over pool tables pretending I didn't know what I was doing, lots of time watching stupid men drink whisky and watch me then I'd take their money. I did it and often. This usually didn't pull down much. Sometimes twenty, usually fifty, if I was lucky and the guy was a moron with a wad of cash, a hundred or even two.

But I figured it was too hot. Who knew what Bud Sharp and his sidekicks were spreading around and how far that would reach? Also, who knew how long this crush would last for Casey and how long we needed to keep our noses clean.

Hells bells.

My brother was half a block away, still grinning like a loon carrying his flowers, heading toward me when suddenly I wasn't walking toward him anymore.

Instead, an arm hooked my waist, my body shifted, my forward momentum shifted with it and I found myself slamming front to front into a long, hard frame.

I knew that jacket. I knew that scarf.

I looked up.

Gray.

He was grinning and his was huge too, dimple and everything.

"You didn't leave."

Hells bells!

"Uh—" I mumbled.

"Yo! Bro! Can I help you?"

I turned my head and saw that Casey was right there. Then I turned my head again and saw that Gray had turned to my brother.

"Hey," he greeted, extending a hand to my brother. "I'm Gray."

"And I'm tickled pink," Casey returned rudely. "Now, you wanna get your hands off my sister?"

Gray looked at Casey then down at me. I tried to move out of the curve of his arm.

It tightened.

Oh dear.

Gray looked back at my brother.

"I'll repeat, I'm Gray. Gray Cody, a friend of Ivey's," Gray stated, still attempting civility but he'd dropped his hand.

"Ivey doesn't have any friends," Casey returned and, like a spasm, Gray's arm curled even tighter around me.

He was silent and I looked between the two of them seeing they were in stare down on the sidewalk in the town square.

This was not good.

"Uh—" I began again.

"You're wrong," Gray said quietly. "She does. Me."

I battled and succeeded and therefore didn't bite my lip.

Casey's eyes sliced to me. "You know this guy?"

"I told you someone stepped in last night and that someone was Gray," I answered carefully but not carefully enough.

And this was when I knew Casey had made assumptions. Casey assumed that some out-of-shape barfly had taken my back. Casey had not considered that a young, tall, handsome man with a confident manner and a natural authority had stepped up for me.

If Casey considered this, we would be three and a half hours out of Mustang, him falling in love with a class act or not.

His eyes narrowed on me and I felt their sting. This was because Casey found this a betrayal. He said no connections. He demanded I play it safe. And me making a friend, even against my will, with a handsome stranger was not playing it safe to Casey.

He cut his gaze to Gray. "Right then, got my gratitude, bro. Now I'm on duty, move along."

Gray didn't move along. Gray didn't tear his eyes from Casey and I didn't know him all that well, but you didn't need to to know he really didn't like what he was seeing.

Gray's eyes flicked to the flowers and back to Casey's face before he said low, "Shoulda been on duty last night..." pause then, "*bro.*"

Oh jeez.

Casey's back went straight or, I should say, straight-*er*.

"All's well that ends well," he clipped and Gray shook his head. Once.

"I reckon you know, bein' a guy and all, you're her brother but you're also obviously not blind. She's out, way she looks, way she moves, even havin' a quiet night, keepin' to herself, that shit might happen. That shit happened. You were not on duty. I wasn't around, shit coulda got worse," Gray pointed out.

"Well, it didn't," Casey shot back. "And as I said, got my gratitude. Now, I'm here and, can't say it straighter, in two seconds you're not."

This was all happening right there, right with me right there.

But all I could think was...

The way I look?

The way I move?

Casey was wrong. In two seconds Gray was not gone.

Instead, he used those two seconds to dip his head to the flowers and ask, "Those for Ivey?"

"None of your business..." pause then, "*bro.*"

"They're not," Gray whispered, his eyes locked on Casey, his arm still locked around me, my front still tight to him but he'd shifted to facing Casey so I was tucked to his side.

"What'd I say?" Casey whispered back. "None of your business."

"Plans tonight," Gray deduced.

Casey opened his mouth to speak but Gray looked down at me.

"You're free for steak and me."

My belly flip-flopped, my heart squeezed and my legs went weak.

Casey got in our space and thus in Gray's face.

"That is not gonna fuckin' happen," he growled.

Gray turned his head and tipped it down the two inches he needed to stare down Casey. This gave me confirmation of his height. Casey was six foot. I was five foot eight. This placed Gray at six foot two.

See? Tall.

"Why?" Gray asked.

"Again, none of your business. Now, one last time, move along."

I could tell by Gray's vibe and the tenseness I felt in his body that things were deteriorating. I knew by Casey's vibe and the look on his face that they were already gone.

I needed to wade in.

"Casey, he's a nice guy. It's okay."

Casey's eyes cut to me. "Stay out of it," he bit off and that made me mad.

Suddenly mad and *really* mad.

For a lot of reasons.

A lot of reasons that had been bugging me, not just then but for a long, long time.

But just then, he was connecting with some woman, buying her flowers, throwing away money *I* won putting *my* ass on the line. Gray was right. He was off having fun and I, as usual, was *not*.

Casey didn't have a lot of fun?

Casey didn't laugh a lot?

I wasn't shits and grins?

Well, he wasn't either.

He was a pain in my behind.

And he had been for a while.

If he could decide Mustang just might be where we put down roots then who was he to decide I couldn't make a connection?

Just one.

Just one since I was twelve *stinking* years old.

He "connected" all the time.

Not me.

And I was not twelve anymore. I was twenty-two. I could drink legally in every state in the Union. I could drive a car. I could vote. I could join the army.

I was an adult, darn it.

And I had been awhile.

I didn't need my big brother looking out for me, and frankly, if we were honest about it (though that was something Casey would never be) for the last at least five years, it had mostly been *me* looking out for *Casey*.

I turned to Gray and said firmly, "I'll be ready at five thirty."

The tension slid out of his body, Gray looked down at me and grinned.

With dimple.

Darn but I liked that dimple.

I smiled back.

"That's not happening, sis," Casey warned, his voice trembling with fury.

I looked at him. "It is."

"Don't be stupid," he hissed and that made me even *more* mad.

"Seriously?" I asked. "Do you see that cut on Gray's forehead, Casey? He got that *for me*. I put those plasters on. You were off having fun and I was in danger and Gray stepped up for me. You should be *thanking* him, not getting in his face. He's a nice guy. He has a lovely grandma. She makes really good preserves. And I'm having steak with him tonight."

Casey's eyebrows shot to his hairline. "You met his grandma?"

"Yes, and she makes really good preserves."

That was when Casey's eyes narrowed on me. "Thinkin' there's shit you left out this mornin', sis."

"You'd think right but I don't ask, you don't tell and I don't ask because even when I did, you didn't tell. My turn," I fired back.

Casey scowled at me.

Then he whispered, "I'm not likin' this shift, sister."

I knew he wouldn't.

But at that moment, standing in a pretty town square pressed up against the warm hard body of a handsome man who was a good guy who took care of his grandma, a grandma that, even in a wheelchair, made delicious strawberry preserves, I didn't care.

Therefore, I made no response.

He kept scowling at me.

I held it and as I did, Gray held me.

Casey's eyes cut to Gray and he demanded ridiculously (and embarrassingly), "I want her home by ten."

Gray burst out laughing.

I rethought my rebellion hearing it and knowing I loved it.

Yes, *loved it*. It was love. It went down to my bones. That was to say, I loved it with not a small amount of intensity. I'd heard it twice and that was how deep his laughter had rooted into me.

Yes, definitely rethinking my rebellion.

"I wasn't jokin', bro," Casey warned and Gray sobered, kind of. Mostly he chuckled while smiling and looked back at Casey.

"You gonna be at the hotel at ten to know?" he asked.

Casey's teeth clamped and his jaw tensed.

That meant no.

And Gray knew it.

"Right," Gray muttered, still sounding amused.

Casey leaned even closer, rolling up on his toes and I held my breath when he got nose to nose with Gray.

"I think you get I'm not likin' this. You do *anything* to my Ivey, you got a problem," he whispered.

"And I think you *don't* get that all men are not like you," Gray returned on a low growl, no longer even minimally amused. "I would never do anything to Ivey or any woman they didn't want me to do. Now back off before I do somethin' to *you* Ivey won't want me to do."

Oh dear.

Casey held Gray's steady stare.

Gray returned it.

I held my breath.

Then I couldn't anymore and therefore announced, "If you two don't stop it, I'm gonna pass out."

Surprisingly instantly, Casey leaned away. When he did, Gray moved back taking me with him.

Casey shot Gray a death glare, modified it only slightly before he swung it to me then he turned on his boot and stomped in the direction of the hotel.

Gray shifted so my front was not tucked to his side, but his front.

I looked up at him.

And at a glance, I knew this was worth it. Enduring that scene was worth it. And this was because Gray wasn't grinning, no dimple, no tender look, no laughter and just his eyes soft on me, but still, I knew it was worth it.

"You okay?" he asked.

I nodded.

"Five thirty?" he asked.

I nodded again.

That was when he grinned.

Oh yes. Definitely worth it.

"Glad his shit kept you in town, dollface," he whispered.

I nodded again. I was glad too. *Very* glad.

He lifted a hand and cupped my jaw.

I held my breath.

Please kiss me, please kiss me. Please, please, please kiss me, my mind chanted.

"See you at five thirty," he muttered, his fingers at my jaw tensed a second then he let me go.

I shifted woodenly and watched him walk to his truck parked on the square.

Then I licked my lips, turned back and headed to the hotel.

ONE HOUR LATER...

I HAD A DILEMMA.

No connections. Play it safe. No roots. Traveling. Hotels. Bars. No one but Casey and me.

This meant I didn't know what I was doing.

I'd never been on a date.

I didn't even know what a VFW was.

I just knew steak was a fancy meal. Casey and I splurged on our birthdays, on Christmas and on Thanksgiving. We saved up (or I did) and made it so. No gifts. Just togetherness, a good meal and a toast that we made it that far and another toast to the hope that our futures would be that we'd keep on making it.

But now, I had a looming date.

With Grayson Cody.

And even though I figured it would only be this one, not for me, but for him, I didn't want to mess it up.

But I had no idea what I was doing.

Casey was staring at the TV, waiting for his dream girl to get off work and ignoring me. When he wanted to hold a grudge, he held it as long as he wanted and he did this by giving me the silent treatment.

But even if he wasn't holding a grudge, I could hardly ask him what to do on a date.

When we'd run he'd been seventeen. He'd only had a handful of dates by then. And since then, his dates included getting some woman in a bar drunk then getting in her pants either in his car or while I made myself scarce and he had fun in our hotel room.

I didn't suspect this was the same kind of date Grayson Cody gave a woman.

My brother couldn't help me.

And I needed help.

And I knew who not only could help, but would.

I just didn't know if I could find her.

But I was going to try.

I flipped closed the semi-stolen, mostly-borrowed library book I was not reading but still was holding close to my face, dropped it on the bed and rolled off.

I grabbed my jacket, scarf and purse, shrugging, wrapping and strapping them on.

Then I hit the door, muttering, "Be back."

Casey didn't even tear his eyes from the TV.

Really, he could hold a serious grudge.

I left him to it, ducked out of the room and hurried through the cold, late afternoon sidewalks of Mustang to the square.

Let her be there, let her be there, let her be there, my mind recited as, head down, shoulders hunched, I walked through the cold.

I pushed through the door of The Rambler and looked right to the bar.

She was there.

Thank you, I whispered in my head.

Her eyes came to me as I moved to the bar, not the opposite end with my back to the wall, the near end with my back to the door.

"Hey," she said, jerking up her chin. "Early tonight," she remarked.

Another go at friendly. That door was still open.

Thank you, I repeated in a whisper in my head.

"Yeah, can I have a diet pop?"

She nodded, grabbed a glass, dunked it in the big ice bin and put it on the counter. Then she shot it with the soda gun.

"Heard Bud and his boys gave you trouble last night," she said softly, curiously and carefully. She expected to be shut down.

I didn't shut her down. I lifted my eyes from the glass to hers.

"Gray knew there'd be trouble. He was looking out for me."

She took in a slight breath and replied, "Gray's that way."

More Gray intrigue.

I didn't have time for Gray intrigue, alas.

I had a date with him that night.

"Anyway, a cop named Lenny showed up and Manny heard the commotion so Gray got backup and it all turned out okay," I finished.

"Len's a good man. And Manny doesn't like trouble at his hotel. Bud, he's a dick. He's no stranger to trouble and Manny, or Len for that matter, especially Len, are no strangers to Bud's brand of trouble."

There it was. Bud spread his jerk cheer all through Mustang. Not a surprise.

"I shouldn't have made that bet," I muttered.

"Don't know, girl," she grinned. "Fifteen minutes to earn five hundred dollars? I'da made it."

I held her gaze. Then, slowly, I grinned back.

She caught it, interpreted it correctly as the opening it was and leaned in instantly. "Where'd you learn how to play pool like that?"

she asked but didn't wait for me to answer. "Seriously, I couldn't believe my eyes. Everyone's talkin' about it."

Oh no. That was not good.

She kept speaking.

"You can't be more than twenty-one."

"I'm twenty-two," I told her.

"Okay," she grinned again, "you can't be more than twenty-two. So, your age, how'd you learn to play pool like that?"

I wasn't used to this. Sharing. I didn't know how to do it. I just knew how not to.

So I told her the truth.

"I didn't. It came naturally. I just picked up a pool cue one day and went for it. My brother flipped out. I can't say I played then like I play now but..." I shrugged, "it just happened. It's just something I can do."

"Cool," she said on a bigger grin.

I liked this, talking to her. It felt nice. Nice enough I could do it awhile. Nice enough, I might even be able to do it for hours.

But I had a mission.

And on that mission, I blurted, "What's a VFW?"

Her head tilted sharply to the side and her brows drew together.

Then her head straightened, her brows drifted apart and she flat out smiled.

"Veterans of Foreign Wars," she answered.

What on earth?

Janie kept talking.

"They got a lodge here. Veterans commune, they do shit, make money, give it to charity, have picnics. I don't know, shit like that. And they make a *mean* steak. Do it as a fundraiser every Friday, but also so they'll have more reason to commune, eat meat and drink beer."

"So, is it fancy?" I asked carefully.

She shook her head and leaned in closer, both arms on the bar. "No, babe. The steak is to die for, to kill for, but it's just a night out.

Everyone'll be there. Cool. Casual." Her eyes held mine and she said softly, "You're good just as you are."

I wasn't sure I was a big fan of "everyone'll be there" but I still nodded.

Then she weirdly begged, "Please tell me it's Gray."

"Tell you what's Gray?"

"Tell me it's Gray who's takin' you to the VFW tonight."

"It's Gray," I confirmed softly.

She smiled huge.

I was surprised. I was also pleased I had her endorsement. But I was lastly confused.

"Why do you want me to tell you it's Gray?"

She shrugged. "Don't know. He's Gray."

"What's that mean?" I asked and it was then Janie studied me.

Then she leaned in even deeper and stated. "Good people in this town, a lot of them. Bad people too but that's the way of the world and luckily, in Mustang, there's fewer than most places. Everywhere, there's always that someone who's better than the good people, better than most anyone and in Mustang, that someone is Gray."

My breath flew clean out of me.

"So," she went on, "you got a guy like Gray, everyone, not just me, but everyone hopes he'll find somethin' great. Somethin' awesome. Somethin' else. Lotsa sweet girls in town gotta say, but none of them'd do the trick."

Eyes glued to mine, she finished.

"Has to be someone great. Someone awesome. Someone who's somethin' else. Like a twenty-two-year-old girl who walks into a bar thinkin' she's invisible and not havin' the first clue she's movie star gorgeous. Like a twenty-two-year-old girl that makes scuffed cowboy boots, faded jeans and a tight Henley look like haute couture. Like a twenty-two-year-old girl who's sweet to cooks in a bar she's never gonna meet because she needs food but she don't wanna put 'em out when it's almost quittin' time. Like a twenty-two-year-old girl that sizes Bud Sharp up, sees his fancy-ass clothes, knows, she takes a good look in the mirror, she could bring him to his knees and make him beg and live the big life even if it's in a small town, and she wants no part of a dick like him. Like a twenty-two-year-old girl who's got her secrets and holds 'em close but cares enough about Grayson Cody, she lays out her cards to make sure, when he asks her on a date, she doesn't go out on his arm and make him look bad. Like you, who could open your door to Gray tonight lookin' exactly like you look, wearin' exactly what you're wearin', and I'm tellin' you he won't be disappointed and no one, not Gray, not anyone in this town, not anyone on this goddamned planet would take a look at you two and not think you belong together."

I'd had a lot of experience hiding behind a guard that was unshakable.

But not enough not to be left breathing heavy with my hand flat on the bar and my eyes trembling with wet as I stared at a woman I did not know who said the nicest things to me that I'd ever heard in my twenty-two years.

"I'll end with this, babe," she said quietly. "I don't know what you got goin' on. It's a small town, you look the way you look, you play pool the way you play pool, you catch Gray Cody's eye and he steps up for you, word's gonna spread. Everyone's talkin'. You decide to let go whatever you got goin' on, I was close on puttin' up a sign in my window. I need help. I don't know what you do but I do know men in seven counties would come to The Rambler to buy a beer from you. You want the job, it's yours. You need a place to hang 'til you get your shit together, I own this joint including up top. Mostly storage and the rest ain't much, but it's got a kitchenette and a bathroom. You're welcome to it until you get on your feet. A month, two. Then, you wanna stay, we talk rent. You wanna find somethin' nicer, you keep smilin', lookin' as flat out gorgeous as you are and sellin' the hell outta beer, we're good. You don't want that and take off, I get that. Life is life. But that offer is on the table. Yeah?"

I was still breathing heavily to stop the wet from spilling over when I nodded.

"Diet's on the house," she muttered then grinned.

I pulled my lips in and bit them.

Then I let them go and grinned back.

I pulled in a heavy breath, grabbed my diet and took a sip.

Then I set it down with great care, my eyes on the glass and my hand executing this maneuver like judges were sitting at the end of the bar who would flip up numbers that would grade my performance.

I tipped my eyes to Janie's and whispered, "Thank you, Janie."

"Thank me with your name," she returned.

"Ivey." I was still whispering.

"Ivey," she shoved her hand at me, "nice to meet cha."

I looked at her hand. Then I took it. I looked back at her.

"You too."

And I smiled.

Chapter 10

I Prefer to Sink My Teeth into Something

T*wo hours and forty-five minutes later…*

"Hey, Gray!"

"Hi, Gray!"

"Yo, Cody!"

We were walking through the VFW, which was what Janie said it was, a lodge. A *full* lodge. Long tables, and lots of them, with bench seats full of people, oldies, young couples, entire families.

Gray had his hand at the small of my back guiding me through.

He knew everybody and they knew him. Thus the called out greetings. He also got a lot of smiles, head tips (women), chin jerks (men) and waves (kids).

I just got a lot of looks and every last one was curious. Friendly, but curious.

Except for a few of the younger women. Their looks were minus the friendly.

Gray led me to the last table where there were two seats available at the end of the benches, the rest of the table full.

I slid on the bench across from Gray thinking I couldn't do this.

I could hustle big, bad, bearded bikers who could break me in two, take their money and clear out of town with Casey driving, gun in his hand, me riding, my baseball bat in mine but this...this I couldn't do.

But I had no choice. I was there so I had to find a way to do it.

I took off my coat feeling self-conscious. Janie said I didn't have to change. But I had a tank that had some nice lace at the top and my cardigan was kind of cute. So I'd put both on. I'd also refreshed my makeup and perfume. I'd lastly added a couple of pretty necklaces and some bigger than usual earrings. It wasn't much but it said something and Gray deserved to have a girl open the door to him who made an effort.

So I made that effort.

And, looking around, no one was in ballroom gowns. In fact, even though it wasn't much, I was dressed better than most.

This gave me relief.

Gray had on what I'd seen him in this morning and afternoon. Dark blue turtleneck, jeans, boots. He didn't look any different at all.

He didn't need to. Gray Cody didn't need to make any effort. He was naturally spectacular.

He shrugged off his leather coat, unwrapped his scarf and, like me, tucked it on the bench between himself and the person next to him.

"Hey, Gray." We heard and I watched his eyes go down the table where more greetings were being called.

He did a chin lift then introduced, "Folks, this is Ivey."

I lifted a hand, looked down the table as a whole and gave a lame wave.

I realized it probably looked lame so I dropped it and tucked both hands between my thighs. As I did this, I took in a bunch of curious, friendly looks, smiles and a few greetings.

Then, to my surprise, that was it. They turned to each other or their meals.

Giving us privacy (kind of).

Wow. That was nice.

"Evenin', Gray. Hello beautiful creature that embodies the reason I put my ass on the line for this country." I heard, my eyes grew wide, my head turned to the gravelly voice and I tipped it back to look at an old guy standing by our table to see him looking down at me. "Gray knows the drill. Gray gets a T-bone, rare, potato loaded and loses the veggies. I gotta know about you. You want a T-bone, which, little thing like you, will kick your ass. A strip, which I recommend. A filet, which melts in your mouth but there ain't much to it. Or a sirloin, which is okay, still recommend the strip."

"Uh...then, I'll, um, go for the strip," I told him.

"Right, then how you want it cooked?"

"Medium rare," I ordered.

"Pansy, but you're a girl, I'll let that slide."

My eyes got wider.

He kept speaking.

"Baked potato or fries, and before you waste my time, a loaded potato comes with butter, salt and pepper, sour cream and chives. If you're gonna eat a potato, I won't like you if you don't get it loaded."

My eyes got even wider.

"Okay then, potato. Loaded."

I mean, what else could I say?

Still, truth be told, I wanted it loaded.

"You want veggies?" he asked.

"Uh...sure?" I asked back.

"Women, they eat the veggies and or make their kids eat 'em. Men are men 'cause they got out from under their momma's thumb and can say a big eff you to vegetables. I carry no judgment, a woman wants her veggies," he informed me.

"Well, that's good," I muttered.

"Still, you could bust my chops, order a steak well-done, a potato plain and ask me to steam the veggies and I'd do it for you 'cause you're just that beautiful."

Wow.

"Thanks," I whispered.

"Though, that said, it'd still be a pain in my ass."

I heard Gray chuckle and I liked it, I liked seeing his face when he was amused but I couldn't tear my eyes off this guy.

"Sonny," a female from down the table called, "there's children present."

Sonny, our unusual waiter, looked down the table and asked, "My seed make that kid?"

I heard Gray chuckle again as my eyes got even wider.

"Of course not!" she cried, offended.

"Then do I care?" Sonny fired back.

I pressed my lips together. Gray's chuckle became laughter.

"Honestly!" the woman huffed.

"That's about it," Sonny muttered then without another word he took off.

I watched him go then my eyes dazedly drifted back to Gray to see the dimple on full display, which did nothing to assist my daze.

"Sonny's a character," he pointed out the obvious.

"I think I got that," I returned the favor.

His dimple pressed deeper.

Seeing that, my mind became consumed with the hope that this date would end with a kiss.

"He went to school with my dad," Gray informed me.

I pulled myself out of my thoughts and nodded.

"Granddad died, he left Dad the place. Dad died, he left it to me," Gray kept sharing.

I nodded again and there it was. His gran was living with him *and* it was her home. He didn't lie and I was glad to know it.

His voice was quieter when he asked, "What's your dad do?"

My eyes slid from his as I felt steel bands clamp around my ribs.

"Ivey," he called and my eyes slid back.

"Don't know my dad."

He held my eyes and I let him.

Then he asked, "Ever?"

I shook my head.

I watched him pull in a soft breath.

I changed the subject.

"What is your place?"

"Say again?"

"What's your place? Is it an orchard, a ranch, a farm?"

"Ranch and orchard. We got peach trees and we got horses."

That was interesting.

"Horses?" I asked.

Gray nodded. "Breed 'em, raise 'em, break 'em, train 'em, sell 'em."

"Oh," I whispered, liking this. I'd never ridden a horse but I thought they were very pretty.

"Mustangs," he went on and my gaze sharpened on him because I liked that more even though I had no idea why. "Or they used to be," he continued and grinned. "Obviously not wild anymore."

"Right," I said softly, really not knowing what he meant.

He must have read my face because he leaned toward me and explained, "Mustangs were and still are free-roaming. In other words, wild. Sometimes, to control the population, they'll let them be captured and adopted. But to be a true mustang, the horse needs to be wild. My great-granddad and his dad before him, before they were managed, used to go out and capture 'em, break 'em, breed 'em. Sometimes we'll adopt to get new blood because we need it since all our horses' ancestry is mustang."

I thought that was fascinating.

"Have you captured any?" I asked.

"Yeah," he answered.

That was even more fascinating.

So much, I smiled.

Gray smiled back.

"Hang around another day, dollface, take you to my barn, show you my beauties," he offered.

I was going to hang around another day. Definitely. Absolutely. I didn't care if Casey's blooming love went up in a fiery ball of flame and he was desperate to beam out of Mustang to another galaxy. I was sticking around because I was going to see Gray's "beauties."

"I'd like that."

He smiled again.

"I've never ridden a horse," I shared and his brows went up.

"Seriously?" he asked.

I shook my head.

"Then we'll get you up on one."

Oh no.

That was when I shook my head. "That's okay. Just seeing them would be nice."

"No way, Ivey. You haven't lived unless you've been on the back of a horse."

"I—" I started but he leaned further in.

"You ride with me. You don't like the feel of it, you're safe. You don't have to control anything. I got it. You like it and want to give it a shot, we'll get you up on one alone. Your call, honey, but you gotta let me give this to you and you gotta let yourself have it. You do, swear to Christ, you'll never regret it."

I ride with him.

I was stuck there. Riding on the back of a horse with Gray.

"Okay," I agreed and earned another smile.

I smiled back.

Then suddenly I felt the mood at our table change. It was swift, palpable, and I would know why when a presence hit the end of the table and a woman's catty voice sounded.

"Same Gray, big spender. VFW on a first date."

My eyes were on Gray and I saw his eyes turn stone cold as his jaw went rock hard and he turned his head and looked up.

I did too.

She was pretty, not beautiful, pretty. Very pretty.

But she thought she was God's gift. It was clear as day.

"Cecily," Gray muttered not in a welcoming way, and I got the feeling he intended to say more but she beat him to it.

Her eyes came to me. "Know you're new in town and every girl in town knows so, fair's fair you should too, this is where he takes all of us."

"Goodness me," a woman down the table muttered.

I stared.

"I should believe this, it's you, but I still don't believe this," Gray ground out but I didn't look at him. I couldn't tear my eyes off her as her venomous gaze swung to Gray.

"We're girls. We don't play games like you boys do." She looked back at me. "Do we, sweetie?"

I knew. That venomous look, I knew.

She had him. She lost him. She wanted him back. She knew that wasn't going to happen, mainly because she was a screaming bitch. If she could do this and convince herself it was okay, she could do a lot of things and think she could convince who she was doing them to—namely, at some point in the probably not-so-distant past, Gray—then she'd lose the person she was doing them to.

Namely...Gray.

Her dark, arched eyebrows shot up and she asked, "Do you speak?" She looked to Gray. "Is she mute?"

I didn't know if Gray intended to answer and this was because I was still looking at her when I did.

"I speak, though I try not to when I don't have anything nice to say and I'm afraid I've been struggling the last few seconds trying to find something nice to say."

Her eyes shot back to me and narrowed.

For some reason beyond me, I didn't shut up.

"I don't know...I mean, I do, since you've made it clear you don't but there are some of *us girls* who think a steak dinner in a family place where the money goes to charity and the waiter went to school with your dad who's passed away is a pretty darned nice first date. It's too bad you don't." My head tilted ever so slightly toward Gray and I finished, my point very thinly veiled. "*Really* too bad."

"Charming," she hissed, not smart enough to keep Gray, not dumb enough to miss my point.

"Funny, that's what I was thinking," I said softly.

She clamped her teeth shut.

"Have you eaten?" I asked when she didn't mosey on her way. I didn't wait for her answer when I went on, "If you haven't, though you've been here, just FYI, the strip comes highly recommended."

"I've *had* the strip," she retorted.

I didn't miss a beat. "Was it good?"

Her nose went up in the air half an inch. "I prefer the filet."

Her meaning was clear.

Total bitch.

"Sonny said, and it's also my experience, there's not much to a filet."

She leaned toward me slightly and said softly, "It melts in your mouth."

I shrugged. "May be just me but I prefer to sink my teeth into something."

At that, Gray burst out laughing, my eyes moved directly to him but not before I noted Cecily's doing the same.

Still laughing, his dancing eyes on me, Gray forced out, "Don't stop, darlin', me and the rest of the VFW are enjoying the show."

Hells bells.

I pressed my lips together.

Gray's eyes dropped to my mouth, his waning laughter waxed and it was then I heard a number of chuckles all around.

My eyes slid to Cecily to see her face had gone red.

"Are you done welcoming me to Mustang?" I prompted and she shot daggers at me with her eyes.

"Enjoy your strip," she replied snottily.

"I intend to," I muttered, Gray's laughter kept sounding as did the many chuckles.

God. Embarrassing.

Cecily, definitely shoving her nose in the air, flounced away.

I sighed deeply.

"That...was...*brilliant*," the woman who had tried to tell off Sonny whispered down the table at me.

I smiled even as I bit my lip.

"Dollface, give me your hand."

That was Gray and I looked to him to see his arm stretched across the table toward me, his big hand turned up. I took mine out of my lap, rested it in his and his fingers curled warm and tight around mine.

"Last night, I bled for you. Cecily is the female version of taking on a battalion of pissed-off assholes. Now I owe you," he said, smiling at me.

"He's not wrong," the man beside me leaned in to mutter then his mutter dropped to a whisper, probably because there were kids at the table. "Thinks her shit don't stink. Probably not a surprise but you aren't special. She spreads that cheer all around. Gets on everyone's nerves."

I nodded to him.

Gray's hand squeezed mine and I looked back at him.

"Thanks for havin' my back."

"You're welcome."

His fingers gave mine another squeeze.

It felt nice.

Sonny arrived and Gray's hand quickly let mine go so both of our arms could vacate the table's surface seeing as, if they did or didn't, either way Sonny was dumping two plates on the table.

Once this was achieved, his eyes locked on mine.

"Next time you have a verbal catfight, you call me before you engage hostilities. Yeah?" he demanded.

Well, that didn't take long to make the rounds.

"Uh...all right," I whispered.

"Clear your plate or you'll break my heart," he ordered.

"I wouldn't wanna do that," I muttered, looking down at my plate.

It looked sensational.

"I hope not," Sonny whispered and his whisper was chock full of something. So much of it, even though him whispering at all would make my eyes shoot to his face, it was the emotion that made them make the journey in record time.

When he caught my gaze, his, which was burning with the emotion in his voice, didn't let mine go.

Then he nodded his head and stomped off.

I watched him go.

I was still doing it when Gray prompted quietly, "Tuck in while it's hot, dollface."

I looked to him.

Then it was me who nodded.

I tucked in.

VFW charity dinner or not, Gray wasn't wrong.

It wasn't only the best steak I'd ever had, it was the best meal.

I loved every bite.

"'Night, Janie," Gray called.

I waved.

"'Night you two," Janie called back also adding a wave and a big old smile.

Gray had his arm around my shoulders and was leading me out the door of The Rambler where, after a delicious steak dinner and conversation that, following Cecily's warm welcome, included the whole table—and that would be the rotating people who sat at it after folks finished and new folks arrived—we had a few beers and a half a dozen games of pool.

During which I wiped the floor with a Gray who didn't mind even a little bit.

I figured this had to do partly with him watching me play pool not only with his eyes on my behind (which I caught more than once and it made me feel warm in a way I'd never felt before) but also just watching me shoot pool.

He was impressed and didn't hide it.

It had always been a job—the hustle, second nature.

That night, playing pool and essentially entertaining a handsome, easygoing, often smiling man I liked a great deal and with every passing second liked even more, it became a whole lot more.

"Honest to God, you just picked up a cue and could shoot pool?" Gray asked.

Obviously, we'd chatted. After the first evasive maneuver I had to make to deflect his question about my dad, Gray made an effort to keep it light, for me.

Not for him.

I learned, when Gray was twenty, his dad died in the car wreck that took away his grandma's legs. Tragic without additional tragic circumstances like joyriding kids or drunk drivers. It was a snowy night and they went head to head with another pickup, both caught ice and the results weren't pretty. His dad died, his gran lost her legs, the other driver lost his arm.

I also learned his mom left his dad when Gray was five after suffering her third miscarriage after she had Gray. She disappeared for twelve years, no word, no sightings, but then came back out of the blue and tried to take up where she left off with both Gray and his father. Gray's dad (still alive then obviously) was not big on this option. Neither was his gran. Neither was Gray, who without evasion cared deeply for them both. His father loved his mother and her desertion of him and his son understandably didn't go over well and her return was worse.

She gave up but didn't leave. Gray told me he ran into her on occasion but didn't give her his time. She was a nurse at the local clinic. Night shifts.

That explained his not getting stitches last night.

I also learned that I was right. He was twenty-five, twenty-six in March.

For my part, Gray learned Casey was twenty-seven, Casey had currently convinced himself he was falling in love and that I had a natural talent playing pool.

It wasn't a fair exchange but I was new to this, I was going easy and I was scared.

I was who I was and I had a sense that he knew who I was and didn't care.

That said, I didn't expect he'd be all that hip on having a pool hustling girlfriend who traveled the continental United States with her brother, playing pool, hustling idiots and returning back infrequently to have steak dinners with him at the VFW.

I didn't know what I was doing or where this was going.

I just knew right then, for the first time since I could remember, maybe the first time in my life, I liked right where I was.

So I was living that moment and doing the best I could.

Gray didn't seem to mind.

"Yeah," I answered his question about picking up a cue and acing pool as we walked into the cold. Gray moved us down the sidewalk toward the hotel, which was away from his pickup, thus clearly stating we were taking a short walk. "I mean, I wasn't as good as I am now but it isn't far off."

"You got a head for numbers?" Gray asked, and I looked up at his profile, feeling his arm around me, my arm, which had slid around his waist, and thinking, strangely, walking tucked to his side and held by him, that it didn't seem cold.

Not even a little bit.

"A head for numbers?" I asked back.

"Yeah. Stands to reason, you can naturally play pool, you got a head for geometry, physics. If you see angles, can instantly assess velocity, force, impact, then you'd have a head for science, numbers."

I hadn't thought of that.

I also left school at twelve so I really had no idea.

That said, I was good with money. For instance, I could assess the percentage of a tip without even thinking about it. I could also without thinking take our bank and divide it knowing down to the penny how much time we had before we needed another score.

Maybe I was.

"Maybe I do," I told Gray. "I hadn't really thought about it. Just thought I could play pool."

"You can't play pool, dollface. You dominate. Never seen anything like it. It's sensational. Like watchin' a master at a canvas. A prima ballerina on a stage." His arm gave me a squeeze and my eyes, which had drifted to our moving feet, went back to his face to see he was grinning down at me. "Not that I ever saw either of those. I'm just guessing."

I grinned up at him.

Then I replied quietly, "I haven't seen either of those either but what you said was nice."

His arm gave me another squeeze. I felt my arm should reciprocate the gesture so it did.

His grin turned into a smile.

I made note of that for future reference.

His gaze moved to face forward.

My eyes drifted down to my feet.

And we both shifted to silence.

It seemed liked seconds had gone by (but it was more like minutes just that I liked walking tucked to Gray in the cold) we were at my door.

Belly full of great food, beer. Time spent in interesting and not demanding conversation. Gray's eyes on me, my eyes able to take in Gray any time I wanted. And Janie smiling on happily. I was lost in the night. A nice night.

No, a *great* night.

The best I ever had. None even came close. Not even when Casey and I scored huge with that idiot with the Rolex who bet five thousand dollars on a single game of pool.

And I'd never been on a date.

So it didn't occur to me that we were at my hotel door and it was the end of our date.

So it also didn't occur to me what normally happened at the end of a date.

Not even when Gray's arm curled me to press my front to his and his other arm slid around me at my waist.

"Be back tomorrow, take you to breakfast at the diner, take you to my place, give you a ride. Does eight work for you?" he asked, his voice soft.

I smiled, liking that I got to go to sleep thinking that was going to be what I woke up to.

Liking it a whole lot.

I nodded.

"Good," he muttered, his eyes dropping to my mouth and then his head dropped and then...then...

Then his beautiful lips were on mine and he was kissing me.

Kissing me!

My first kiss.

It wasn't a stealth attack but I was still surprised and this worked in my favor because the touch of his mouth to mine, the hardness of his body against mine, his arms around me, his warmth, his smell, all that was him, I liked it. So much, I got lost in it and my body automatically melted into his, my arms around him going tight, my elbows bent, forearms running up his back either side of his spine. My hands felt leather and under that hardness and they pressed in.

Then Gray touched his tongue to my mouth.

My stomach dipped instantly, tingles shot down the fronts of my thighs and my lips opened instinctively.

His tongue slid inside.

Oh my.

That was nice.

Oh *my*.

That was *nice*.

My fingers fisted in the leather, my knees got weak, more tingles shot through my legs but these were different. Stronger. Racing up not down, straight between my legs as Gray's arms got super tight and he held me super close and my tongue intuitively danced with his.

He looked good. He sounded good. He smelled good. He felt good.

And now I knew he tasted good.

Sublime.

The best taste to touch my tongue.

Absolutely.

Then it got better. His arm around my shoulders moved, his long fingers ran up the back of my neck, sifted in my hair, cupped the back of my head and that felt lovely.

He used his hand at my head to tip mine to the side, his slanted the other way and the kiss went deep.

Way deep.

Straight through my mouth, down my throat, through my belly to spasm between my legs even as it seared straight into my soul.

I whimpered involuntarily, that sound a sound I never made and a sound that spoke volumes.

At it, Gray moved us, shuffling me back. I hit door, Gray's entire body pressed into mine and the kiss hit the stratosphere.

When he tore his lips from mine I found my hand had somehow made its way into his leather jacket, curled around and my fist was now in his sweater. My other hand had plunged into his soft, thick hair, holding his head to me and I was up on tiptoes, squeezing myself tight to him.

I blinked hazily into his eyes as he muttered, "Fuck."

"What?" my mouth said without me telling it to.

"Your brother is unpredictable, Gran would lose her mind I took you home and there is no way in hell I'm movin' somethin' that hot and sweet forward on the bench seat of an old, cold, dirty pickup."

I stopped breathing.

"Say goodnight, Ivey," he growled, not letting go of me.

Something was happening and I might not have had a date and that might have been my first kiss—the greatest first kiss of all time—but I wasn't naïve.

I knew what was happening.

My brother was my brother and he got himself laid regularly. And I spent most my time in seedy dive bars, or just bars, around men. They said things, with their mouths and with their eyes.

I knew exactly what was happening.

And I liked that it was happening between Gray and me.

I delayed too long in doing as ordered. I knew it when Gray's arms got tight and his hips pressed into my belly.

"Say...*goodnight*...Ivey," he growled again.

"Goodnight, Gray," I whispered.

"Fuck," he whispered back, touched his mouth to mine and let me go.

At the loss of his arms, his heat, his strength, the cold smacked straight through me.

"Get inside," he demanded.

I nodded, jerked my head down, dug the key out of my purse and turned to the door. I opened it, took a half step in and turned back.

Gray was still where I left him.

"Lights on, darlin'," he said softly.

I didn't tear my eyes from him as I felt the wall for the switch and flipped it on.

"Right, get in. I wanna hear the chain."

I nodded but didn't move.

"Now, Ivey."

I nodded again but still didn't move.

He grinned and I saw the dimple.

And I fell, right then, *right then*, straight, fast and hard...in love.

"Eight, baby," he whispered.

"Eight, Gray," I whispered back.

"Get warm, honey."

I nodded. "Thanks for a nice night."

"We'll have more."

We'll have more.

I felt tears sting my nose as my mind sent my gratitude heavenward.

Thank you, God.

"Eight," Gray repeated.

I smiled.

So he could get out of the cold, I scurried in, closed the door, flipped the lock and set the chain.

Then I moved to the curtain. Trying to hide, I peeked out but I didn't need to try to hide.

He was sauntering away.

I watched, smiling.

When I lost sight of him, I moved from the curtain and looked around the hotel room.

I wrapped my arms around my belly.

Then I smiled so big it hurt my face, I twirled around like what I didn't know was a teenager, danced to the bed and dropped on it on my back, giggling the whole way.

Chapter 11

I Was Free

T*welve hours later…*

Gray pulled back on the horse's reins and although the view was stunning, the snowy plains, the flowing creek, its sides crusted with ice twinkling in the bright sun, the far off mountains blue against the skyline, I didn't want him to.

This was because, being held tight against Gray with one of his arms around my belly on top of a magnificent equine beast, I didn't want to stop. Not ever.

Not ever.

Still, he did.

Then again, we were far from his ranch-slash-orchard (and I saw, in daylight, the rows and rows and *rows* of densely planted, short peach trees that nearly surrounded the house and the outbuildings that also undoubtedly in spring were amazing) so we'd have to climb back on to get back.

Again, something to look forward to.

Something to look forward to.

I didn't know if I could get used to that. I'd never had that either, until last night.

I loved it even though I was so excited for the morning to come, I didn't sleep a wink. And I didn't care that Casey didn't come back before I left again. I just wrote him a note, got ready and was waiting impatiently by the time Gray knocked on my door.

Breakfast at the diner, meeting his "beauties," which were just that (there were twelve of them, *twelve!*) and now this.

A ride over his land.

And there was a lot of it.

He shifted. Throwing off a long, heavy leg, he dropped down then his hands came up to my waist and pulled me down. Then his gloved hand curled around mine, which was also gloved since he went into the house and grabbed a pair of his gran's that I could borrow.

Grandma Miriam was not there, by the way. She was in town with some ladies, "knittin' or whatever they do, probably just jabberin'," (as Gray said).

This too surprised me about Grandma. She was in a wheelchair so, stupidly, I didn't think it was easy for her to get around so I guessed she wouldn't.

Obviously, she did.

Gray led me to the edge of the creek, his horse trailing behind us since Gray still held his reins. He stopped, dropped my hand but curled an arm around my shoulders and looked to the creek.

I curled my arm around his waist and looked to his profile.

"Is this your favorite place?" I guessed, and he stopped looking at the creek to grin down at me.

"One of 'em. Got a lotta land, dollface, and it's gorgeous land. So got a lotta places."

I could see that. We'd been riding awhile, maybe ten minutes and not at a sedate walk (which was fun). Everything I'd seen had been a candidate for top spot.

He turned his head, jerked his chin in front of him and my eyes followed.

When they did, he shared, "Across that creek, Bud Sharp's daddy owns that land."

Wow.

"Really?" I asked, staring at it.

"His daddy tried to buy ours from mine. His daddy's daddy tried to buy it from my granddad. This goes on, darlin', for four generations. Four generations they wanted their hands on Cody land."

That explained that.

Gray went on with brutal honesty.

"Bud wanted Cecily before me, had her after me."

My body jolted.

No. Now *that* explained *that*.

His arm gave me a squeeze and I looked up at him to see his eyes on me.

"Before her was Connie. Before her was Donna. Before her was Debbie. All the way back to junior high when he picked up with a girl named Emily after I got tired of makin' out with her at recess." He grinned again. "Which was around about the time she got braces. I liked my lips the way they were. Bud's were torn up for a month before he cottoned on."

I didn't want to find this amusing because it was kind of scary in a lot of ways. One of those being that he started kissing in junior high which put him around twelve or thirteen and I thought that was kind of young. And another was that he'd been kissing at that age and I'd just had my first kiss last night. But I couldn't stop the small giggle from escaping.

Gray's grin became a smile.

I bit my lip and looked back across the creek, letting it go and noting, "He didn't look much like a rancher cowboy to me."

And he didn't. Smooth hands. Nice clothes. Gray's clothes were nice, masculine, decent-quality, attractive but durable and not showy. And his hands were nice, beautiful actually, but that didn't mean they weren't callused. He was a man who worked with his hands. Bud Sharp was not.

"Buddy Sharp has got a lot of problems. One of 'em's bein' a pansy-ass. He doesn't like hard work. Sends his dad over the edge. Got some degree, don't know what, works one county over at the flagship branch of that county's bank. Heard word, since Bud spread it, he makes big money. He's got two sisters. Daddy Sharp is not feelin' much joy with his son. You got land, you pass it down to your boy you spend a lifetime trainin' to work it. You do not pass it down to your daughter's husband unless you have no son."

"Daddy Sharp share this with his son?" I asked quietly.

"Frequently and publicly, which means also frequently privately," Gray answered.

"So, seeing as Buddy is not into ranching and probably couldn't care less about your land, he took the family feud with you in a different way."

I felt Gray move and my eyes went back to him to see his movement meant he was looking at me.

"Not a family feud, Ivey, we get along fine. They make offers, we decline. They got twice as much land as us, though, not near as pretty." He grinned yet again and I returned it. Then he continued, "They run livestock, got two orchards, a vineyard, they make wine. I hire hands for peach season and bring in help when I'm breakin' a horse. Other than that, it's just me. Jeb Sharp, he's got five ranch hands, full-time. I lost my mind, accepted an offer, they'd be happy to expand their operation. The answer's no, Jeb don't care."

"So what's Buddy's problem?"

"Fuck if I know," he muttered, looking back across the creek. "Though my dad lived his life tellin' me often he loved me and was proud of me. He died and I knew those two things down to my bones. Don't know what would drive me if my dad was openly disappointed in me for bein' just who I was which wasn't bad until I became an asshole."

I again couldn't hold it back and laughed silently, this shaking my body so Gray looked back down at me, the dimple out.

I sobered and said softly, "You are who his father wants him to be."

"Say again?"

I turned and pressed my front to his side, tipping my head way back. "Gray, you are who Jeb Sharp wants his son to be. And if he doesn't mind frequently and publicly telling his son he's disappointed in who he's become, it probably stands to reason that the personification of that, right across a creek, has passed his lips on more than one occasion."

Gray's eyes drifted across the creek as he muttered, "Well, fuck me."

"Then again, maybe Jeb Sharp doesn't say anything and Bud Sharp just looks at you and knows. So, he bests you somehow, with women or earning money or whatever, he proves to his father and everyone that he's better." Gray looked back at me and I advised, "Maybe you should throw him a bone."

That got me a treat, the best gift I ever received. And this was, while Gray burst out laughing and I got to watch and listen, his body also shifted so we were front to front, his other arm stole around me and he held me tight.

When he sobered but was still smiling big and beautiful, his eyes tipped down to me and he asked, "And what do you reckon I should throw him, dollface?" Before I could answer this unanswerable question, his face got warm, his arms got tighter and he kept talking. "'Cause see, just found me something I like a lot, Bud likes her just as much and she's a bone no fuckin' way I'm gonna throw."

I felt my body ease against his just as my legs trembled.

"Gray," I whispered.

One of Gray's hands drifted up my back, my neck and held me at the base of my head.

"You're the prettiest thing I've ever seen, Ivey," he said softly and my body eased more into his even as I felt my eyes sting with tears.

I battled for control as he went on.

"I got shit to do today and it sucks, but soon, I gotta put you in my truck and take you back. Sayin' that, after I'm done, I'm gonna drive back into town and pick you up. I want you in my house eatin' dinner tonight then I want you to stay with me and watch TV. Your brother's got a place to be, I talk to Manny after I drop you off, you give up that room because I 'spect you need the money. No strings, no funny stuff, you sleep under my roof but in your own bed. We take that at your pace. But he's screwin' around with whatever he's screwin' around with and you and me are gettin' to know each other, you don't need to blow whatever stash you got on a hotel. You with me?"

I was but I wasn't.

"Gray, your gran," I whispered.

"Love her, she helped raise me, but, honey, I'm a man and I make the decisions that pertain to my life. It's my house even though it's both our homes. I'm not gonna lie, she's not gonna like it but I also don't care. She's an adult, you are and so am I. She'll have to deal."

"I'm not sure that's cool," I said quietly.

"Maybe not but it's the only time I've ever done it so I hope she gets my point and, knowin' that now, I hope you do too."

Wow.

I got it.

I got his point, definitely.

And I loved his point.

I didn't respond, just looked into his blue eyes with their dark, russet tipped lashes.

"Ivey, darlin', you with me?"

"If she feels uncomfortable enough that I feel it, will you take me back to the hotel?" I asked.

"Absolutely," he answered.

I gave him more of my weight then I whispered, "I'll try not to walk in on you in the bathroom."

He grinned. "Didn't complain last time."

No, he didn't.

I grinned back.

His grin died about a half a second before his eyes dropped to my mouth then his head dipped down and he kissed me.

It was nearly better than the first except this time, he didn't push it, I didn't whimper and it didn't careen out of control. It was wet, it was deep and it was sweet.

And I loved every second of being in his arms on a snowy plain by a creek in the cold with his mouth on mine.

Every blooming *second.*

He lifted his head, eyes locked to mine and muttered, "Let's get you back so you can deal with your brother, I can deal with my shit and then I can bring you back home."

Home.

That was what he said.

Home.

I loved that too.

"Okay," I whispered.

Gray grinned.

THREE HOURS LATER...

I WALKED the streets of Mustang.

Casey had come back and Casey was super okay with letting the hotel room go because, "My girl, she's all over me. It's cool. I'll crash with her. You and me will hook up for lunch at noon tomorrow at the diner."

He didn't ask about my first-ever date.

He didn't ask if I got home by ten (I didn't but it wasn't that far after).

He didn't care that I was crashing at Gray's.

He just was rabid to get back to his girl (after, of course, he begged me for another hundred dollars, which, of course, being me, I gave to him).

So he took his bag, the car, I dropped mine off with Manny at the front desk who assured me Gray had talked to him. And even though we checked out late, he wasn't going to charge us the extra day. I paid him for the time we stayed and then...I was free.

For a day, I...was...*free*.

I walked down the sidewalk of the square only just able to stop myself from whistling. Halfway down, I turned right and pushed open the door.

My eyes went to the bar.

Janie's eyes came to me.

My body went to the bar.

Janie's eyes followed me.

I put my hands on the bar.

Janie's eyes didn't leave me.

My mouth opened and this was what it asked, "That job still open?"

Janie smiled huge and this was how she replied, "Take it the date with Gray went good."

At that, it was my turn to smile huge.

Chapter 12

I'll Wait

S*even hours later…*

"She doesn't even know how *to cook*," Grandma Miriam hissed at Gray in the kitchen while I sat in their comfortable, lived in, countrified living room that had crocheted doilies on the backs of the couch and armchairs (yes, *doilies*), my eyes glued to a TV that came nowhere near to drowning out her voice.

"Gran, Ivey's in the next room," Gray growled.

She ignored him. "Who's ever heard of a twenty-two-year-old girl who doesn't know how to cook?"

"Cecily knew how to cook and still, everything she made tasted like shit," Gray returned.

"At least she knew," Grandma Miriam retorted.

"And Nancy was so damned flighty, she knew what she was doin' but still, she'd forget and every time I went to her house for dinner, the place smelled like it had just been badly renovated after a massive explosion because she either flat out burned the shit outta something or something boiled over, the gas went out of control, burned the wallpaper off the wall and I'd begin my date wielding a fire extinguisher," Gray shot back.

I didn't want to laugh because I was mostly terrified out of my mind seeing as Grandma Miriam seriously didn't like me and didn't mind me knowing, but it must be said, Gray was funny.

"She still knew how to do it," Grandma Miriam rejoined.

"Yeah, and so do I and so do you and, it comes to that, which Gran, this is our second date so why you got yourself in a snit, I don't know, then you teach her or I teach her," Gray responded.

"I'm in a snit because before date one, you got yourself a cut over your eye because of that girl's troubles and this might be date two but it's night two that girl's sleeping under this roof."

"In the guest bedroom."

"Grayson Cody, look at me. I'm seventy years old and I had four sons. *Four*. And I was married to your granddaddy. Do you think after all that experience with Cody men that *I don't know*?"

Oh dear.

"First," Gray clipped and I bit my lip at his tone, "I would not disrespect you like that. Second, I wouldn't do it to Ivey. I'm a Cody, Gran, and I'm more intimately acquainted with your other three boys' bullshit than you are these days, but I'm my father's son. Remember that."

Another bit of intrigue from Gray.

Grandma Miriam was silent.

Obviously Gray made his point.

Then Grandma Miriam decided to argue a different one.

"Don't care you're five or twenty-five, Grayson Cody, you need to watch that dirty mouth."

Gray clearly didn't feel like taking this admonition to heart considering I barely heard but did still hear him mutter, "Fuck me."

"Gray!" Grandma Miriam snapped.

I bit my lip again to stop myself from laughing because it might be scary but it was still funny.

There was nothing from Gray and then nothing from Grandma Miriam until I heard her declare, "I'm watching the box in my room."

"Suit yourself," Gray replied.

"I'd like to do it on my bed," she told him.

"Right, you wanna get ready for bed? Or you wanna watch awhile and call me later?"

"Watch awhile," she said much more quietly.

"Then let's go, darlin'," he muttered.

This time I was biting my lip because they could have an out-and-out and it ended with Gray putting his gran in bed so she could watch television comfortably and not in the presence of the girl her grandson was suddenly dating that she didn't like all that much only to go back and deal with her when she needed to get ready to go to sleep.

And I thought that was very sweet.

Grandma Miriam wheeled through calling out her lie that, though it had been a really long time since I went to church, I was pretty certain God frowned on as much as He disliked curse words, "Just feel like watchin' a different show than you and Gray, child. I'll say my goodnights now."

"Goodnight, Mrs. Cody," I called back and noticed as she wheeled around the stairs she didn't look at me.

Gray, following her, did.

"Be back in a minute, dollface."

"Okay," I said softly.

They disappeared.

I looked back at the TV.

Suffice it to say, dinner didn't go that well. Gray came to get me and we got back to his house before the meal had been prepared. Upon arrival, Grandma Miriam tried to press me into service and before I gamely waded in and commenced slicing off a digit or blowing up their kitchen, I confided in them that I'd never cooked.

Gray didn't say a word, didn't even give me a look, though it terrified me to admit that. Still, it wasn't something you could hide so, if we went beyond a second date, he'd eventually find out so I had to.

As evidenced by the fight that happened after I did manage to assist Gray in clean up, we all sat down and watched a sitcom then Grandma Miriam told her grandson she needed "a word," she didn't take to this too well.

I felt him before I saw him round the doublewide doorway to the living room. Then I watched him, ready to make my speech only to be cut off when he did something that took my breath away.

And what he did was pluck me right out of the couch and into his arms whereupon he entered the couch to lie on his back with me on top but tucked partly to the back of the couch.

I struggled to get my breath back then I struggled to get my wits about me. That (kinda) accomplished, I pushed up slightly with a hand to his chest and looked down at him.

He had his beautiful head with its thick gorgeous hair resting on a flowery-patterned pillow that had ruffles at the sides and his eyes were on the TV until he felt mine on him and they moved to me.

"I think maybe I should go back to the hotel," I whispered and his arm, which was curled around my back, got tight.

"Ivey—"

"She's uncomfortable."

"She'll get over it."

"Okay, maybe, but now, she's uncomfortable and this is her home, and my guess, and you can correct me, but it has been a while. No one should feel uncomfortable in their home."

"That include me?"

I shut my mouth.

His other hand came up and he tucked hair behind my ear but left his hand there, fingers in my hair, palm under my ear.

"She'll get over it," he said softly.

I pushed it carefully, "Gray, honey, you promised that if her discomfort made me uncomfortable, you'd take me back to town. That's happened."

"Ivey, honey, how much money you got left?"

That shut my mouth again.

"You guard a lotta shit, give me that." It was his turn to push.

"Six hundred, twenty-six dollars and sixty-seven cents."

He shook his head against the pillow, his mouth moving like he didn't know whether to grin or frown.

Then he muttered, "And sixty-seven cents."

I bit my lip because I knew, knowing it down to the penny, that said it all.

Gray held my eyes a moment before he stated softly but firmly, "She'll get over it."

He was looking out for me.

This knowledge washing over me, the way it did, the way it felt, I blurted, "I got a job at The Rambler today."

Gray's body went completely still under mine.

Then he asked, "Say again?"

"Janie and I chatted and she said she was looking for someone. I asked if that someone could be me. She said yes. I start Monday."

He stared at me, body still, mouth unmoving.

Seeing as this was the second date I'd ever had, it was kind of weird though I didn't know much about dating. Still I thought lying stretched out with your date on his couch while his grandmother nursed her snit in the next room and in a few hours you'd be going to sleep in his guest bedroom had to be weird for anyone. The only man I'd ever dated was Gray, not to mention the only man I really ever knew outside our parade of "uncles" was Casey, so I didn't know what to make of his response.

"Gray?" I called, it was tentative and that was not hidden in the slightest.

"Painful," he muttered strangely.

I tipped my head and kept his gaze as I asked, "What?"

Suddenly, I wasn't tucked between him and the couch. Suddenly, I was on my back on the couch with Gray's, long, hard body on mine and it was my head on the flowery, ruffled pillow staring up at him.

I found it hard to breathe and not because he was heavy (though he was but he was holding most of his weight up on a forearm in the pillow beside me). Just because I'd never had a man on me.

That man being Gray, I liked it.

A lot.

"Painful," he repeated, "seein' as you hustle pool. You shouldn't. You had one date with me. It was fuckin' fantastic. You felt it just like me because you givin' that up means you wanna see where this is goin' just as much as me and my gran is in the next room and I really, *really* wanna show my appreciation in a way that at this juncture I can *not*."

Oh my.

"Don't look at me like that, dollface, and don't touch or kiss me or we *will* be goin' back to Manny's but we'll both be spendin' the night," he warned.

Oh...*my*.

"Uh...how am I looking at you?" I asked.

"Like that," he answered, his eyes moving over my face.

I bit my lip because I didn't know how to help, but more, I didn't know if I wanted to.

Then I pointed out the obvious, "I'm not touching you, Gray, you're lying on me."

"Baby, no shit. I feel every inch of you and if I trusted myself right now to move, your ass would be in the armchair across the room and I'd be headin' upstairs to a cold shower."

Oh.

My.

"Gray—"

"I'll add, at this point, don't speak especially if it's to whisper my name all breathy like that."

I pressed my lips together.

Gray's eyes moved to them.

My eyes got bigger because recently any time that happened, a second later his mouth was on mine. He'd only given me two deep, sweet kisses, but before he dropped me off and since he picked me up, anytime his eyes moved to my lips, his mouth then moved to touch them.

Yes, even in front of his gran (twice).

This didn't go over too well either.

His gaze moved back to mine and when it did it didn't settle but roamed my face before he muttered, "Prettiest thing I've ever seen, on my couch, under me, her fantastic, fuckin' hair all over my pillow."

To that, I blurted, "This is your pillow?"

His eyes came back to mine.

"Yeah."

"It's ruffly."

Finally he grinned and muttered, "Yeah."

"Did you pick it?"

"Fuck no."

Well that was a relief.

My thoughts must have been written all over my face because Gray burst out laughing. And it was safe to say, standing in his arms, watching and hearing him do it was amazing but lying underneath him and watching, hearing and *feeling* him do it was even better.

By the time he semi-sobered, so did I because something he said penetrated.

"You know I hustle pool?" I whispered.

The amusement fled his eyes and his face got closer when he answered, "Yeah."

I guessed that. Still, it didn't feel great having it confirmed.

"How?" I asked.

"The bar your brother was casin'? The Alibi?"

I fought against biting my lip and nodded.

"My uncle owns that bar and my other two uncles hang there. Your brother marked one of them and started playin' him. He's shifty, can be mean, but he is in no way stupid. They followed him, caught sight of you, guessed the play. I was there, they told me about it, described you and I knew exactly who they were talkin' about seein' as I could barely keep my eyes off you when you were in The Rambler. I found you, warned you off."

"Your uncle owns that bar?"

He nodded. "He's shifty and can be mean too but doesn't go down that road as often."

Something else he said penetrated.

"You could barely keep your eyes off me at The Rambler?"

He grinned. "Dollface, you're not the only one with the ability to watch someone in a way they don't know you're watchin'."

Hells bells.

"You knew I was watching you?"

"All night long."

Darn.

His grin turned into a smile before it faded and he whispered, "You walked out before I could make an approach and you didn't even glance my way. Saw you in the playground, you told me you were stayin' at the hotel, swear, findin' out you were driftin' through hurt like a mother. Didn't get it then," his face got closer, "get it now."

My heart started thumping.

Gray wasn't done.

"Glad you're takin' a chance on a decent life in a decent place that'll treat you kind."

My heart started thumping harder.

Gray still wasn't done.

"And glad you're takin' a chance on me."

My heart began to thump wildly as tears filled my eyes.

"Gray—"

"Prettiest thing I ever saw," he whispered.

More wet in my eyes.

"Gray—"

"Now on my couch."

A tear slid out the side of my eye.

Gray caught it with a thumb.

Still whispering, he shared with me, "My dad taught me good

things come to those who wait. He was a patient man and he taught that to me. I never lived anywhere in my life but here but that don't mean I don't know the ways of the world. I know somethin' led you to that life but I look at you, nothin' hard about you, not your attitude, not your mouth, not your eyes, nothin'. Whatever led you to that life wasn't good but you didn't let it make you hard. There'll come a time when you'll give that to me. And you take your time, Ivey, I'll wait."

Another tear slid out of my eye followed immediately by another one out of my other eye. And then another. And more.

Gray caught the ones he could catch with his thumb but the others slid down my temple and wet my hair. I stared into his blue eyes with their russet tipped lashes and thought, but did not say, he was the most beautiful thing I'd ever seen and it wasn't just his outward beauty that made him that way.

His eyes moved to my trembling lips, he dropped his head and touched his mouth to mine.

Then he rolled, him to his back, me tucked to his side and murmured, "Now, dollface, let's relax in front of the TV."

I rested my cheek to his shoulder, slid my arm around his stomach and whispered, "Okay."

His arm around my back gave me a squeeze.

My eyes blinked away the wet, my hand lifted from his gut to wipe my temple then I put it back.

Then, even though this was the first time I ever lounged on a couch with a man watching TV, I thought it was unbelievably comfy.

And it came naturally.

Chapter 13

Silly

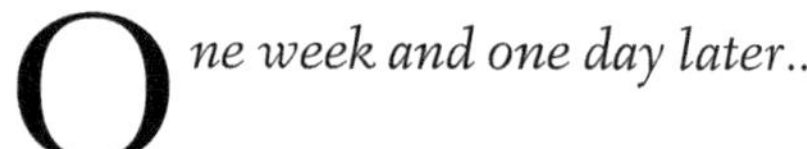

O*ne week and one day later…*

"FUCK," Gray whispered roughly against my lips and then his tongue was in my mouth again.

Yes.

We were upstairs at his house and he had me pressed deep against the wall by the door to the bathroom. Part of my skirt was bunched up at my waist because his hand was in my tights *and* my panties, cupping my behind, skin against skin. His other hand was up the back of my sweater, wrapped tight around, fingers curled so the tips were near to the side of my breast. I had yanked his shirt out of the back of his trousers and my fingers were exploring the muscled plains of his back, my other hand was in his hair, holding his mouth to mine.

It was heated. So heated I was liquid in his arms and if he didn't have such tight hold on me, I'd sink to my knees. Pressure was building between my legs, my breasts were swollen, nipples rock hard and pressed tight to his chest. I couldn't get enough of his mouth, his tongue, his hands or his body and he couldn't get enough of me.

"Gray!"

That was Grandma Miriam calling from downstairs.

I heard it, I knew Gray did but neither of us stopped, that was how into it we were.

"*Gray!*"

It came again and he tore his mouth from mine.

"*Fuck!*" he clipped and my eyes opened halfway to see his were fiery and I was already hot but seeing his beautiful eyes looking pissed at the same time very turned on, another flood of wet saturated the area between my legs.

"*Gray!*" Grandma Miriam shouted again.

"Coming!" Gray shouted back and I was turned on, I didn't want to stop but we had no business starting. We were going to church. We were supposed to be in the truck in ten minutes so even though it got heated as it always got heated, we both knew we couldn't take it anywhere. Not before church. Not in this house. Not with Grandma Miriam there.

"Sorry, dollface," Gray muttered, gently sliding his hands out of my clothing and I grinned at him.

"That's okay," I whispered.

His eyes got lazy. It was a sweet, beautiful, appealing lazy and I lifted up on my toes to touch my lips to his because I couldn't stop myself.

His arms gave me one last squeeze before his hand smoothed the skirt down over my bottom, though this was copping one last feel and I knew it. The skirt was long and full and the minute his hand went out of my pants, it dropped to my ankles.

I let him have it mainly because I liked it, but more I liked that he wanted it.

He leaned in and touched his lips to my forehead before he turned and sauntered down the hall shoving his shirt back into his trousers. I watched until he disappeared down the stairs, still leaning against the wall so it would hold me up. Then I took a trembling breath and grinned.

I pushed away from the wall and rounded the door to the bathroom, flipping on the light. I went to the basin and looked in the mirror.

Grandma Miriam was shrewd, she'd take one look at my swollen lips, my dreamy eyes and she'd know Gray and I were making out.

Well, it wouldn't be the first time she saw that.

Suffice it to say, the last week had been eventful. In fact, I'd never lived a week so eventful.

Or so fantastic.

After going to church last Sunday with Gray and Grandma Miriam (in jeans, which was mortifying and made worse when Grandma Miriam glanced askance at them the second I hit the bottom of the stairs), Gray dropped me off in town and I had my lunch at the diner with Casey.

I thought he'd take the news that I got a job and was staying in Mustang no matter what explosively.

But I didn't take into account how loved up he was. Casey and his mystery woman (I still didn't know her name) were bonding, seemingly as tight as Gray and me. In fact, he hurried through lunch since it was Sunday, her day off and he wanted to get back to her. He was even excited and proud that I'd nailed down a job.

He was all for staying in Mustang. Didn't utter a word of protest. Not a peep.

He still didn't ask about Gray. He also didn't ask if I was crashing at Gray's or if Gray was taking care of me.

But he did ask for money.

So I gave him two hundred dollars and then I went to the department store and blew a wad of cash on a new outfit. It was just a skirt, a sweater and a pair of tights. But I did it so the next time I went to church with Gray and Grandma Miriam, she wouldn't give me a hard look about my outfit.

And I liked it. I hadn't owned a skirt in so long, I didn't know if I actually ever did.

Further, it was nicer (thus, more expensive, unfortunately) than anything I'd ever owned. It was a long, full, black wool skirt that had a graceful line that went down to my ankles and a matching, thick but fitted wool turtleneck sweater. My cowboy boots would have to do but luckily, my black ones were the nicer ones.

After I went shopping, Gray picked me up and I spent part of that Sunday afternoon convincing Gray I'd be safe in the room above The Rambler that Janie offered me.

I then spent another part of that Sunday afternoon assisting Gray in unearthing and boxing up stuff to take to the room. This was because Gray called Janie and she told him there was a double bed, a couch and nothing else up there. Another part of that afternoon was spent watching with some fascination as Gray brought in an old coffeemaker that had quit working and he fiddled with it for a while to make it work again.

For her part, Grandma Miriam wheeled in and out of places Gray and I were. When she did this, she did it wearing an expression that said she didn't know if it was brilliant news I was not going to be under her roof, a constant temptation for Gray to turn heathen, or if she was convinced I'd disappear with their castoffs and live the life of luxury shooting up on skid row with drugs I purchased hocking her stuff.

Monday morning, Gray drove me into town and we met Janie at the bar. She showed me my new space and Gray carried up the boxes. She was right. It was small. A room, against one side there were cupboards, minimal countertops, a half fridge she had to turn on and an old, narrow stove. There was a bathroom with all you needed but no tub, just a shower and no shower curtain. There was a couch. There was a double bed, no pillows so it was lucky Gray packed two for me.

Janie went home. Gray went to do stuff Gray had to do. And I unpacked a bit, made the bed, but I was supposed to be at work at eleven and I was.

And that was, essentially, it for my week.

But that was everything.

My life hit a pattern unlike any it had had before.

I went to the general store for cleaning stuff and the department store for a shower curtain.

I spent my mornings cleaning, doing my minimal unpacking, popping to the store and putzing around.

At work I was mostly a waitress but also made some drinks. My hours were eleven to eight. It was not taxing and considering I could make change quickly on the fly and found I had a head for memorizing orders, even complicated ones, I took to it by the second day. Janie was thrilled.

So was I. My shift meant I worked the lunch *and* dinner crowd and I was right, the bar was way more populated during those times. Tips were nothing to sneeze at and I could not explain how unbelievable it felt every day to have cash in my purse and know the next day I'd earn more.

Earn it.

I loved it.

My first day, Gray came in for dinner on my shift and then went upstairs with me after it so he could deliver an old TV he got for me from somewhere. Then we made out on my couch, and before it got too heated, he went home.

The second day, Gray came in half an hour to the end of my shift. I stayed another half an hour to sit next to him, drink a beer and shoot the breeze with Janie. Then we went to my room, made out on my couch, and before it got too heated, he went home.

The third day, Gray came in half an hour to the end of the shift, he took me to his place after it and we watched TV with Grandma Miriam who had not thawed even a little bit toward me. Then Gray helped her get to bed, he came out, we made out on *his* couch and then he took me home before it got too heated.

This went on until yesterday, my first day off, Gray met me at the diner for breakfast then he took me to his place to start teaching me how to ride a horse.

But after he got a docile mare saddled up and we were about ready to walk her out so Gray could show me how to climb on, he gave me a new pair of gloves he bought for me.

They were beautiful. A sandy suede with attractive stitching and they were lined with soft rabbit fur.

I looked at the gloves then him, back to the gloves then I decided, instead of bursting into tears seeing as he was the first person to give me a gift since Casey and I made our getaway, I would throw myself at him.

So I did.

Gray caught me and since there was no Grandma Miriam in the stables, no work the next morning, no nothing, we ended up (seriously!) in a haystack and Gray gave me the best present in the variety of presents he'd been giving me.

Lips on my lips, tongue in my mouth, body pressed to the side of mine, hand in my jeans, his long, strong fingers working magic, he gave me my first-ever orgasm.

It was *amazing*. Mind-boggling. The fact was, after having it, it was so spectacular I couldn't focus on his face for at least a full minute.

And when I did that handsome face was grinning at me in a way that was so sexy I nearly had another one.

And it also hit me that he gave me that and he didn't get his own.

"What about you?" I whispered.

"I'm inside you for the first time, dollface, it's not gonna be on a bunch of hay."

The hay was warm and I liked the smell of it but it was also scratchy and although the air in the stables was not as cold as outside, it wasn't toasty warm either.

Therefore, I saw his point.

So we got out of the hay and he gave me my first horseback riding lesson.

I was pretty good, Gray even said so.

But what he gave me in the hay started something. Something I wasn't experienced enough to understand fully but intuitively I felt that he liked giving it to me, he liked what he saw when he did and because of that, the floodgates opened.

A week of making out, heavy petting, getting used to him, his taste, his smell, his hands, his body, discovering all of that was fantastic. I loved every second. But I would understand after he gave me what he gave me in the hay that, before, he had it under stringent control.

Because, after, that control was gone.

And, it must be said, it probably helped that him giving me that, knowing what that felt like, how beautiful it was and wanting more of that from Gray, my control was gone too.

All day yesterday after our time in the hay, when his eyes dropped to my lips, he didn't drop his head to touch his to mine. He dropped his head, his mouth hit mine, his tongue drove into my mouth and then we went at each other like there was no tomorrow. He'd press me against the wall, the counter, take my hand and drag me out of a room his gran was in and there he'd press me against a wall and lay a hot and heavy one on me. Lots of tongue, lots of hands and it felt like, for the both of us, it took a mammoth effort to pull away.

I loved it. I loved that he liked touching me, tasting me, holding me and letting me know he did. And I loved doing those things to him.

In fact, I loved everything.

I loved Mustang.

I loved my little room even though there wasn't much to it, not even personality (yet). It still was mine and for a girl who carried everything she owned in a bag, that room was a huge step up.

I loved Janie. I loved my job. I loved our customers. I loved having cash in my purse. No, I loved having cash *I earned* in my purse and the way I earned it being normal, real, not to mention legal.

I loved making coffee in the morning from my coffeemaker, pouring it in my cup (well, ones I'd borrowed from Gray, but still, I'd have my own soon) and standing by the window at the front, watching the town of Mustang wake up. I loved pouring my own cereal using my own milk. I loved going to the corner market on the square to get bits and pieces. I loved going to sleep in a bed I knew I'd go to sleep in the next night, and the next, and the next.

And then there was Gray who I loved most of all.

Truly, completely...I fell hard and I didn't mind the fall, it didn't hurt a bit, so I stayed down.

Since I was going to church with them and I spent all day at Gray's yesterday, instead of taking me back into town only to go back in and pick me up in the morning, I crashed in his guest bedroom.

And I spent half the night trying to find sleep instead of throwing back the covers, wandering down the hall, finding Gray and convincing him to disrespect his grandmother in their home.

Luckily, I succeeded in this endeavor.

But I had the feeling that it wouldn't be long before I had Gray, *all* of him, and I...could not...*wait*.

I looked at myself in the mirror and even to me, taking in my swollen lips, dreamy eyes, I saw that I looked happy.

And that was something else I'd never seen. I'd never had. Never felt. Not in my life.

"Dollface." I heard Gray say and at his strange tone of voice, I whipped around to see he also had a strange look on his face.

I studied him a moment and saw it was concern.

"What's going on?" I asked, moving quickly to him.

"Don't know. It's Gran. She's in her bathroom, tellin' me to call her friend Shirley. She says I can't go in. She doesn't sound right."

Oh dear.

I held his gaze even as I made it to him then moved by him and hurried into the hall, down it and down the stairs.

Grandma Miriam's room was around the stairs and at the end of the back hall that ran parallel to the front hall, which went to the kitchen. Gray told me he renovated their old den with a handicapped accessible bathroom after she had her accident but I'd never been back there.

Still, upon entering her room, it didn't look like a renovated den. It looked like it had been a bedroom since the house was built. Clearly, he'd moved everything as she had it wherever she used to sleep and put it in here.

Again, an indication of how sweet Gray could be.

The bathroom door was closed. I went to it and knocked.

"Mrs. Cody, are you okay?"

Silence then, "Gray, call Shirley?"

"Gran," Gray called from behind me, "Shirley lives forty-five minutes away. Ivey's here, you need somethin', she'll help you out."

Gray had shared that his grandmother's spinal injury was located low on her spine and it was a "partial," which meant she had total control of her torso and some control of her legs. That said, they were weak and the control unpredictable so her legs couldn't support her if she was in a walker or they would give out at random times. They knew this because they'd tried.

He also told me a nurse came every day but Sundays and Wednesdays to help Grandma Miriam get showered. Grandma Miriam's best friend Shirley, a retired hairdresser, came every Wednesday to give her a shampoo and set. But she could mostly clothe herself just with the use of the parts of her body that she had but also she had a bunch of tools she'd been trained to use at the rehabilitation hospital. He shared further that from all that wheeling and moving herself around, she had the upper body strength of weightlifter and she could also do her bathroom business. From what Gray said and what I'd seen, she was incredibly self-sufficient, though Gray had assisted in some of this. For instance, he'd installed a mirror over the stove so she could cook on the two front burners and see what was happening on the stove by looking up at the mirror.

It was ingenious.

It was also sweet.

But Gray did not help her with personal stuff. She changed into her nightgowns. He just lifted her into bed, or out of it. He didn't dress her and he didn't bathe her.

And now she was behind a closed door in the bathroom.

"Call Shirley!" she shouted and I understood Gray's concern. She sounded funny, not herself. It wasn't pain but I didn't know her enough to know what it was.

Though some of it was impatience and irritation, I knew her enough to hear that.

I looked up at Gray whose jaw was hard. He also looked impatient as well as worried and he was moving to her phone on her nightstand.

Before he made it there, I turned back to the door, knocked twice, put my hand to knob and called through the door, "Mrs. Cody, I'm coming in!"

I turned the doorknob back and forth a couple of times just to give her time before I pushed open the door and went in.

I closed it swiftly behind me even as my heart jumped into my throat.

She'd fallen off the toilet.

How, I didn't know. But she was on her side on the floor, her panties pulled awkwardly up, the skirt of her dress shoved down. Her chair was in an awkward place, tilted and resting on the side of the tub like she'd run into it when she fell and tipped it over. She'd gotten both panties and skirt twisted somehow, probably panic and embarrassment so her skirt was tucked in her panties in places it would be hard to get to since she had to roll back and forth in the small space she had to do it. And that rolling probably made it worse.

"I said, call Shirley," she whispered and I didn't have to know her very well to know she was mortified.

I didn't answer and I didn't look at her face. I just walked right up to her, got down on my knees and righted her clothes. I did it swiftly, efficiently, and didn't say a word. Then I wrapped my arms around her, pulled her up, rolled her to her bottom and scooched her so her back was to the vanity cabinet. It was awkward to do all that, the space was small and with the chair wedged in, it didn't help.

Then I turned to the toilet, closed the lid and flushed it.

Only then, when I turned back to her, did I catch her eyes.

"Are you hurt?" I asked.

She pressed her trembling lips together and shook her head.

"Sure? No pain?" I pressed.

She nodded.

"Do you think I can get you up and in your chair without calling Gray?"

Her eyes held mine and I saw brightness glistening on the bottoms but she didn't answer.

"Mrs. Cody," I began again, "can I get you in your chair or do we need to call Gray?"

"I don't want him to know I fell," she whispered.

"Right," I whispered back. "Can we get you in your chair?"

"I was reaching for something. Silly. I knew better," she told me, still whispering.

I scooted closer to her and took her hand. "We all do silly stuff but now we have to get to church. I'm not a weakling but I don't know how to do those transfers Gray talks about. Can you talk me through it so I can get you in your chair?"

She stared into my eyes and nodded.

"Bring it over here, child, then make sure the wheels are locked. I'll talk you through it."

I nodded back, gave her a small smile then did as she said and kept doing it until we had her up, her skirt down, her bottom in her chair and her feet resting on the pedals.

"Need to wash my hands, Ivey," she said softly. "But I was reaching for my perfume. Can you get it for me?"

I saw the perfume on a standing shelf across and just down from the toilet and I could see how she'd think she could make it as well as see how she did not.

I moved it to the vanity countertop as she washed her hands.

"Was running late," she said to her hands as she wiped them on a towel. "Thought I'd multitask, save time."

"Jesus!" Gray shouted from outside. "You wanna give me a clue? Is everything all right in there?"

My eyes went to the door at his first word then they went to Grandma Miriam and I saw my wide eyes reflected on her face.

Then, to my shock and utter delight, she burst out laughing.

"We're fine, Gray, keep your pants on!" she shouted back after she quit laughing. "Ivey's helpin' me with my perfume!"

Silence, then through the door, "For fuck's sake, I thought a black hole swallowed both of you."

At that, to my further shock and still utter delight, her eyes caught mine and she rolled hers.

She grabbed her perfume bottle, spritzed it on and shouted, "Grayson Cody, we're about to go to church and you're giving us that mouth!"

"Fuckin' hell." We heard him mutter then, "Right!" he shouted. "I'm gonna go warm up the truck."

Grandma Miriam expertly whipped around her chair, leaned in, threw open the door and wheeled out, forcing Gray, who was standing in the door, to jump out of the way.

And as she did, she replied, now sounding happy as a clam, "You do that, honey."

Gray scowled at her then he looked at me, the scowl fled and his brows went up in a clear question.

I ignored his question, pressed my lips together, put my hands to the back of her chair and started pushing. Her hands, surprisingly (again!), left the wheels and she let me.

As I did this, I stated, "Let's get our coats on while Gray starts up the truck."

"Good idea, child," Grandma Miriam muttered.

I looked over my shoulder at Gray as I wheeled her to the door. "See you out there, honey."

He stood stock-still at the side of her bathroom door and stared at me.

I wheeled her around the doorframe and lost sight of him.

Ten minutes later, Grandma Miriam's chair folded in the back, Gray at the wheel, his gran in the passenger seat, me scrunched between them on the bench seat, we headed to church.

Seventeen minutes later…

Standing beside Gray in the Fellowship Hall, we watched Grandma Miriam do her socializing exactly like she did last Sunday (and I enjoyed watching it). This proved what Gray had told me that she was born in Mustang and lived her whole life there seeing as she knew every single person in that church.

I felt Gray's arm slide along my shoulders and then I felt his lips come to my ear.

"You gonna share?"

I pulled my head back, he did too and we locked eyes.

"You need to move the shelves in her bathroom so she can reach them better from the toilet," I whispered.

His blue eyes flashed exposing disquiet and understanding before he nodded and muttered, "Right."

I gave him some of my weight and smiled.

Gray's eyes dropped to my mouth and luckily, seeing as we were in a church, when his mouth dropped to it right after it was only for a touch.

Then he moved us forward so we could commandeer Grandma Miriam and get her in a pew.

Chapter 14

Feels Good Doesn't It?

N*early two hours later...*

"Maybe we can go see a movie?" I suggested.

Gray was driving. I was sitting in the passenger seat. We were headed back to his house.

Grandma Miriam had informed us after more communing in the Fellowship Hall when the singing, sermon, praying and more singing was done, she had made plans (just then) with her friend Shirley to go to Shirley's daughter's house for Sunday lunch. Then Shirley's daughter and her husband were going out and Grandma Miriam and Shirley were going to watch Shirley's daughter's kids.

She wasn't going to be home, she didn't reckon, until close to ten.

"You can," she began, her eyes slid to me, her mouth twitched then her eyes went back to Gray, "order a pizza or something."

"Think I can feed myself and my girl," Gray had muttered then surprisingly, with no further ado, he leaned right in, kissed his grandmother's cheek, grabbed my hand and dragged me right out to his truck.

During this short, fast trek, I had asked if Shirley needed any help with Grandma Miriam and her chair but Gray assured me that Shirley's daughter's husband knew the drill and would sort it.

And away we went.

Now we had the whole day. I was off again and I wanted to do something normal people did.

Back in the day, when I was still a kid, Casey would take me to see movies. Not many of them, it was a treat, but he did it and I loved it. I loved movie popcorn. I loved being in a dark cinema where you felt alone even though you weren't, your vision filled with what was on screen.

But when I grew up and learned that movies were an extravagance we couldn't afford, I put a stop to it.

Now I made my own coffee. I poured my own cereal. I went to grocery stores (kind of, if the corner store could be classed as that, but I figured it could since most of what they carried were groceries). I had a job. I owned a skirt. I had my own place.

I was nearly normal.

I wanted to do something normal.

And I hoped Gray did too.

We turned into the long lane that led up to his house and as we did, he muttered, "We're not gonna go see a movie."

I looked to him in surprise. This was because he sounded preoccupied. This was also because it occurred to me in that instant that Gray gave me everything I wanted and I was surprised he denied me.

Not that I'd ever asked for anything. Not the finest of steak dinners no matter that it was served at the VFW. Not for him to pay for my breakfast when we went to the diner. Not for a pair of gloves I knew just looking at them, but definitely by the feel, they were way on the other side of expensive.

But he gave them to me all the same.

Then it hit me he had a beautiful farmhouse, a bunch of land, decent clothes and a great leather jacket but the first two had been left to him and he had upkeep. He also had a beat-up pickup truck that had to be at least a decade old and a grandmother who needed a nurse to come in five days a week to take care of her.

Maybe he couldn't afford expensive gloves, taking me to the diner *and* a movie.

"My treat," I said brightly and it could be my treat. It wasn't like I was going to retire on the Riviera within a year, but without a hotel to pay for and with Janie giving me the room for two months for free I could take us to a movie *and* save for all the stuff I needed to start my life.

And I was looking forward to that. Getting my own car. My own mugs. My own silverware. Buying my own comforter. Replacing Gray's TV with a new one.

I couldn't wait for that either.

"We're not goin' to a movie, baby," Gray murmured, his voice sweet, soft but still preoccupied.

"Okay," I whispered.

Maybe he didn't like movies or maybe he didn't like going to the theater. Maybe on my next day off, I'd go. Though I didn't know where the cinemas were. I knew they didn't have one in town. And I didn't have a car so I couldn't get there unless I asked Gray to drop me off and pick me up which I wasn't going to do.

So maybe I'd wait until I had my own car which might be November, but I hadn't seen a movie in the cinema in years. I could wait until November.

Gray parked where he normally parked beside the house and his door was open nearly before he had the old girl shut down. Mine creaked as I threw it open. I hopped down and it creaked as I slammed it.

I jumped because Gray was right there, hand in mine, and he was dragging me to the house.

What on earth?

I mean, he held my hand and he did it a lot. Usually, he slid his arm around my shoulders and held me close to him, but holding my hand wasn't unheard of. He even waited on his side of the truck when we got to his place for me to round it then he took my hand or slid his arm around my shoulders so we could walk the short distance to his house.

But he'd never come to my side, grabbed my hand and dragged me to the house.

Up the three wooden steps to the porch, past the porch swing to the front door and in. There, he stopped us, closed the door and immediately shrugged off his leather jacket and tossed it on the piece of furniture next to the door in his hall. It was one of those things that looked like a weird seat with armrests and a super tall back that had a mirror in it. The seat opened up so you could store stuff in it and there were hooks all around the mirror.

As he did this, I pulled the strap of my purse over my head.

The instant I got it cleared, Gray grabbed it and tossed it on his coat.

I blinked and froze.

Gray didn't.

He shrugged off his suit jacket (incidentally, Gray wore a suit to church and it looked *amazing* on him, dark blue with a dark blue-gray shirt under it and a phenomenal tie—I loved him in jeans but I had to say, that suit on him looked fabulous). He threw that on his jacket and I looked up at him.

"What—?" I started but he grabbed my hand and dragged me up the stairs.

It was then I knew what and my belly dipped.

Grandma Miriam was out of the house.

We had it to ourselves.

Until ten.

And yesterday, the floodgates had been opened.

Here comes the flood.

Oh my.

My heart jumpstarted, ticking over fast so by the time we got to the top of the stairs, I felt every beat.

When we got to the top, instead of going left to my room, he took us right.

To his.

I'd never seen his room even though it was across from the bathroom. The door had always been closed.

For some bizarre reason, I couldn't wait for that either.

In record time Gray had me down the hall, his hand went out, turned the knob and he pulled me into his room.

I understood his hurry, I knew his intent, but still, walking in his room the first time, I came out of myself and just stared.

This was because it was like we walked into a different house.

No doilies. No flowers. No pastel carpets. No pretty quilts.

The walls were the color of his shirt, a dark blue-gray. The furniture was heavy, masculine, dark wood, all angles, squares, rectangles with no-nonsense manly etching in the drawers and cabinets.

The house was tidy and clean, although full of stuff.

His room wasn't tidy and clean or full of stuff. No trophies he won playing sports as a youngster, ribbons displayed.

Over the bed there was a huge black and white photo of the Colorado Mountains that I knew was taken by Cotton, a famous photographer who lived in said mountains. There were jeans, boots, long-sleeved tees and flannel shirts in tangles on the floor. Books on the nightstands, so many of them, they overflowed to the floor. There was change in a small bowl on one of his dressers. Sturdy, manly matching lamps on the nightstands and another one on the low bureau.

And that was it. No other decorative touches. Nothing.

And the bed was huge.

Huge.

Squared off head and footboard with slats, dark gray cover covering a down comforter, dark blue sheets. There were six pillows —*six*—in disarray at the head of the unmade bed.

"Boots off, darlin'," Gray muttered, my body jolted and my eyes flew to him to see him pulling at the knot in his tie.

"Wh-what?"

"Boots..." his eyes locked on mine and the fever in them corresponded in heat flooding my body, "*off*."

Oh...

My.

I dropped my head, lifted my foot and pulled off my boot. I did the same with the other.

I'd just straightened when Gray was in my space and moving, rounding me close, herding me as he unwrapped the scarf from around my neck and tossed it aside.

My stomach dropped again, my heart started thumping again and heat gathered between my legs.

He moved forward, shuffling me back. Hands to my jeans jacket, he pulled it over my shoulders, down my arms and then it was gone.

My mouth went dry.

Then one of his arms wrapped tight around me, the fingers of his other hand drove into my hair. Cupping my head, he tilted it, his slanted the other way and his mouth crushed down on mine.

His tongue was sliding in my mouth as I fell backwards, my arms automatically wrapped around him and he landed on top of me in his bed.

Oh yes, it was oh *my*.

My breath went out of me taking his weight but he rolled instantly so I was on top even as he continued kissing me.

I didn't care about my breath being gone. I was used to being breathless. Gray kissed me to that state all the time.

His hand left my head, both went into my sweater, up, my arms were forced up, my head jerked back and *whoosh*! It was gone.

I no sooner processed this fact before I was on my back again, Gray's mouth on mine but his torso was angled away from me because his hands were on the buttons of his shirt.

I got lost in his kiss before he arched his back completely, whispering, "Help me out, dollface, I want to feel you skin against skin."

Oh yes. I wanted that too.

But more, I wanted to see his chest again.

With shaking hands I started helping him undo the buttons on his shirt until they were undone. He tore it over his shoulders, down his arms and it, too, was gone.

My eyes had a nanosecond to drink him in.

Just as I remembered. Fantastic.

Then his mouth was back to mine, his tongue in my mouth, his warm, hard chest crushing my breasts, his hands on me, my hands on him and he felt so good, every inch, every centimeter.

His hands slid around my back, I felt the fingers of one at my bra then it was loose. He lifted up and it was also gone.

Over the last week, Gray hadn't avoided my breasts. When we were making out on his couch, he'd cupped one over the bra, his thumb gliding across my nipple and that was fabulous. And yesterday, in the haystack, his hands under my clothes, he paid them a considerable amount of attention.

But he'd never seen them.

Suddenly, uncertainty slithered in as he again arched his back, his eyes gliding down my body and he took me in.

It hit me then this was going fast. Really fast.

And I was a virgin.

I needed to slow things down.

"Gray—" I whispered, his eyes went from my body to mine and I clamped my mouth shut at the look in them.

It was blistering. It was appreciative. And it was carnal.

I was again breathless.

"Prettiest thing I've ever fuckin' seen," he murmured, then he came back to me. But he did it by twisting his torso even as his hand slid up my ribs to cup the bottom of my breast. He lifted it, his mouth was there and he drew my nipple sharply between his lips.

Heat shafted through me, my back left the bed and both my hands slid into his hair as I whimpered.

And that was it. I was lost. It was all mouths and tongues, licking, sucking, biting, hands roaming, nails scraping. I heard the zip go down on my skirt then it was gone then my tights with my panties. I heard the zip on Gray's trousers and suddenly he was naked. I didn't see it, I was too busy running my tongue up his neck, one of my hands gliding along the skin of his back, the other one over the skin of the defined muscles at his stomach. I heard his swift intake of breath as they trailed and then he adjusted. Jerking me with him until I was on my back, Gray's weight on me, his hips were rolling. My legs opened automatically, his fell between, his hands raced up the back of my thighs, hooking the back of my knees, yanking them up and he drove inside.

My back arched and I cried out, not in pleasure, in pain as that surprising sensation seared through me.

Gray's body went statue-still for a moment, still buried inside me then just his head came up.

My neck righted and my eyes opened as his hand framed one side of my face.

"Jesus, Ivey," he whispered.

"I kinda..." I hesitated, "got excited and forgot to, uh..." I paused again, "mention I was a virgin."

"How the fuck did that happen?" he asked.

What a bizarre question.

"Um...when you don't have sex?" I answered in a question.

He stared at me and his face got that near to tender look. But he did it one better because he got that look even as his eyes warmed in a way I hadn't seen before (and Gray's eyes were almost always warm). In a way that made my body warm all over. His lips tipped up in a grin and his dimple popped out.

Sensational.

"Yeah, my beautiful Ivey, but how the fuck does a girl like you reach the age of twenty-two and not have sex?"

My belly dropped again but this time not in a good way.

"Like me as in a pool hustler?" I asked softly and his thumb immediately slid out to stroke my cheek as his face got closer, his grin disappeared but the tender took over his expression.

"No, dollface, like you. Like the most beautiful girl to hit Mustang, fuck, maybe the entire state of Colorado in a century. Like that kind of girl."

My belly didn't drop with that. It flipped.

"In my life, I haven't made a lot of connections," I told him and the grin can back.

"You're connected now, baby."

I was. I definitely was. In a lot of ways.

All of them good.

I returned his grin.

His hand left my face, slid down my shoulder, arm, in between us and down.

"Wrap your legs around my hips, Ivey. I'm gonna take care of you so you can take me," he ordered gently, my whole body trembled and his grin turned into a smile.

"My girl likes that," he whispered.

"Yes," I whispered back.

His thumb hit the spot, pressed in and rolled.

My eyes closed and my neck slightly arched.

"And my girl likes that," he growled.

"Yes," I breathed.

He kept pressing and rolling. I held on tight. He kept doing it. I held on tighter, lifted my face and shoved it in his neck. He kept doing it and started moving inside me slowly.

Oh *yes*.

That felt really good.

I turned my head and gasped in his ear, "Gray."

He stopped.

My limbs clutched him and I gasped again, "Don't stop!"

He kept going.

And going, thumb swirling.

Oh yes.

Yes.

"Gray," I whimpered in his ear.

"Right here, Ivey," he whispered in mine.

Right there, as right there as he could be.

Instinctively, I lifted my hips, rocking them up with each of his strokes.

When I did this, Gray groaned, his strokes went deeper then they started going faster, harder, his finger pressing and rolling.

Yes.

More, faster, harder, deeper, I held on tight.

Yes. That felt really, *really* good.

"Gray," I gasped.

"Right here, baby."

"Oh my God," I breathed then there it was.

My head flew back into the pillows, my fingers plunged into his hair and fisted, I cried out then moaned loud then just felt it, lips parted, no breath, experiencing the beauty as it washed over me.

Better than in the haystack.

Better than anything in the world.

The best.

When my body relaxed under him, his thumb left me and his hand pulled one of my arms from around him. His fingers lacing through mine, he lifted our hands and pressed them in the pillow beside my head. Lifting up on his other forearm that he was bracing his weight on in the bed, that hand slid up and his fingers tangled in my hair as his head came up, his eyes locking on mine and he kept thrusting.

I kept rocking my hips and taking him, digging my heels into him to do it, watching him moving inside me, and he was so beautiful, it was arguably better than what he'd just given me.

Then he drove deep, his fingers laced through mine tightened, his other hand fisted in my hair, pulling my head slightly to the side and his face disappeared in my neck where he groaned against my skin.

I liked that. The sound, the feel. It was beautiful.

Okay, no.

That was better.

He stayed buried inside me and I held him close to me until his breath came to almost even and his mouth started nuzzling my neck, his fingers never unlacing from mine.

And there it was.

A week and a day ago I was a girl who owned a bag of stuff and not much of it was good.

And now I was lying in a huge, masculine bed, on soft, dark sheets, wrapped around the most beautiful man I'd ever seen, and I was a girl who had everything.

And at that thought, it came right out of my mouth.

"How can one day you have next to nothing and then a week and a day later you have everything?"

Gray's head came up, my eyes went to his and it was there, that tender look as he lifted the hand he held, twisted it and brushed his lips against my knuckles.

That was so sweet, seeing him do it, feeling his lips, my heart skipped a beat.

He let my hand go, his came back to my face, his thumb moving out and gliding along my lip as he answered, "Don't know, dollface, but feels good doesn't it?"

Oh my.

He felt the same.

"Yeah," I whispered against the pad of his thumb.

"Yeah," he whispered back.

Then his thumb swept away and he replaced it with his lips.

I thought I had everything a moment before, but just like Gray, wrapped around him, still connected to him, his mouth on mine, he gave me more.

Chapter 15

King of Mustang

T*wo hours later…*

Gray was wearing nothing but jeans. He was lying on his back in his bed, four pillows cushioning his head, shoulders against the headboard. He had a plate on his stomach that had a jumble of crackers, slices of cheese, a cut up apple and a handful of store-bought cookies. On his nightstand were two freshly opened bottles of beer.

Lunch.

I was wearing my panties and his dress shirt, four buttons done up. I was lying on my side at his side, one of my legs thrown over one of his, my head in my hand, my elbow in the bed.

I had lazed in Gray's huge, awesome bed while he did the taxing work of walking downstairs, cutting some slices of cheese and apple, dumping out some crackers and cookies and grabbing a couple of cold ones then walking it back up.

So he was right in what he told Grandma Miriam. He could feed himself and his girl.

After we had sex, we cuddled, we whispered then we fooled around some more. But Gray didn't take it all the way.

"Coupla days, honey, don't wanna hurt you again," he murmured against my neck, his hands sliding soothingly along the skin of my back.

I didn't want to wait a couple of days. Sex was fantastic. Or maybe just sex with Gray was fantastic.

Then again, I'd bled a little (which was semi-embarrassing and only stopped being that when Gray didn't make a big deal of it) and it had to be said, I ached and I did it in a way that didn't invite further attention to that area.

So we'd wait a couple of days.

I could wait a couple of days for Gray.

For Gray, I'd wait an eternity.

I reached to his belly, put a slice of cheese on a cracker and shoved the whole thing in my mouth.

I saw the plate tremble on his stomach, my head tipped back and my eyes (enjoying their journey) drifted up to him to see he was smiling but his eyes and the rest of his body were laughing.

"What?" I asked through a full mouth.

"Jesus, dollface, there's more downstairs. You don't have to stuff your face."

I chewed, swallowed and told him, "I don't want to get crumbs in your bed.

"I don't care," he told me.

"No one wants to sleep in crumbs," I informed him.

"I'll brush them out," he informed me.

I scrunched my face. "Euw. No. In this room, they'll never be swept up. Yyou'll be walking all over them, they'll get in your socks and then you'll get ants in the summer."

He was still smiling but his head tilted to the side and he asked, "First, *euw*?"

"Yeah, euw."

"No one says *euw*."

"I just said it."

He kept smiling at me when he replied, "I stand corrected. But I will point out that only a woman with a beautiful face and more hair, all of it gorgeous, than is fair to the rest of the female population on top of a fantastic body, who says my name breathy when she gets hot or she's in the mood to be sweet, which is often, and sounds even hotter when she comes then gets an unbelievably sexy look in her eyes when she comes down can say *euw*."

I stared at him actually *feeling* my heart swell.

Then I pulled myself together and noted, "That's a lot of conditions."

His eyes held mine and his reply was quiet. "I know."

Oh my.

To hide the blush I felt creeping up at his compliment, I dipped my chin and reached out to grab a slice of apple.

"Second," he started and my attention went back to him. "The crumbs won't get lost forever. Macy comes every other week to clean the house and do the laundry."

I tipped my head deeper into my hand. "Macy?"

"My Uncle Olly's third wife."

There were only five words there but a lot to go over.

"Uncle Olly?" I prompted.

"Yeah, Uncle Olly. Oliver. Dad was the oldest. Oliver after him. Frank after him and then Charles. They're all named after famous cowboys."

Cool.

"Really?" I asked.

"Yeah, Dad's name is Abel after Abel Pierce. Olly after Oliver Loving. Frank after Frank Eaton and Charlie after Charles Goodnight. Their last names are my dad and uncles' middle ones."

That was still cool even though I had no idea who all those people were.

"I don't know any of those people," I confessed.

"Not a lot of people do. Gotta be a cowboy to know cowboys and my granddad was a definite cowboy."

That was cool too.

"Are you?"

"Got a bit in me but it isn't the same, not like he tells it, not like he said his daddy told it. Those days are long gone."

Alas, they were.

"So Olly's been married three times?" I asked.

"Olly, three. Frank's just got rid of his second and is workin' on his third. Charlie's still in his second but, the way things are going, I don't see that lasting very long."

"Wow," I whispered, Gray grinned and I noted, "They've been through a lot of women."

"Hard men to live with."

"Sounds like it."

"Lucky Macy's got more piss and vinegar in her than most. Olly owns and runs the bar. Macy owns and runs Olly. Gran and her don't get along but Macy don't care. She still comes every two weeks, cleans the house, does the laundry, does the ironing, puts flowers all around because Macy likes flowers and that's her way, and then she leaves."

Well, that explained the flowers.

"She and your gran don't get along?" I asked.

Gray shook his head. "Macy wants peace in the family. Gran can hold a grudge. Dad being firstborn son meant he inherited the land. Me being his only son meant I inherited it. When Dad died, her boys wanted their slice and didn't mind letting that be known. They didn't shut up about it, Gran lost her mind. They'd been marrying, divorcing, carousing and brawling for years, none of this she liked and all of it, dollface, they still do. So when Dad died and they made their play, got slapped back and wouldn't let it go, she was done. She hasn't seen any of them in years except when she can't avoid them if she's in town, and then she ignores them."

This concerned me.

"Are they still wanting their slice?"

He shook his head again. "They gave up. None of 'em are bad seeds, they just got a lotta stupid in 'em. Woke up, paid attention, saw they had a nephew who lost his dad, a mom who lost her son at the same time she lost her legs and they lost their brother. They got their heads outta their asses. All of 'em, in their way, none of those ways good but still, they did it, extended an olive branch. It was too late. Gran was done."

I felt my face get soft when I whispered, "That's kind of sad."

"Yeah," he replied quietly. "It is. But Codys have owned this land for six generations, Ivey, and it's always been that way. Tradition. Firstborn son to firstborn son. Over the years, the others lived on the land and worked it. My uncles never did. They turned eighteen, took off and wreaked havoc elsewhere. Gran wasn't a big fan of that either. But for six generations, it's been the same. Started as ranchers and horse breeders. Granddad sold off the livestock and put in the orchard." He grinned again. "Looks better, smells better and a lot less hassle. But we've always had the horses. The town of Mustang is called Mustang because my great-great-grandfather refused to have the town named Cody after him but he captured, broke and bred mustangs so they named it that instead."

I blinked in shock at learning this information. Then I stared.

Gray kept talking.

"So, seein' as the Codys were the first to settle in these parts and the town grew up around them and their ranch, tradition is kind of important."

"The town of Mustang is named Mustang because your family captured, tamed and bred mustangs?" I asked on a breath.

"Yep."

"The town of Mustang is named Mustang because your family captured, tamed and bred Mustangs?" I repeated like he didn't answer.

He smiled big and repeated his answer of, "Yep."

"So, you're like Mustang royalty."

His smile got bigger and his beautiful body shook when he again repeated, "Yep."

"Wow," I whispered.

That smile grew wide and white and his body shook more as did his voice when he remarked, "You're lyin' in the king of Mustang's bed, wearin' his shirt after he took your virginity, dollface. Now, aren't you lucky?"

I kept my eyes glued to his and I knew he was joking but my answer was deadly serious when I said, "Yep."

He heard it and his smile faded. Then he grabbed the plate, reached across me, dumped it on the bed behind me and his arms were around me, hauling me up his body.

Then he was kissing me.

He tasted of apples and Gray.

It was delicious.

His hand went up his shirt then down in my panties and I had about three seconds of thinking how much I liked his hand in my panties before we heard a knock on the door.

My head came up and both of our gazes turned to the opened door of his bedroom.

Gray muttered an annoyed, "Fucking hell, I get a day with my girl in my house all alone and someone's at the goddamned door."

He didn't move. Lying mostly on top of him, I didn't either.

Another knock came, this one louder.

"Is your plan to ignore it?" I said low, like whoever was out there might hear me if I didn't.

"If that's possible," Gray replied, not talking low.

We stayed locked together and silent, our eyes to his bedroom door.

Another knock came, even louder and the caller knocked for longer.

"Shit," he clipped, rolled me to my back then let me go and rolled out of bed.

Guess it wasn't possible to ignore it.

He tagged a random, dirty, long-sleeved tee from the floor and tugged it over his head.

He was still pulling it down his chest when his gaze came to me and he ordered, "Don't move. I'll be back."

"I'll be here."

His gaze held mine then it moved down the length of me, heated and then my cheeks heated.

Another knock came at the door.

"Shit," he bit out, turned on his foot and stalked out the door.

I pulled myself up, rearranged the pillows so they were behind my back and then bent down to grab the plate.

It was on my thighs and I was munching, still careful of the crumbs no matter what Gray said, when I heard it.

"I do not deal with you, motherfucker, I deal with my sister!"

My body locked.

Casey.

Why on earth was he shouting and what was he doing here?

And how did he even know where Gray lived?

I hadn't seen him since he took off from the diner. Neither of us had cells, we couldn't afford them. But he knew where I worked and told me he'd pop by. He didn't and I got so busy with work, Gray and happily living a normal life, I had to admit, I didn't really think about it.

In fact, truth be told (guilty truth), I was kind of enjoying the break.

Now he was here and shouting.

Then he shouted more.

"Stand aside, goddamn it, and let me see my sister!"

I put the plate on the bed, rolled out quickly and hustled on a jog-run out of the room, down the hall and halfway down the stairs.

It was only halfway because I saw Gray standing, blocking Casey at the front door. But Casey caught the movement on the stairs, his eyes came to me and the minute he saw me his face twisted in fury so ugly, I froze on a step.

"She's wearin' nothin' but your shirt," he said quietly, his eyes sliding to Gray.

Gray's head turned and his eyes came to me.

"My *sister* is wearin' *nothin'* but *your shirt*," Casey semi-repeated and Gray's head started to turn back to Casey but not fast enough.

I sucked in breath then cried out, "Casey, no!" as Gray's moment of inattention put him off-guard giving Casey the opportunity to get the drop on him, and he did. Casey dipped a shoulder and lunged. Catching Gray in his chest, he powered him back five steps.

That was all he got.

My breath clean left me as—swiftly, efficiently and with experience clearly borne of lots of practice—Gray's body rolled away from Casey's shoulder.

Casey went flying, righted himself quickly, turned, immediately stepped toward Gray and aimed a punch at him. Gray dodged it but came back swinging and caught Casey on the jaw with a vicious blow. While Casey was reeling, Gray moved in, now dropping his shoulder. He caught Casey in the belly and didn't push him back. He lifted him up, turned on a bare foot and, with long, fast strides, he walked out the door.

I raced after them and hit the cold outside, dashing down the porch, watching Gray bounce Casey up and over at the end of the porch sending my brother flying to land on his behind, back and elbows into the cold snow beside Gray's cleared front walk.

Oh God.

That had to hurt, not only his body but his pride.

I plastered my front to the side of Gray's back and stared down at my brother, completely at a loss of what to do.

"Get inside, darlin'," Gray ordered on a growl, and my head snapped back to look up at his profile, seeing his angry eyes locked on my brother, his entire face hard with fury.

"*You fuckin' slut!*" Casey shouted. Gray's already tense body went rock-solid and my eyes flew to my brother who was scrambling back on all fours, snow flying all around. He pushed up to his feet and kept shouting. "*You fuckin' whore!*"

Gray's fury escalated sharply, so much so it filled the cold air with crackling electricity. He came unlocked and started advancing but my arms quickly circled him and got tight so he stopped.

"Casey, don't," I whispered.

"I don't believe this!" Casey was still yelling. "I don't fuckin' believe this *shit*!"

"Casey, *don't*," I begged.

"Take my eye off you for a week, *a fuckin' week*, and you're on your back for a fuckin' *cowboy*!" Casey clipped.

"Gray means something to me. We're seeing each other and he *means something to me*," I returned, feeling Gray's body tense again but my attention was focused on my brother.

"You don't know shit. You don't know what anything *means*," Casey fired back and I started to get angry.

"How do you know what I know?" I asked sharply. "News flash, I'm not twelve anymore, Casey. I'm a grown woman and I know what I'm feeling, how deep it runs and what it means."

"You're so full of shit," Casey retorted.

"Why? Why do you think that? Why, when you meet some woman, in a day you're falling in love and expect me to believe in that and give you time to explore it? Why aren't you prepared to believe in me when I'm feeling the same way and why won't you give me the same?"

At that, Gray's body again went rock-solid but I was still entirely focused on my brother.

So I kept talking.

"Why, instead, when I don't see you for a week, are you here now, shouting at me and calling me ugly names? I didn't do that to you."

"It isn't what you think it is, Ivey, it's hormones rulin' your head," Casey returned.

Seriously?

My *stupid* brother!

"Is that what rules you every time you hook up with some woman somewhere? Are you stuck in your teenage years ruled by hormones?" I shot back. "Again, Casey, *wake up*. I'm not twelve. I'm not sixteen. I'm *twenty-two*. I've been around just like you. I've met my fair share of folks, just like you. I've been hit on enough to know when I actually *want* the attention. And I know what I'm feeling. I know when what I'm feeling means someone is growing to be something important to me. I'm not stupid. I'm not emotionally arrested at age thirteen. I *know*."

Casey changed the subject, moving straight down his well-trodden path of emotional blackmail with, "I spent a lifetime lookin' out for you."

"Then first, you didn't do a very good job, and second, good news for you, man, your job is done."

That came from Gray in a deep, rumbling, angry voice and Casey's eyes sliced to him.

"The fuck you say," was Casey's bizarre reply.

Gray must have thought it bizarre too because he didn't reply.

"She's my sister," Casey told Gray something he already knew.

"Yeah, I know," Gray returned. "I also know she's movin' on, that's her choice and she's takin' it. You're not down with that, I'll see to it that you come around to Ivey's way of thinkin'."

Hells bells.

Casey's eyes narrowed and then they moved to me.

"I see, sis. I've been replaced."

"Then you don't see because that's not it at all. Or you do see and you're just bein' a dick," Gray stated. Casey looked back at him but Gray wasn't done. "Now, seein' as you looked out for her awhile, you'll also see she's standin' on a porch in thirty degree weather wearin' a shirt so I know you'll want her to get warm. So maybe you'll share with us what you're doin' here so we can be done with that and I can get my girl back in my house."

When Gray didn't move, extend an arm to the front door or give any indication this conversation would happen anywhere but where we were currently standing, Casey snapped, "Right, so I see you're happy to have my sister in your bed but you won't invite her brother in your house."

"No, I won't," Gray confirmed. "Woulda but you fucked that by makin' your own way in and doin' it with your shoulder in my chest. You cool down, get your head outta your ass and prove to me you're not an asshole, you'll get that invitation. Though, I'll warn you, after the way you've acted and the shit that came outta your mouth directed at my girl, that's gonna take a while. So today you're not gonna feel my hospitality. Now we got that straight, what the fuck are you doin' here?"

Casey's eyes went shifty and I instantly knew what he was doing there.

"You wanna give me a second alone with my sister?" he requested, trying to force his voice to normal but the irate still came out.

"No," Gray replied shortly and said no more.

Casey glared at him.

Gray didn't move or say a word.

I opened my mouth to speak but Gray got there before me.

"Tomorrow, nine o'clock, I meet you at the diner. I'll have five hundred dollars with me." I sucked in breath and my body went still but Gray wasn't done. "You'll take it and be happy with that. You get no more. Not from me, *never* from Ivey."

"Gray," I murmured, giving his middle a squeeze. But he didn't move, didn't look down at me, didn't tear his eyes from Casey.

Casey didn't move either, just stood on Gray's front walk, glaring up at him.

"Am I wrong?" Gray asked into the silence. "You're here to hit Ivey up."

Casey visibly clenched his teeth.

Yep. Just as I knew and Gray knew, Gray was right.

My brother.

Gray continued, "Five hundred dollars. Tomorrow at the diner. Nine o'clock. Then you're done and you do whatever you gotta do but Ivey isn't part of it. Get me?"

Casey didn't move or speak.

"You get me," Gray muttered then ordered, "In your car, man, off my land, and until I give the all-clear, you don't come back. You do, the door doesn't open. I pick up the phone and call the cops and I know you don't want that. And you don't know me so I'll educate you, I do not make threats. You with me?"

Casey remained immobile and silent.

Gray waited.

I waited.

Then Gray was done waiting.

"Car, Casey," he said softly and finished with, "now."

Casey glared at him before he transferred it to me, turned and stomped to his car.

I watched, holding on to Gray, trembling and not with cold.

Gray watched too, shifting only to wrap an arm around my shoulders and pull me deeper into him.

Casey got in his car, reversed too fast and sped down Gray's lane.

When we lost sight of him, Gray immediately turned us and walked me swiftly into his house, shutting and locking the door.

I pulled away, looked up at him and whispered, "I'll give you the five hundred dollars tomorrow to give to Casey."

I had it. Yes, tips were that good. But it would be a huge hit.

"You fallin' in love with me?"

Gray asked that and when he did my thoughts about my tip money going to Casey went up in flames and so did my cheeks and most of my body.

"Sorry?" I was still whispering.

"Are you falling in love with me?" Gray asked.

I stared in his deep blue eyes with their russet tipped lashes.

Then I said quietly, "Yes."

Suddenly it was me that was over Gray's shoulder and we were going up the stairs.

Fast.

"Gray!" I cried, my hands holding on to his waist but he said not a word and we were up the stairs, down the hall and in his room in no time flat.

Then I was flying through the air before I was flat on my back in Gray's bed.

Then Gray was on top of me.

"Right," he said, both his hands moving to frame my face, "I wanna be inside you. Jesus, God, I wanna be inside you. But I can't have that, I can't give you that, so I'm gonna give you my mouth then teach you how to give me yours. That good for you?"

Oh my.

"Yes," I whispered.

"Good," he whispered back.

Then he kissed me.

Then he gave me his mouth.

After that he taught me how to give him mine.

It was unbelievably awesome.

And we were so into it, neither of us noticed we got crackers, cheese, apple and store-bought cookies all over the bed.

Chapter 16

I Looked Out for Me

T*hree weeks and three days later...*

I OPENED my eyes and saw my pillow illuminated by weak, early-morning-in-February Colorado sun.

But I felt Gray's long, warm body curved into my back, his steady breath on my neck and his arm tight around my belly.

This was the third time we'd slept all night together.

I couldn't wait for the day when it would happen all the time.

But it sucked that it happened last night because of what Casey did.

I closed my eyes and snuggled backward into Gray. He responded in his sleep by pressing deeper into me, taking me partly to my front, his arm curling tighter around me.

That was Gray. He gave even in his sleep.

I sighed.

Then the last three and a half weeks washed through my brain.

In those weeks I was surprised to find that normal was not boring and this didn't have to do with Casey until last night.

I had always hankered after a routine, a pattern, steady money, steady life. But I found that Casey and I being on the road half our time, hanging in bars the other half and occasionally hustling someone at pool had more steadiness than everyday life.

This, I decided, had to do with the fact that steady meant most my time was spent with Casey.

In normal, my time was spent with everyone in Gray's life and everyone who came in the bar which was to say pretty much everyone in Mustang.

For instance, Janie loved her man Danny and he was loveable. I'd met him, Gray and I had had a drink with him and Gray had known him for years. He was a big, burly bear of a man with a full beard, lots of long hair, an easy smile and a booming laugh. But that didn't mean Danny and Janie didn't fight and do it a lot. Which meant Janie came in complaining about him a lot. Their relationship was passionate and volatile and Janie didn't mind sharing it. In detail.

Another example was that I met Macy, Gray's aunt, and I didn't need to spend ten years honing the art of reading people to read instantly she had piss and vinegar. I knew this when she came right in the bar, all five-foot-four, square-bodied, big-boobed, permed-fluffy-mouse-brown-hair of her and gave me what for for taking a job with Janie at Mustang's rival bar.

Then Janie got in her face on my behalf and I (and the patrons, the male ones looking on avidly) thought I'd have to break up a catfight. But surprisingly, when Janie explained I was restarting my life and my job came with the room over the bar, Macy backed down.

That done, she turned her attention to me and announced, "So Mirry doesn't ride your ass the rest of your life, you better learn how to cook. Lessons start your next day off. My house. Hear you don't have a car so get Gray to get his fine ass in that POS truck a' his and get *your* fine ass to my house. Eleven o'clock. You're makin' lunch."

With that she stomped out.

My next day off, grinning, Gray dropped me off at Olly and Macy's house.

I learned how to make hamburgers and fries.

It wasn't that hard.

Then came Gray's Uncle Charlie who looked a lot like Gray if Gray had an extra twenty or so years, drank and ate five times more than he did and spent the vast majority of his time with his behind on a barstool or in a Barcalounger. And when I say Uncle Charlie came, I mean he came straight into the bar, straight up to me and started straight-talking.

"Shee-it, seein' you from afar was enough, up close, I'm in love."

Yes, that was his opening line delivered while doing a head to toe and back five times.

Then came, "Also hear you're the shit at pool. Got a guy at The Alibi that needs a lesson. When you're off tonight, get Gray to bring you in. I'll set 'im up then you get your cue. See you at nine."

He left before I could say word one.

Needless to say, when Gray came in that night with the intention of having a beer in the final half hour of my shift then taking me upstairs to cuddle, fool around and then make love, he was not super-delighted with the change in plans as decreed by his uncle.

I knew this when he stared at me after I gave him his open bottle of beer, his lips to the mouth of the bottle but not taking a tug, his eyes aimed around the bottle at me, his body unmoving. Then, when I got done telling him his uncle's plans for that night, the bottle hit the bar, Gray's boots hit the floor and he was gone.

About an hour later, when I was in my room reading a library book I'd legally borrowed (yes, I had an address so I also had a library card!), Gray showed up. He stalked to me, plucked me out of the couch, planted us in it with me on my back and him on me and declared, "Your decision is you're through hustlin' pool, you're through hustlin' pool. You got an offer you wanna accept, up to you. But no one tells you to hustle pool and no one...and that means *no one*...uses you to hustle pool or for any fuckin' reason. You with me?"

His face, his tone, the look in his eyes and the way he held his body even while lying on top of me made me answer what I'd answer anyway, "Yes."

At my answer, Gray dispensed with the cuddling and got right into the fooling around then making love.

And I decided, if that was my reward (even though I liked cuddling, definitely), I'd agree to just about anything Grayson Cody decreed.

Every once in a while, after my shifts but definitely on my days off (when I wasn't at cooking lessons with Macy), Gray took me to his house. After our bathroom drama, Grandma Miriam's attitude toward me changed. That was to say, she now tentatively liked me which meant I was open for her to boss me like it seemed she bossed everybody.

This included such comments as, "You have such a pretty figure, Ivey, and you're always in jeans and cowboy boots. You need some pretty skirts and heels." And, "Every time I see you, you're wearing different perfume. A girl has to have a signature scent. You need to settle on one and stay there." And, "You really need more than a jeans jacket in Colorado. You need to get yourself down to Hayes for a winter coat. A nice one. Long. Wool. I think for your coloring, camel. Good timing since they're having their winter clearance sale." And, "You have such lovely hair, child, but there's so much of it. You should get yourself an appointment at Stacy's and get it cut, probably to your shoulders."

This last was unfortunately timed to come while we were at the dinner table eating the spaghetti I made (I was really getting the hang of ground beef) and Gray was sitting there.

Mostly, since he did it himself, he ignored Grandma Miriam bossing me.

This, he didn't ignore.

"She's not cuttin' her hair. Ever," Gray declared, and Grandma Miriam looked to him, and even though she'd known him since birth, she clearly misjudged his tone and the look in his eyes because she kept right on talking.

"She has a beautiful head of hair, Gray, but you're a man. You don't know anything about these things. A shorter style will become the shape of her face."

"She's not cuttin' her hair. Ever," Gray repeated and there was even more steel in it this time.

"Gray!" Grandma Miriam snapped. "It's not for you to say. It isn't *your* hair."

"Yeah, it is. You know *how* it is and even if you wanted to pretend you didn't, you don't want me to explain how it is. What I will explain is that it's...not...*yours*," Gray returned.

Grandma Miriam snapped her mouth shut and her cheeks got pink even as her blue eyes flashed. I quickly excused myself, rushed from the table and ran to the bathroom where I burst out laughing.

I think they heard me.

I didn't care.

What could I say? They were funny.

Later, after Gray and I made out in his truck before I went to my room, I promised him I'd only ever cut my hair to get a trim.

This got me another hard kiss then, against my lips, a soft, sweet, gentle, "Thanks, dollface."

And I made my promise honestly, but at Gray's soft, sweet, gentle gratitude, it became a vow.

Being a waitress in a bar in a small town I quickly discovered that we had regulars and if they sensed you were turning local, they sucked you in. They did this by sharing their lives with you, showing you pictures of their kids, telling you what movie they recently saw and that you *had* to see it. They also did it by advising you about the restaurant a town over that had an unfortunate result to a recent health inspection and writing down a recipe that took four different napkins that you *had* to try.

Stuff like that.

Stuff I liked.

Though it had to be said that I might have been getting the hang of hamburger meat, a recipe that took four napkins was currently beyond my capabilities. Still, I kept it.

I also met Gray's two best friends. Shim, a tall, gangly, sandy-haired man who was a hand on Jeb Sharp's ranch and was engaged to Chastity, a seriously petite and curvy blonde who looked cute with him regardless of the fact he was eight inches taller than her. And Ronan, called Roan, who was about two inches taller than me, worked with Janie's man Danny at some local place that processed gravel (who ever heard of such a thing, processing gravel? Still, from the way they explained it, that was what they did). Roan seemed dedicated to the task of expanding his beer gut, had no girlfriend and a fondness for telling long-winded jokes that were hilarious. And he had a million of them.

They started to become regulars at The Rambler and I liked it because they obviously liked me and I obviously liked that.

Unfortunately, working at one of the town's two bars meant that Buddy Sharp, his sidekicks Jim, Ted and Pete and Gray's exes, specifically Cecily, came in every once in a while. Just as Shim, Chastity and Roan made it clear they liked me, Buddy, Jim, Ted, Pete and Cecily made it clear they did not.

I didn't let this bother me because, fortunately, even though they didn't like me and didn't mind me knowing it, that didn't mean they didn't tip.

Twice (before last night), Gray braved the wrath of Grandma Miriam as backed by God and His Word the Bible and he arranged for his cousin, Audie, to spend the night at his house to look after Grandma Miriam so he could stay with me.

I doubted this went down too well. What I knew was, however it went down, Gray and Grandma Miriam kept it between them because when I went over to his house after, she bossed me but she didn't say anything about it. Nor did she give me any indication she was angry or disappointed in Gray or me.

I figured this was because Gray laid down the law that he was a man, I was his girl, his private life was his private life, and even though he lived with his grandmother, that was the way it was going to be. I also figured part of Gray's law was that she didn't bypass him with her aversion to our modern relationship and pass it on to me.

So she kept mum on the subject and Gray did what he pleased.

And luckily, what he pleased meant I had him all night in my bed with me.

And I liked that.

So having a job, a place, a boyfriend and a routine wasn't boring.

But it was beautiful.

Until last night, and it wasn't Bud Sharp or Cecily or Mustang making my life not what I wanted it to be.

It was Casey.

And, after last night (I hated to admit it because I owed him everything), but for a long time, making my life be nothing I wanted it to be had been all Casey.

It was quarter to eight, fifteen minutes before Gray was due in but also after the dinner rush. Folks ate early in Mustang, the dinner rush starting at five and ending at seven. Then things got quiet and it was just Janie and me and a few regulars until, on weeknights, around nine thirty, ten, Janie saw things pick up but not so much she couldn't handle it on her own. On the weekends, it was a different story but she had another girl who worked part-time to help her out with that.

I was days. Or days until eight which was mostly days and evenings.

So it was quiet, me on the outside of the bar and Janie on the inside, shooting the breeze, and there were only four other people in the bar.

I was winding down from work but winding up to see Gray. We'd been together a month but I had been right. I wasn't used to him or his beauty. I looked forward to it all day. I started getting excited about it when it got close then felt the splendor of it when he finally walked through the door.

And this escalated after our relationship became physical.

Since she didn't mind sharing personal stuff with me, I tested the waters and I told Janie about it. When I did, she told me having an orgasm your first time was so unusual, it was exceptional.

"Though," she went on quietly, "not surprised that a man like Gray gave that to you. What I will say is that I sure am glad you gave a man like Gray what you had to give him."

It must be said I really, really liked Janie.

The first time being great, it kept getting better. Gray told me his father taught him patience and I learned that to be true. I didn't know who taught him gentleness but that was true too, out of bed as well as in it. Nudity, touching, tasting, sharing, kissing, holding and making love was safe with Gray. I didn't feel self-conscious, not ever. He communicated, not with words most of the time, with his eyes, his hands, his mouth. He guided. He taught. He listened. He paid attention. He discovered what I liked (and we both enjoyed it, me more, obviously) and he showed me what he liked (and we both enjoyed it, him more, hopefully).

And it just kept getting better and better.

Janie told me that, too, was unusual.

So I looked forward to Gray, to talking to him, to being with him then cuddling with him and finally *being* with him.

And I looked forward to it *a lot*.

So I was in a good mood, in a good place, fifteen minutes away from Gray and unprepared for Casey to storm into the bar.

But even if he'd come in at high noon and I had hours to wait for Gray I would have been unprepared. Because even though Gray met him at the diner like he said and gave him five hundred dollars of his own money (something we had quiet words about and he refused to allow me to do it, I didn't like it but it clearly meant something to him so I let him), I hadn't seen Casey since that day at Gray's.

And also because I was not then nor ever would be prepared for what Casey would do and say to me.

It went like this...

He walked right up to me, manner hurried, things on his mind, places to be. I knew him well so I knew that.

I just didn't know what was on his mind, where he wanted to be and I would never have guessed he would take for granted wherever that place was, it would be with me.

When he made it to me, he said, "Come on, Ivey, let's go."

I stared at him and asked, "Where?"

"It's fuckin' cold up here. Tired of cold. I'm thinkin' southern California, San Diego or maybe Tucson."

San Diego or Tucson?

"What are you talking about?" I asked, so caught in my new life, what he was saying didn't dawn on me.

He focused more on my face. "Next stop. San Diego. Tucson. Maybe Phoenix. Pack your shit. We're on the road tonight."

Was he crazy?

"Casey," I said softly, "I'm not going to San Diego or Tucson. I've got a job. An apartment. I'm not going anywhere."

That was when he really focused on me.

Then he declared, "Yeah you are. You're comin' with me."

It hit me belatedly that his relationship with the mystery Mustang woman had crashed and burned.

"Oh Casey," I whispered, moving to him, "did you break up with your girl?"

He jerked up his chin, eyes hard, hiding emotion he didn't want anyone to see but I knew him. He couldn't hide from me.

"Bitch ousted me. Just like that. Said pack your bags, out tonight. So I packed my bags, I'm out, we're on the road and this shithole is in our dust."

I studied him and I saw he wasn't lying when he talked about her after they met. He liked her. And he was hurt.

"If you guys have had a fight, maybe you should give her a night to cool down. Go see her tomorrow. Talk it out," I advised.

"Ivey," he snapped. "You're not listenin' to me. We're *gone*."

"Honey, seriously, give her the night."

"Yeah, give her the night," he hissed sarcastically, then went on in the same vein. "You gonna let me crash on your couch? Oh, I know, your friendly cowboy'll let me crash at his pad."

This meant he didn't have any money.

"Yes, for the night, Casey, I'll let you crash on my couch," I offered cautiously at the same time trying to figure out how I'd convince Gray that was an okay idea.

"Fuck that," he returned. "We're goin'."

"Casey, honey, I'm not going and if she means something to you, you shouldn't either. You should give it a shot, work it out."

"Relationship advice from my fuckin' sister," he muttered.

"Well, yeah, Casey. I know you. I love you. And you're obviously hurt so I'm looking out for you and advising you should try to work it out."

He leaned in, his face twisting, and spat, "I'm not *hurt*. Bitch wanted to tie me down. Yammerin' on every night, 'Casey, you go to the plant and talk about a job?' and 'Casey, darlin', saw an ad in the paper, sellin' cars, you'd be good at that.' Sellin' cars. Fuckin' crazy.

That's not me. I tell her that, she doesn't listen to me, just keeps at me with that shit. Fuck that, I'm done."

At this speech it finally broke through. It dawned crystal clear that for the last month as I started my normal life with my job and my room and my boyfriend in this town, Casey had been going through the money I gave him, Gray gave him and undoubtedly his girl gave him. And no doubt he'd done it stupidly. And she was done giving money to him, feeding him, putting a roof over his head and a pillow under it. He probably promised her he'd step up. He didn't. And she was done.

"Maybe you should take a second, think about what she said and look into those things, Casey," I gave my suggestion hesitantly. "You don't know. You might like it. I know I like waitressing. It's fun. Maybe you'll like doing something steady too."

"Are you fuckin' nuts?" Casey shot back. "This isn't my life and it isn't yours. We're goin'."

"Okay, if you've decided it isn't your life, that's fine for you. But it is mine and I'm not going anywhere," I replied.

"We're goin'," Casey repeated.

"You can but I'm not," I returned.

And that was when he shocked me straight to my core.

Because that was when my brother Casey lost it completely doing something he'd never, ever done to me.

And what he did was grab my arm, dip his face half an inch from mine, shake my arm hard and hiss, "Pack your *fuckin'* bags, sis, we... are...*goin'*."

Looking into his furious face, feeling his fingers wrapped tight around my arm, hearing Janie whispering probably into a phone behind me, I knew it.

I knew it then.

He needed me.

I understood it before but not in the same way.

He couldn't make his own way. He couldn't put gas in his car. He couldn't feed himself.

Unless he used me.

Used me.

When Gray got angry with his uncle and made his declaration about no one using me, he didn't mean Uncle Charlie. He meant Casey. He'd barely been around us but he'd seen it even before me.

That was why there were no connections but that rule was just for me. That was why I had to play it safe when he didn't.

He found his girl who made his heart race, it was okay for me to find whatever I found.

But when he was done so was I.

I was his meal ticket.

I was all he had.

A long time ago, he was all I had. But as we got older, that had shifted. And instead of Casey finding us something safe, something steady, something right, something good and moving us into that kind of life, he was too scared or too dumb or too addicted to the hustle to do that.

And he couldn't hustle anyone without me.

So he kept me under his thumb and used me.

"Take your hand off me," I demanded quietly, but he didn't.

His fingers tightened so much the pain magnified and he shook me again, this time my body going with it.

"Not gonna say it again," he ground out.

I twisted my arm savagely but he was holding on so tight I didn't get free and it hurt more so I stopped doing it and my voice rose with anger and a little bit of panic when I repeated, "Take your hand off me!"

He shook me again, leaning into me so I had to bend back, and shouted, "Get your shit and get in the car!"

I twisted my arm again, it hurt again even more but he *still* didn't let go and I shrieked, "Casey, *take your hand off me*!"

"Dude, do as Ivey says," Barry, one of the two men (I was right back when I made my guess) who sat hunched with his friend Gene nearly every night at The Rambler was now standing close to Casey and me.

Casey's neck twisted and he spat, "Stay out of it."

"Let her go and move back," Gene ordered, standing to Casey's other side.

Casey's neck twisted the other way. "Fuck *you*!"

"One last shot, dude, you let her go or we make you," Barry warned and Casey looked back at him.

"Yeah, right, fat ass, like you can do that," he snarled, lip curled.

"Casey!" I snapped.

He looked at me, started to shake me again then Gene put two hands on his shoulders, Barry wrapped one around the wrist of his hand that had hold of me and they both pulled him away from me.

It was then it began. Casey tore loose and went back at them fighting.

"Oh God," I whispered. "God!" I cried. "Casey! Stop it!" I shouted.

He didn't stop. He took on Barry and Gene and he underestimated them.

Pure Casey.

They might be big boys but then again they were *big boys* and there were two of them. Casey had speed and agility but they had bulk and numbers and they got him down on his belly, his arm twisted around his back, Gene's knee in it for good measure and Barry turned to Janie.

"You call Len?" he asked and she nodded.

"Lenny and Gray," she confirmed.

I closed my eyes then opened them quickly.

A squirming, infuriated, Casey demanded, "Let me up, asshole."

I got as close as I dared and told my brother, "Casey, Janie's called the cops and Gray and you do not want to be here when either of them get here. Trust me. If I ask Gene to let you up, will you promise to get out of here quick?"

"Fuck you, you stupid, selfish *cunt*! Fuck...*you*!" Casey yelled.

This was a bad idea and it was very, very bad timing.

It was a bad idea because I had gabbed with Barry and Gene on more than one occasion. I saw them nearly every night for a month. I liked them, they liked me and they didn't like anyone calling me the c-word, even my brother.

And it was bad timing because he said it precisely as Gray stalked into the bar.

So Gene got one second to twist Casey's arm so brutally he cried out in pain and I feared he's snap it right off before Gray pushed him aside.

He rolled Casey to his back, jerked him to his feet, pushed him off and invited in a low, rumbling, seriously angry voice, "Let's do this."

The last time they went head to head, Gray had dumped him right on his behind in the snow, but Casey, my stupid, *stupid* brother, did not hesitate.

And Gray instantly commenced beating the shit out of my stupid brother while I stood straining against the arms of Barry that were holding me back and shouted at them to stop.

They didn't.

Not until Lenny showed up in uniform, badge on his chest, gun on his hip, and he pulled Casey from the hold Gray had on Casey's collar to keep him steady while he slammed his fist repeatedly in my brother's face.

Casey went flying, shaking his head, so addled by the blows he didn't even throw his arms out to catch on to anything.

Lenny planted a hand in Gray's chest, arm straight, eyes locked to Gray's and voice growling, "Stand down now, Gray."

Gray's chest was rising and falling fast, his jaw was hard, a muscle jerking in his cheek. His eyes were locked on Casey who was swaying and still shaking his head, trying to shake the sense back in.

A fruitless endeavor.

Lenny gave it a minute, holding Gray's eyes to ascertain he got a lock on it. When he did, Lenny stepped back and dropped his arm.

Then he asked the bar at large, "What we got here?"

Peg, the barfly who, like Barry and Gene, was there every night, piped up and apparently, even though she was usually always borderline sloshed, that didn't mean she couldn't pay attention.

"That guy came in mouthin' off at Ivey. She tried to be cool with him. He didn't listen to a word she said. He got physical, wouldn't stop. Barry and Gene stepped in. They warned him to stop, he wouldn't. They got him off her then he called Ivey the c-word and Gray was walkin' in, heard him and justifiably whaled on him."

Although this was succinct and all the truth, albeit with a bit of opinion thrown in, Gray had heard Casey call me the c-word but he didn't know Casey had been physical with me. Hearing Peg, his gaze cut to me, he took me in and unfortunately I wasn't wearing one of my long-sleeved Henleys but instead a short sleeved tee and he saw the angry, red welts on my arm left by Casey.

Fortunately, Lenny knew Gray. His glance was faster and he had a hand in Gray's chest by the time Gray's gaze cut back to Casey, his body leaned forward in preparation for launching another attack and his rage filled the room.

Gene edged closer to help Lenny control the situation and Barry's arms got tighter so I didn't do anything stupid.

"Keep your shit, Gray," Lenny growled, arm up but now his weight was in it.

Gray continued staring at Casey.

"Gray, son, listen to me. Keep...your...*shit*," Lenny repeated with variation and additions.

For a scary second, Gray continued staring at my brother before he pulled in a deep, audible breath, his rage saturating the room eased, and he took a step back.

Lenny dropped his arm.

Then he looked at Casey. "You thinkin' clearly enough to hear what the witness said?"

Casey was bleeding from the lip, nose and a cut by the side of his already swelling eye but he was also back in the room and I knew this because he was scowling at Lenny.

He didn't reply.

"It go down like that?" Lenny asked.

Casey continued scowling.

"It went down like that," Janie chimed in from behind me.

"Exactly like that," Gene confirmed.

"Yeah, just like that," Barry, still holding me in his arms, threw in.

Lenny looked at each of them then back to Casey.

"Now, I can take you in for disturbin' the peace, assaulting your sister and scrappin' with Gray. This means I gotta also take Gray in. I'm seein' you probably like that idea. But Gray's got no priors, he's got no outstanding warrants, he's got family local who'll look out for him and he's got a certain reputation, so a judge will probably not go hard on him. You, I don't know. You, I figure need to think smart right about now about how you wanna play this. Usually, I don't mind arresting people. It breaks up my night. Tonight, I'm not feelin' it. So you lucked out, you play it smart and get your ass outta this bar. But my kindness comes with conditions. When I say get your ass outta this bar, I mean get your ass outta my town and while you're at it, outta my county. You feel like communicatin' with your sister, who clearly has the urge to share her pretty face with the folk of Mustang for a spell, you send a greeting card. Are you reading me, son?"

Casey glared at Lenny then he shifted his glare to me.

"I gave it all for you," he whispered.

That went in like the plunge of a blade but not for the reasons it used to.

And because of that, I returned, "And then I started giving it all for you. Difference is, I was twelve, Casey. I had no one else and I needed you. When I started to be able to give back, you were twenty and you just took it from me."

My brother had it in him to wince before he kept at me.

"You're all I've got."

"I'm sorry, honey, but you aren't all I have. Not anymore," I replied quietly.

On my last word, Barry's arms moved from around me and Gray's arms took their place.

Casey's eyes went up over my left shoulder then his face twisted and they came back to me.

"Did what I did because I loved you, sis."

I knew that. Way back when, I knew it. Casey was everything to me and I was everything to him. Before we ran, we had a mom who was less than nothing, and we had a lot of troubles and a whole lot of nothing else.

All we had was each other.

But now that had changed.

"Then keep loving me and let me keep what I found," I whispered.

I watched him swallow.

Gray's arms got tight.

My eyes filled with tears.

Without another word, looking down to his feet, my brother turned away and walked out of the bar.

I knew he had no money, no skills, nothing.

I had no idea where he'd go, what he'd do, how he'd get there and how much trouble he'd catch when he landed wherever he landed.

And it killed me.

But one thing my brother Casey taught me was to look out for myself.

So the tears slid silently out of my eyes, down my cheeks and Gray turned me in his arms to face him. My arms closed around him, I shoved my face in his chest and I concentrated on that rather than running after my brother and giving him all of my money just to keep him safe for a little while.

Instead, for the first time since I was fifteen, I didn't look out for my brother.

I cried in Gray's arms and looked out for me.

"DOLLFACE, KNOW YOU'RE AWAKE."

I blinked at the pillow, sighed and turned to face Gray.

He looked beautiful in the sunlight, in the moonlight, in the lights of the bar, in the light thrown from a TV.

But he never looked more beautiful than in the morning with his head on a pillow beside me.

"Hi," I whispered, sliding my hands up his chest and his lips curved up.

"Hi," he whispered back, his arm not around me shoving under me so both of them could gather me close.

He dipped his chin. I tipped my head back and he brushed his mouth on mine.

Then his hair slid across the pillow as he pulled slightly away but gathered me even closer.

"You doin' okay?" he asked, his blue eyes studying me.

"No," I answered honestly.

"You'll get there," he muttered.

I would. It would take some time but I would. And it would hurt but I would still get there.

"He's a man," Gray went on. "It's time he acted like one, baby. Took care of his own shit. You still haven't shared and I told you I'd wait, I'll wait. But I know this, what you were doin', and I get the impression you been doin' it awhile, it is wild-ass luck you two made it this far without some kinda tragedy. And he's a man. Those tragedies he could face are a far sight fewer and a far sight easier to move on from than what a woman could take. He put you out there. You. A miracle you didn't get chewed up. You didn't. Hold on to that. Hold on to the decent you carved out for yourself and let go of the shit."

"He's all I had for a long time, Gray," I whispered.

"Yeah. And what you said last night is true. He's not all you have anymore, Ivey. You're with people who give a shit about you now."

When I opened my mouth to speak, his arms gave me a squeeze and he went on.

"I mean give a shit about you in a healthy way not some fucked-up, dysfunctional way born of whatever-the-fuck you two had goin' was born of. I get that you love him. I get he's your brother. I get that you worry about him. But he shoulda sorted his shit *and* yours a long time ago. I also get that this has come to you. Don't let guilt and worry fog that, darlin'. You're on the right path. Don't allow him to veer you away."

I held his eyes then, nodding, I dipped my chin and pressed my face to his throat.

Gray tilted his head back and sifted his fingers in my hair. Then he kept doing it.

I let him because I liked it, it was soothing and after he did this for a while, I asked his throat, "You know what I wish?"

"I can guess, dollface, but tell me anyway."

"I wish I'd met your dad because I would like to have had the chance to meet the man who made a man like you."

His hand stopped and his body went completely still.

My head tipped back and his tipped down and I saw instantly he didn't guess correctly. His eyes held surprise and something else, something I'd never seen on him or anyone.

But whatever it was, it made the area around my heart get warm.

"Gray?" I called when he didn't say anything.

"You still fallin' in love with me?"

I stared, my cheeks now getting warm and opened my mouth to answer affirmative when he went on.

"'Cause you should know, baby, I'm already gone for you."

My mouth stayed open only because at that point it was hanging open.

Then I snapped it closed and asked, "You love me?"

"Yeah," Gray answered.

"You love me," I stated but it was still a question.

Gray grinned, dimple and all, and he repeated, "Yeah."

Tears filled my eyes and I whispered it again, "You love me."

Gray's grin faded, he rolled me so I was on my back and he was mostly on me. His face got really close and he whispered back, "Yeah."

I stared into his blue eyes with their russet tipped lashes and shared quietly, "I fell for you after you first kissed me."

And quietly back from Gray I got, "I win since I fell for you that night at my kitchen table when you blew on me."

Oh God.

When I blew on him.

Oh God!

He went blurry as tears filled my eyes.

"Say you love me, Ivey," he ordered.

"I love you, Gray," I did as ordered.

"Good, baby, because I love you too," he whispered.

Finally, he kissed me.

Then he made love to me. He did it slow. It was sweet. It was beautiful. And if I had any questions that I was on the wrong path, which I did not, I wouldn't anymore.

I'd driven all over the country and back again probably eight times.

But finally, I was going in the right direction.

Chapter 17

Veer Crazily Under My Feet

S*ix weeks and a day later…*

"Fuck, I shoulda planned for this," Gray muttered, lips at my throat and I knew what he meant.

We were naked in my bed. We'd finished. It was fabulous. So fabulous, as usual, we wanted to start up again.

And he needed to get home to Grandma Miriam.

His hands slid up my sides, one moving in to cup my breast but my fingers curled around his waist.

"Get off me, Gray, you gotta go home to your gran," I whispered, even though I really didn't want to, and he growled against the skin under my ear.

I shivered.

His head came up, his hand leaving my breast to frame my face. "Love her, you know it darlin'. My mom left and she stepped up and was there for me. When she lost her legs, I vowed I'd pay her back and she could depend on me no matter what, no matter how long it lasted. But, right now, I wish my uncles weren't assholes and most of my cousins didn't hightail their asses outta Mustang to get away from their asshole daddies 'cause this shit is killin' me."

I knew what he meant about that too.

Audie was good for once a week and Audie had stepped in for us with no notice when we needed him, going to Gray's after Casey did his thing at The Rambler so Gray was free to stay with me. But Audie made it clear that was all Gray got. And Grandma Miriam refused to let anyone but Audie, Gray or me help her with things at the house.

But tonight was a special night.

Tonight, I'd bought a new outfit, including heels and hose, and tonight Gray had taken me for a fancy dinner at Jenkins. Tonight, we drank wine and ate steaks that were really good but not as good as the VFW. Still, they had fancy sauce that tasted awesome and Jenkins had superior desserts that were phenomenal.

Gray had even dressed up.

It was fun. Better than the movies Gray took me to which I loved. Better than most everything.

Except for his birthday, his birthday we had at his house, Shim, Chastity, Roan and Audie came over. Grandma Miriam made a cake and I helped with dinner and we had a blast.

And Audie stayed and Gray and I came back to my place where he stayed.

And he'd loved my present but not so much at first.

It was a scarf given to him in March and when he opened it, he grinned at me and teased, "Dollface, it's March. In about a day I won't need a scarf for another eight months."

To which I returned, "When I saw you walking up to me in the playground that first night, I thought that a scarf said you had a woman who cared about you. And a man having a scarf does say that. So you've got two women who care about you therefore two scarves."

After that, he kissed me then he made love to me and that was when he told me he loved his present.

So that was the best.

But his frustration now was about more than just this being a special night.

We had two and a half months of this and Gray wanted me falling asleep at his side and waking up there just as much as I wanted to do it.

I knew this because he told me.

Incidentally, that made me cry too, just like when he told me he loved me.

"I'm gonna talk to her," Gray decided, and my eyes got big.

"Sorry?"

"I'm gonna talk to her about you movin' in," Gray replied.

I blinked rapidly then told him something he already knew, "You can't do that."

"I sure as fuck can."

"Gray!" I cried. "She'll lose her mind."

"Better 'n both of us doin' it. I gotta drag my naked ass outta your bed one more time, get dressed, go home and go to sleep alone when that is the *last* thing I wanna do, dollface, I'll lose it. And you want me to go about as much as I want to."

"Actually, less," I informed him. "At least you have Mrs. Cody's strawberry preserves to wake up to. Macy's graduated me from hamburger to roasts to casseroles and now I'm just cracking desserts. I haven't made it to breakfast and definitely not preserves so I still wake up to boxed cereal or toast, so you're ahead of me on that score."

Gray stared down at me a second then burst out laughing, collapsing on me then rolling so I was on top.

I lifted my head and he lifted his hands, tucking my hair behind my ears then holding it there, still chuckling.

"Just an FYI, dollface, for a guy, preserves do not make up for goin' to sleep alone when he can go to sleep with your face, hair and body and wake up to your smile, your breathy 'hi' and your ability to make me laugh."

I allowed his compliment to settle deep as I muttered, "Good to know."

"Though, seein' as I love you, I'll pinch a jar of Gran's preserves and bring it to you. She inventories that shit so she can call Macy out when she steals it and ream her ass but I'll take that hit for you."

I grinned at him and replied, "Thanks, Gray. And, just so you know, if I had a grandma I could steal jam from and catch flack for it, I love you enough to do it for you too."

He shook his head, grinning, dimple out, before he lifted up and touched his mouth to mine.

Then he rolled me to my back and touched his mouth to mine again.

He lifted his head, looked me in the eyes and muttered, "I gotta do this or I won't."

I knew it. I knew by his words that it wasn't easy leaving and it was getting harder.

I loved that just about as much as I hated it.

And I knew it because it wasn't easy letting him go and it was getting harder.

"Okay, honey," I whispered.

He lifted up, kissed my forehead then slid out of the bed making sure the covers never left me, but still, once out, he pulled them to my shoulder. I slid my hands under my cheek and watched him dress. When he was done, he got close and smoothed my hair back, leaned deep and kissed my temple.

I turned my head, lifted a hand and caught the side of his neck before he pulled away.

"Thanks for tonight, honey," I said quietly.

"Anything for my girl," Gray returned quietly. "See you tomorrow. I'll talk to Audie, see if I can get him to take an extra night."

I knew that wasn't going to happen because Gray did this daily. But I was glad he wanted to try.

I nodded. "That'd be good."

"Say you love me, Ivey."

"I love you, Gray."

He grinned, gave me the dimple, then whispered, "Love you too, baby." He bent again, touched my lips with his and whispered against them, "'Night."

"'Night," I whispered back.

Then he was gone, using his key to lock the door behind him.

I closed my eyes, sighed and threw back the covers, got out of bed, pulled on undies and a nightie, put away my pretty new dress, my pretty high heels, dumped my hose in the hamper, washed my face, brushed my teeth, turned out the lights and went to bed.

And I did all of this not knowing the path to beautiful I was on was going to veer crazily under my feet.

Five hours fifteen minutes later…

"Ivey!"

I woke with a start, my heart racing and a hand shaking me.

"Ivey!"

I scooted across the bed, terrified.

"Ivey, sis, it's me," Casey whispered.

I blinked at the shadow in the dark.

What on earth? How did he get in?

"How'd you get in?" I asked.

"Doesn't matter, Ivey, I don't have much time. I don't…I don't have much time, honey, they're after me."

Oh God.

"Who?" I asked, moving toward the lamp by my bed.

"Don't turn on the light!" Casey hissed, and I stopped dead.

"Who's after you, Casey and why can't I turn on the light?"

"'Cause I'm worried they're close and I don't want them to know where you live."

Oh God!

I shoved up to sitting and demanded to know, "What's going on?"

"I ran into some of our history."

Oh God!

No.

What we'd always feared.

Always.

"Casey," I whispered.

"Worked me over," he whispered back. "Bad dudes. Serious bad dudes. Wanted to finish me off. Don't even know how I got away. Just know I did and they followed me. You turn on that light, you'd see. It's bad, sis. They're pissed, they wanna do me and while they were workin' me over they asked for me to give up you."

I closed my eyes.

Then I opened them. "Right, I'll get dressed, we'll go to Gray."

"Are you *crazy*?" he hissed. "There are five of them, Ivey, they're on a mission and they got hardware. You want your cowboy steppin' up for you and gettin' his denim shirt filled with holes?"

My heart started beating wildly.

No, I didn't want that.

"We'll go to the police," I told him.

Something filled the room. Something I forgot seeing as Casey had been out of my life awhile. Something that was not good. And it was something that told me Casey messed up big.

"When I left you, Ivey, I was hurtin'. Did somethin', we go to the cops, they might put two and two together and know it was me."

God!

My *stupid, stupid, STUPID* brother.

"What'd you do?"

"What I did, they nail me, I'll do five to ten in the local penitentiary."

Yes, my stupid, *stupid* brother.

"Get up, pack a bag, we gotta go," Casey ordered.

At that, my heart clenched.

"Go?" I whispered.

"Go, honey, *go*. We gotta *go*."

"But I can't. I have a job, rent to pay..."

Gray.

"They followed me, they'll find you. Won't be hard, Ivey and all these folks, someone shields you, they'll buy it. You cannot do what you're doin'. You and me, we gotta evaporate, sis, to stay alive and to keep these folks safe."

"Who are these people, Casey? Where did we play them? How are they here?" I asked.

"I'll explain on the way," Casey evaded.

"Casey!"

He turned the light on, just for a flash, but in that flash I caught his mangled, swollen face. He plunged the room back to darkness as I sat frozen in my bed, his image burned on the backs of my eyes.

"Get up, get dressed, get packed, Ivey. We don't got a lotta time if we have any at all."

I sat in the bed, breathing heavy.

Then I told my brother, "I have to write Gray a note."

"Sis, I told you, *we don't got a lotta time.*"

"I'm writing Gray *a note*!" I hissed.

"Fuck! Whatever! Just do it and *let's go*!"

Heart beating wildly, lungs working overtime, I got up, got dressed, got packed and wrote Gray a note.

Then I stole out into the dark spring night that was still cold but not freezing and took off with my stupid, stupid brother.

Buddy Sharp

Eight hours, twenty-three minutes later...

"You gotta go to her place, she left a note," Casey whatever-the-fuck-his-name-was mumbled in his ear.

"That's been seen to," Buddy Sharp told the moron. "Be sure to lose this phone."

"Good phone, shame to dump it," the idiot replied.

"Yes, it would be, so do whatever you want. It isn't me who has to explain the phone to your sister."

There was a pause then, "See your point," he muttered.

Fuck, this guy was a total, fucking idiot.

"You go to the bank in Cheyenne I told you about, you'll find the rest of your money just like I explained," Buddy informed him.

"Right," he kept muttering.

"This is done. You do not come back. You do not hit me up again. You do not bring that bitch back here. And you make certain she doesn't come back or what me and my boys did to your face to convince her to go with you we'll do for real and we will not stop. Is that understood?"

"Jeez, bro, I speak English. I know the deal I agreed to."

"No communication between her and Grayson Cody at all. She tries to phone, you stop her. She tries to come back, you tie her down if you have to. She sends a fuckin' birthday card, you infiltrate the United States Postal Service to steal that thing. I've paid you ten large to make this happen, you fuck it up, I'll find you and you know I will. I got the resources and I got the motivation. Now is that understood?"

"Seriously, bro, I'm not an idiot."

He was wrong.

"We're done," Buddy stated then disconnected

He looked out the window of the bank.

Then he grinned.

Six hours *and thirty-six minutes later…*

The door to Buddy Sharp's apartment opened and Cecily walked through, lugging a bag and grinning.

Buddy didn't grin on the outside but he sure as fuck was smiling on the inside.

"You take care of it?" he asked.

"Got in right after I saw them take off. Got everything that was hers. There was a bunch of stuff, looked like it was Janie's or something, sheets, an old TV, shit like that. Left that."

"Tomorrow, you get your girls talkin'. They saw the brother. They saw her go with him. Right?"

Cecily nodded. "They're all set and my cousin in Grand Junction is gonna come for a visit and talk about friends of his that got hustled at pool by a blonde with attitude and a lotta hair."

That was when Buddy nodded then asked, "Did you get the note?"

Her grin got bigger. She dumped the bag, opened her purse, pawed through it and came out with a folded piece of paper.

Buddy took it from her.

He read it.

Then his lips curled into a sneer.

He took it to his fireplace, grabbed a match, struck it, set it to Ivey's note to Gray and it caught fire.

He threw it in the fireplace and watched it burn to ash.

Only then did he smile.

That done, *it* done, he turned to Cecily, threw her on the couch, pulled and tugged her clothes just enough to provide access to the areas he wanted and he fucked her even though she was still mostly dry. Then again, Cecily was shit in bed, never loosened up, never got very wet.

And it never occurred to Buddy Sharp that she didn't because he didn't put enough effort into getting her that way.

All the time he drove his cock into Cecily, he did it with his eyes closed.

And he did it visualizing Ivey.

Chapter 18

Fathoms Deep in Concrete

T*wo years, eleven months and one week later...*

I LOOKED in the mirror over my bathroom basin and saw it.

Hard behind my eyes, hard around my mouth.

I stared.

Then I pulled my hair away from my face and secured it in a ponytail.

It happened often. Still, after nearly three years, it happened. The memories coming back to me. Sometimes it was okay, I could deal. Sometimes it hurt like a mother.

But every year on that day, it killed.

Gray's birthday.

I went back. When I got shot of Casey, I went back to Mustang.

I called beforehand, five times, and each time Grandma Miriam answered and put the phone down on me. I called his cell too but that number was no longer in service. I also called The Rambler, twice, and both times Janie put the phone down on me.

I didn't get this.

So I went to Mustang.

And I drove right through.

Because while driving, on the sidewalk right on the square I saw Gray strolling with a pretty girl about my age, his arm locked around her neck, pulling her close, his face near hers, aiming his dimpled smile straight at her.

So I drove on through.

I'd been gone three months.

Three.

And I'd been replaced.

Really, I shouldn't have been surprised. Before me there was Cecily and Connie, Donna, Debbie, Nancy, all the way back to Emily.

For three months I'd had not one thing to smile about, but not Gray. Strolling down the street with his arm around a pretty girl and giving her his dimple.

How could I ever have convinced myself that he would want me? A pool hustler. A virgin who, until him, had never been kissed.

I shouldn't have been surprised.

But I was and that hurt like a mother too.

Devastation so complete, it left my heart in tatters.

It killed me to admit it but my stupid, stupid brother was right.

I should have played it safe.

Now I did. I'd learned my lesson. It took months just to breathe easy, scared my heart would shred with just a breath. But once I succeeded in that, as it healed, I went to work. Layer by layer, block by block, I built a cement wall around my heart. Then, right up next to it, another. Then up next to that another. And another. And another. Until my heart was fathoms deep in concrete.

Fathoms deep.

No one would get near it again.

My mother was a slut, a bitch and a loser. The men she brought into our house were dangerous and she didn't care.

One in particular.

And she didn't care about him either.

My brother saved me then used me to guard the fact he, too, was a loser.

And the first man I loved didn't give a shit I was gone. His grandmother didn't. His friends didn't. I disappeared into the night, left a note about the trouble I was in and he just moved on.

Just moved on.

So I was done. I was through. No one else got to my heart.

And so yeah, some of that cement I used to protect my heart had made it to the backs of my eyes, settled around my mouth. So be it.

Smart men took one look at me and they knew. Dumb ones got the point another way and this was usually me laying it out for them.

No one got close.

Ever.

I'd learned to play it safe and that was the only way I'd play it until I stopped breathing.

I heard the car honk and my head turned in the direction of the front of my house.

Then I moved out of my bathroom to my bedroom, grabbed my designer bag from my stylishly flowered down comforter cover and walked on my high-heeled, strappy designer sandals through my house to the front door, out of it and to the waiting car.

"How's my girl tonight?"

I turned my head to the dressing room door and I saw Lash coming through.

Lash was my boss. Lash owned the club. Lash had taken one look at me serving drinks in a skimpy outfit in a casino and hired me on the spot. Lash was a tall, built, handsome man who looked as macho alpha as they came but was a closeted gay.

Of all Lash's girls, only I knew that.

All Lash's girls thought he was doing me.

Lash and I let them.

Best boyfriend to have, being the beard to a handsome, rich, gay guy, trust me. If I could share this secret without exposing Lash's, I would. Every girl should know it. It would save a lot of heartbreak.

I knew he was gay because Lash was my one and only true friend in this world and I was the same to Lash.

He knew me. He knew everything about me.

And I knew the same about him.

And I knew he'd guard my secrets with his life as he knew I would his.

"Doing good," I replied, looking back at the large mirror with its big, round lights, putting the makeup brush back to my eye and sweeping.

My makeup was already heavy. It was always heavy but that was show business.

"Got a big crowd?" I asked.

"Honey, this is Vegas and my headliner has the best tits, ass, legs and head of hair in this entire fuckin' city and you've lived here almost three years, you know this and livin' here for three years, you know this is sayin' something. Men got dicks. And lotsa them roll in and outta this town daily. So yeah, even though it costs a hundred and fifty dollars to try real hard to see you then leave and spend the next year convincing yourself you caught a glimpse, the place is fuckin' packed," Lash answered.

By the way, I discovered I had two talents.

I could play pool.

And I could strip.

That was to say, strip like Lash's girls stripped.

I was the headliner of Lash's burlesque show. Front row seats cost three hundred dollars. The back seats one hundred and fifty.

Lash had twenty girls.

But they all came to see me.

I knew this. Lash knew this. The girls knew this, one of the reasons why my one and only true friend in this world was Lash because, even though they pretended, they all hated me behind my back.

Three hundred dollars for a front row and I danced two times during the show. Both times for five minutes, two of those minutes in nothing but sequined panties and spike-heeled, fuck-me shoes with two huge, feathered fans held around me, and no one ever saw a thing.

I had long legs, great hair, a firm, round ass and a pretty face, but it wasn't that.

The way I danced could make a man who'd depended on Viagra for a decade get hard.

So, clearly, the talents God bestowed on me led me to the path of my life.

I'd learned the hard way to follow and not veer off to try and find some ridiculous dream that included imperfect town squares and handsome cowboys with cute dimples, but just go where life led me.

Even if that was a burlesque show run by a closeted gay man.

I made serious cake. Lash paid me a mint. And he sent a driver to get me and take me home mainly because the losers in the audience often thought they could fuck with me in the parking lot or trail me home.

Brutus (not his name—what I nicknamed him—his real name was Freddie), my driver was two hundred, fifty pounds of black man on a six-foot-five-inch frame.

The losers who trailed me home drove on by when Brutus got out to open my door.

I also got my own dressing room. This was because I was the headliner.

This was also because Lash knew his other girls secretly hated me.

It wasn't a lavish dressing room with chaise lounges and silk screens.

But it was better than sitting with those bitches who were fake being nice to me.

Lash came up behind my chair and put his hands to my shoulders as I dropped the makeup brush and went for the sequins I'd stick around my eyes.

"Right, Ivey, I asked, you answered, you lied, I'll ask again," he said softly. "How's my girl tonight?"

At his strange question and tone, my hands arrested and my eyes went to his in the mirror.

"I'm doing fine, Lash."

He held my gaze in the mirror a beat.

Then he whispered, "It's his birthday."

My throat constricted.

That was Lash. Something like that, he wouldn't forget.

Then again, the first one he lived through with me I got drunk, blathered out the whole story and ended the night sobbing in his arms.

So that kind of shit made you remember.

"I'm fine, honey," I whispered back.

He continued to hold my gaze. Then he squeezed my shoulders. Then he dropped his handsome head and touched his beautiful lips to my shoulder.

He let me go, and walking out, reminded me, "You're on in ten minutes."

"Right," I said to his back.

He went through the door.

I looked at myself in the mirror.

God, seriously, I loved Lash.

I leaned forward and stuck sequins around my eyes.

I WAS three and half minutes into the dance.

I could hide the hard in my eyes and around my mouth with makeup and spotlights.

They weren't looking anyway.

All they saw was hair and flesh and all they could take in was the way I moved.

I started in a bra, corset, panties and feathered fans. I had ten sets. Purple with hints of pink and pale pink fans. Emerald green with hints of peacock blue with baby blue fans. Shocking pink with hints of red and red fans.

It went on.

I loved my getups. They were the bomb. And they were the bomb because Lash laid out a wad to get me the best.

The corset went first. Then the bra went. That was when the fans came in handy.

It was all twirls, bends, deep squats, sticking out and swaying my ass slowly, fan flashes and come-hither looks that came with a come-hither smile and fake bedroom eyes that weren't hard to affect mostly because the makeup did all the work.

The men ate it up.

Two dances, ten minutes, six nights a week and Lash paid me five hundred dollars a night.

The best gig *ever*.

I was whipping my fans back to front, torso bent slightly forward, head tipped back, lips parted, ends tipped up. I could feel my hair tumbling down my back, my ass pointed out and swinging slowly, when my come-hither eyes moved through the tables at the side of the stage and I saw him.

Gray.

Gray.

My heart stopped beating and my eyes locked to his but I didn't stop dancing.

Oh no.

The show must go on.

Even if the love of your life who crushed your heart who you hadn't seen in three years, was sitting by a stage while you were essentially doing a striptease on said stage.

He looked good. God, amazing. The same, a little older, as he would look seeing as he was older, three years older.

Today.

He was sitting, lounged back, one arm out, forearm resting on the table, ankle resting on his opposite knee.

Yes, he looked amazing.

And he looked *pissed.*

I tore my gaze from him to see Shim and Roan with him.

Boys trip to Vegas.

Fuck me.

Gray's friends didn't look happy either.

My eyes left their vicinity. I worked the stage, the crowd, my body and my fans.

I knew how this happened.

I didn't let Lash use me for any of his promotional materials and I explained to him why. If someone I hustled in the past happened into Lash's club, they might not recognize me. If they did, they certainly couldn't get through the bouncers or Brutus.

But if I was on pamphlets and billboards, that was a different story.

And they might try to find me.

It sucked for Lash at first, but then he loved it when he found it worked in his favor. Pictures told a thousand words but mouths had a bunch more and if people talked about me, and if you couldn't see me unless you paid to see me and you wanted to see me, you paid to see me. Not on a billboard, pamphlet, poster or magazine ad.

And I danced under the name "Rue." Lash made it up, thought it was funny. His name was actually Lash, his parents gave him that name. He wanted me to call myself "Larue" but I convinced him that was too corny.

So Rue it was.

Only a select few people in the inner sanctum (namely, Lash and Brutus) knew my name was Ivey.

No one knew I danced here unless they saw me.

And not a lot of people would recognize me under all this makeup, big hair and sequins.

Not to mention, most men didn't look at my face.

I finished the dance, took my applause like a professional, smile on my face. Then I got the fuck out of there, flashing one of my fans in a farewell wave per usual as I strutted offstage, back bare, ass covered in sequined emerald-green panties, come-hither look thrown over my shoulder, other fan pressed to the front of me.

Once out of the spotlight and backstage, I ran to my dressing room.

I tossed down the fans, snatched up my robe and pulled it on, tugging the belt tightly.

Then I paced.

Gray was out there.

Gray was out there!

God.

God!

Could I go out there for the next dance?

I had to go out there for the next dance.

But Gray was out there.

And he looked amazing.

And pissed.

Why did he look pissed?

What did he have to be pissed about?

He certainly didn't have anything to be pissed about.

Hell, he was lucky I didn't jump off the stage and beat him with my feathered fan.

He was a dick like all men were dicks (except Lash, but it was my experience gay men weren't dicks except, according to Lash, to other gay men, primarily lovers turning dick before becoming ex-lovers—the way of the world no matter which way you swung).

I went to my dressing table, snatched up my phone and called Brutus.

"Yo!" he answered, the sounds of the club in the background

seeing as when Brutus wasn't picking me up and driving me home, he was a bouncer.

"Brutus, baby, it's Ivey."

"Woman, my phone tells me who you are. You don't have to identify yourself every time you call me."

Brutus said this a lot.

He went on.

"And, my name is not fuckin' Brutus."

He said this a lot too.

As you can see, Brutus wasn't a big fan of his nickname.

"Listen, can you pick me up out back tonight after the show?"

"Why?" he barked, alert at that. I only asked him that when I got a bad vibe or someone sent something to my dressing room who was in the audience and repeat with the bad vibe.

I'd learned.

"Just a feeling," I told him.

"You got it, Ivey," he told me.

"Thanks, honey," I whispered.

"Shee-it, bitch, do anything, you whisper to me."

Brutus was a tough guy, macho man, bodyguard-esque, driver/bouncer, but he was also a big softie.

"Later," I said.

"Later, babe," he replied.

I disconnected.

I took in a deep breath.

Then I sat down at my dressing table and got down to the annoying twice nightly business of doing my makeup because different colored outfits meant different colored makeup.

And as I did this, I hoped that I didn't get a message that Gray wanted to come back and see me.

I shouldn't have worried.

I didn't get a message.

And during my second number, Gray, Shim and Roan's table was empty.

Chapter 19

Tragedy

In my high-heeled designer sandals, designer jeans, cute designer top with my big, slouchy, scarily-expensive designer purse on my shoulder, I walked out the back door of the club.

The black Lincoln Lash owned that Brutus drove (not only me but sometimes Lash or VIP guests) was parked five feet away, lights on, ready to roll.

I moved to it, my heels clicking on asphalt, when I heard an unmistakable voice say, "Ivey."

I stopped dead.

Gray.

Shit.

Shit!

I clenched my teeth, swallowed, got my shit together and turned.

It was lit well back there. There were cameras. Bouncers randomly and often did walk-throughs. Lash didn't fuck around. The girls parked out there.

That was all good except now.

I could see him well.

And he was no less tall, broad or beautiful.

"Gray," I replied, tipping my head back as he walked to me and got close.

"Yo! No contact with the talent!" Brutus shouted, and I turned my head to look over my shoulder, seeing he was out of the car and moving our way.

"It's okay, baby, he's all right. I know him. He's an old friend."

Brutus stopped and stared at me. He'd known me the two years he'd been working there. As far as he knew, I fucked Lash and Lash was my only friend.

His attention went to Gray then back to me then Gray then me.

Finally he jerked his chin up and called, "I'm just in the car, Rue. High sign, you need me. I'll keep my eye on you."

"Thanks, honey," I called back, watched him walk to the car, give us one last look then fold his big body behind the wheel.

I looked back to Gray.

His gaze was on the car then it came to me.

Then he murmured, "Old friend."

Fathoms of concrete, years of building it, and just hearing his voice, miles of it disintegrated.

"Boys' weekend in Vegas?" I asked.

"Roan's gettin' married," he answered.

"Anyone I know?"

"Don't know. Probably. Probably not anyone you'd remember."

I remembered everybody, every second in Mustang, every person I met, every fucking thing.

I didn't tell him that.

"So stag weekend?" I guessed.

"Yeah," Gray confirmed.

I fell silent.

How did people do this?

I had one boyfriend, one lover, so I didn't run into them everywhere I went. I didn't have any experience with this kind of thing.

Well, whatever. I was me and I might be hard but I wasn't rude.

"Would you like to go somewhere? Get a drink? Brutus will drive us."

"No, Ivey, I wouldn't fuckin' like to go somewhere and get a fuckin' drink."

It took everything but I didn't step back. I didn't still. I didn't press my lips together nor did I swallow against a suddenly dry throat.

I didn't even flinch.

Yep, he was pissed.

"Jesus, fuck, you take your clothes off for money," he whispered like he couldn't believe it.

"Gray—"

"Three years ago, only eyes that saw that body were mine. Now thousands of fuckin' guys have seen it."

This was true.

"Your point?" I queried on an eyebrow raise.

"My point?" Gray flashed back, his eyes narrowing.

I sighed and asked, "Do we have to do this?"

He stared at me and I felt emotion shifting off him, filling the air, sliding into my nostrils, down my throat, suffocating me and suddenly his hand shot up. Thumb and finger capturing my chin, before I could do anything about it he tipped my head back, leaned in and studied me close.

He got three seconds in before I tore away from his touch.

My eyes sliced to him and before I could say anything, he did.

"Hard," he growled then finished, "as nails."

"Shit happens," I hissed, the guard crashing down.

What could I say?

This was Gray and he was standing in front of me three years after he crushed me acting pissed.

"Yeah it does. You let it. You seek it out. Shit definitely fuckin' happens."

He was right about that. I let it, Casey and I sought it out. It happened.

And when I finally, *finally* got shot of it, I went back to the only home I'd ever had and found that other shit happened and that was worse.

"Christ, I'm standin' right here lookin' at you and it's like I've never known you."

"Are we done here?" I asked tersely.

"We're done," Gray answered immediately but neither of us moved. We just stood there, staring at each other.

Finally, Gray ordered, "Walk away, Ivey."

Then, out of nowhere, in my head I heard his voice order, *Say you love me, Ivey.*

Say you love me, Ivey.

Say you love me, Ivey.

And I heard my voice reply, *I love you, Gray.*

I held his stare and didn't move.

Neither did Gray.

And then he dealt the death blow.

"I told you tragedy would strike. What I didn't know when I was sayin' that shit was that the tragedy would be the sweet, funny girl who was the prettiest thing I'd ever seen would turn into a hard bitch in fancy clothes gettin' paid to pretend every night, twice a night, she was a whore."

I held my breath.

Gray finished, "Fuck me. Tragedy."

With that he turned on his boot and walked away.

I watched him until he rounded the corner of the building and disappeared.

Then I walked to the car, opened the door and slid into the passenger seat.

I was buckling my seatbelt when Brutus asked quietly, "Everything okay, Ivey?"

"Everything's okay, Freddie," I whispered, felt his shock when I used his real name but looked out the side window.

We got five miles from my house before it overwhelmed me.

Brutus helped me up to the house, took the key from me, opened the door and held me on my big, expensive, comfortable couch while he called Lash and I sobbed.

Then Lash came over.

Lash slept in bed with me mostly because I cried the whole night clutching him in my arms until I passed out.

Freddie slept on my couch.

Chapter 20

A Barrel of Laughs

F*our years and two months later...*

"Ivey, babe, phone!" Lash shouted, and I looked from watering the big pots of flowers with my hose to Lash who was standing in our French doors.

"Who is it?" I asked.

"Don't know. A lady. Says it's urgent."

Great.

A mysterious lady calling the home phone saying it was urgent.

Clearly, I urgently needed a timeshare in Boca.

Lash was such a pushover. How he became a millionaire was anyone's guess. The only thing I knew was that, regardless of being gay, he had a good eye for gorgeous women, a talent for finding ones who had what it took on the stage, no aversion to essentially selling tail for a living and, not unusually for a gay guy, a flair with costumes and interior décor.

I released the handle, the spray stopped, I set the nozzle on a lounge chair and headed to Lash.

We'd made it official. We didn't get married or anything but we moved in together three years ago. We did this because I was a determined celibate who had sworn off men and Lash, for his own reasons, needed to keep his reputation as a ladies' man when he was anything but.

I personally thought his reasons were a little screwed up. But they had a lot to do with the fact that he had a ball-buster of a mother who lived close who made Grandma Miriam look like a sweet, old granny who baked cookies (which she did), crocheted doilies (which she also did) and pinched your cheek, smiling at you with bright eyes that shared irrevocably that anything you did was hunky-dory with her (which she did *not*). Lash got to brag his lie that he nailed down the finest piece of ass in Vegas and I got relief from men thinking they could best the challenge that was me.

Luckily, Lash wasn't only hot. He was also big and had learned to take care of himself so most men didn't mess with me.

And anyway, if they did, Brutus had my back. I didn't dance anymore, I managed the house. Still, Brutus had my back. He still picked me up and drove me to the club every night but Lash took me home seeing as we lived at the same place.

Brutus did this now because he was my second true friend in the whole world.

See? Totally told you shit like women sobbing their hearts out because the man they loved with everything that was them crushed it then unexpectedly showed up at a performance where you were stripping, ripped it out and crushed it again would do that shit to you. Hot, strapping gay guy. Big-ass, badass black guy. Anyone.

I made it to Lash. He handed me the phone then leaned in and kissed my cheek before he wandered away.

Seriously. Who needed a real lover when you had a handsome, affectionate man who adored you, put a beautiful house over your head, gave you a great job, lavished you with fabulous clothes, shoes, purses and jewelry and would never break your heart?

On this happy thought, I put the phone to my ear and greeted, "Hello?"

"Ivey?" A-somewhat-familiar-but-I-couldn't-place-it voice asked.

"Yes, this is Ivey. Can I help you?"

"This is Janie. The Rambler? Mustang? Do you remember me?"

My heart spasmed, clenching so tight I could barely breathe. I reached out a hand, practically stumbling until it caught the back of a chair and I held on.

Something had happened to Gray.

She'd never call me unless something had happened to Gray.

Something bad.

"Of course I remember you, Janie," I said quietly.

"Right," she said efficiently. "Well, I don't reckon you'll give a shit but you should know that Gray's about to lose his land."

My body jerked and my heart spasmed again and it didn't hurt any less than the first time.

"What?" I whispered.

"He's about to lose his land. In fact, he's about to lose everything. All of it, the house, the trees, the horses, everything. Shim and Roan came back after Roan's thing and told everyone about you then Roan goes back to Vegas all the time and heard you hooked up with a millionaire so you're the only one we know who's got the kinda money who could help him out. I know you probably don't give a shit and Gray'd lose his ever-lovin' mind he knew I was even makin' this call much less tellin' you his troubles, but this is Gray, this is Mustang and it's the least you could do."

There was a lot there.

First, it killed me everyone knew I danced for a living.

Second, it killed me she thought I wouldn't give a shit about Gray.

Third, it killed me that Gray would lose his ever-lovin' mind if he knew she was calling me.

And last and most importantly, it killed me that Gray was about lose his land.

"For you," she went on, "probably a drop in the bucket, seein' as you're shacked up with a hotshot. But for Gray, it's his land. And you should know, the bank that holds the note is Buddy Sharp's bank."

My body jerked yet again.

Oh God.

She wasn't done.

"And you should also know, Buddy Sharp is scrapin' together money to buy that note. So, they foreclose, the bank won't own it and Jeb Sharp won't own it. Buddy will."

Oh God!

"How did this happen?" I asked.

"Mirry's not growin' younger through the years," she snapped like I should know that which I should, but honestly, no offense to Grandma Miriam, but she was seventy when I met her over seven years ago. I was kind of surprised she was still alive.

Janie continued, "Got to the point Gray couldn't take care of her, his uncles are all assholes, his cousins proved to be too, so he had to put her in a home. He's self-employed, got no insurance and he's Gray. He didn't put her in a shithole. He put her in the best place in the county. Had a bad crop of peaches last year, the bills from the home, a bad year with crops, shit happens."

"This is awful," I whispered.

"Well...*yeah*," she snapped again like someone would say, "No duh."

"So, what about his uncles, his cousins, can they help?"

"Did I not mention they're assholes?" she asked.

"Yes, I know that Janie, but this is their family's land. It's been in that family for six generations," I reminded her.

"Yeah, well, 'bout twelve years ago, Gray's daddy died and they wanted their bit. They didn't get it. Seems that left a sour taste in their mouth so they're not feelin' like steppin' up. So they're not."

Those assholes!

I controlled my bizarre flash of temper because, really, this had nothing to do with me (anymore) and asked, "I...uh...how much does he need?"

"You kickin' in?"

My back went straight and I repeated. "How much does he need?"

"Are you kickin' in?" she repeated too.

"Yes," I said instantly and I had absolutely no clue why.

"Right, I'll get Shim or Roan to find out what they can find out. I'll call you back."

"I don't want him to know it's coming from me," I said quickly.

"Well...*yeah*." There it was again, the "No duh."

"Janie," I said softly, "I'm helping out."

"You know, it took a lot for me to make this call, way you cleared out on Gray, way you cleared out on *me*. So, I appreciate it and all that you aren't a total bitch and are gonna help out, but don't think you doin' it means anyone's gonna kiss your ass."

I wasn't breathing.

Therefore I had to force out, "The way I cleared out on Gray?"

"Yeah, one minute, he's at home takin' shit from Mirry because he told her you were movin' in, the next minute, I'm callin' him because you didn't show up for your shift. The next thing we know, people saw you take off with that brother of yours. Then the *next* thing we know, rumors are pool hustlers are on the game in Grand Junction. You tried, I'll give you that, gave it a go. Too bad you couldn't manage not to walk all over Gray while you were doin' it. I could find another girl. Lot harder for him to do it."

Even though my heart was beating like a sledgehammer against the wall of my chest, my blood pressure was also skyrocketing.

"Actually, it wasn't hard, seeing as when I came back three months later to explain, I saw him cuddling on the street with a pretty little brunette so, please, I know you're tight with Gray and you think he's one step down from God, but don't bullshit me."

"What?" she whispered.

"I think you heard me. And also, I've never been to Grand Junction except to drive through it. The last game of pool I hustled was before I went to Mustang. I haven't taken a dollar from the game since Buddy Sharp, and I didn't hustle him. So if people were trash talking me after I left, they can go fuck themselves. And as for you and Gray believing it, the same goes for you. Now, although this catch-up phone call has been a barrel of laughs, I've got flowers to water. Call me when you know how much he needs and I'll get it to you. Take care of yourself, Janie."

I beeped the phone off and threw it on the chair.

Then I deep breathed and I did it for a long time.

Lash walked in and asked, "Who was it, babe?"

I looked to my fake boyfriend, smiled bright and lied, "Nobody."

Then I walked out of our fabulous living room through our fabulous French doors to our fabulous flower bedecked cool deck around our fabulous pool and I grabbed the hose and recommenced watering.

Chapter 21

Artillery

T*wo days later…*

I WAS AT THE CLUB, sitting at the way back around the corner of the bar, three stools next to me empty, Brutus standing against the wall guarding me.

Unfortunately, he needed to do this. I hadn't danced for long and I hadn't danced in a while, but still, Rue the burlesque dancer was a Vegas legend.

And I worked the house.

This meant I hired, fired, scheduled and managed the waitresses, the bartenders, the bar and the floor.

Part of me managing the floor was getting tricked out every night, putting on amazing dresses that exposed a fair amount of flesh (in a classy way, I thought, and so did Lash, considering he chose and bought all my dresses for me), high-heeled, fuck-me shoes and expensive jewelry. Often, I wandered the floor smiling, touching men's arms, shoulders, hands, leaning down and brushing their knees or the outside of their thighs with my fingertips all the while inspecting their tables and the state of their drinks. If they were half done, I'd give the high sign to a scantily-clad waitress and convince them with a practiced, come-hither smile that, even though they were only halfway done with their drink, they needed another one.

I sold a tremendous amount of booze. Lash told me that within a month of me taking over the floor, the bar's turnover doubled.

This was why he paid me a shitload and kept me in amazing dresses, shoes and jewelry. This and the fact that the waitresses and bartenders worked his nerves. They were always screwing each other then getting in fights, breaking up and taking that shit to work. When I took that off his shoulders, he was beside himself.

This was also because he adored me.

So I was visible. You paid your money, there was a chance you'd still see Rue. She wouldn't be dancing on the stage in high heels with fans, but it was better. She would be working the crowd and she might come close, you might see those bedroom eyes, that hair and that smile right in front of you, and if you were lucky, she might touch you.

Men were pretty stupid on the whole, I thought. Dropping that kind of money to see women dance nearly naked (that said, Lash's girls were the shit, no one in Vegas was better than them and even I had to admit there was an immense sensual beauty to it) and getting wound up because some woman touched your thigh and bent over so you could look down her cleavage...

I mean, really?

Whatever. It kept Lash in the lap of luxury and Lash kept me in the lap of luxury so who was I to complain?

"Ivey, beautiful, got a sign from Patrick," Brutus said in my ear, hand on the flesh at the small of my back exposed by the low dip of my dress. "May be trouble across the floor. Gonna give him backup. Be right back."

I looked from the notes I was making on the schedule on the bar, a martini glass filled with straight-up cranberry juice next to it, twisted my neck and smiled over my shoulder at him, giving a nod.

His hand pressed lightly into my back and then he moved through the tables across the floor.

My head bent and I went back to my schedule.

I liked it back here. The lighting was dim and it seemed far from the crowd. It was the farthest place in the room from the stage so no one wanted back here. With Brutus at his post, the darkness, the distance from the stage, which was why everyone paid to be there in the first place, I had privacy.

Not that night.

I would learn this ten seconds after Brutus left when a voice came in my ear.

"Do not stick your nose in with Cody."

My neck twisted and I stared in shock at Buddy Sharp standing next to me wearing a hard expression, his eyes glittering mean even in the dim light.

Yes, Buddy Sharp.

What the fuck?

"I'm sorry?" I asked.

"Small town. Word travels. Janie's a stupid bitch. I know she's called you. Do not stick your nose in that business with Grayson Cody."

I felt something snake across my skin, it wasn't good. In fact it was really, really bad.

He'd come to Vegas to warn me off personally. He lived in Colorado, not Italy, but still, it wasn't an hour's drive.

And I did not think this boded well. I didn't know what it boded but I had the distinct impression something was going on, something I didn't know or get and it was something very, very bad.

Very, very bad for Gray.

I stared into his eyes.

Then I told him, "What I do or don't do is none of your business."

He got closer, threateningly closer, and there was no mistaking it. His face was all I could see and the mean shown from his eyes, wetting the air all around with acid.

"You step in for Cody, you'll wish you didn't. Stay the fuck away from Cody and Mustang. You get me?"

Yes, something was happening and it was very, very bad.

For Gray.

I held his eyes, I held my space and I held my shit when I ordered, "Step back, now."

He didn't step back.

"Do not try me. Do not fuck with me. You do not exist for Cody and you do not exist in Mustang. You make even a single move to change that, you'll regret it," he warned.

"Step..." I hissed then leaned into him, "*back*."

"Do not fuck with me," he whispered and the way he did, the acid in the air saturating those five words, I felt true fear.

"Rue, we got a problem here?"

Thank God, Brutus.

I didn't take my eyes from Buddy as I answered Brutus.

"Yes, this gentleman is no longer welcome in the club. Please escort him out, Freddie. Now."

Freddie put his hands to the back of Buddy's shirt, clenching in, and Buddy tried to shake him off but no way in hell could Buddy shake off Freddie. Hell, the Incredible Hulk would have some issues shaking off Freddie.

My eyes moved from Buddy to Freddie, they locked with his and I said softly, "Eighty-six. Life. You see him, you take him down and I'll deal with the police later."

Brutus nodded, jerked Buddy around and I watched him frog march Buddy to the door.

Then I swallowed.

After that, I breathed deep.

It was there, insidious, crawling through me, I felt it.

Worry.

And if I didn't get a lock on it, I knew it would consume me.

I took a sip of cranberry juice and another deep breath.

Then I got a lock on it.

I went back to my schedule.

Seven twenty the next morning…

The phone rang. I opened my eyes and saw an ivory satin pillowcase and my body felt Lash's curled into the back of it, his arm wrapped tight around me.

Yes, Lash and I slept together. We didn't start this way, but the minute I moved in was the minute his mother started showing up unannounced in the morning, using her key and surprising us. A lifelong Vegas resident, an ex-showgirl (hence her naming her son Lash), she was beside herself with glee Lash hooked up with me, the Vegas showgirl to beat all Vegas showgirls.

She was not beside herself with glee catching us in separate bedrooms.

Questions were asked, nosy ones, and after the fourth time it was clear she wasn't buying Lash's excuses that we'd had a rip-roarin' the night before.

So Lash talked to me.

I got him. He loved his mother and she was unfortunately the kind of mother who would not accept who he was. Growing up, his dad was a trucker and not around a lot, his mother a showgirl and therefore mostly on her own, she took care of him. Being a showgirl, this wasn't easy but she did it, she did it well, she liked doing it thus she didn't complain. She loved her handsome boy.

She just didn't want him to be gay.

This was coupled with the fact that Lash's father was a man's man. I got the impression that Lash's dad would be more approachable on this subject but not by much. He was proud of his son, his son's occupation, his son's reputation and his son's success. I got that Lash loved his dad and was loath to take that away and I got why he didn't.

Lash also worked the hotshot, playboy angle for business. Many of his VIPs would not be down with hanging with a gay guy but instead preferred to think they were tight with someone who was just like them, ambitious, wealthy, aggressive and sexually predatory. Lash, of course, *was* all that except the last part, his prey was a different gender.

And anyway, I loved Lash. He took care of me in a variety of ways. If he needed this, it was my small way of returning the favor.

I didn't mind sleeping with him. We whispered to each other before falling asleep, talking about our days, what the next one would bring...whatever. It was nice.

And he cuddled and I liked that, the affection, the closeness.

And he had satin sheets and they were the freaking *bomb*.

I felt Lash shift, his arm going from around me. I heard the beep of the phone and his deep voice sleepily saying, "'Lo." There was a pause then, "Right here." He rolled back and said sleepy-growly to me, "Gotta say, not a big fan of takin' a call for my girl from a man at just after fuckin' seven in the fuckin' morning."

When he sounded sleepy-growly like that, it was one of the few times I wished he wasn't gay.

I saw the phone in front of me and, sleepy myself, I took it without hesitation.

I put it to my ear and greeted, "Hello?"

"Ivey?"

My heart stopped beating.

Gray.

It was Gray.

I shot up to my forearm and asked, "Gray?"

"Yeah."

Oh God.

I felt Lash's chest press to my back.

"Gray, what—?"

"Know Janie called you. Don't want your money. Stay out of it."

My heart started beating again but fast.

"Gray—" I began.

"Don't want your fuckin' money, Ivey. Stay the fuck out of it."

My temper started rising.

"Gray, it isn't—"

He cut me off again. "Fucked, Janie phonin' you. Totally fucked. I do not need this bullshit and I do not want your money. Stay out of it."

My temper shot to the stratosphere.

He wanted to be a macho man rancher cowboy without a ranch or horses, fine. Pride goeth before the fall.

Whatever.

His problem.

Not mine.

Not mine.

"Fine," I snapped.

"Fine," Gray clipped back.

I wasn't done.

"And, do me a favor, you want me out of it and everyone wants me out of Mustang, keep Mustang away from me."

"Not a problem, Ivey. Janie won't be phonin' you again," Gray assured me.

"I'm not talking about Janie. I'm talking about Buddy."

Silence, then, "What?"

"Buddy," I hissed. "He showed at the club last night, got in my face, threatened me, told me to keep my nose out of it just like you just did. Except, even though your voice isn't filled with peaches and cream right now, he was a lot less nice about it and his meaning was clear. So clear, I had to have him forcibly removed from the club. So, Gray, you want me out of it, keep me out of it not only with you and Janie but also that hideous troll. I don't need his kind in my life. Do you understand me?"

"Buddy came to your club?" Gray asked quietly.

"Yes. He came, got in my face and threatened me. And he was not joking. He meant it. I didn't like it. If you want me out of your shit, keep your shit away from me."

Gray was silent.

I wasn't.

"Good luck, Gray. I hope you sort it out. Have a nice life."

I beeped the phone off.

I threw it on the satin comforter.

Then I exploded, "God!"

"Babe?" Lash called.

I shifted and flopped down on my back.

His eyes caught mine and his hand came up to cup my jaw.

"Babe," he whispered.

I felt the tears wet my eyes and again I deep breathed.

"Oh my girl." Lash kept whispering, handsome face soft, eyes warm and worried. I'd eventually told him about Janie's call. This was our way. I eventually told him everything. He also knew about Buddy's visit last night.

I went on deep breathing.

Then I got a lock on it.

"I'm okay," I finally whispered back.

Lash's head tipped to the side. "Sure?"

God, I loved him.

"Sure, honey."

He studied me. Then he leaned in and kissed my forehead. He settled back down and adjusted me so we were spooning again.

"Go back to sleep, babe, yeah?"

We were never home before two in the morning and we were never up before nine.

Lash was right, we needed sleep.

"Yeah," I agreed softly.

Lash's arm pulled me closer.

It took a while, it was tough, too much happening in my head, too much worry gnawing my belly, too much artillery battering away at the walls around my heart.

But eventually I found sleep.

Chapter 22

Shot to the Heart

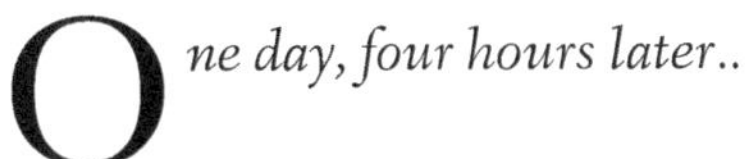

One day, four hours later...

The phone was ringing and I was in the sitting room, standing with Lash and his mother Rhonda, listening to them talking about how they were going to redecorate it (again). Lash had lived in his house five years and redecorated every room at least once. This would be the sitting room's third look.

Seriously. How Rhonda didn't cotton on her son was gay, I had no idea.

"I'll get it," I mumbled, moved into Lash, leaned up and touched my mouth to his.

His hand came to my waist and gave me a squeeze.

This wasn't fake. This was us. Affection. Pure.

Maybe that was how Rhonda didn't cotton on. No one could see through that because there was nothing to see.

I walked out of the room, went to the phone, beeped it on and put it to my ear. "Hello."

"Ivey?"

Shit. Janie.

"Hello, Janie."

She was silent a second, then, "I...I...oh, Ivey, I'm really sorry. I told Roan and Shim I called you. They had to know so they could find out what Gray needed but I forgot Roan has a big mouth. He told his wife Stacy, she owns the salon and her mouth is bigger. Word traveled. Got to Buddy, got to Gray. I had no idea Buddy would, he would..." she paused then went on, "do what he did. That wasn't cool. I'm sorry you had to deal with that."

"Not a problem, Janie, just as long as he doesn't come back. Don't worry about it."

"It's, I think..." another pause, then, "it was really nice how you wanted to step up for Gray, but he talked to me and he was kind of..." again a pause, then, "not happy."

I bet.

She kept going.

"So, he's going to do his thing and we need to stay out of it. But, again, it was really nice of you to want to kick in."

So Gray was going to go forth and lose his land, lose everything.

Men.

Stupid.

I tried not to let that hurt, but when I failed I tried to pretend it didn't hurt.

I was better at that.

"Right, well, I hope he works it out," I told her.

"No chance of that," she muttered.

I didn't want to, I really didn't want to...

But I did.

And what I did was ask, "Sorry?"

"Movin' Mirry out next month, Ivey. Gray can't afford the home anymore. They're puttin' her in some state funded place. Never been there but I got a coupla customers had people in there. They say it isn't all that nice. For her, seein' as she's in a wheelchair, they reckon it'll be worse. Guess it's not super-clean and the staff isn't all that attentive."

Shot to the heart, I stood still and steady but I was reeling.

Janie wasn't done.

"Gray's beside himself but what can he do? He can't pay the bills. Got buyers comin' in from everywhere, sellin' all his horses. Every last one. Tryin' to raise money to pay on the note. First time in over a hundred years that ranch won't have mustangs on it. Town is reeling. You wouldn't think it would be a big deal, but it is. Old-timers sayin' it's the end of an era. And even me, only lived here half my life, still, I feel it. It's a loss."

Another direct hit, I felt myself going down.

She didn't stop.

"And that fuckin' family of his, won't even take care of their momma. It's crazy. No one gets it. Leavin' Gray to be picked over by the buzzards, that's already totally uncool, but leavin' their momma to go to that place?"

She stopped abruptly and went silent.

I hit the dirt, lifeblood oozing out of me.

"I'm sorry, Ivey," she whispered. "I shouldn't lay this on you. Sorry. Gray was seriously pi—" She stopped again and then continued, "I guess, thinkin' on it for a spell, you had your reasons to pick up and go without explanations to even Gray. And, thinkin' on it, you were a good gal. And I'm glad you found your place where you can be happy. I guess I just wish that was with Gray so he could be happy."

More blood sinking into the earth.

I needed to fight it.

"I left him a note," I whispered.

"What?"

"I left him a note, Janie. I don't know what he told you and I know Gray is a good guy and you care about him so I don't want to color how you feel about him, but he isn't giving you the full story. He knew exactly why I left, what I was doing and that I intended to come back as soon as I could. Why he didn't share that with you, I don't know. I guess he had his reasons and years have passed so it doesn't matter now."

"You didn't leave a note," she told me.

"Janie, I did."

"Where?"

"In my room," I paused, "your room, whatever."

"Ivey, I went up there with Gray and there was no—"

Seriously? Why were we going over this?

I shouldn't have said anything.

"Right, Janie, I'm sorry," I cut her off. "But my man's mother is here and I can't talk. I'm sorry all this is happening to Gray, what you're feeling, what the town's feeling. It's awful. But you'll all get through it. I know you will."

"Ivey—" she started, but I kept talking.

"You take care and be well. Bye."

I beeped the phone off.

I stared at it.

It rang again but I didn't answer it.

When I didn't, Lash shouted, "Babe? You gonna get that?"

"No, letting it ring," I called back. "Tell you later," I finished.

Nothing from Lash.

The phone stopped ringing.

Then it started again.

I didn't answer and Lash didn't shout.

It stopped ringing and didn't start again.

I kept staring at it.

But I didn't see it.

The only thing on my mind was the only woman who was even close to a mother to me even if it was just for a blink of my life was going into a shoddy, state-funded nursing home that wasn't very clean and didn't have good staff. And the only man I ever loved was losing everything he had, everything he loved, everything his family had built for six generations. And the only town that ever felt like home was losing a huge piece of its history.

And with that on my mind, I found my feet moving.

They moved to Lash's office where they took me to his chair.

Then my hand moved to turn on the computer and wield the mouse.

I did what I had to do.

Then I went to my purse, got my car keys and called out to Lash and Rhonda I'd be back in an hour.

I went to my bank.

I went home and walked straight to Lash and my bedroom.

I started packing.

Then Lash walked in and saw what I was doing.

I told him my plans.

Then Lash started packing.

Lash went to the computer and did what he had to do.

Then he phoned Brutus.

The next day, Brutus drove us to the airport. But he didn't drop us off.

He parked and went with us.

Chapter 23

Scarlet Lady

It was a nice place. You could tell that right off the bat. Very attractive building, one story, sprawling. Extensive lovely grounds, safe walkways through them, lots of flowers lush even in May in Colorado.

I could see why Gray picked this place.

She was bossy but she loved him and Grandma Miriam deserved to be around pretty.

I walked up to the front door, huge-ass, movie star, black shades on my nose. My body encased in crimson. A see-through blouse with puff sleeves that fit me like a glove, body-hugging blush camisole under, sexy, alluring, but just hints you could take and let your imagination soar. Skintight, crimson pencil skirt that hugged my ass, hips, thighs and went down to my knees. Crimson slingbacks with a pointed toe and a high, lethal heel. Smart, thin, crimson leather clutch tucked under my pit. A ruby pendant surrounded by diamonds at my throat, not huge, not small, but still, it had to be said, borderline ostentatious. Matching studs at my ears. Tennis bracelet dangling from my wrist. All of this given to me by Lash including the jewelry on our one year anniversary of moving in together.

I gave him a Rolex.

It was his second.

Still, my fake boyfriend loved watches and I loved him so Rolex it was.

I picked the outfit because if Mustang thought I was a scarlet lady then I was going to show them they hadn't seen anything yet.

Lash and Freddie trailed me, leaving the shiny, long, black, shaded-window, rented Lincoln at the curb.

Freddie was carrying a briefcase.

I pushed right in through the door and went directly to the reception desk.

"I'd like to speak to the Home Administrator," I announced, shoving my sunglasses back into my hair.

The receptionist blinked at me then she blinked at the tall, built beauty of Lash settling on one side of me and after that she blinked at the enormous, powerful black beauty of Brutus taking my back before her eyes came back to me.

"And you are?" she asked breathily.

"I'm Ivey Larue."

Yes, I had my last name changed to Larue. Firstly for me because it meant getting shot of the only thing I had left that I shared with my mother and Casey. Secondly, I did it as a present upon moving in with Lash. He loved it so much, tears hit his eyes. He was butch so that was a surprise and told me exactly how much he loved it.

I kept talking.

"I'm here to pay for Miriam Cody's stay for a year."

She blinked again but this time she added her mouth dropping open.

Then she whispered, "What?"

"I'm here to pay for Miriam Cody's stay for a year."

"But...Mirry's movin' out next month," the receptionist told me.

"Not anymore," I replied.

"I...should we...I don't know..." Her eyes were darting everywhere, taking all of us in. Then she pulled it together, focused on me and said, "I'm not certain sure but I think we need to call Gray."

"I would prefer you didn't do that simply because I don't have the time. I have two other stops scheduled and a dinner reservation tonight. I'd like to do this and move on," I told her.

"Are you doing this anonymously?" she asked.

"No," I answered. "You're welcome to tell Mr. Cody and his grandmother about my gesture, I just don't have time for you to call Mr. Cody at this juncture."

"Your, uh...*gesture?*" She sounded dumbfounded.

"Indeed," I replied.

"I, well, you know, a year on a private room like Gray has for Mirry is..."

Then she told me how much it was.

I immediately divided it to monthly.

Jeez. No wonder Gray was losing the ranch. Holy crap.

I turned and looked over my shoulder at Brutus. He stepped up, slapped the briefcase on her counter, flipped the latches and opened it, twirling it around so she could see the stacks of money in it.

Her eyes bugged out.

Then they shot to me.

Then she whispered, "I'll just go get the Administrator."

"I'd be grateful," I replied.

Then I smiled.

WE SETTLED AT THE DESK, the man in his cheapish but well-fitting suit across from us, Lash in the chair beside me, Brutus standing at my back with his briefcase.

I saw him when I walked in.

Buddy Sharp sitting behind a huge desk in a glass-walled, corner office.

He'd undoubtedly moved his way up in the last seven years.

Dickhead.

The loan officer's eyes settled on me.

"This is highly unusual, Ms. Larue, and I must inform you again that I cannot discuss the details of Mr. Cody's loan with you."

"I don't want the details. I simply want to know how much it will cost to bring his payments current, including any penalties, and how much you'll need for me to pay his payments for a year in advance. I will then give you the cash. You'll print out and provide me with a statement for this transaction and send a copy to Mr. Cody," I told him.

"Again, Ms. Larue, this is highly unusual," he told me.

"That may be so but that doesn't interest me. I have very little time, sir, and I have more business to see to today, so if you'll just..." I paused, twisted my neck, looked up at Brutus and he did the brief-case trick, this time on the corner of the loan manager's desk. Once it was open and the loan manager was facing the cash, I kept going. "Give me a figure, we can proceed."

Freddie and my shtick didn't work a treat like the last time, unfortunately.

"Ms. Larue," the loan manager started, "unless you've arranged with Mr. Cody to invest in his property, this is essentially a gift and the Internal Revenue Service needs to be informed of any gift to an individual that's over five thousand dollars. What you wish to do is well over five thousand dollars. There will be taxes to be paid."

"That's not your concern," I replied. "That's between myself and Mr. Cody."

That was a lie. I was never going to talk to Gray again. I paid for Grandma Miriam's nursing home. I got his land safe. He could pay the taxes on me doing it.

His eyes slid to Buddy's office.

My stomach curled.

Lash saw it and stepped in.

"It is highly likely that an established institution like this refusing payment on a citizen's loan regardless of where the money was coming from might be misconstrued, and definitely would be questioned, by certain authorities, especially if the property in question were to end up in the hands of an employee at the bank that refused the payment. Indeed, it might lead to an inquiry. And it's equally highly likely that inquiry would be uncomfortable and public. It is my understanding that Mr. Cody and the land he owns has a special meaning to the people of the county next to yours, which would no doubt garner further attention should you refuse payment to keep that land safe in the family that has tended it for six generations. Ms. Larue has explained her intentions as well as the fact that we're facing time constrictions. I'd be grateful if you would quickly consider what I just explained and didn't delay further."

The loan officer watched him talk then he took in Lash's suit that was *not* cheap, his Rolex, his haircut, his tan and his dentist office whitened teeth. Then he took in all that was Brutus. Last, he took in me, my outfit, the blouse of which cost more than his suit, and he might not know that, but it was so exquisite, he could guess, and my jewelry.

Then he made an intelligent decision.

He turned to his computer and muttered, "I'll just call up the account."

I let out a silent breath.

Thirty minutes later, our briefcase lighter, we rose, exchanged handshakes but we didn't move to the front door.

We moved to Buddy's office, Lash leading.

He had a man in there but Lash didn't hesitate to open the door and step in.

I stepped in behind him.

Brutus stepped in behind me.

"I apologize for disturbing you but unfortunately my message can't wait," Lash announced, eyes on the man in Buddy's visitor's chair, then they went to Buddy. "Rue explained to me about your visit, that you threatened her with violence and made her uncomfortable. You did this in her place of employment. Regardless of where you did it, no gentleman, in fact, no real man threatens a woman. *Ever*. See that it doesn't happen again."

Buddy stared up at him, speechless, face a mask of fury.

The man sitting in his visitor's chair stared up at Lash, speechless, face a mask of shock.

Lash wasn't done.

"It's only fair to warn you that from here we're going to the Mustang Police Station to inform them of your activities at my club in Las Vegas. It's my understanding you work here but live in Mustang. In about an hour, the local police will know about your threats."

Buddy didn't move and didn't speak and neither did his visitor.

Lash turned, put a hand to the small of my back and started guiding me to the door, Brutus trailing.

But he stopped at the door and turned back.

"I understand you're a big fish in a small pond," Lash said softly, his deep, cultured voice carrying a more eloquent threat than Buddy could ever hope to pull off. "But I'll explain that if you want to swim in the ocean, you must understand that the ocean is populated by sharks and sharks never sleep."

On that fabulous finale, he turned and guided me out while Brutus followed.

Lash and I were in the back seat of the Lincoln, Brutus at the wheel aiming the car to the road to Mustang, when Brutus remarked, "Lash, pure class. Sharks never sleep."

I turned to Lash, leaned into him and grinned up at him. "It was, honey. That was a stroke of genius."

Lash grinned down at me and muttered, "Came to me on the fly."

"I loved it," I whispered.

"Good," he whispered back.

I leaned up and touched my mouth to his.

Brutus watched in the rearview mirror.

The three of us were close, but still, Brutus thought Lash was banging me. Maybe Lash would let him in one day. It wasn't my call but I had hope. I didn't want any secrets amongst my posse.

Like a real family.

I settled into Lash's side, curled in, head to his shoulder, arm around his stomach. His arm curled around my waist and his head turned to look out the window.

My eyes moved to the rearview mirror, catching Brutus's.

Then I smiled.

IT WAS Lash and Freddie's play. They called it, I didn't like it but they wanted it for me.

So we didn't buzz under the radar into Mustang.

Upon my brief and final return, they wanted me to make a statement. So we did.

Our shiny, shaded-window Lincoln rolled right up to the square and parked. Then Brutus got out and opened the door for Lash and I. I alighted and Lash unfolded his long, fantastic body out behind me.

I had my sunglasses on. Lash was also wearing shades. So was Brutus.

I strutted across the street, Lash's hand on my back just over my ass, Brutus Lash's wingman.

We caused a sensation. I knew it because I felt it. I didn't know if anyone watching remembered me and I was in the zone, wanting to get this done and get out of there, so I was blocking them all out.

Two down, one to go.

Looking around even though I didn't want to, I noticed I was right all those years ago. The square in summer had perfectly tended, dazzling green turf and healthy, abundant, colorful flowers burst forth from the urns. However, I did not guess there would be huge, vibrant planters with trailing greenery hanging from the streetlamps.

That was a nice touch.

We walked up the courthouse steps, in, and followed the sign to the police section. Then we walked up to the front desk.

"We'd like to speak to an officer named Lenny," Lash announced.

"You mean Cap?" the man behind the desk asked, his eyes shifting through all of us, alert.

Seemed like Lenny moved up too.

Good for him.

"Likely," Lash answered.

"What's this got to do with?" the officer asked.

"We would like to report threats made to my lady friend by Buddy Sharp," Lash answered, tipping his head to me.

The guy stared at him. Then he grinned.

Not a Buddy Sharp fan.

No surprise.

He grabbed the phone.

Five minutes later, down a hall I saw Officer...no, *Captain* Lenny coming at me. Surprisingly, he didn't try to hide his surprise at seeing me.

"Ivey," he greeted, his eyes moving through Lash and Brutus then back to me. "It's been a long time.

"Captain," I replied. "Please meet my partner, Lash Caldiwell." I motioned to Lash who shook Lenny's hand. "And this is Brutus." I motioned to Brutus who jerked up his chin and kept his place behind me and just to my side, close to my back. Lenny read this correctly and didn't go for a handshake.

His eyes came back to me.

"Heard about what happened to you in Vegas, Ivey," he said softly.

I had no doubt.

"Ms. Larue is here to make a statement," Lash put in and Lenny looked at him and back to me.

"Think the situation was covered by Gray," he stated.

I felt Lash tense beside me when he requested, "Perhaps you'll explain."

Lenny sighed and looked at me. "I believe you informed Gray that Buddy paid you a visit."

"I did," I confirmed.

"Well, after you did that, Gray paid Buddy a visit. It was public. It was heated. And there's not a lotta people in three counties that don't know Buddy's an assclown, but now there's not a lotta people in *seven* counties who don't know that seein' as Gray was pissed and when Gray gets pissed it's serious and he don't care who's around. Gray managed to keep his hands off Buddy, which is good. He's got enough problems without his ass bein' in the tank. But his message was pretty clear."

Lash took my hand but even though that felt nice, nothing could stop my heart from beating as hard as it was beating.

Lenny kept speaking.

"Anyway, Ivey, incident occurred in Vegas. That is way outta my jurisdiction. Nothin' I can do."

"I understand that, Lenny, but what he said to me, something is happening. Not only did he threaten me and I'd like that down in an official capacity somewhere, it was clear he had some machinations he was instigating or had already started against Gray. If my statement is on record somewhere, wherever that may be, something happens to me or Gray, then the breadcrumb trail has already been laid," I told him.

Lenny was alert always but at my story he got more alert.

"He make threats against Gray as well as you?"

"Not directly." I shook my head. "No. That isn't true. To me, directly, to Gray, indirectly."

Lenny rolled his tongue along his lower teeth behind his lips, his eyes working.

Then he stepped back, extended his arm down the hall and stated, "Let me introduce you to one of our officers who'll take your statement."

My heart eased.

Lash started moving me, Brutus behind, but as I got abreast of Lenny, I stopped. They stopped with me and I caught Lenny's eyes.

"Thank you, Lenny," I said softly.

"My job, Ivey," he replied quietly.

He'd said that to me before and I remembered it like it happened yesterday. The memory hurt like a mother but I didn't let it show, nodded and walked down the hall with my two best friends.

We were sitting at a fabulous restaurant in the middle of nowhere with expensive steak dinners sitting in front of us. They weren't VFW delicious but they were nothing to sneeze at.

Leave it to Lash to sniff out elegance and extravagance in the mountain plains in Colorado. Not only the restaurant but the hotel spa, also in the middle of nowhere, where we were spending a couple of getaway days.

I was smiling at Lash who'd just said something Lash-like to make me smile. I'd grabbed my wineglass and was lifting it to my curved lips when Brutus spoke and Lash and I looked at him.

"Right, just gonna take this moment to say, not sure I get this, you two, what you're doin', dumpin' a wad on this fuckin' guy who broke Ivey's heart." He looked at me and his voice dropped soft. "What I do know, you doin' this, but I already knew it before, is that heart is made of pure gold, baby. That guy is fuckin' whacked for losin' hold a' you. What you did today, I would never do. But I'm proud a' you that you had the strength to do it."

My heart swelled, tears filled my eyes and I whispered, "Thank you, baby."

"You're welcome, baby," Freddie whispered back.

Lash found my thigh under the table and squeezed it.

I breathed deep, got a lock on it and looked between the two of them.

Then I smiled.

Chapter 24

Nothin' Better Than You

N*ine thirty the next morning...*

I WAS RETURNING from having breakfast with Lash, walking down the hall toward our room.

I'd lost Lash for the day. Gym, Jacuzzi, sauna, shower, haircut at the house salon, professional shave and manicure. Just his time at the gym would be over an hour. He had a popular club in Vegas that took a lot of his time but he liked to work on his body and he didn't often have the time to get a good workout in. Rarely a sauna. Never a professional shave and manicure.

It was cool that, after taking his time to deal with my business, he was going to get something he liked out of it.

I'd also lost Brutus for the day. Even though he worked at his body too and Lash was footing the bill, Brutus's activities didn't involve long gym visits and salon services. They involved a smooth, mocha-skinned beauty who worked hotel reception that he eyed up, nailed down and with whom he was currently behind closed doors with a Do Not Disturb sign. Today was her day off so they had lots of time.

Brutus got his own treat.

As for me, I was at a loss for what to do. My life *did* include regular spa treatments. We had a pool at home I used often. I spent a lot of time shopping because I liked it and could afford it and my life was generally stress-free. That was, when the people of Mustang weren't paying me threatening visits or firing at the defenses I'd built around my heart with bazookas.

I was looking forward to getting back to that.

But for the next couple of days, I wasn't sure what to do.

Yes, there I was. *Me.* Except for drifting through the club fake-flirting with men, my life was a vacation.

Fancy that.

I decided I'd order up room service, slip into something comfortable, call up a bunch of movies and spend my time lazing in bed with a movie marathon.

I didn't do that at home and I thought that would be awesome.

I slid my keycard in. The light went green, I pushed down the handle, slid the card out and pushed open the door.

Then something warm and hard was at my back pushing at me and the door.

I started to cry out, twisting around, my shoulder slamming into something solid, my head jerking back, and I saw him.

Gray.

The cry strangled itself in my throat and I didn't struggle as Gray pushed us in until we cleared the door. Then he stopped, facing me, shutting the door behind him and standing in front of it.

I took three quick strides into the room and whirled.

Shit. He looked good.

No.

He looked fucking *great.*

Time had been kind and I shouldn't have been surprised, I knew it would be. The way he was made, there was no other way it could be. But I also saw photos of his dad at his house. His father never lost it either.

It wasn't like it had been thirty years. Gray was just thirty-three.

But he wore it well just as he'd wear fifty-three, sixty-three, and if he was lucky, eighty-three.

"How did you find me?" I asked, tearing my gaze from all that was him to look into his blue eyes.

"Dollface, you came to Mustang and made a splash. It was impossible *not* to find you."

It happened and he kept speaking but he saw it and when he was done talking his brows shot together.

My body had jerked like it took a blow.

And this was on his first word.

Dollface.

"Ivey?" he called, his voice softer, a thread of concern drifting through it.

I pulled my shit together and straightened my shoulders.

"Get out."

The concern vanished and his face got hard again.

"Oh no, we're gonna talk."

"You and I don't have anything to talk about," I informed him.

"Twenty-four hours ago, you're right. We didn't. Then you strutted your ass through two counties laying a thick trail of your man's money and gettin' in everyone's face about it, especially mine, so now we do."

"It's done, there's nothing you can do about it so just leave and move on," I advised.

"You're right again, Ivey. It's done and there's nothin' I can do about it but that don't mean I got nothin' to say about it. I'm gonna say what I gotta say and you're gonna listen."

Really?

Why couldn't these people just leave me alone?

"Is this necessary?" I snapped.

"Yeah, to me, yeah. You, Ivey, *you* waltz into Mustang and bail my shit out usin' another guy's money? What the fuck?"

"Gray—"

"That was not cool," he cut me off, his voice starting to go rough with building fury. "Shovin' your man and his money in my face, Ivey. That...was not...*cool.*"

"It wasn't his money, Gray, it was mine," I shot back, Gray leaned back and the surprise showed on his face. I took that and went with it. "So you can stop being macho man rancher cowboy pissed off that another man sorted your shit. Now you can start being macho man rancher cowboy pissed off that a woman sorted your shit. But, for God's sake, do it somewhere else."

"It was his money," Gray pressed, the surprise moving out of his face, the fury back in.

"It wasn't, Gray," I pressed back.

"It was, Ivey. You live with him. You fuck him. He uses you and your hair and your ass and your legs to make the money he pays you so it's his money. Christ, all these years, you never learned. It just got worse."

Melted steel shot through my veins encasing my spine and as it did I lost my mind.

"How dare you?" I hissed.

"Pretty easy," Gray clipped back.

"You have no idea how it is between Lash and me."

He leaned in, expression, posture and, when he spoke, his tone telling me his anger was escalating right along with mine.

"Darlin', you forget, *I saw you.* You swayed your tight ass right in my face. I paid three hundred dollars for the seat at that show as did a hundred other men around that stage. You can talk for a year and you will never convince me that the man you fuck gave you all that money. He's using you just like your brother. Except, unlike your brother, he gets to fuck you a different way and you're so goddamned stupid, *you let him.*"

"You don't know how it is," I snapped.

"I know exactly how it is," he bit back.

"No you don't, Gray. Lash is gay."

I was so furious at the way he was speaking to me, what he was saying, it just slid out.

And a miracle didn't happen a nanosecond afterward where my words evaporated before they hit Gray's ears. I knew it by the shock that settled on his face.

And I had to instigate damage control, pronto.

"You can't tell anyone," I breathed.

Gray stared at me and didn't say a word.

Frantic, I rushed to him and repeated, "You can't tell anyone. No one knows. No one but me. You can't tell anyone."

Gray looked down at me, still speechless, and I lifted a hand, curled it into his tee and leaned into him.

"Gray, you have to promise me, not a single word. He trusts me. I'm the only one in this world he trusts. I know everything about him, he knows everything about me. The only reason he gave me that gift was that he trusted me to keep it safe." I leaned deeper, rolling up on my toes. "Please, please, Gray. He's my best friend in this world and he trusts me. You have to promise me you won't breathe a word to anyone about what I just said."

Gray's eyes moved over my face and when they did they took their time but he still said nothing.

"Please," I whispered, feeling the tears shimmering in my eyes, hearing the desperation in that one word and Gray's hand came up, fingers curling around mine at his shirt, holding it tight and warm.

"Ivey, who am I gonna tell?" he whispered back.

"No one, please, promise me," I begged, and his fingers squeezed mine.

"I promise, darlin'."

I stared in his eyes searching for any sign he was lying to me and when I saw none I sucked in breath.

Then I realized I was leaning, breasts to his chest, my hand curled in his shirt with his hand holding mine, so I yanked my hand free and took two steps back.

Gray watched me do this and he kept watching me even as I stopped. His face held no fury. No residual shock.

But he was still studying me, eyes alert, something working at the back of them.

I heard a phone ring, it was coming from Gray's ass, but he ignored it and I did too.

I pulled in another calming breath, let it go and with it got my shit together.

So, being together, calmly I told him, "I don't understand what made me do it but I did it and it's done. If it wounds your pride, I'm sure you'll get over it. But Mrs. Cody was kind to me, eventually, in her way, and I didn't like that she would not be in a clean place where she liked being. And Mustang was kind to me in its way and I didn't like that it was losing its legacy. So I had the means to do it and I did it. Please accept that, move on, and I will too."

His phone stopped ringing only for it to start up again.

But he ignored it and kept looking at me.

When his phone quit ringing again without him speaking, I started, "Gray—"

"She's in there," he interrupted me on a murmur, "just saw her."

I felt my brows draw together and I asked, "Sorry?"

His phone started ringing again, he muttered, "Fuck," reached to his back pocket, pulled it out, looked at it and put it to his ear. "Janie. Now is not the time."

I stared at him, really wishing he still wasn't so beautiful, really, *really* wishing I hadn't blurted out Lash's secret and lastly wishing that he would just go away and I could get on with my movie marathon.

That marathon would most assuredly include a couple of boxes of Kleenexes but whatever. I'd survived before, I'd survive again.

I just had to hold it together in the now.

I moved across our large room that started with a kind of sitting room. This led through a large open doorway to another room that held a king-size bed off which was a huge, pristine bathroom that was at the end of a wall that was filled with cabinets, cupboards and a built-in wardrobe. There was a mirror behind a shelf covered in various-sized crystal glasses, a mini-bar that wasn't so mini, a safe behind a cabinet, shit like that. It was spacious, comfortable and elegant. A serious upgrade and it was sweet.

No half-measures for Lash, ever.

I sat on the end of a chair, crossing my legs, my spike-heeled, strappy-sandal-shod foot bouncing as I heard Gray say into his phone, "Yeah, I found her. I'm with her now."

Great. Janie and Gray were talking about me.

I put an elbow to my crossed knee, my head in my hand and kept impatiently bouncing my foot waiting for this to be done, him to be gone and me to be free to have nervous breakdown number five gazillion as pertains to Grayson Cody.

Gray's back shot straight before I saw his body freeze.

Oh no.

My body froze with him.

Then he whispered, "What?"

He listened.

I waited.

His eyes came to me.

Oh no!

What was Janie saying?

"Say again?" Gray asked into the phone softly. He listened again. I stared as his face changed to something I didn't get but whatever it was scared the hell out of me and as I did this I tried (thankfully successfully) to force myself to keep breathing. "Right," he said quietly then again, "Right. Later."

He disconnected and turned to me.

"What?" I asked when he didn't say anything but he didn't answer, just looked at me with that expression on his face that scared the shit out of me. "What, Gray?" I pushed.

"You wrote me a note?" He was still talking quietly.

Shit.

This again.

I stood and crossed my arms on my chest. "Yes, Gray. Seven years ago I stole off in the dark of night, but before doing it, I wrote you a note. This happened *seven years ago* and those words are the only words I'm going to give this shit. It's over. It's been over for seven years. I'm not going over it."

It was like he didn't hear me and I knew this when he asked, "You came back?"

Okay, now, he *really* didn't want to get into this.

"Listen, you said what you had to say, we had it out, now can you just leave?"

"You came back," he stated, again not listening to me.

"Gray, I asked relatively nicely and I'll do it again. Please leave."

"You came back," he repeated and I uncrossed my arms from my chest, planted my hands on my hips and snapped, "Yes, I came back."

"*Why didn't you come to me?*"

I took a step back because I had no choice. His words came at me in a roar, a wall of sound that was physical, beating into me.

"I—" I started, thrown, stunned, scrambling, unable to think.

"Why the fuck didn't you come to me, Ivey?" His voice was deep and rasping, it was so abrasive.

"Gray—"

"Why *the fuck* didn't you come to me?" he shouted, and once again, I lost it.

"Because I saw you, you *asshole*!" I shouted back, leaning in. "I saw you with a pretty brunette walking down the sidewalk, smack in town, your arm around her, holding her close, smiling in her face. Like only three months before you'd held *me*!" I kept shouting. "I knew about Cecily and Nancy, all of them, all the way back to Emily, all your history. Twenty-five and Mustang's resident player who played *me*. So do not stand there and pretend you didn't get my note and do not stand there and bullshit me that this is about me leaving. This is about you and your pride and needing to get something off your chest. Whatever. You did it. Now get *the fuck* out."

"I wasn't with another woman, Ivey," he ground out, eyes locked to mine, his burning.

"Bullshit, Gray, such fucking bullshit. *I saw you with her.* I was not seeing things. It was not the dead of night. The sun was shining. You were smiling. Do not...*bullshit me.*"

"I wasn't with another woman," he repeated.

"*Do not bullshit me!*" I leaned forward to shriek.

He didn't move, not a muscle, just stared at me.

Then he whispered, "Brunette."

"Yes, Gray, she was a brunette. Switching it up again. Cecily was too."

His eyes held mine and I noticed his chest was rising and falling deeply (just like mine). He tore his gaze away from me at the same time he tore his fingers through his hair. He dropped his hand and when his eyes came back to me it took everything I had to keep my feet at the pain etched in his features.

"I didn't get any note," he whispered. "And that girl was my cousin Chandler. She went to Auburn back then. She was back for summer vacation. Outside Audie, she's the only cousin I like. Fuck, I'm closer to her than I am Audie. Closer to her than anyone but Gran."

Every word hit me like a blow, each carrying too much force I couldn't stop myself from swaying back. I hit chair and steadied.

"You should have come to me," Gray said softly but each word held at least a ton of weight.

I couldn't process that. If I gave those words time, they would crush me.

Instead, I whispered, "I left you a note."

He shook his head. "I was outta my mind when you disappeared. Looked everywhere for you. Janie and I went up there. Swept clean. Nothin' there but the stuff you borrowed from me."

My heart was beginning to race and something was crawling in my belly, tearing at the lining, trying to get out.

"That isn't true," I said quietly. "I packed in a hurry. I left clothes behind. Books. Shoes. I told you I'd be back."

"There was no note, Ivey. There was nothing left of you at all."

It was my turn not to hear him.

"I told you I'd be back," I whispered as that thing tore through the lining of my stomach, infiltrated my system, rushed to my brain.

"Baby, there was no note."

"I told you I'd be back," I repeated in a voice so soft there was nearly no sound because in that instant it hit my brain, all of it.

It never made sense.

Until right then.

Casey.

And all that acid leaking out of my shredded stomach drenched my system. I couldn't hold it back anymore so I turned and dashed straight to the bathroom. I hit the tiles painfully as I fell to my knees, sliding. I tagged the toilet and barely got the lid up before I let fly.

Breakfast. Gone.

My back arched and bowed with the strength of sick pouring out of me but I could vomit forever and never get it all out.

It ran in my veins.

It *was* me.

Vomit. Sick. Filth.

Fucking *Casey*.

My stupid, fucking, loser, dickhead, user, asshole *brother*.

"Ivey, baby, Jesus, you're scarin' me," Gray's voice whispered from close, his hands shifting my hair away from my neck. I couldn't endure his touch so I lurched away.

Throwing myself on my ass in the corner, pressed between the wall and tub, I saw Gray crouched by the toilet start moving to me.

My arm flew out straight, palm up toward him, and I cried, "Don't!"

He stilled.

"Don't," I whimpered, dropping my arm.

I looked at the wall, reached out, grabbed a towel from the rail, pulled it down and gathered it close like a security blanket, holding it to my body, the edge of it to my mouth.

Gray closed the toilet lid, flushed it, sat on it and leaned his elbows into his knees before he begged, "Dollface, talk to me."

"He had money," I told my bent knees, curling them closer, wrapping one arm around.

"Get outta that corner, honey, come with me. We'll talk in the other room."

I didn't move.

"He had money. A lot of money," I semi-repeated.

"Ivey—"

My gaze stayed glued to my knees. "I thought he'd stolen it. Now I don't know. I don't know where he got it."

Gray was silent.

I kept talking.

"He said they were after him, us. They'd beaten him badly. I saw that. But months we were on the run. He never pushed the hustle. Never asked for money. Never dropped a con. I looked through his stuff and found the money. I just thought he stole it."

"Please, baby, let me come to you, get you off this floor."

I ignored him.

"I never saw them. He told me they were following us but I could spot a tail. I was better at it than him. He was acting weird. All over me. Never left me alone. Never. Never let me get near a phone. Twitchy. God, so damned twitchy. It freaked me out."

"Right, Ivey, I'm comin' to you."

I kept ignoring him even as my ass was suddenly off the bathroom floor, Gray's was on it and mine was in his lap.

I held my towel to my mouth, looked into his eyes and kept talking.

"Something was up with him," I whispered.

"Yeah," Gray whispered back, holding me close, holding my eyes, his holding clear concern as he kept his gaze locked to mine.

"I never got it. Never. In the end, I thought he'd made his play just to get me back so we could go on the hustle again because he couldn't make it without me. But I don't think it was that. I don't know what it was, but all that money, Gray. I don't think it was that."

"So you got shot of him and came back to me," Gray said quietly.

I nodded vaguely. "I promised you in the note that when the danger was gone, I would. But I can sense danger, Gray, and as we ate up the miles, town to town, state to state, days into weeks, I never felt it. We weren't being followed. Casey lied to me. The way he was acting, all over me, all sweet to me, but watchful, jittery, it wasn't right. I couldn't get a lock on it then I thought I figured it out. I stole his car, left him behind and I went back to you."

Gray closed his eyes and leaned his head back against the tile.

He opened them and looked at me. "And you saw me with Chandler."

Tears filled my eyes and I nodded.

"Fuck, baby," he whispered, staring at me.

"I thought you saw my note and didn't care. I thought you moved on. I thought you didn't want my hassle. I thought you didn't care I had bad men after me. I thought," a tear slid out of my eye, "I thought you didn't care."

"I loved you, Ivey, and I thought you cleared out on me."

"I wrote you a note." My voice broke on those words.

He pulled in breath and sighed.

Then he asked, "That fuckin' brother of yours, he have the opportunity to grab that note?"

I thought about it and nodded but added, "He couldn't grab my stuff, though, Gray. And I left stuff. Not a lot of it but it meant something to me. I worked for it, earned it. My skirt, my dress, my heels. I wouldn't leave that behind. I wouldn't leave *you* behind."

"Fuck, I wish you'd have fuckin' come to me," he growled.

"Casey said they had guns. Said they'd shoot you. I couldn't go to you."

"Okay, then, I wish you'd have fuckin' come to me when you got back."

"You were with another woman," I reminded him.

"She was my cousin, Ivey, and you knew me better than that."

"You were my first kiss," I blurted, he blinked and his arms spasmed around me.

Then he whispered, "What?"

"You weren't just my first lover, Gray, you were my first *everything*."

That pain I saw earlier slashed through his features and his arms again spasmed but stayed tight around me.

I kept talking.

"I wasn't experienced enough. I thought I wasn't..." I shook my head. "I was a pool hustler virgin who you'd given her first kiss at age twenty-two. You were too good for me, I knew it and I figured you figured it out too so you moved on to better."

"Baby, fuck," he hissed on a near snarl, his eyes narrowing and his arms going super tight. "There was *nothin'* better than you."

And right then, yes again, I lost it.

Six words that held the impact of a nuclear bomb disintegrating years of work building a wall to protect my heart. All of that gone, demolished, rubble at...six...words.

There was nothin' better than you.

But I didn't lose my temper or lose my mind or blurt my beloved friend's secrets.

I lost hold on my emotions. Tears sliding from my eyes, body wracked with sobs, I fell face-first into his shoulder and just cried.

Gray gently pulled the towel from my grasp, got up from the bathroom floor and took me with him. He moved us out of the bathroom as a whole. Then we were down on the bed, Gray's back to the headboard, me held close, his arms tight, his knees cocked, cocooning me in all things Gray.

All things Gray.

I wanted to glory in this. I wanted to burn it in my brain so I'd have it forever. But I didn't have it in me. All I did for a long time was just cry.

Shit. Just like always.

All these years, years of tears and Grayson Cody never leaked out of me.

Still crying, suddenly I felt his body tense and we were up. He held me close with one arm around my back but carefully dropped the arm behind my knees. My sandals hit floor but he held me tight to him, his body still tense and I would know why when I heard, "What the fuck?"

Lash.

My face, still stuffed in Gray's chest, turned and I saw Lash.

The problem with that was Lash saw me.

And he lost his mind.

Quickly advancing, he whispered menacingly, "*What the fuck?*"

"Calm, man," Gray warned, his arm coming up, held straight, palm down, a caution at the same time a placating gesture.

"You did it to her again. She used up every fuckin' penny in her savings account to cover your ass and here you are and here *she* is, a fuckin' mess *again* because of you," Lash shot back and as he spoke, Gray's body got tighter and tighter.

"Lash—" I murmured, shifting to go to him but Gray's arm locked tight.

"Calm down and I'll explain," Gray ordered.

"Fuck that, let her go and get the fuck outta here, and for fuck's sake, if you *ever* gave even one, little, microscopic shit about her, stay out of her life," Lash returned.

"It's not what you think," Gray told him.

"It's exactly what I think, asshole. *You* did not pick up the pieces. *You* probably enjoy your birthday when every year that fucker comes around, she locks her shit down so tight so it doesn't come flyin' apart it's a wonder she can move. You do not take her back day and night, keepin' the wolves at bay so she won't get a wild hair up her ass, let one of 'em in, give so much of her heart there's nothin' left so they can destroy her again. Do *not* fuckin' stand there with her in your arms, her face red and wet and tell me I don't know what this is. I know what this is, motherfucker, and I know you need to get out."

"I thought she was yours," Gray lied quietly, for Lash, *for me* and I felt something warm glide through me, shocking my system as it drifted through a cold I thought would never go away.

But Lash's head jerked, realizing what he gave away before he covered.

"Rue's not anyone's. She's Rue's."

Gray let it slide and told him, "Somehow, we got played."

"What?" Lash clipped.

"Somehow...we got *played*," Gray repeated with an added hesitation and some emphasis.

Lash crossed his arms on his wide chest. "What the fuck does that mean?"

"I see, she's with you, that what's gonna go down next is not gonna go down well with you, but before she took off Ivey left a note I did not get explainin' what went down with her. I thought she bailed on me. She did not. So someone played us. We don't know who but Ivey just figured out her brother was more than likely involved. Knowin' her brother, and I don't know you, man, but I hope you've been saved meetin' that piece of shit, this is undoubtedly true. This rocked her and it's rocked me. Worse, Ivey came back and saw me with my cousin. She didn't know it was my cousin but it was. Chandler's livin' in Denver now but I show Ivey a picture, it'll prove what I say is true. We got played then there was a misunderstanding and we lost seven years to that shit. So what's gonna happen next, you love her like you obviously do, you're gonna have to give it to her and at the same time you're gonna give it to me."

Lash was staring at him clearly as stunned and thrown as I was, pain also in his face, understanding, heartbreak, all of this for me but Gray didn't give him any more time.

His arm that was still held out toward Lash came to me, his hand cupping my jaw, tipping my head back until he caught my eyes.

Then the pads of his fingers dug in and the look in his eyes, the burn there, burned through my insides.

"We cannot take this further with him here. But we gotta talk about this, Ivey. We were played. I don't know who or why or how but I got some good fuckin' guesses. Someone took you away from me and used Casey to do it." He dipped his face close and that burn in his eyes grew hotter corresponding to the heat in me. "Never before, never since have I felt for any woman, fuck, *anyone* the way I felt about you. I want that back. I want my girl back. She's in there, Ivey. I saw her and you got it in you to give her to me. But you gotta make that decision, dollface. You gotta think about it, make your decision, and I hope when it's made, you'll come to me. You know where I live. I'll be waiting."

I lost sight of his deep blue eyes with their beautiful russet tipped lashes when his face moved in even closer. He touched his mouth to mine then he let me go, strode by Lash, through the room and disappeared out the door.

My eyes moved to Lash who was twisted and looking at the door.

He twisted back and his eyes came to me.

Mine again filled with tears.

"Fuck," I hissed, lifting my hands to cover my face.

I felt Lash's arms close around me and heard his whispered, "Babe."

"Fuck," I repeated, that word breaking.

Lash's arms got tight.

More tears came.

Lash had forgotten to take something to the gym and came back for it thus missed his Jacuzzi, sauna and salon appointment so he could deal with me.

Fuck.

Chapter 25

Keycard

Lash Caldiwell

E*ight hours later…*

"Dude does somethin' to piss me off, can I lay him out?" Freddie asked, him driving, Lash in the passenger seat watching the orchard trees pass by as they neared the quaint farmhouse.

"I'm thinkin' you're not gettin' who this guy is to Ivey," Lash replied quietly.

"Right," Freddie said and Lash knew he saw him as Lash did. Sitting on his porch swing, arm stretched out resting along the wide back of the swing, beer bottle in his hand.

Grayson Cody.

Ivey didn't have a picture of him but she'd gone into detail describing him.

Lash thought she was glorifying a memory.

But she had not come close.

The faded jeans, the tight, gray t-shirt stretched across the wall of his chest, those shoulders, that hair, that ass, those long legs, those fucking *eyes*.

Jesus.

He was not Lash's thing, too butch (*way* too butch) but that didn't mean Lash couldn't appreciate all that was him.

Freddie parked behind a rusted out, old, light blue pickup truck that really needed to be put out of its misery.

As they drove up, parked and even now, Grayson Cody's long body kept swaying in that swing but his eyes never left the car.

Lash turned to Freddie, pulled in a breath and stated softly, "Okay, my man, in a minute you are gonna hear a bunch of shit that's gonna knock your socks off. So, two seconds to prepare, Ivey is my best friend, outside you my only real one, as you know. What you don't know, she is not my lover. She's my friend. And I'm gay. You tell anyone, I'll shoot you and you know I'm not fucking with you about that. Deal with it. We gotta move on, like, *now*."

Freddie's eyes were big but Lash didn't have time for Freddie. He turned and folded out of the car.

Then he walked through the thick, green grass to stand at the side of the porch opposite Grayson Cody.

He'd scanned his surroundings while they drove up so he kept his gaze steady on Cody.

But he got it. He got it just with that man. With the way he looked and with the way he held her, touched her and spoke to her. He also got it with all that was around him. The peach trees, the faraway mountains, the fields that were waves of green and wheat brown, this house.

He got it.

He got why this man was the one and only man for the beautiful Ivey Larue.

Now Grayson Cody needed to get it.

He heard Freddie get out, his door slam and he knew Freddie was leaning against the car.

Cody's eyes flicked to Freddie and back to Lash.

Then he asked the right question.

"How is she?"

"Not good," Lash replied and watched Cody's square jaw go hard even as his body remained relaxed, lounging and swaying in that porch swing.

Ivey would look cute, curled up against him in the crook of that arm thrown wide.

It was time to get this party started so Ivey could live a life, curled up against her man, in that swing, in the crook of that arm thrown wide.

"She's Ivey so she told me what she told you about me," Lash shared and Cody stared at him a second then jerked up his chin.

He gave him no more.

Lash crossed his arms on his chest, settled in and stated, "Now I'm here to tell her secrets."

Lash watched with no small amount of fascination as his body went alert.

Very nice.

Lash went on.

"I do this for her and that means you get something out of it. She has no clue we're here. She finds out I did this, it could swing either way for me. But what I know of her, how she feels about you, the opening you gave her, I'm hoping she'll find it in her to forgive me. But you're about to get a gift, and if you don't handle it with care, you answer to me and Freddie."

He jerked his head back to indicate his friend at the car but didn't take his eyes off Cody.

Lash also kept talking.

"Not now, but eventually, you have my promise that you'll pay if you break her again. We will make you hurt worse than the hurt that has crushed down on her her entire life. Not just the seven years she's been jacked up about you but all the twenty-nine she's endured. And when I say you handle it with care, I say that the next twenty-nine and beyond better make up for every minute of the last, and if you don't break your back to do that for her, I'll break it for you. Do you understand me?"

His gaze was laser sharp. He was listening. He was hearing. He was beyond interested.

But Grayson Cody didn't say a word.

Lash decided to take that as an affirmative and kept going.

"You told her you'll be waiting. My advice, Cody, is to start gettin' impatient really fuckin' fast. You don't, she'll slip through your fingers because my girl has no intention of coming to you. You know snippets of her past. You saw her strip. You said shit then and you said shit today and she's spent the day convincing herself that she's done her penance for not believing in you by bailing you out and now the best thing she could do for you is let you live your life. You need to disabuse her of the notion you think she's a step up from a whore and you need to do that quick-like."

That got him something.

A clipped out, pissed off, "*Fuck.*"

"Right, I get you, my man. You were her first, you're that type of man, seein' her do what she was doin' would rile you. Type of man you are, pissed off, you'd share. You need to make fast work of rightin' that wrong."

That got him something else. The swing tipped back as Cody leaned forward, boots to the porch, elbows to his knees, gaze still locked to Caldiwell.

"You need to move your fancy-ass Lincoln so I can get my truck out," he demanded.

Lash smiled.

Then he said softly, "I'm not done."

"Well, finish it, man. I don't got a lotta time."

Lash's smile got bigger before it faded from his face.

He dropped his arms, took two steps forward and crossed them again.

"Her momma was bad news."

Lash heard Cody suck in a hissed breath but he kept talking.

"You think about all the ways a momma could be bad, Ivey's momma went one better. Ivey and her brother had two different fathers. Neither of them knew their dads. Ivey because hers is in the penitentiary for twenty-five to life for murder one.

Lash lifted a hand and dropped it, still talking.

"A caution, I found that shit out. She has no clue about that either and I haven't told her. He was just gone by the time she could cogitate and her mother never shared. Casey didn't know his dad because even his momma doesn't know who his daddy is. They did not grow up in a safe home. Only thing Casey knew all his life was lookin' out for his little sister. Feedin' her. Gettin' her dressed. Gettin' her to school."

Lash drew in a deep breath, kept his gaze locked to Cody and started into the *really* bad shit.

"She grew up, started gettin' pretty, with the man parade Momma had in and outta that house, Casey's protection had to shift. He loved his sister. He grew watchful. He took her back. What he feared would happen, happened. One of Momma's men got an eye for Ivey and started makin' plays. Casey could only do so much. Momma was blind to that shit, and even if she wasn't, she didn't fuckin' care. So he kept on comin' over."

Lash ignored Cody's jaw visibly tightening and went on.

"One night, Casey heard shit he didn't like and did what he always did lookin' out for his sister. He walked in on his twelve-year-old sister fightin' off a biker. Casey took a baseball bat to that shitbag motherfucker, bashed his head in, packed them up and stole the very little there was that was worth something. Cleaned out the biker's wallet, his passed-out mother's purse, her car, took off and never looked back. Then he did the best he could."

Another deep breath and Lash gave more.

"Now, I looked into this shit after Ivey told me about it and that guy didn't die. It was touch and go but he didn't die. He isn't right, surviving a head wound like that, but he also isn't dead. Still, police were lookin' for Casey and Ivey Bailey for a while. Years passed, trail got cold, case went stale, it's done."

Grayson Cody didn't move, didn't even twitch but his eyes were burning laser sharp into Lash.

So Lash kept going.

"I know you know him and think he's a piece of shit. What I heard, he is. But Casey saved his sister from a fate one step down from death. And he did it when she was at an age where that kinda shit, shit that could fuck up a grown woman for life who was strong, could seriously fuck up a sweet, innocent twelve-year-old girl so she'd never be the Ivey you know and I know. He kept her alive, he kept her safe and he made it so he could give Ivey to you, me and Freddie. He fucked up along the way but I think you get why she stayed tied to him, loyal and felt she owed him."

Lash hesitated a beat to let that sink in before he carried on.

"I don't know this new shit that's come out and what she's told me of him, I can believe he'd be involved. What you need to know is, there is one person on this earth who could tear her from you and that was him. He came to her, fucked up, face mangled, scared outta his brain. Or tellin' her that shit. She loved him. She owed him. She went with him. But you gotta get she went thinkin' she was comin' back. He also convinced her you were in danger and not just you, the entire town of Mustang. So, just like yesterday, she acted fast and not thinkin' to keep you safe. And, while I'm sharin', she thought you replaced her, you tore her shit right up, shredded, my man, tatters. She believes this entire town thinks she's trash. And still, she got word this town was rocking and it took her five minutes to decide to lay out her savings to steady that boat."

Lash watched Cody close his eyes and drop his head.

To that, Lash called out, "I'm not done."

He then watched Cody's muscled back bow as he drew in a deep breath before Cody tipped his head back to look at Lash.

"There's been no one since you," Lash whispered and immediately, he saw it, felt it. Cody's body went statue-still but the air around him started undulating with the depth of emotion coming off him. "She danced for me but only for me. She was a waitress when I found her. She never dated. Never had a boyfriend. Nothing. Not even another kiss. You were her one and only, Cody, and you still are."

"Move your fuckin' car," he growled instantly.

"What?" Lash asked, Cody's beer bottle landed with a thud on the porch by his boot and he surged to his feet sending the porch swing flying.

"I said, move your fuckin' *car*."

He walked forward, dropped down off the porch and walked right by Lash to his truck. He opened the door and it creaked loud.

Lash turned to him, saw Cody pause, change direction and stalk back to Lash.

"Keycard," he demanded, hand up, palm up.

Lash's lips twitched and he dug out his wallet.

"You get another room tonight, man," Cody went on.

"Right," Lash muttered, pulling out his keycard and handing it to Cody who tagged it swiftly, turned and stalked back to his truck. "Better move the car, Freddie," Lash called but Freddie was on it, smiling a huge-ass, motherfucking, white smile.

Freddie got in and barely got the car out of the way before the truck reversed then swung around and sped down the lane.

Lash sauntered to the Lincoln and folded in the passenger seat.

After he got his door closed and seatbelt on, Freddie took the lane a lot more slowly.

"I think that went well," Lash muttered.

"Fuck yeah," Freddie muttered back.

There was silence.

Eventually from Freddie, a quiet, "Dude, you're gay?"

Lash sighed.

Then braced.

Then affirmed, "Yeah."

"I *so* have a cousin I need to introduce to you. You are totally his type," Freddie replied. Lash's eyes cut to him, Freddie glanced at Lash, back at the windshield and again he smiled a huge-ass, motherfucking, white smile.

Lash looked to the lane and stopped bracing about half a second before he started grinning.

Chapter 26

Say It

The door opened.

I was lounging across the bed in my black satin nightie. It had spaghetti straps that crisscrossed over a mostly exposed back, a hem that hit me right at the bottom of my ass, slits up the sides to my waist. With that, I wore a pair of little, black panties (all of it Lash bought me, he didn't only have an eye for good eveningwear, costumes and interior décor, he was hell on wheels in the lingerie department).

I didn't tear my eyes away from the movie I'd rented from the hotel selection as I called out my greeting to the returning Lash.

He'd gone places unknown, explaining he had "shit to do." I didn't question this. Lash owned a successful club. He often had "shit to do." So much of it he couldn't escape it and I knew some of it would eventually leak into our getaway.

So, eyes never leaving the TV, I called, "I think warning the catering staff I was in meltdown over a hot guy was overkill, honey. They didn't give me a breadknife with my room service and 'forgot' to bring it up even after I called so I had to pry open my baguette and spread my pâté with a fork."

There was silence as I felt Lash's presence near the bedroom area.

Then, "You don't look like you're in meltdown over a hot guy."

That wasn't Lash and my eyes flew to the wide doorway that led to the bedroom area where Gray was lounging, shoulder against the jamb, arms crossed, ankles crossed, lean hips hitched, eyes on me.

I was on my side, head in hand, elbow in the bed, but seeing him I shot up to a straight arm, hand in the bed, and stared, my breath clean leaving me.

Gray's eyes held mine then they traveled down my body and his entire expression changed to one I hadn't seen in seven years. One for just over two months I saw often. One I never forgot, not for a day, and one that had a profound effect on my whole body.

"Jesus, fuck," he muttered.

"How did you get in here?" I whispered.

His gaze moved to mine, his arms uncrossed, and between two long fingers he held a keycard.

But he didn't answer.

"How did you get that?" I asked.

He casually shoved the keycard in his back pocket, re-crossed his arms on his chest and kept his eyes on me, but he didn't speak.

"Gray?" I called.

"You sleep with him."

It was a statement not a question.

I held his gaze and for some ridiculous reason explained quietly, "We whisper about our days before we fall asleep and he cuddles. I like that. Not feeling alone even when I'm asleep."

Gray pushed away from the doorjamb and started toward the bed, saying, "I'll remember that."

At his movement, I pushed up to my knees and scooted back, asking, "What?"

"I'll remember you like to whisper about your day before you fall asleep and you like cuddling. I'll remember that. Though, already knew that last part."

I hit headboard and changed directions, scooting quickly off the bed, repeating, "What?"

Gray changed directions too, moving to round the bed toward me, saying, "I think you heard me, Ivey."

What was happening?

"What are you doing here?"

He was almost at me as he said, "Told you we had to talk. We're gonna do other things first, *then* we'll talk."

At his presence, his movements *and* his inference, my heart leapt into my throat then my feet leapt onto the bed. I ran across its wide expanse and jumped down the other side, eyeing the doorway, knowing I was acting like a lunatic, not caring even a little bit and then seeing Gray had changed directions and was again coming at me.

He had a mind to do it he'd get to me fast. I knew it. I didn't have a prayer.

"Wait!" I cried putting a hand up but he didn't even slow.

But he did speak.

"Honest to God, dollface, you need to stop running around in that fuckin' nightie. You're killin' me."

I was breathing fast even though I was not moving, not able to get a lock on all that I was feeling.

Panic, a little bit.

Confused, definitely.

Excited...

Oh yeah.

Panic, as it does, won out and I made a dash toward the seating area not even knowing why I was doing it. But I was caught with an arm around my belly, hauled back into a hard body, walked back swiftly then I was going down. Gray landed on the bed, I landed on Gray then he slid me off him and rolled right on top of me.

Yes, that was what I said.

Right on top of me.

I took his heavy weight, I loved his heavy weight, and I looked into his heated eyes.

Oh God.

"Gray—" I whispered.

"*Fuck*, Jesus, *fuck*," he hissed and his forehead dropped down to mine. "I missed you sayin' my name like that."

Tears filled my eyes and my heart started beating triple time.

"What's happening here?" I kept whispering.

His head went back up and his hand came to frame my face, his thumb sliding out high across my cheekbone under my eye.

"Please don't cry anymore, Ivey."

I pulled in a trembling breath in an attempt to get a lock on it, succeeded in that endeavor and repeated, "What's happening here?"

"I need you to know I don't think you're anything but Ivey."

My head shook slightly with confusion and I asked, "Sorry?"

"You're not anything but Ivey. Way those two guys got your back, you never have been."

"I don't..." I cleared my throat because my voice came out croaky, "I don't know what you're talking about."

"I don't think you're a whore. I don't think you're trash. I don't think you're anything but Ivey, the prettiest thing I ever saw seven years ago and seriously the prettiest fuckin' thing I've ever seen five minutes ago wearin' that fuckin' nightie."

My body froze under him and my eyes froze on his face.

Gray wasn't done speaking.

"I loved you then. I love you now. I've loved you every day for seven years. You left, flashback to my mom, flashback to my dad pinin' for my mom. He loved her, Christ, he loved her. Ate away at him when she left. He never got it. Never. And that pain dug deep and grew bitter so when she came back he never forgave her. Three years they lived in the same town, he never forgave her. She came to his funeral and she looked crushed. She actually *looked* it. Like her world just ended, and even now I see her and that haunts her eyes, what she lost, what she threw away, what she'll never get back. And that was me when you left, Ivey. I knew it was happening to me, I felt it, I understood it, I lived it with my dad and knew it was happening to me and I didn't do fuck all to try to stop it."

He couldn't be serious.

This couldn't be happening.

"You love me?" I breathed.

His eyes didn't leave mine and the intensity didn't leave his.

"Yeah."

"You love me," I stated.

"Yeah."

"Every day for seven years?"

"Every day, every minute, every second since you blew on me."

Oh my God.

Oh my God.

I stared into his eyes.

He was serious.

This was happening.

Oh my God.

Gray's thumb slid across my cheekbone again and he said gently, "Now, you get that, can you relax so I can kiss you then I can fuck you then we can talk about important shit. After that, I'm gonna fuck you again then we'll go to sleep and while we do, we'll cuddle."

I stared at him again before I whispered, "Say it."

"Say what?"

"Order me to tell you I love you."

The instant the words came out of my mouth, his eyes closed, a shadow of pain crossed his face and he dropped his head to the side of mine.

He remembered.

He missed that too.

He missed it badly just like me.

His hand found mine, his fingers laced tight and his lips went to my ear.

And there he whispered words I longed to hear for over seven long years, "Say you love me, Ivey."

I turned my head, my arm stealing around him, and I whispered back, "I love you, Gray."

His head lifted, mine kept turning and we both went for it, our mouths colliding.

We had a lot of making up to do. Seven years.

And it was clear both of us had the same thing on our minds.

Desperate, even greedy, mouths taking, tongues driving, hands bumping into each other's, I tore his shirt over his head then I yanked at his belt. Gray took over and I multitasked, moving down, pulling off his boots, his socks then tugging at the legs of his jeans.

Then he was naked, gorgeously naked and hard—hard *everywhere*. He rolled back into me and, *whoosh*!—my panties were gone then, *whoosh*!—my nightie was gone and then we really went for it. Driven. Near frantic. Like one or the other of us would disappear into thin air and we had only that moment and the next and the next.

Gray's fingers between my legs were making me whimper into his mouth and my hand stroking his cock was making him groan into mine and he shifted.

He lifted up, jerking me up as he went. He positioned me, my legs opened to straddle his hips, his arm was around my waist and he pulled me down on him, filling me.

Gray filling me, inside me, connected to me.

Yes.

My hands went into his hair, fisting, my head fell down, my forehead crashing into his and I rode him. Moving up, driving down, again, again with the same desperation we'd both had since we started. My mouth was against his, our breath mingled. I kept going and my mouth moved, lips open, tip of my tongue trailing, down his cheek, along his jaw.

God, I loved the taste of him.

Always did.

His hands slid up my back, gathering my hair, holding it at my neck in his fists, his arms tight around me as I kept riding him.

It didn't take me long, it had been over seven years, it came fast, and I gasped, "*Gray*."

He heard it, knew it was coming and he twisted me. I landed on my back, he kept thrusting and his mouth came to mine as it swept through me. Bright, burning, beautiful, I moaned my orgasm into his mouth.

Both his hands went behind my knees, jerking up, and still mewing through the glorious aftermath of my orgasm, I kept taking him, rocking my hips to take more, give more to him. He buried his face in my neck, grunting with each thrust, his hands shoving back my knees and I knew he was close.

"Baby, I wanna see," I whispered and his head came up.

My hand moved to one of his, took it. He twisted his, laced his fingers with mine and pressed it into the bed beside me as he kept driving into me.

"Missed you," I kept whispering, watching his face, drinking in his beauty. "Missed you so much, Gray."

He held my eyes and kept moving as he whispered back on a groan, "My beautiful Ivey."

"Missed you, honey."

Then he gave it to me. His cock drove deep, his head shot back then it fell forward, his forehead to mine and I watched it move through his face as his hips bucked into mine again, again, again, again and one last time before he stayed rooted and his weight hit me.

When I sensed it was fading for him I whispered yet again, "Missed you."

Gray closed his eyes, slanted his head and he kissed me, wet, deep, yes, God, yes, I missed him.

His lips slid from mine to my jaw, my ear, down and started nuzzling my neck as his hand left the back of my knee. My calves shifted to round him, his free hand went up into my hair and he moved our linked hands to press them to his chest, sandwiching them between us.

Finally his head came up but his eyes didn't come to me. They went to my hair and I watched him watch his movements as I felt his hand sift through it like he was arranging it, fanned across the comforter.

He took his time doing it, his expression absorbed, before his eyes came to mine.

"You never cut it," he noted softly.

"Never," I confirmed.

"It's longer now."

It was. A lot longer.

"Yes."

His gaze held mine and I saw something flash in his, more pain but understanding.

"You did that for me."

I did. I never cut my hair except for trims and I did it for him.

"Yes," I whispered.

"Didn't have me, knew what that meant to me and did it for me."

I pressed my lips together. His voice was rough, thick, it sounded tortured like he had to push the words out.

"Fuck, Ivey," he whispered.

I closed my eyes and lifted my head to shove my face in his neck.

He squeezed my hand then I felt him turn his head so he could say in my ear, "Gonna get off you now, dollface. You need to put your sweet nightie back on. We got shit to talk about and I want you to feel safe while we do it. Yeah?"

I pulled in a trembling breath, nodded, my face moving against his skin. He gently slid out, rolled off me and took me with him. Then he rolled out of bed, taking me with him when he did that too and setting me on my feet in the circle of his arms but he didn't let me go.

I tipped my head back and looked at him to see he was looking down at me.

"You gotta know, I also want you to put that nightie and those panties back on because I like them a fuckuva lot."

Then he grinned and gave me the dimple.

I had a nanosecond to make a choice.

Take in that dimple for the first time in years, how it made his extreme masculinity so damned cute, remembering how much I loved it, feeling that love still, having it back and burst into uncontrollable tears again. Or take in that dimple for the first time in years while standing naked in his arms after he told me he still loved me then made love to me and keep my shit, move forward with Gray to put the past behind and move the fuck on.

I chose option two.

And therefore I grinned back. It was tough, the pain wanted to burst through so my grin trembled on my lips. But I did it.

He saw it, a shadow crossed his features but he made the same decision as me. I knew this when his head dipped, his mouth touched mine, he again lifted it and his arms gave me a squeeze.

Then he ordered, "Get dressed, honey."

I nodded and moved to grab my nightie and panties. I pulled the nightie on over my head, moved to the bathroom, cleaned up, donned my panties and came out.

Gray was buttoning up his jeans, his chest was bare, the TV was off, and the minute I moved into the room, his eyes came to me.

"Come here, dollface," he murmured.

I went there. The instant I made it to him, he picked me up like a groom would carry his bride and he walked us to the bed. Then we were in it. He spent some time grabbing pillows to stack behind his back before he settled with head and shoulders against the headboard, me tucked to his side, my head to his pectoral, his chest all I could see.

God, was I really here with Gray?

To prove it to myself, my arm snaked across his flat abs and my leg lifted and tangled with one of his.

Yes. He was real. I was there with Gray.

"Do you think it's weird that I sleep with my fake, gay boyfriend?"

That was me. I blurted it right out and for a second I wished I had the power to shove it back in. But then I felt Gray's body shaking and I knew he was laughing.

I lifted my head to look at his face and again got the dimple.

Damn, but I loved that fucking dimple.

And he was definitely laughing.

I loved that too.

"Yeah," he answered.

I stared at him as it dawned on me.

"It is," I declared. "It is weird that I sleep with my fake, gay boyfriend."

Gray's body started shaking harder and the word was also shaking when he repeated, "Yeah."

Great.

His arm around me tightened and he slid me partially up his chest so my face was closer to his still smiling one.

"Shit that's weird to a man from Mustang, Colorado is probably not weird in Vegas. There's probably nothin' you could do that would be weird in Vegas."

I'd lived in Vegas for a long time therefore I knew this was totally true.

Gray wasn't done.

"And he loves you near as much as I love you. And you love him. I see his play, I get it, and the way you love him, I get why you'd give that gift to him. You got somethin' outta it too and way he loves you, I get why he'd give it to you. You love someone, you do shit like that, and that, Ivey, is *not* weird."

Okay, well, good to know the seven years had not changed the fact that Grayson Cody was understanding, generous, kind and loving.

What he would say next would prove that seven years had not changed the fact that Grayson Cody was a serious macho man rancher cowboy.

And I knew this when the amusement shifted out of his face, it got serious, his arm got tighter and he stated, "That said, that shit stopped about half an hour ago."

"Right," I whispered.

"Right," he whispered back.

Totally a macho man rancher cowboy.

Therefore, it killed me but I had to be honest and I felt it was fair to warn him, "You know, a long time has passed. I've changed. I'm not the Ivey you knew. You were right that night you saw me. I'm hard as nails. I'm not a pushover anymore."

That was when he gave me the gift of Grayson Cody that I missed most of all.

His arm squeezed tight, his body shook deep and he burst out laughing.

I watched it. I loved it. I loved it no less than I always loved it. But I didn't laugh because I was being deadly serious.

Gray looked down at me, saw my serious face and pulled me further up his chest so we were eye to eye still, incidentally, chuckling.

Then he muttered, "Bullshit."

"It's true," I told him.

He kept grinning and repeated a muttered, "Bullshit."

My hand moved to curl around his neck and I said softly, "No, seriously, Gray, it's true."

Gray's grin faded and he got serious too.

"They came to me, both a' them."

"What?"

"Your fake, gay boyfriend and that mammoth black guy. They came to me."

I blinked before I whispered, "Sorry?"

"Keycard?" he asked and my body stilled as it hit me. "He gave it to me."

His hand came up, fingers sliding into my hair at the side, holding it back and he continued.

"He told me everything, Ivey, everything about you. Both of them came but your fake boyfriend laid it out. Those two men would do anything for you. They'd walk through fire for you. You were hard as nails, those men, who they are, what they do, what they've undoubtedly seen, where they live, they would not give one shit about you. You were hard as nails, you wouldn't take a coupla phone calls from Janie, hightail your ass up here and sort my shit. You wouldn't give a fuck where Gran was stayin'. You thought I moved on from you in three months, you would not save me from losin' my land. You thought everyone in Mustang thought you were trash, you would not protect their legacy. You are not hard as nails, Ivey. You're just Ivey."

"Shut up, you're going to make me cry," I snapped, fighting tears, and again Gray burst out laughing, both his arms moving around me to pull me more on top of him and hold me tight. "Gray! I wasn't being funny!"

"Dollface," he said through his continuing laughter, "women who are hard as nails do not cry at the drop of a hat and I've not spent a lot of time with you in seven years but a lotta the time I've spent with you, you've been bawlin'."

This was true.

Shit.

"Well, when I see Lash and Brutus and you see me kick their ass, you'll see my hard."

His face got that near to tender look I also missed a whole helluva lot and he replied quietly, "You'll give them attitude, no doubt, but you're as devoted to them as they are to you and you know they did that shit for you so it'll be a show and they'll know that too."

He was right.

I decided to change the subject, not to a better one but change it anyway.

So, hesitantly, I asked, "What did Lash tell you?"

"Everything."

Fabulous.

Unfortunately, I needed detail.

"What's everything?"

Gray didn't hesitate. "That he knows you told me about him. That you took to heart that shit I spewed when I was pissed at seein' you on that stage and I had to get my ass in gear or I was gonna lose you again. That your mother was fucked up. What went down that put you and your brother on your path. How your brother took your back which explained your loyalty to him, something, darlin', I was glad to know because it was somethin', no matter how much I chewed on it, which was a whole fuckuva lot, I never got. And last, that you mighta done what you did on that stage but there was no one but me."

Well, there it was. Lash told Gray everything.

Therefore there was a lot to go over.

So, again hesitantly, I started, "So you know about who I am? I mean, where I came from, what Casey did, how I grew up?"

"Yep."

And he was here.

Right then, moving on.

"You were seriously pissed when you saw me dance, Gray."

"Yep."

And he was still here but still, that concerned me.

"That happened," I reminded him. "I can't erase that from my past."

"First, Ivey, I was seein' you for the first time in three years after I thought you cleared out on me. Like I said earlier, my shit was fogged with what my mother did so I didn't think about it. I didn't think that maybe there was a reason and maybe I should look into that and find you. I just thought history was repeating itself. Did I like you dancin' like that for a bunch a' men to watch, get hard, go home and jack off for probably the next ten years, eyes closed, thinkin' of you?" he asked.

He didn't wait for my answer, he answered for me.

"No. I didn't like it at all. But I was more pissed about seein' the woman I love for the first time after she cleared out on me. You coulda been walkin' down a street and I woulda been pissed. It just was not good you were doin' what you were doin' which aggravated my anger. Then you were how you were in that parking lot because you were hurt and pissed at me. If you were Ivey that woulda gone different."

He gave a short shake of his head and kept talking.

"Fuck, I went there and waited for you not admitting to myself but definitely hoping that I'd walk up to you and under all that makeup you wore would be my Ivey and you'd give me back my girl. You weren't Ivey. Your guard was up, understandably, I get that now, but that was all I could see. That pissed me off worse, I mouthed off, said stupid shit because *I* was pissed but," his voice suddenly dropped soft and low, "I didn't like what you were doin', baby, not for a room full of people. But you were beautiful up there. Amazing." He grinned. "My girl, everything she does, every-fucking-thing, she does it better than anybody. We gotta get you some of those feathered fans, but from here on out, you got a one man audience."

I glared at him even though I liked all he said, I loved having that explanation, and as always, I adored his compliment. It meant the world to me.

Still.

"I don't dance anymore, Gray," I informed him.

He kept grinning and muttered, "Reckon I could get you to do it for me."

He definitely could.

"Whatever," I muttered back and his grin became a smile.

I rolled my eyes.

Then I gave up the fake attitude and smiled back.

Gray took in a deep breath and lost his smile as his eyes changed, their intensity burning into me.

And when he spoke again, he did it gently, quietly but firmly.

"Seven years we lost, dollface, we both did shit, we lived our lives and we've probably changed. But I know who's in my arms and I know what I felt back then, what I felt for the years in between and what I feel now. You got a life in Vegas, friends who are devoted to you and I can see it's a good life. I cannot give that kind of life to you.

You sortin' my shit doesn't mean I don't have a shitload more problems, but even when I see my way clear of that I can't give you a life like your fake boyfriend does. You also know I'm not leavin' my land."

He took in another breath but held my gaze captive as he went on.

"So, the important shit we gotta talk about is that I want you back, in Mustang, in my home, in my bed. I do not want to spend time explorin' that option before we get that. I've lost seven years and you have too. I just want you with me, in my house, in my bed. And you gotta decide, knowin' what you got and knowin' you gotta give that all up and knowin' what I can give you, what you're going to do."

"Well, I think I should probably help Lash deal with my replacement but then I'm moving to Mustang," I replied instantly and Gray's arms got tight a second as he blinked slow.

Then he asked, "What?"

"First, I love you," I stated. "Second, she's bossy but I love Mrs. Cody. Third, Mustang was the only home I ever really had until Lash gave me one. But Lash is a good man and he has a lot of love to give. He'll eventually find a partner. I know this, always have and always dreaded it. And it's probably time he pulls his finger out, quits spending his time looking out for me and starts thinking about his own happiness."

It was my turn to take a breath but I did it for a different purpose than Gray did. That being to hold my temper (an endeavor, incidentally, that kinda failed).

And I kept talking.

"And last, something is happening in Mustang. That something involves Buddy Sharp, that something is not good, and the target is you. Yesterday, I foiled his plans, but if he's still aiming punches at you after seven years, then me doing what I did yesterday is not going to stop him. And Mrs. Cody is in a nursing home in a wheelchair, someone has to have your back and that someone is me. So, Gray, you get Ivey but I've been around the block. I'm an ex-Vegas showgirl. You might not see hard but no one fucks with someone I care about and I might be a pushover for you but Buddy Sharp better watch his shit because if he tries to fuck with you again, I'm gonna bring him down."

Gray stared at me and he did it so long I wondered if I went a little overboard.

Then he grinned and murmured, "Fuck, darlin', you're cute when you're tryin' to be a badass."

Trying to be?

"I'm being very serious," I informed him.

"I see that, baby, you're still cute."

"Seriously, Gray, I was the headliner at a burlesque show with twenty other girls who hated me and spent their time trying to stab me in the back. Now, I run the floor of that burlesque show and I've got a bunch of waitresses and bartenders who keep bringing their personal lives into Lash's club so I have to deal with their crap. No joke, when I get going, I can be hell on wheels."

Still grinning, Gray shifted, rolling us so I was on my back and he was on top of me, doing this muttering, "Gonna look forward to that."

"You might find it unattractive," I told him honestly, and I hid it, but to me, fearfully.

He stopped grinning and locked his eyes with mine.

"Dollface," he started, "you in your fancy-ass red getup with your smooth operator that no one in a million years would believe is gay, your humongous bodyguard and your shiny Lincoln, rollin' through Mustang, kickin' ass and takin' names in a classy way happened yesterday and it's already lore. I had so many fuckin' phone calls, from Janie, Shim, Stacy, Sonny, Ang, describin' that shit in detail, I had to turn off my phone. Yesterday, you were hell on wheels *for me.* This is not news. And I do not find it unattractive. And if shit goes down I'm gonna look forward to you rollin' that out to have my back."

Oh. Well then.

That was good.

"Okay," I whispered then smiled at Gray.

Gray didn't smile back.

Instead he asked, "You really movin' to Mustang?"

"Yes," I answered immediately.

"You're movin' to Mustang."

"Yes, Gray."

He stared at me.

Then he whispered, "My girl's movin' back to Mustang."

Damn it all to hell!

My eyes again got wet and I whispered back, "Yes, Gray."

He held my eyes and murmured, "Don't cry, Ivey."

I took in a trembling breath and murmured back, "Okay, Gray."

He drew in a breath too. Then his gaze dropped to my mouth.

I knew what that meant.

And Gray gave me what it meant.

Five minutes later, arms locked around each other, lips locked together, tongues dancing, heart rates escalating, a knock came at the door.

Gray's mouth broke from mine and his eyes went to the door.

"Lash," I murmured and his eyes came back to me.

He touched his lips to mine, rolled off me and the bed, grabbed his tee from the floor and strode to the door pulling it on.

I watched, uncertain if I should aim my eyes at his shoulders, his back or his ass.

I picked his ass.

He opened the door and I heard Lash say quietly, "I got a room, my man, but I need my shit. Gave you time. Hope it was enough."

"It was enough," Gray replied, opening the door and stepping aside.

Lash stepped in as I moved off the bed, my eyes on him.

His eyes came to me and he stopped. Gray closed the door and I moved but Lash didn't.

He was worried I'd be pissed.

I smiled at him so he'd know I wasn't. Over the years he gave me a lot and a couple of hours ago he set about giving me everything. How could I be pissed about that?

Lash smiled back, relief in his.

Seeing that, I stopped walking and ran.

He caught me in his arms and mine closed around him tight.

Face in his neck, I held him tighter, moved my mouth to his ear and whispered, "Thank you, honey."

His arms gave me a squeeze and he replied in a whisper, "Anything for you, babe. Anything."

"I love you, Lash."

"I know, babe."

That was when I burst into tears.

Yes, again.

Two seconds later, Lash transferred me into Gray's arms and Gray held me close as Lash wandered around the room packing.

"She do this a lot?" Gray asked, one arm tight around me, one hand sifting through my hair.

"Oh yeah, usually about you, though, never about me," Lash answered, sounding amused.

"Told me she's hard as nails," Gray shared, still holding me close, hand sifting through my hair.

At that, it was Lash who burst out laughing.

Jeez.

I pulled my face out of Gray's chest, dashed a hand across my wet cheeks and snapped, "I am!"

It was then, both of them burst out laughing.

Now I was getting mad.

"I'm a hard as nails, badass Vegas showgirl who's been around the block," I declared.

"Okay, babe, keep tellin' yourself that," Lash muttered, shoving underwear in his bag, grinning.

Right.

Whatever.

I pulled out of Gray's arms and looked up at him.

"Have you had dinner?"

He looked down at me, dimple out which made my irritation vanish but I didn't let on.

"No," he answered.

"Do you want room service?"

"Yeah."

I looked to Lash. "Do you want to join us?"

Lash looked to me then to Gray, smiled huge and answered, "Fuck no."

"You're welcome," I told him.

"I'm not," he told me.

"But—"

"Babe, you love me, I get that. But your man does not want me here and I orchestrated this so I'm cool with bein' kicked out. Reunite. Enjoy it. You deserve it." He came to me, wrapped his hand around the back of my head, kissed the top then he let me go and stepped back. "Me and Freddie'll see you two at breakfast."

With that he walked into the bedroom area and disappeared into the bathroom.

I looked to Gray and said softly, "You could have made him feel welcome to have dinner with us."

"Dollface, no way in *hell* he's welcome to have dinner with us," Gray replied softly back.

I glared at him thinking he was probably right.

"Baby, come here," Gray ordered. "You're too far away."

"I'm two feet away."

"Ivey, for seven years you've been two states away. You're too far away. Come here."

My heart swelled, my belly curled in a really nice way and I went there.

And when I got there I found he was again right. *Really* right.

And when I made it the two steps to him, I was right.

Right where I wanted to be, right where I belonged.

Held tight against the long, lean frame of Grayson Cody.

My head pressed back into the pillows as it washed over me.

At the same time, Gray shoved his face in my neck and I heard it come over him.

We came simultaneously. We'd never done that before.

It was brilliant.

The fingers of both his hands were laced through mine, holding them over my head pressed into the pillow. He was buried deep and staying right there. My legs were up, knees bent, thighs tucked deep to his sides.

We said nothing, just came down, joined, close, holding hands, tucked tight, Gray's breath drifting against my neck, mine his shoulder. We needed no words. We'd had them. We'd need more but not now. Now was about what he'd just given me, I'd just given him, both at the same time, our bodies as close as they could be, our fingers laced, sharing space, breath, a bed, our time, our lives.

What we should have had for seven years, this, more of Gray's dimple, his laughter, maybe children, creating a family.

We felt it, both of us, I knew it. I knew it was searing through his mind too. We took that moment after being found again to experience the loss, mourn it so we could let it go.

I loved him then and now so desperately, it hurt. But if what happened didn't happen, I wouldn't have Lash, I wouldn't have Freddie. It sucked I couldn't just have it all without the pain in between but I'd learned life didn't have that in store for me. I wasn't a victim, life didn't give that to anybody.

But I had it all now.

All of it.

Everything.

Gray's lips moved to my ear and he whispered, "Say you love me, Ivey."

Yep. I had it all.

Everything.

My fingers squeezed his hands and I whispered back, "I love you, Gray."

I felt his sigh on my neck before he said softly, "You gotta clean up, okay, but come back to this bed in that nightie but no panties."

We weren't done.

Yippee!

"We're not going to sleep?" I asked to confirm.

"Yeah, we are."

Oh. Bummer.

Gray kept talking.

"But when I wake up, be it morning or middle of the night, I don't want anything in my way that wastes my time."

Brilliant.

I grinned.

He kissed my neck, pulled out and rolled off me.

I rolled into him, kissed his chest then rolled off the bed and did what I was told.

Back in bed, tucked tight to Gray's side, my arm around his stomach, my head on his shoulder, my leg tangled in his, he'd pulled my nightie up to my waist so his hand was cupping the bare cheek of my ass and my eyes were drifting closed when Gray called, "Ivey."

"Yeah, baby," I answered sleepily.

"Thank you for takin' care of Gran and savin' my land."

My eyes shot open.

"Pay you back," he went on.

"Gray—" I started, also starting to lift my head but his other hand came up, fingers in my hair cupping the side and he held it down.

"Not with money, baby, but swear to Christ, by the time you leave this earth, you'll feel I paid you back."

I started deep breathing.

Gray asked, "You gonna start bawlin'?"

"Maybe," I mumbled, that one word trembling.

"Shit," he muttered.

That was when the tears stopped threatening and I grinned.

Then I pressed deeper.

Gray's hand slid through my hair and went away.

"Love you, honey," he whispered.

"Love you too, baby," I whispered back.

"'Night."

"Goodnight."

And shortly after, my eyes drifted closed and it was.

A very good night.

Chapter 27

No Stone Unturned

Lash Caldiwell

After breakfast with Cody and Ivey, Lash and Freddie were coming back from the gym, finished working out, and they both saw them. Fifteen feet ahead standing at the glass doors that led to the attractively landscaped pool.

And they both stopped.

Ivey was wearing a slightly see-through silk robe Lash bought her, its glimmer was bronze. Under it, a gold bikini.

Cody wearing his jeans, boots and gray t-shirt from yesterday.

He had his hand light on her hip, his other hand was bunching her hair at the back of her neck, his neck was bent, his lips on hers.

She was leaned partially into him, up on her toes in her muted bronze, slim-strapped Havaianas flip-flops, the swirly pattern visible on the soles. Her hand was to his abs, her other hand curled around the side of his neck.

Something happened and the kiss changed. Cody touched his tongue to her lips or Ivey hers to his or just the fact hit them that they were together, close, reunited after seven years of heartbreak.

So they forgot where they were.

Cody's hand slid from her hip back and down to cup her ass. Ivey's hand slid from his neck up and into his hair. Her body pressed close, she got up on the tips of her toes and her hand at his abs became an arm tight around his back. Both their heads slid into deeper slants. Their mouths were open and the kiss turned visibly carnal.

"Fuck me, seein' that I see now you were never in there," Freddie muttered at his side and Lash grinned. He and Ivey were openly affectionate but they never made out and certainly not in a public corridor by the pool of an exclusive hotel spa in the Colorado plains. "Watch that shit any longer, I'll need a cold shower," Freddie kept muttering.

Freddie was not wrong. Lash was gay but *that* could turn pretty much anyone on.

The kiss ended in a way it was obvious neither participant wanted it to end. Freddie and Lash didn't move as, lips nearly touching, Cody and Ivey whispered to each other. Cody smiled. Ivey returned it. He touched his mouth to hers, gave her a squeeze then he lifted his lips and kissed her forehead.

Finally he let her go and she turned to the doors to the pool. She threw a beaming, radiant smile over her shoulder at Cody and sashayed toward the pool deck.

Lash Caldiwell knew who he was and how he was for a very long time. But that didn't mean watching Ivey Larue's ass swaying in bikini bottoms didn't remind him that more than once in the seven years he knew her that he considered switching sides.

Lash took his eyes from his friend and they went to Cody and he remembered instantly which side he was on.

He also saw that Cody was watching Ivey walk to the pool too. Lash's view of him was only a hint of his profile, Cody's head turned mostly away, but even that showed pain.

Lash barely knew the man but he knew and loved Grayson Cody's woman. For Ivey Larue there was one man on earth for her.

Seeing Cody now, that expression on his face, loss close to the surface, Lash knew with no doubt there was one woman on earth for him.

The burn he'd been fighting anytime over the last day that he thought about what was done to them fired in his chest.

He beat it back when Cody turned and started walking their way. He caught sight of them and jerked up his chin.

Lash returned the gesture. Freddie probably did too.

You loved Ivey, you saw those two together, even for a second, they won you over. It was the simple matter of fact that, at a glance, you knew they belonged together.

That said, Lash had thought that it would take Cody some effort to win over Freddie who was arguably more protective of Ivey than Lash. An occupational hazard, he'd seen many men eyeing her, he'd warned others off, he'd stepped up for her frequently, he'd had her back for six years.

But he accepted Cody easily.

Lash knew what it was—that beaming, radiant smile.

Ivey was happy.

That was all it took.

Cody stopped at them. "Gotta get back to Mustang. Got shit to do. Ivey says you guys are leavin' tonight. She wants us all to have dinner. Know a place, I'll call for reservations." One side of his lips twitched and he said, "Warnin', won't be fancy."

"Food good?" Freddie asked and Cody looked at him.

"Yep."

"Works for me," Freddie muttered and both sides of Cody's lips twitched.

Then his amusement fled and his gaze slid between both Lash and Freddie.

"You got time before I leave, I need it. Shit you need to know."

Lash went alert as he felt Freddie do the same.

"Do we need privacy?" Lash asked and Cody studied him before he looked over his shoulder toward the pool.

His eyes came back to Lash and he nodded.

"Right, let's go," Lash murmured and led the way.

Conversation was scarce as they made their way to Lash's room. Inside, Lash took a seat in an armchair and rested his arms along its sides. Freddie took his place at a wall, shoulders to it, arms crossed on his chest, habit. It was a stance he assumed often when he was close to Ivey.

Cody stood in the room, muscled legs planted slightly wide, arms crossed on the wall of his chest.

Christ, Lash thought as he took him in. He'd noticed it but only in a vague way as other things took his attention. But, if this man lived his entire life in a small town or not, he was not someone to fuck with. Everything about him screamed it.

Which made Lash wonder why it was clear that for years someone had been fucking with him.

Then it hit him, Cody was a challenge.

He presented a challenge. Man like that with looks like that coupled with natural authority, easy confidence, a lesser man with a sick twist in his head would stew on that, want to take him down a peg.

Obsess about it.

Fuck.

"I can assume," Cody started, "you both are in the know 'bout all that went down, then and now."

"You'd assume correct," Lash replied. He'd briefed Freddie on the way to visit Cody the day before.

Cody nodded. "That shit you all did a day ago, that shit'll rile Bud Sharp."

"Not a surprise, dude," Freddie said. "Saw the guy, one glance, instant dick."

"Right," Cody replied, then, "You get that, you'll probably get that he had a focus. Now he has two."

Freddie and Lash had talked about this but having it confirmed made Freddie growl.

Lash sighed.

"Rue," Freddie grunted.

"Yeah," Cody confirmed. "I figure she's told you about our history. Somethin' that was probably throwaway to her was not throwaway to Bud and if you don't know about it, you need to know about it. Man hates me. He's been gunnin' for me since junior high. May have a lock on why but still don't get it."

He gave that a beat to settle in before he continued.

"But Ivey bested him at pool and when I say that, she made short work of makin' a fool of him. Worse, he was hopin' to get in her pants at the same time and he's not used to not gettin' what he wants. Whole thing lasted maybe half an hour. Still, he rounded up his boys to pay her hotel room a visit. What they intended to do, I have no clue. I'm not a man like that. Four men, one twenty-two-year-old girl, turns my stomach, but I could guess. She beat him in two games of pool and didn't respond to his flirtin'. Whatever four men could do to a lone girl in a hotel room is not fair payback for that, then again, it's not fair payback for anything."

He stopped talking, the air in the room was thick, and when neither Lash nor Freddie spoke, processing their own thoughts, Cody gave them time then he carried on.

"With you two, she bested him again a day ago and not a handful of people in a bar saw it. Probably by this point, everyone in two counties is talkin' about it. He is not the kinda guy who makes a lot of friends. Folks in Mustang, his home, especially are not real fond of him. They are eatin' this shit up. Janie's spreadin' what went down with Ivey and me and if Ivey had folks who didn't think much of her, what you all did a day ago and with Janie sharin' what went down, that's gonna change if it hasn't already. They're lovin' this and Buddy Sharp is gonna feel that and he isn't gonna like it."

Cody quit speaking, letting that sink in, then he went on, and when he did his voice got quieter and his tone made both Lash and Freddie—already alert and hyper-attentive—become acutely so.

"Last year, had a situation with my trees. Had to cut down and burn a quarter of my orchard." He took in a breath, clearly still pissed about this, then kept speaking. "They were diseased. Shit happens in my business, you roll with it. I was expanding operations anyway. Seein' as I had a bank loan to pay, planted a fuckload of trees two years before. Still, it'll take time for those to produce. But this disease hit the mature trees."

When he stopped, Lash said softly, "Sorry that happened, Cody," and Cody's eyes focused on him.

"Yeah, me too. Sucked. My granddad planted those trees."

Lash nodded.

Cody kept going.

"Weird part of that is no other orchard had this problem, and when I say this, not only no other orchard around Mustang but no other orchard in the entire fuckin' state of Colorado. That shit isn't unusual. It's impossible."

Fucking hell. This information ratcheted the danger level up about seven fucking notches.

Knowing it, Freddie pushed away from the wall and Lash leaned forward to put his elbows on his knees.

Cody kept speaking.

"There's an origin to that kinda shit and that kinda shit spreads. No origin could be traced because there was no other outbreak in the entire western half of the United States. And I caught it quick so it didn't spread."

"Someone diseased your trees," Lash guessed.

"Yeah," Cody answered. "And that's not all."

Fuck.

"What?" Lash prompted.

"Had a mare go down, sick, had to destroy her," Cody answered.

"Jesus Christ," Lash whispered, sitting back.

"Right," Cody replied. "That's tough. Again, shit happens and it's happened to me. Rare but it has. Two months later, had a stallion go down."

"Fuck me," Freddie muttered.

"Right," Cody repeated. "Now *that* shit has never happened to me. Talked to the vet, he investigated, stallion was poisoned. Stallion had the same symptoms as the mare. Fair guess, they both got slipped the same shit."

"Goddamn it," Lash clipped.

Killing horses, living beings.

Now the danger level ratcheted up about fourteen notches.

Fuck.

Cody kept on with his story. "No way I can afford a security system, so I rigged the doors to the barn with a shotgun, the blast aimed to wake me not take anyone out. Month later, that shotgun blasted."

"You see anyone?" Freddie asked.

"They got outta there quick, so no. And I have not had any more problems with my horses," Cody answered.

"Well, you sorted that," Lash muttered and Cody's eyes cut to him.

"No, I didn't. That shit stopped but this situation is not over. Can't patrol my land twenty-four seven, don't got eyes in the back of my head and it is clear someone is gunnin' for me. I don't have to reach real far to know who. And now, Ivey's movin' in."

"Fuckin' *shit*!" Freddie bit out and Cody looked to him.

"And she's movin' in," he stated firmly. "He's not gonna take more of her away from me. I don't know how but I been chewing on it now since Ivey and I had our thing yesterday. It's not a stretch to get that Buddy Sharp somehow found Casey Bailey and paid him to take Ivey away from me. I'm not an idiot. My trees, my horses, I reported it. Len and the Mustang Police Department know what's goin' down. They sniffed around and found nothin'. They're on the alert though." Cody looked at Lash. "But I want Casey."

Lash's brows went up. "You want Casey?"

Cody looked back to Lash. "He loves his sister. He's fucked up but he loves his sister. It isn't healthy but it's there. Sayin' that, these last years, she bailed on him, left him behind, took his car, he might be pissed and that love might have died. I do not give one fuck about that. He's gonna talk. He's gonna say who paid him, how much and what the play was. He owes that to Ivey and Ivey and I need to know, not only because we deserve to know but because, to fight the fight I got on my hands, I need all the information I can get. And you're gonna find him."

"Yes, I am," Lash said low.

Cody nodded. "Get on my feet, you keep track of what it costs, I'll pay."

"No, you won't," Lash told him.

"Man, this is my shit. Shits me but I need you. And I'll pay," Cody returned.

"Cody, this is your shit and it's also Ivey's. Do you not get by now we have her back and when I say that, I say that with *everything*?" Lash replied.

Cody held his eyes and reminded him quietly of something Ivey announced excitedly at breakfast, "She's movin' to Mustang."

"She told us that at breakfast, Cody, I remember," Lash said quietly back.

Cody explained his point, "She comes here, you lose her and all she is to you, your life, your club."

Lash shook his head and stood before he said softly, "You've been apart awhile but you know Ivey. You know her. She might be moving to Mustang but I'm not losing her and I never will."

Cody held his eyes then he tipped up his chin.

"I'll find Casey and I'll find out what went down," Lash told him.

"Right," Cody muttered and continued to hold Lash's gaze in order to communicate further without words being said.

Gratitude.

Lash took it then asked, "This private chat, this mean you want us to keep this shit from Ivey?"

Cody nodded again. "Yeah, but temporarily." He grinned. "She's all fired up to prove she's a badass, hard as nails ex-showgirl and do that by takin' on Buddy. She knows this shit, she'd lose her mind. She needs to sort her life with you, feel good about that, have time with you both." His gaze swept through Freddie then went back to Lash. "I want her to have that. She knows this, she'll hightail her ass to Mustang and let loose. I'll wait, give her this information when the time is right. She won't be kept in the dark forever, just for now."

"Understood and thank you," Lash said quietly.

Another chin jerk then Cody looked at Freddie and back to Lash. "Shit to do."

"Of course, see you at dinner," Lash muttered.

Another glance through both of them, another chin jerk then Grayson Cody strode to and out the door.

The minute it closed, Lash took a deep breath to calm the burn in his chest.

That done he turned to Freddie.

"Find me that motherfucker," he ordered quietly. "No stone unturned, Freddie, do not count the cost. And when he's found, I want him brought to me."

Freddie held his gaze for a long moment.

Then he grinned.

Then he shoved his hand in his pocket and got out his phone.

Chapter 28

Welcome Back to Mustang

T*hree and a half weeks later…*

To SAY I was freaking out when I drove my deep purple Lexus 250C up Gray's lane toward his farmhouse would be an understatement.

I was totally freaking out. The palms sweaty, heart fluttering, brain consumed with panic type of freaking out.

Three and a half weeks ago, Gray and I had our dinner with Lash and Freddie and afterward Gray talked me into going with them.

I didn't want to leave him.

"The sooner you get started on that, the sooner you're with me," he whispered to me in our bed in the hotel room in the dark.

I saw the wisdom of this and gave in.

So I had over seven years without Gray, just over a day with him, then off to Vegas I went to have another three and a half weeks without him.

This was no fun. Wrapping up my life in Vegas but most especially my life with Lash and Freddie in it was not a ball of laughs. And being separated from Gray didn't help.

But obviously, this separation was different. Mainly because Gray called at six thirty every morning, waking me up. He also called at eleven o'clock every night, right before he went to bed.

At first, these early morning calls troubled me. As crazy as it sounded, I wondered if he didn't trust me and he did it thinking he'd catch me in bed with Lash.

Then it hit me this wasn't it. This was when Gray started his day and he wanted to start his day with me.

And this hit me because on day three, he flat out told me then stated, "We got different schedules so if when I'm callin' don't work for you, dollface, and you want me to call at different times, say it. I'll stop what I'm doin' to say good morning or I'll wake up to say goodnight."

There you go.

He trusted me.

And he'd stop what he was doing to say good morning or wake up to say goodnight.

I liked that.

So obviously since I liked why he was calling at those times and what he said, I'd replied softly, "No, honey, I'll wake up with you when you start your day and I like being the last person you talk to before you go to sleep."

"Then that's what you'll get, baby," Gray replied softly back.

Of course, I also called him during the day when I had something to say, like telling him when I'd accomplished the task of boxing everything up. Then asking him when he'd be around to accept delivery. Then telling him when the movers were coming to get it and when he could expect them to arrive. Or telling him about a waitress we had who'd slept with two bartenders and three bouncers, was trying to pit them against each other and was working my last nerve (or I should say with this I called him to moan about it). Or telling him my joy at learning Lash had shared his secret with Freddie. Or just telling him I missed him, loved him and was thinking about him.

And every time I called him, Gray stopped what he was doing to take the call from me.

Yes, even when I moaned for half an hour about the waitress, he stopped what he was doing, listened like he had all day and pretended really well that he was interested in what I had to say.

On day four of our separation, while I was still sleepy and whispering to him, Gray introduced me to phone sex. Later, he'd tell me he'd never done it.

Obviously, I hadn't either.

Incidentally, Gray was a natural.

It wasn't better than the real thing but it would do in a pinch.

But now, most of my belongings were already at Gray's. I'd sold everything from my old house when I sold my old house and moved in with Lash. Thus, with my usual fastidious saving, considering I was a girl who once never knew where her next dollar was coming from and I didn't want to be that girl again, I had a wad to drop on sorting Gray's problems. So it was mostly just personal items. I had a couple of suitcases in my trunk. And I had my car.

And I had me.

I'd taken two days to drive to Colorado even though it was really just a one day haul, about ten hours. But Gray nor Lash *nor* Freddie would allow me to do this because they didn't want me to get tired. I explained I'd had ten years of driving long hauls with Casey and I was a current badass, ex-Vegas showgirl, so tough enough to haul my ass across two states in ten hours. This was clearly not enough evidence for them seeing as not a single one of the three believed I was a badass *or* tough so Gray decreed no more than seven hours the first day.

It killed me to be only three hours away from Gray in a hotel. But I saw the merits of this although they weren't the same merits Gray saw.

My merits were that after three hours of driving the next day, I'd still be refreshed when I got to him. Not to mention, before I left I had time to primp but there wasn't enough time in the car in the summer heat for the bloom to go off the rose.

Obviously, I drove with the top down. I mean, I had a kickass convertible, it was summer, I'd be crazy not to.

So two days it was.

But the overwhelming excitement of being back with Gray mixed with sadness of leaving behind Lash, Brutus and my life had now been replaced with panic.

We'd spent two and a half months together seven years ago. He was twenty-five, just twenty-six. I was twenty-two. We were young. What we had flamed fast and bloomed bright but we'd never lived together.

And a lot had happened in between.

I was worried this was a terrible mistake. I was worried that eventually the badass, hard as nails ex-Vegas showgirl that I totally was (no matter that anytime I said that to Gray, Lash *or* Brutus they laughed their asses off) would show through and he wouldn't like it. I worried we wouldn't get along.

I worried about everything.

And now I was here.

Shit.

His farmhouse in sight, I saw him come out the door. He was headed across the porch before I even got close. By the time I parked, he was down the steps, waiting for me.

Nope, even though it was only three and a half weeks, nothing had changed about him. Faded jeans, tight navy blue tee, head to toe beauty.

God, I hoped I didn't disappoint him.

I parked just beyond the porch so I didn't block his truck (and he had the same truck I was both horrified and gleeful to see). I barely had the ignition switched off before he was at my door.

I undid my seatbelt, twisted my neck, tipped back my head and smiled nervously at him from behind my shades.

Yep, nothing changed. Total beauty even through sunglasses.

"Hi," I whispered.

Then I squealed.

This was because Gray leaned over my door and plucked me right out of my convertible. I squealed again as he tossed me over his shoulder. With long, fast strides he rounded my car and headed to the porch.

I wrapped my fingers around his waist and cried, "Gray!"

He kept walking fast, up the porch steps across the porch.

"Gray! Put me down!" I snapped.

He didn't put me down. He kept going, into the house, straight to the stairs, muttering, "Jesus, top down, probably got third degree burns."

"I lived in Vegas for seven years, Gray," I told the small of his back, head and hair hanging. "I've been introduced to sunblock."

He ignored me and kept muttering, "My girl's got a purple car."

"It's tyrian gray," I stated, though that was the official color name, it was still totally purple.

"Whatever," he kept muttering, taking the stairs.

Taking the stairs.

Which meant going upstairs.

To his room.

My mouth got dry.

Up we went, down the hall then in his room, across it and I was flying through the air to land on my back in his bed.

I pushed up on my elbows, already breathing heavily, already turned on. I lifted a hand and pulled off my sunglasses. Then I stared at him standing by the bed staring at me.

His eyes moved down my body (cute black sundress, skintight, buttons all the way up the front, halter top and *fabulous* strappy black heels).

His gaze shot to my face and he whispered, "My girl's home."

My breath caught and my heart missed a beat.

Gray's hands went to his tee and I watched him pull it over his head, exposing his unbelievably amazing (still) chest.

That's when I started panting.

I scrambled to my knees, walked on them to the edge of the bed and my body hit Gray's. His back bowed, my head tipped way back, his arms sliced around me, my arms curved around him and his mouth hit mine.

Then his tongue drove in my mouth.

I whimpered in his.

His hand went under my hair and I felt it tug at the bow that held the straps of the halter top. He broke the kiss but demanded roughly against my lips, "Get this thing off, honey."

He let me go and, my eyes still locked with his, my hands went instantly to the buttons of my dress. His hands went to the belt of his jeans. It took effort, my fingers were shaking, but I undid buttons as did Gray. Then he got rid of his boots and socks. Then he got rid of his jeans and my hands stilled after releasing the last button that was mid-thigh.

Oh yes, I missed him. *All* of him.

Gray didn't hesitate and surged toward me.

I went to my back, he landed on top of me and his mouth took mine at the same time he spread the dress open like unveiling a present. His body came to mine and I felt his skin, his heat, his muscle against me, and I arched into him.

He broke the kiss, went to his knees straddling me and his hands went under my arms. He hauled me up the bed and away went my panties. He spread my legs wide, dropped between them and suddenly his mouth was on me.

My knees cocked, my hips surged up, my heels digging in the bed and my fingers drove into his thick hair.

Oh God, yes.

Oh God, *yes*.

"Gray," I breathed.

I loved it when he did this, *loved it*. Seven years ago, three and a half weeks ago, I loved it.

His hand went between my legs, fingers gently spreading me open as his tongue lashed then his mouth sucked deep.

"*Gray*," I breathed, it came out deep, throaty, mainly because a half second after I said his name he made me come.

Still feeling it, I lost his mouth. My eyes dazedly opened as I felt the backs of my knees hooked around his arms and his hands were on my hips dragging me up his thighs.

Then he was inside me, pounding deep.

Still feeling it but coming down, I watched him watch me as he thrust into me, my body jerking with each thrust, his eyes burning, his handsome face turned on, his fingers digging into my hips yanking me to him as his hips drove into me.

My legs and torso moved, tensing, lifting. I wanted to go to him, touch him, fold into him, kiss him, but he buried himself deep, started grinding and growled his order of, "Lay still, Ivey. Your hair all over my bed, your body *in* my bed and me in you, I wanna see."

My legs tensed into his arms automatically as another shot of heat penetrated me at his words and I whispered, "Okay," and relaxed back.

Then I watched my man fucking me.

And I liked watching.

Oh God, this was *hot*.

"Fingers between your legs, baby," Gray muttered low, his voice thick.

I did as I was told and once I did, my neck arched, my head pushing back into the bed and my eyes closed.

Yeah, this was hot.

"Ivey, look at me," Gray rumbled and it took effort. I liked this. I liked being in his room, his bed, open to him, feeling him driving inside me, knowing he was watching me touching myself as he fucked me. I liked it a lot.

But for him, I gave him my eyes and a full body shiver trembled through me at the hot, dark look on his face.

He must have liked what he saw too because his fingers dug further into my flesh and he pulled me harder into him, plunging faster and deeper into me.

Oh God, oh yes. Oh God, oh *yes*.

This was *hot*.

"*Gray*," I gasped then I came again, harder, stronger, overwhelming. So much I didn't feel his arms leave my knees or his weight hit me or his face bury itself in my neck until I started coming down.

My arms and legs circled him then his hips started bucking in a way I knew.

"Honey, give it to me," I breathed, his head came up, his hips drove deep, he stayed planted and I watched as he gave it to me.

When he finished his face went back into my neck. One of my legs slid down to curl around his thigh, the other one slid from around him, sole of my foot to the bed but I pressed my inner thigh to his hip. My hands moved along the contours of his back, feeling his skin, his muscle, his heat and memorizing it as I did his weight, his cock still inside me, his smell.

God, he smelled good. I forgot that. He smelled like outdoors and man.

He moved his head, his lips came to my ear and he whispered, "Welcome back to Mustang, dollface."

I blinked at the ceiling. Then I burst out laughing.

His head came up and his grinning eyes came to me and, lucky for me, his lips were grinning too so I also got the dimple.

I controlled my hilarity and remarked, "I hope you're not Mustang's welcome wagon, honey, and that was all just for me."

His grin slightly faded, his head dropped and his lips touched mine before he pulled back and said quietly, "It's all for you, Ivey."

All for me. All of him was all for me.

I sighed.

Then I smiled.

Gray's eyes took in my smile before they moved to mine and he ordered gently, "Say you love me, Ivey."

My body eased under his and I whispered, "I love you, Gray."

"Welcome home, dollface."

My hand moved to cup his jaw as my lips whispered, "Thank you, baby."

His gaze got lazy before he gave me the dimple again.

SIX HOURS LATER…

MAKEUP REFRESHED, a spritz of perfume, having run my fingers through my hair, re-donning my fitted, fabulous black halter-top sundress and strappy, spiked-heeled black sandals, my hand in Gray's, we were walking across the porch.

And I was trying not to hyperventilate.

Because it was Friday.

And being Friday, we were heading to his truck to go to town for VFW steaks.

I was not ready for this.

Not at all.

"Maybe I should change," I suggested as Gray walked us down the porch steps.

"You look beautiful, darlin'," Gray replied on a hand squeeze, leading me around the porch and toward his truck.

The rusted out wreck grew closer and closer as my anxiety grew more and more.

"I have a lot of unpacking to do. Maybe I should get started on that," I tried.

"Ivey, you don't have a job. You have plenty of time to unpack," Gray pointed out, walking me to the passenger side of his truck.

Okay, shit.

Okay, *shit*.

I didn't want to face down Mustang, not now. They knew I was a burlesque dancer. They knew I was shacked up with a hotshot who they would never know was gay. These people went to church. They lived in a small town. They were not hardened, seen it all, done it all residents of Vegas.

They would think things about me.

They *already* thought things about me.

I knew it.

I could handle this if I had time to prepare. But a day full of having sex with Gray broken up to eat turkey and Swiss sandwiches and have whispered conversations as we lay naked in his bed, fingers trailing, bodies seeking and gaining contact, legs tangling, lips brushing, did not prepare me for dinner at the VFW where most everyone in the town of Mustang would be.

Shit.

Gray stopped me at the passenger side door of his truck, pulled it open and it creaked loudly. My thoughts of everyone in Mustang judging me fled and my eyes shot down to the door.

A smile slowly rose on my lips.

"Get in, honey," Gray muttered and I looked up at him.

"Same truck?" I asked softly and he focused on me.

Then he grinned.

God, that grin. All the shit that went down, it still came easy.

"It runs, so yeah," he answered.

"How much do you have to work on it to make it run?" I asked.

"Dollface, it's American made so not much."

He was totally lying. This thing was still running on a wing and a prayer.

Whatever.

"It's twenty years old, Gray," I told him.

"It's fifteen years old, Ivey."

I felt my brows draw together and I asked, "Is it?"

His lips twitched and he answered, "Yeah."

"Looks older," I muttered.

"Get in, Ivey."

"Way older."

"Get in, Ivey."

"Way, *way* older."

Gray burst out laughing, hooked an arm around my waist, pulled me into his body and kissed me, hard and closed mouthed.

He lifted his head and ordered, "Get...*in*, Ivey."

"All right, all right," I muttered, turned and climbed in.

The door creaked loudly when Gray slammed it.

I smiled again as I looked around the interior.

Candy bar wrappers. Gum wrappers. Chip bags. Receipts. Empty pop cans. The ashtray open and filled to overflowing with change that had fallen down and therefore was also on the floor.

Gray's door creaked loudly, he angled in then it creaked loudly again as he slammed it.

He'd fired the old girl up, reversed and we were on our way down the lane when I queried, "Have you tidied the old girl up since I left?"

"The old girl?"

"Your truck."

"Right," he muttered, I looked at his profile to see he was grinning. Then he answered, "Probably."

"By the looks of it, I'm not sure you're telling me the truth."

Gray glanced at me then back out the windshield before he replied, "Ivey, I'm a guy. This is a truck. It's not a new truck. It's not even a five-year-old truck. It's a fifteen-year-old truck. I don't *tidy* anything and definitely not a fifteen-year-old truck."

"Now you'll often have a classy albeit ex-showgirl in your truck Gray," I reminded him.

"Good, so you can tidy it," Gray replied and I giggled.

I looked out the windshield as Gray turned us on the road to Mustang. "So, if you don't tidy anything, are you saying that even with Mrs. Cody gone, Macy still comes to clean your house?"

"Yep, every two weeks."

"That's weird, Gray," I noted softly.

"Why?"

"Well, you're a grown man and you have use of all four limbs, ten fingers, ten toes. Not to mention, your uncles are assholes and she's married to one of them."

"Yeah, they are. But they don't come and clean my house. Macy's not an asshole. Macy also knows I planted a shitload of trees two years ago, adopted more horses and had a fuckload of problems. So I've been busy and one of the things I don't have to get busy doin' is cleanin' my house. It's cool she does it and I'm grateful. Though," I turned my head to see he'd done the same to glance at me grinning before his eyes went back to the road, "she doesn't leave flowers anymore."

"Well, at least there's that," I muttered and Gray chuckled.

"By the way," I began to note after he quit chuckling, "you leave your ashtray open like that with change in it, you're practically begging for someone to break into this wreck."

"They wanna make that kinda effort for four some odd dollars of change, they can have it."

There you go.

We fell silent as the old girl's wheels took us closer to Mustang.

Shit.

As if sensing my thoughts went back to my worries, Gray said gently, "No one thinks bad things about you, baby."

Right.

"Gray, you wouldn't know. If they did, they wouldn't tell you. But I'll feel it."

"They know we got played and they know what you did for me, for Gran, no one thinks shit about you."

We would see.

I didn't reply.

When I didn't, Gray ordered, "Give me your hand, Ivey."

I looked to him to see he had an arm extended to me, palm up. I put my hand in his and his fingers closed around tight.

Then he whispered, "No one thinks shit. They did, you think I'd put you in my truck and take you to town?"

He had a point there.

"No," I said quietly.

"Then relax."

I drew in breath.

Then I said, "Okay."

His hand gave me a squeeze and he repeated my, "Okay."

We drove to town, Gray holding my hand between us on the bench seat and me trying to be calm. The Gray I knew seven years ago would never make me endure something unpleasant. And, as far as I could tell, the Gray of now would be the same.

He parked, our doors creaked, we got out and Gray came around my side to claim me. He did this by sliding an arm around my shoulders and pointing me to the front doors of the VFW lodge. I slid my arm around his waist and let it pour over me, walking again with Gray, tucked to his side close, his arm around me.

Behind those doors might be good people who nevertheless held judgmental thoughts about me.

But I had Gray.

I'd be okay.

Gray pushed through the doors taking me with him.

Seven years hadn't changed this either. The long tables with their benches were packed. Conversation hummed through the large space. And the smell of steak was in the air.

We took two steps in, me in my expensive dress and shoes, Gray in his jeans and tee.

Eyes came to us.

I should have changed. I was *way* overdressed.

More eyes came to us.

I definitely should have changed.

More eyes and conversation started dimming.

No greetings were called out to Gray as he led me down the aisle between the two sides of tables and it dawned on me maybe I *couldn't* do this.

We hit a table where there were empty spaces across from each other three folks in, and Gray stopped me. But by this point the lodge was silent and I knew all eyes were on me.

I didn't have my heavy makeup, my sequins or a spotlight to hide behind.

No, I couldn't do this.

Gray's arm tensed around my shoulders, my head started to tip back as my body curled close to his so I could whisper to him I wanted to leave when it happened.

Someone started clapping.

I turned my head in that direction and I saw Sonny walking down the aisle toward us, his hands smacking against each other, the sound booming loud in the silence of the space and an intense expression on his face.

What on earth?

Someone else started clapping and I whipped my head around to see Janie's man Danny was doing it and as my gaze hit him he rose to his feet.

Someone else started clapping and my attention again turned to see Barry and Gene both rising from their seats, their gazes on me, their faces split in grins, their hands cracking together.

Another someone started clapping. Then another. And another. Suddenly everyone around us was getting to their feet, clapping, hooting, catcalling and someone shouted, "*Way to go, Ivey!*"

What on earth?

All of a sudden, I was no longer held in the curve of Gray's arm but tugged into a tight embrace, iron bands clamped around me and in my ear a man whispered, "Saved Mirry, saved Gray, saved Mustang. Welcome home, Ivey."

I pulled my head back and saw Sonny had hold of me.

I stared in his still intense eyes as his arms gave me a tight squeeze and he said again, "Welcome home."

That was when me, tough, badass, hard as nails ex-Vegas showgirl Ivey Larue burst out crying.

Publically.

Okay, evidence was suggesting that maybe Gray, Lash and Brutus were right. I wasn't all that hard. Instead, I was a big softie.

Shit.

The iron bands released but I was shuffled into Gray's embrace as everyone kept cheering.

For me.

I shoved my face in his chest and kept crying.

Gray's body moved so his lips were at my ear where he muttered, "Told you they don't think shit about you. Or, at least, not bad shit."

"Shut up!" I snapped, this muffled by his tee since I snapped into it then my body jerked with a sob.

"Pipe down! Pipe down! You don't shut up, I can't get their orders and feed Ivey." I heard Sonny shout.

My body was again shuffled and I heard Gray ask, "Can you shift? I want my girl sittin' at my side."

"No problem, Gray," someone answered as the applause started to die then Gray came back to me.

"Dollface, you wanna unplant your face from my chest so we can sit down and eat?"

"Not really," I told his chest.

"Honey—"

"I have a feeling my makeup is messed up."

"First, they got a bathroom. Second, I don't think you get it that these folks don't give a shit. You're Ivey. You saved my ass. You saved my land. We got ripped apart and now we're back together. And, bottom line, they like you."

This appeared to be true on all counts. A standing ovation was hard to deny.

I shoved my hands up between us and swiped at my cheeks hoping I wasn't doing more damage.

I tipped my head back and looked at Gray.

"Well?" I asked.

"Bathroom's at the front, off to your right," he answered.

Great. He gave that answer and he barely had to look.

He grinned and dipped his head to touch his mouth to mine.

He shouldn't have done that. He really, really shouldn't have.

Because when he did, the whole lodge again went crazy.

Great.

He lifted his head no longer grinning but smiling huge. I rolled my eyes, dashed my hand across my cheeks and pulled at his arms.

Gray let me go.

I walked to the bathroom lamely giving out waves to people who were clapping and shouting after me.

I hit the bathroom and tried to repair the damage.

And as I did, I stared into the mirror and saw Gray, Lash and Freddie were right.

There was no hard behind my eyes, no hard around my mouth.

I just looked happy.

"Welcome back to Mustang, Ivey," I whispered to the mirror.

I grinned.

Then I went to go eat a fantastic steak.

An hour and a half later...

Gray's arm around me, mine around him, he was walking me up the sidewalk toward The Rambler.

Three feet from the door I came to a dead halt in a way that Gray had no choice but to stop with me.

I looked up at him. "Okay, I could do the VFW, I can't do this."

Gray turned into me and curled his other arm around me.

"Honey, Janie can't get away from the bar and she wants to see you. She feels shit for some things she said. You gotta give her that."

I shook my head. "It's not that."

His eyes held mine. "Then what is it?"

I pressed my lips together and looked to the door of The Rambler before turning my eyes back to Gray.

Then I whispered, "I was happy there."

He closed his eyes.

I sucked in a deep breath.

Gray opened his eyes and his arms gave me a squeeze. "Ivey—"

"And not only that, but this is...the VFW and now this. It's our first date, Gray."

"I know that, Ivey," he replied instantly. So instantly, I blinked.

That was why we were here. Why he pushed me to go to the VFW. Why we were going to The Rambler.

He was giving me our first date again.

Oh my God.

How sweet was that!

"Gray," I murmured, again feeling overwhelmed, this time in a good way, and he gave me another one of his grins.

"No shittin' you, dollface, I could have started our first date with you naked in my bed for hours, I woulda taken that. I could have that date knowin' you'd end it in my bed, I'd take that too. That was the best date I ever had, but, gotta say, this one's better."

I stared at him a beat before I burst out laughing.

His arms gave me another squeeze and when I sobered I saw him smiling down at me.

"Come on, Janie's waitin'," he said gently.

I nodded, he let me go with one arm and turned me to the bar.

We entered and I braced. The applause was awesome and I liked it, I liked why I got it, but I didn't want to go through it again.

I didn't.

Barry and Gene had transferred their asses from the benches at the VFW to their seats at Janie's. Peg was at the bar as usual. It was Friday so the crowd was not heavy but it wasn't light. And Janie was behind the bar.

Yep, God liked her. Seven years and she still looked great.

I saw her mouth move saying my name but I didn't hear it. Then she moved to the near end of the bar.

Gray walked us toward her as Peg called out, "Hey, Ivey," like the last time I saw her was yesterday.

I smiled at Peg. "Hey, Peg."

She grinned semi-drunkenly back. It was early. She wasn't sloshed. Not yet.

Jeez. Peg.

Well, at least she hadn't died of liver damage.

I turned again to see Janie had cleared the bar and she was coming at me, smiling tentatively.

"Hey, Janie," I said and her smile got bigger before it wobbled.

God, I hoped she didn't cry. I didn't have much makeup left. If she cried, I would and another bout would take the rest.

She made it to me and folded her arms around me.

I returned the favor.

I'd never hugged her and now I had proof that her breasts weren't fake.

"Hey, Ivey," she whispered.

My arms went tighter.

So did hers.

Neither of us moved.

Then her arms got tighter, her head turned and in my ear she started, "Years ago, I hung up on you when you were tryin' to find Gray. And a month ago, I said some—"

"Don't," I cut her off and pulled my head back, keeping my arms around her and finding her eyes. Her head went back too. "It's over. I get it. You do too. Don't." I grinned. "That's done. Everyone's moving on. I'm home."

She studied me carefully, eyes moving over my face, they flicked up to Gray then back to me where she grinned and asked, "Wanna job?"

I started laughing.

She smiled bigger but she stated, "No joke, wanna job?"

I stopped laughing and stared at her.

She *wasn't* joking.

Wow.

Could I go back to work at The Rambler after wearing thousands of dollars of dresses, jewelry and shoes every night at Lash's club for years?

I didn't know.

"Can I have a couple of weeks to settle in and think about it?"

"You can but job might not be there because, seriously, I need some help. But you think and even if that job goes, I'm sure you'll find where you wanna be. It seems to happen that way, you hit Mustang."

"Experienced that," I muttered and she smiled again.

"Two beers, Janie," Gray ordered, moving in to claim me. When he had me at his side with an arm around me, he went on, "Me and Ivey're gonna play some pool."

"You got it, Gray," she murmured and grinned at me.

I grinned back and Gray turned me to the pool tables.

He got the balls while I got the cues.

This felt weird, this felt good and this felt sad.

I decided to focus on the former two.

Gray racked the balls. I gave him a cue. Janie brought our beers.

"Flip to break?" I asked.

"What's the point?" he asked back.

I grinned and walked to the head of the table, leaned over and set my cue to the ball.

"Go easy on me, dollface," Gray called and just my eyes tipped up to him.

"Not a chance."

He smiled.

I looked at the table and let fly.

Balls scattered, two went down.

I hadn't lost my touch.

Good to know.

Seven hours later…

I woke tucked in the curve of Gray's body, his arm around me.

I didn't know what time it was. I just knew, after Gray took me home, we had sex, and after, he cuddled into me in order to go to sleep at a time when it was way earlier than I was used to going to sleep. Lash and I didn't hit his ivory sheets until two or three in the morning nearly every night.

It took me a while to find sleep but now I was awake like I could face the day.

It would take a while to get used to this.

But now, I had an idea and, lying there wide awake, I decided I was going to go with it.

I carefully slid out from under Gray's arm only for it to tighten and bring me back.

"Where you goin'?" he rumbled in a sleepy growl.

Oh yes, I liked that. The growl and that he didn't want to let go of me.

I liked them both.

A lot.

"Bathroom," I lied. "Be back." That wasn't a lie.

He let me go.

I slid out of bed.

Then I moved through the house. Curtains open everywhere, moonlight shining in lighting my way. There was no one around to look through those windows, no need to shut the drapes.

For some bizarre reason, I liked that too.

I hurried down the hall and found my boxes in the guest bedroom. Then I searched for the box I wanted. As quietly as I could, I opened it and dug through it until I got to what I was looking for.

I did what I had to do and walked back to Gray's room.

The sheets were up to his waist, he was still on his side, his exposed back to me.

I put a knee to the bed and trailed the tips of my red, feathered fan down his back.

Immediately, he rolled to that back and just as swiftly, in my shocking pink sequined panties and nothing else, I flipped a fan open to cover my top and threw a leg over him to straddle his hips.

"Jesus," he muttered, voice already thick.

I grinned, not outside. Inside.

"You wanna turn on the light and make this multisensory?" I asked quietly.

"Darlin', only person in this room who's gonna move for the next half hour is you. I'd like to see you try to turn on the light and hide from me."

I could do that, totally. I was a master of the feathered fan. It had been years since I danced but you didn't forget that kind of thing.

"Half an hour?" I asked.

"Yeah."

"Gray, my dances lasted five minutes."

"Private ones go on awhile."

He had an answer for everything.

He also wasn't done.

"And, five minutes in, you lose the fans."

That time I grinned on the outside.

Then I moved and turned on the light.

Gray moved too, to wrap his fingers around the sequined panties at my ass.

I bent toward him, fan spread wide between us and whispered, "You're not allowed to touch the talent, baby."

His fingers dug in as he did an ab curl and went up to sitting. I moved back with him and held the fan between us.

But I got a good look at his face and, getting it, I also got a good quiver somewhere in me.

His hands moved up my back and he answered, "Fuck that."

"I thought you said I was the only one going to move," I reminded him.

"Changed my mind," he muttered, one hand still sliding up my back, one hand going back down to slide in my panties.

Oh yes.

"Honey, I can't move my fan, there isn't enough room," I pointed out.

The hand heading up disappeared then the fan did when he jerked it out from between us.

"Gray!" I snapped but it came out breathy.

He moved and I was on my back on the fan spread out under me on Gray's bed and Gray was on me.

"You're ruining my performance, you know," I informed him.

"Now, why don't I believe that?" he asked me but didn't wait for me to answer.

He kissed me.

Then he did other stuff to me. I did stuff to him. And we did stuff together.

Incidentally, for Gray, it wasn't about the fans.

It was about the panties.

Important information to have.

An hour later, my fans and panties on the floor, my body tucked back into Gray, I didn't have even a little trouble falling asleep.

Chapter 29

Green Acres

T*hree days later…*

"Gray—"

"Ivey."

"Gray!"

"Ivey."

We were having our first fight. Our first fight *ever*.

Three days I was in Mustang living with Gray and we were fighting.

This sucked and it sucked mostly because Gray was being proud and stubborn and wouldn't *listen to me*.

I learned a lot about Gray in the last three days, mainly that I didn't pay much attention to Gray in the two and a half months I'd had him before. I was so engrossed in starting my new life I didn't pay any mind to his.

And there was a reason he started his day at six thirty. In actuality, he got up at five thirty which was pure *hell* and totally *insane*. But he was so used to it "sleeping in" (which he did on Sunday) meant he rolled us (yes, I said *us*) out of bed at seven and this was *after* we'd made love.

And the reason Gray started his day so early was that, apparently, being a macho man rancher cowboy that had a huge amount of land, horses and peach trees was a lot of work.

For instance, the horses needed to be fed, watered and exercised and their stalls mucked out. This would be a lot, actually too much, for the twelve horses he had when I knew him seven years ago. But in an attempt to cover the loan, which he got to cover Grandma Miriam's stay in a swanky retirement home, he adopted more horses three years running.

Now he had twenty.

That was a lot of horses.

Mostly they just stood there blinking but they did require water and sustenance to survive and didn't have the means to feed themselves and no one deserved to hang out in a space covered in excrement, so they also required a lot of work.

And so did the land.

I would come to understand that peach trees didn't just bear fruit you picked come peach season and a big old ranch couldn't just sit there and look pretty. All of this took maintenance.

The grasses had to be mowed and this wasn't just the patch of lawn around the house. This included the area by the lane running up to the house (which was a long way), the area by the road to Mustang (which was a long way) and the area around the peach trees and outbuildings (which were big areas). Then of course, there was the patch of lawn around the house.

There were also fences that needed to be run to make sure they were in good repair seeing as Jeb Sharp owned livestock and, although he had fences too, Gray told me, "Shit happens and it's happened." Gray didn't want any of Jeb's cattle on his land so both tended their own fences. Not to mention Gray rode the land and inspected the trees often in order to exercise the horses, make sure there were no poachers or squatters and that the peach trees were doing whatever they had to do.

Then the outbuildings needed to be kept in good repair, so did the tractors and mowers.

You also had to go into town and buy and haul back feed and hay for the horses, stuff for the trees, shit like that.

Some of this he told me, some of it I saw him do. Although it was a lot of work, one could not say that watching Gray on a horse or driving the ginormous tractor with the thingie on the back that cut grass, the back of his tee stained with sweat, a tattered baseball cap on his head and his tanned-brown arms glistening in the sun was not engrossing.

It was.

Very.

As I knew years ago I would never get used to his beauty, I knew then I would never get tired of watching Gray work his land.

Ever.

That said, it was clearly a lot of work.

So much Gray worked part of the day Saturday but he took off Sunday then worked all day Monday from six thirty to quitting at five.

Flat out (except for lunch).

Ten hours.

Jeez.

Even before I knew this, we talked on Saturday morning as I'd broached the subject that I was there, unemployed and I could help. Unfortunately, I had suitcases and boxes full of designer clothes and high-heeled shoes and you couldn't muck out a horse stall in Christian Louboutins. Or you could but you'd be an idiot. So I missed helping out on Saturday seeing as I didn't have the proper gear.

Though Gray did teach me how to feed and water the horses which wasn't very taxing except you had to remember which horse was which since he had eight mares in foal and they needed different food than the others.

But you still couldn't do it in high heels.

Therefore we took a trip to Hayes department store in town on Saturday afternoon so I could stock up on durable western wear. We moved on to a big, somewhat frightening and rickety tin building on the outskirts of Mustang so Gray could stock up on horse food.

Monday morning, wearing my new duds, I gamely followed Gray to the barn, mucked out one stall and decided it was definitely *not* for me. Serious visions of *Green Acres* except Gray was never an attorney who gave up the big city to force me into a life of torture on the farm.

Luckily, Gray thought this was funny and I knew this when he roared with laughter like I was hilarious before his gloved hand hooked me around the neck and he tugged me to him for a hard kiss, which was still hard even though he laughed through it.

After the kiss, he let me off the hook.

His roar of laughter had some to do with me clearly not wishing to spend my days shoveling horseshit but it had more to do with me faking being taken over by the spirit of Eva Gabor.

So I went into the house, cleaned it, did laundry, unpacked the rest of my stuff and made sure he had a good lunch and dinner, activities that took most of the day.

Lash had taken over my cooking lessons, so now I had a full repertoire. Though Lash didn't make casseroles and I wasn't sure how Gray would feel about me making lobster thermidor. But I could do a sandwich and I did—a big, grilled, delicious one at that.

After lunch, Gray went out to do macho man rancher cowboy things. I did a quick inspection of the cupboards and took a not-so-quick trip into town to buy groceries. This meant I could make him my fabulous, homemade beef Stroganoff for dinner.

Dirty plates still on the table and us sitting around it finishing our beers, Gray complimented me on the culinary strides I'd made since he last ate my food.

I then decided we needed to get down to the nitty gritty of life.

So we started talking about money.

This was a bad idea. Very, very bad.

Not, surprisingly, when I told Gray that I was living with him and I wanted to kick in, not only finding something that didn't involve horseshit to help out, but also financially. I didn't entirely wipe out my savings (though it was vastly depleted) and I had a healthy checking account so I wasn't destitute. I could help. I could also find a job.

Gray easily agreed to me being responsible for getting and paying for food and household items. I agreed he'd pay household bills. And the ranch account would pay for things for the ranch (like horse food).

That part was easy.

No, what got us into a sticky situation was Gray being honest about his finances in so far as telling me when he recently was looking to raise money to keep afloat, he sold four horses (that meant he'd had twenty-four!) but that was not what riled me.

He told me he also sold some furniture from the house and was looking to sell more.

Now that...

That semi-riled me.

And it got worse because somehow we veered from talking about him selling stuff in the house to his uncles and they...

Well, they would rile anyone.

It was just that they *really* riled me.

It went like this.

"You sold stuff from the house?"

That was me sounding horrified and mentally inventorying my

memory of the place from seven years ago to see if I could figure out what might be missing.

"Yeah."

That was Gray, nonchalant like everything in his house wasn't a treasure, which it *was*.

"Why did you do that?" I asked gently and his head tipped slightly to the side.

"Uh...because I was flat broke, losing my land and my gran was being moved to a state-funded nursing home."

These were all good reasons that in my horror at learning this news I didn't consider.

But still.

"Gray, this house, it's like, like...a museum of Cody history," I told him quietly and carefully.

"Ivey, this house was on the verge of not being Cody anything."

Another good point.

Gray kept going.

"I had a foreclosure notice. I was goin' down. If I sold the horses, all of them, I'd significantly decrease my ability to make money should I save the land. But it didn't look like I was going to be able to save the land and I still needed money to survive, to eat, to put a roof over my head while I figured out what I was gonna do with the rest of my life, so shit had to go. This place is full of junk. I sold three pieces, they made me seven grand. Three fuckin' pieces and I got seven grand. And I never liked the look of 'em anyway. Those pieces and those four horses, with you paying the loan current and beyond for a year and lookin' after Gran, I'm liquid again. Money in the bank and I can build on our future. So, when you were back in Vegas, I had the guys at the auction house take a walk through and they think they can find private buyers for five more pieces."

Oh dear Lord.

My eyes got big. "*Five?*"

"Yeah," Gray replied, entirely unaffected about selling off Cody history. "And they think they can take other shit off my hands. They say the private sales could be fifteen or twenty K and if they auction the stuff they're eyeballin', I could get another three to five more."

Oh God.

If he kept going, the house would be barren and not charming anymore.

On that thought, I muttered, "Maybe I should take that job with Janie."

"No," Gray returned firmly. "Maybe you should do what you said you were gonna do. Settle. Get used to a new life and take your time to land where you wanna land."

"I liked working there," I reminded him.

"Yeah, seven years ago before you became a Vegas showgirl then ended up the fake girlfriend of a millionaire," he reminded me. "Ivey, honey, three days ago, you didn't even own a pair of tennis shoes. Now you're sayin' you're gonna shuffle drinks for below minimum wage and small town tips?"

Yet another good point, which I was beginning to find annoying.

I decided to be calm, rational and slightly emotionally manipulative.

"Honey," I said softly, "I like the house the way it is."

"Baby," Gray said softly back, "I'm glad but that shit's gonna go and, trust me, you won't miss it."

There you go. Emotional manipulation didn't work with a cowboy.

"Do you need money that badly?" I asked cautiously.

"We're good for a while but there's nothin' more comin' in until the crop comes in and those mares drop their foals and they can be sold, which is near to a year away. So, yeah. I sell seventeen thousand dollars worth of crap, no. I do that, we breathe easy."

This was where the conversation veered to his uncles and yes, it was me who veered it that way.

And I did this by deciding, "Then you need to talk to your uncles."

Gray sat back in his chair. "Say again?"

"You need money, they need to give it to you."

"Ivey, that's not gonna happen."

"Why, because they're assholes?"

"That and I wouldn't take a dime from any of them."

"Gray—"

"Seriously, Ivey, don't go there."

It seemed I was not treading as cautiously as I thought and it hit me then that this was really none of my business.

"You're right. It's none of my business. It's your house, your land, your money. I shouldn't have mentioned it."

I said it in a conciliatory manner, clearly backing down but, again, it was the wrong thing to say and I knew it instantly when Gray's eyes narrowed and the room filled with his pissed-off vibe.

"My house, my land, my money?" he asked quietly but not his soft, sweet quietly. A different quietly. A ticked-off quietly.

I didn't get it.

"Well, yeah."

"You sleep in this house?" he asked.

"Well, yeah," I repeated.

"Go to the grocery store and come back home, a home that's on this land?"

I saw where he was going.

"Yes, Gray, but—"

"Turn on the burner to the stove that's gas, gas paid for by my money?"

I leaned toward him. "Gray—"

"You're here, Ivey, you're my girl, this is where you're gonna stay. This is your home, your land, what's mine is yours, all of it, including my money, what there is of it. You're sittin' at this table after eatin' dinner here for the third night in a row but your ass *should* have been sittin' right there every night for seven years. Unfortunately, that shit starts now and didn't start then. You'll find your way in Mustang whatever that way's gonna be. You don't wanna muck out stalls, you don't have to. Like I said, you'll find what suits you in Mustang but also here, in this house, on this land… with *me*."

"Okay," I said softly.

"Okay," he replied, still ticked off and I partially got it because I should have been sitting at that table with him for seven years and I felt that loss as acutely as he did.

But I didn't get all of it.

So, tentatively, I started to ask, "So, uh…what you're saying is I have a place here—"

Gray, still pissed, cut me off, "Yeah. That's what I'm sayin'."

"I wasn't done, honey."

He stared at me.

Something new, Gray could get grouchy after a day of working hard as a rancher cowboy.

I tried again. "What I was saying is that you obviously want me to feel comfortable here…with *you*, so why can't I go there with your uncles?"

It was then I could tell that *I* had a point this time and Gray, too, found it annoying.

"They should help protect their legacy," I told him.

"It's no longer their legacy. They carry the Cody name but they are not part of this land. They made that point sittin' on their hands watching me drown. They drew that line. I'm not drownin' anymore. They still stay to their side."

"Right, I get that but what about Mrs. Cody?"

His brows drew together. "What?"

"Your gran, Gray. How long has she been in that home?"

"Four and a half years."

"Then, say you take responsibility for your share, which obviously you'd want to do, at three quarters of her home fees for as long as she's been in there, they owe you two hundred and seventy K, which means each one of them owes you ninety."

"No they don't."

"Gray, yes they do."

"They don't have anything to do with that either," Gray stated.

"How's that?"

"They made that choice too."

"Gray, they don't get a choice with that. She's their mother."

"Yeah, a mother, when I asked him to kick in, that Frank reminded me about half a dozen times in the last four and a half years was a mother who held a grudge and didn't speak to him since that shit went down after Dad died. His mom ignored him for years, he didn't feel like ponying up to keep her in a clean place she likes that has good food and staff who like to work there and the residents get the benefit of that. The other two agreed."

"My point is still valid, he doesn't get that choice."

"Funny since he took it."

Now I was getting mad.

"Sorry, but them trying to horn in on your inheritance, land they hadn't worked since they were eighteen, and Mrs. Cody being justifiably pissed about that is not grounds for them to turn their back on their mother in her final years," I snapped.

"Ivey, honey, they don't see it that way."

"Well then someone has to *make* them see it that way and if you aren't going to do it, that someone is going to be me."

"Ivey—"

"No." I shook my head, leaning in, now definitely mad. "No, Gray no. All my life I wanted two things, just two...a home and a family. They were fortunate to be born in a good one of both and they've shit on both and that is *not* right. That shit does *not* play. And I'm going to The Alibi and explaining these things."

His ticked off vibe disintegrated and his face was near to tender when he said softly, "I get you, dollface, but you aren't gonna get anywhere and I don't *want* you to get anywhere. We're solid. Fuck them."

"No, they aren't going to get away with that shit."

"You're not going there, Ivey."

"I am, Gray."

"You aren't, Ivey."

"I am, Gray!" I snapped. "They sat back and watched you drown. That is not cool in and of itself. Family legacy or not, you're just plain family and they should look out for you. But the fact is, you were drowning *because* you were taking care of *their* mother and that is absolutely, one hundred percent *not right*. They owe you ninety grand each and I'm gonna get it."

"You won't go to The Alibi because it's a waste of time. I won't take their money," he returned.

"That's okay because I will."

His ticked off vibe came back before he said, "You won't, Ivey. Shit's fine now. I'm taken care of and so is Gran, you've seen to that. You've done enough. I don't need them."

"It'll be a lot more fine when you have two hundred and seventy K in the bank. So fine, I bet you can use that money to pay off the note in full and get out from under that weight. And, by the way," I added, "if, God willing, Mrs. Cody lives past her tenure that I paid for at that home, they're doing their part then too."

"They're out of it."

"It's impossible to be out of it!" I cried. "They're family."

"Ivey, you are not goin' to The Alibi."

"I most certainly am."

"You definitely are not."

"Gray—"

"Ivey."

"Gray!"

"Ivey."

And there we were.

It must be said, I was Lash's fake girlfriend for years and I never fought with him.

And I thought at that juncture Gray should know that.

"You know, I was Lash's fake girlfriend for years and I never fought with him. Three days into living with you, we're at it."

Gray snapped his mouth shut, his jaw flexed, his eyes flashed then a muscle jumped in his cheek. Watching it I realized what I just said and that, even though Lash was gay, he'd had me for nearly the entire seven years Gray did not, including four years of that in his bed.

And I knew Gray felt that, deeply.

Therefore, I was a total idiot.

Shit.

My mind was working through ways to make things right and/or apologize when Gray surged out of his seat, rounded the corner of the table and pulled me out of my chair and into his arms.

I was bracing, considering I thought this odd and had no clue where it was going when I felt his body shaking and I was tipping my head back to look up at him when he burst out laughing.

I blinked.

Still laughing, he dipped his chin and looked at me.

"Glad to hear you got on so well with your fake boyfriend."

He wasn't mad.

Still.

"That was a shit thing to say, Gray, and I shouldn't have said it," I said quietly.

"It true?" he asked.

"Well, yeah," I answered.

"Were you pissed?"

"Well, uh...yeah."

"Ivey, honey, I could let myself go down the path of envy about the time that guy had with you and let that shit fester in my gut until it becomes bitter and leaks out to you. Instead, I've decided to be pleased as fuck you found a decent man to look out for you when I wasn't around to do it. You guys got along, way I see it, it's like gettin' along with your best girlfriend. I know he's a guy and, lookin' at him, first instinct is to stake my claim. But he's not about that and I gotta learn that because with you comes him."

Now I remembered why I loved Gray.

He wasn't done.

"Furthermore, if you actually *were* fuckin' him, you'd argue. No doubt about it. Since you're fuckin' *me,* dollface, get ready because we can't have what we have in bed without some of that passion leaking out into life. You have opinions. I will too. They clash, we'll battle our corners. Just as long as we go to bed in the same bed every night and eventually find a way to sort our shit, we'll be good."

"But, we didn't fight before, Gray," I whispered.

His face softened with understanding before his equally soft voice replied, "First, seven years ago, you were findin' your way to you. Now you've found you. The badass showgirl is out." He grinned and gave me a squeeze. "And second, we lucked out. You had so much other shit goin' on, that took focus so we didn't have anything to fight about. My uncles were assholes back then and if we didn't see eye to eye about how to deal with them, I hope you were or eventually would be in a place to tell me what was on your mind even if I didn't agree with it and it ended with us having words."

Yeah, I remembered why I loved Gray.

"Okay," I said softly and his face dipped closer, turning serious.

"You're home, Ivey. You're safe here to do what you want, eat what you want to eat, be who you wanna be and you're safe with me. Always. To do all that, you gotta just be you and feel free to speak your mind."

Yep, totally remembered why I loved Gray.

"So, are you cool with me going to The Alibi?" I asked.

He grinned and I got another squeeze.

But he answered, "No."

I was relaxing into him but at his word, I tensed.

He kept talking.

"But I can't tie you to the fencepost. So you do what you gotta do. Now, I say that knowin' that they are no way in hell gonna give you ninety K, not a one of them. So it's a waste of your time. But you don't mind wastin' it, it's your time, not for me to say."

"What if I get them to give me the money?" I asked.

"They won't."

"Do they have it?"

"Those miserly bastards?" he asked.

"Uh...yeah," I answered uncertainly because I didn't know if they were miserly or not.

"They have it."

"So...?" I trailed off.

"They won't give you the money."

"And if they do?"

Gray studied me.

Then he muttered, "We'll see."

Truly, I didn't know if that was a win, loss or stalemate in the fight stakes. I was going to do what I wanted to do and Gray was convinced it was a fruitless effort.

So, I guessed we would see.

And thus endeth our first fight.

It wasn't that bad and the best part about it, just like when he had an out-and-out with Grandma Miriam years ago, after it was done, it was done. We stretched out, cuddling on the couch in front of the TV. Then we stretched out not cuddling but doing other things in bed. After we were done with those things, we lay in bed cuddling and whispering about our days and what the next day would bring.

Then we slept and we did that cuddling too.

Chapter 30

Good Things Come to Those Who Wait

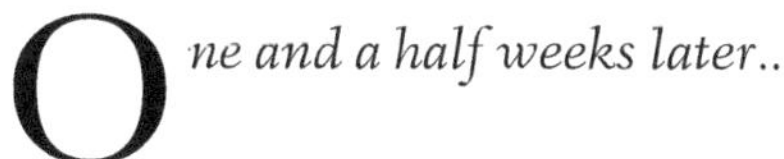

One and a half weeks later…

Like the last time I hit Mustang, it happened and it happened quickly.

I found my place easily.

Slotted right in.

And that place was with Gray on his land and it was being the me I'd come to be.

So there I was, in the grocery store in Mustang in my classy, high-heeled sandals, my designer jeans and a sophisticated but casual top. I'd dumped my big, designer bag in the child seat in the cart. I had makeup on, had spritzed with expensive perfume and my hair was long and wild like Gray liked it.

And I was in this getup perusing the grocery shelves in a small town on the plains of Colorado because this was me.

And there was a new part of me coming out seeing as all things to do with the ranch didn't involve horseshit.

First, I took over feeding the horses. This wasn't tough. I was getting to know the horses so I knew which to feed what but it did take time. Time Gray was glad he could use doing something else.

Second, once Gray taught me how, I took over releasing them from their stalls and leading them into the big paddocks Gray had so they could get some sunshine, walk around and be free.

Third, Gray restarted my horseback riding lessons and did it by taking me riding with him when he rode the ranch, further helping him keep the horses exercised but also helping me learn the lay of the land.

Fourth, he'd called Macy and released her from cleaning duties and I took over that, grocery buying and cooking.

Fifth, I took over the phones. Gray got a lot of calls about his peaches, his horses and his stallions who he loaned out and charged stud fees. He started telling folks who called his cell to call the house and gave me a crash course in breeding and peaches. I took to it easy as I took to everything easy and I dealt with them.

Sixth, I took over paying the bills and doing the ranch accounts. I had a head for figures and I had the time and Gray didn't so he had no problem relinquishing this to me. So he did.

And last, Gray taught me how to drive the small riding mower he had so I also took over mowing the front lawn and the areas around the house.

I'd also taken the time to clean out Gray's truck and I was right. He hadn't tidied since I left, or if he did, he did a half-assed job, and I had the date on an old receipt as proof.

I threw myself into my new rancher's stylish girlfriend role and loved it. I could wear my high heels into town, my western duds while out with the horses and work on my tan by wearing one of my bikini tops and short-shorts while on the riding lawn mower.

Gray loved it too (especially me wearing my bikini top on the lawn mower).

I knew this because his days went from being ten hours long to eight. I knew this also because I made Gray a blueberry cobbler that I served warm with gourmet ice cream and he told me it was the best thing he'd ever eaten. I further knew this when he walked by the vase of flowers I'd put on the cabinet under the window in the kitchen, stopped, looked at it awhile then looked at me grinning.

And I knew this because he told me so.

The more I learned, the more we lived together, the more I settled. I knew where my new place would be in Mustang—at Gray's side, doing my bit to work the ranch. And, if we could swing it financially, that was where I'd stay, making sure my man got what he needed while doing my part.

I loved it.

Every second.

So, surprisingly, green acres was the place for me.

The only blight on the last week and a half was the Tuesday after Gray and I had our first fight. After he was done working, he took a shower and we got takeaway pulled pork sandwiches from The Rambler and took them to Grandma Miriam.

Although Gray again tried to calm me, I was anxious about seeing her. I left Gray but she had one son who was left behind by the love of his life and then she had a grandson it happened to too. She loved Gray and I figured Grandma Miriam might not be forgiving even after what I'd done to save the land.

But when we made it to her room, my anxiety disappeared and something else far more difficult to deal with took its place.

Because there was a reason Gray had to put his gran in a home, and one look at her, I saw it.

The seven years had not been kind to her. She'd lost weight, she'd gained wrinkles and the flash of matriarch bossiness in her eyes had disappeared. Gray had told me that time had marched fast for Grandma Miriam, it had done it marching all over her, and he hadn't lied. She had pain from her spinal injury, and that and age just wore her down. She started losing strength and having more and more troubles doing things for herself.

But even knowing this, I was not prepared for just how frail she was. How the life seemed to have seeped right out of her, and seeing it, it knocked me emotionally to my knees.

I hid it because the other thing I noted instantly was that she was far more anxious at seeing me. So much so she appeared terrified.

And this was because Gray told her everything. She knew he and I had been played, she knew what I'd done to save her and the ranch, and seven years ago, she put the phone down on me five times. She knew we'd been played, but still, she felt responsible for keeping us apart by being stubborn and ornery.

It took a while to talk her around, make her understand that I didn't blame her, I got it that she, like Gray, was flashing back to Gray's mom and this taking so much effort hurt too. Because the Grandma Miriam I knew would let this sink in, snap back and then start being bossy.

She didn't.

The visit went as well as it could. She wasn't needy or whiney. She seemed in good spirits. She just wasn't the woman I knew.

Though, she did have it in her to mutter, "Pleased to see you in a skirt and heels, child, though that skirt is a little tight."

That was the only flicker of Grandma Miriam she gave me.

And this devastated me.

So much, I was virtually silent on the drive home. Gray asked if I was okay and when I lied to him that I was and he didn't believe me, he let it go but asked for my hand and held it all the way home. I just sat in his truck staring at the passing landscape, letting the visit seep into me.

When we got home, I changed into jeans, got a glass of wine and went to the porch swing.

About two minutes later, carrying a bottle of beer, Gray joined me.

Shifting me then settling me with my back to the side of his front, his arm around my chest, my head on his shoulder, he murmured, "Talk to me, Ivey."

"She isn't her," I whispered.

"Told you that, honey."

He did. He'd never put her in a home if there was a little spitfire left, I knew that anyway. But still, he told me what to expect.

"You're you and I'm me," I went on to explain. "You're thirty-three, still hot, still vital, still Gray, and I'm still me. She's not her."

"Ivey—" he started, but I interrupted him, tears gathering in my eyes.

"Whoever did this to us, they took that away from me. I got you back but her I lost. I know she declined, I just saw it. But it was slow and I wasn't here for her and now it's done and I'll never get that back. I got you back but I'll never get that back and that hurts me, Gray. In the end, she liked me, she trusted me and she could have come to love me and I was already growing to love her. They took that away from her and they took that from me and it hurts."

Gray drew in an audible breath as his arm gave me a squeeze but he didn't reply.

Then again, there was nothing to say. I spoke the truth, he knew it and there was nothing either of us could do.

So I just lifted my legs, knees cocked so my soles were on the porch swing beside me, my weight on Gray and he held me and sipped his beer while I sipped my wine. My eyes were on the meadow beside his house where the horses were wandering, the tears I was shedding for losing Grandma Miriam silently rolling down my cheeks.

Thus visits to Grandma Miriam as often as I could were added to my schedule. I couldn't go every day, but since my first visit, I'd been there four times. I didn't stay hours but I brought her flowers, then a box of chocolates, then a plant to spruce up her room, then a book because she liked reading. I sat with her. I chatted with her. I held her delicate hand with its loose papery skin and liver spots. I tried to make her laugh and often got a smile. And I did this because the woman I knew for a short time who I liked and respected might be gone but this woman remained and I was going to give as much as I could and take as much as I could get in the time remaining.

And doing it, my decision to have it out with Gray's uncles had been firm but it was then planted in concrete.

Okay, so they may never pay Gray what I thought they owed him. But they'd get a piece of my mind.

I hadn't yet done that because I knew I was so pissed I'd probably screw it up. And anyway, I had other stuff to do to look out for me, for Gray and settle in our new life together.

So there I was, wandering through the grocery store, our menus planned for the next several days, a grocery list resting on top of my purse and my cart filled with what we'd need.

Mustang's grocery store, called Plack's, was like everything else in Mustang. One town over, a town Gray told me was established about a decade after Mustang, was different. Mustang was day, that town, the town of Elk, was night. Mustang might be the county seat but Elk was the hub. They didn't mind demolishing and rebuilding. They had two strip malls, a huge-ass cinema with six screens, massive home and do-it-yourself stores and two big, chain grocery stores.

But not Mustang. Mustang didn't have anything like that. And the citizens of Mustang didn't care. Except to use the cinema (where I'd gone with Gray when I was there before), Mustangians stuck to their patch. Thus everyone in Mustang went to Plack's.

The hotel was on the southeast corner of the courthouse square, the elementary school at the southwest, the library at the northeast and Plack's at the northwest.

It had not been built in 1912. By the looks of it, I'd guess the 70s. And it had never been renovated. The building was small for a grocery store, the aisles were narrow and the shelves were packed. But, with increasing experience, I noticed they had everything. They might only have a couple of boxes of cake mix rather than a stacked row but they still had every type you could buy. Not that I got cake mixes. I was the stylish girlfriend to a rancher cowboy. I might wear high heels but I still baked cakes from scratch.

Seeing as they had everything you might need, you didn't need a big chain store that also had a pharmacy and sold toys, homewares and inexpensive clothes if you had Plack's. And anyway, the pharmacy was on the square and you could get toys, homewares and (it had to be said) not inexpensive clothes at Hayes.

So I was in Plack's contentedly dwelling in my rancher cowboy's stylish girlfriend zone, perusing the chiller cabinet cheese selection looking for crumbled bleu to put on the steaks I was going to be broiling that night when it happened.

I heard someone call, "Ivey."

My head came up, my fingers around a package of bleu cheese (see? they had everything at Plack's) and I saw Cecily in the company of a girlfriend bearing down on me.

Shit.

Gray and I had gone into town a couple of times to have a beer at The Rambler so I had the opportunity to get updated on gossip. Not to mention, being together for two weeks, Gray and I had time to talk with each other.

I knew what had happened to his trees. I knew what had happened to his horses. And I knew that Gray (rightly) suspected Buddy. I also knew this freaked me out but I sensed Gray needed me to keep it together. Someone was poisoning his horses. He didn't need to worry about me.

I further knew that Buddy and Cecily got married about a year after I left. With this information came the knowledge they had two children, both girls. And I knew that Buddy had gone from loan manager to branch manager and now he was Vice President of the four branches of the bank that were in the next county. So I knew (but had not seen) that Buddy and Cecily lived in a "God-awful monstrosity" (Janie's words) on the eastern outskirts of Mustang opposite Gray's ranch. They lived large for Mustang and didn't hesitate lording it over the entire town.

In other words, they weren't popular...still.

Now I saw that I'd been right those years ago about what would befall the woman Bud Sharp took as wife.

Cecily had had six years of marriage and two children with

Buddy Sharp but she didn't settle into life, marriage and motherhood with any kind of security and definitely no contentment. She was ten pounds underweight and looked gaunt. Her hair was styled in a fashion that was becoming but trendy and I knew with one look it took her at least a half an hour with a roller brush and a hairdryer to pull it off. She was made up and her clothing very nice (not, I was gleeful to see, as nice as mine). But it didn't suit her simply because she wore it with a desperation that I didn't think she knew anyone could see but was obvious to me.

She worked out a lot, probably watched every morsel that passed her lips and likely never left her home without her fancy clothes, her hair done and her face put on.

She was either terrified Buddy would cheat on her or knew he already did and she was terrified he'd find one he liked better than her. He'd then scrape her off, leave her high and dry with two kids and she'd spend the rest of her days in Mustang running into Buddy and her younger, prettier replacement.

I liked this. I knew liking it might make me a bitch but I also didn't care.

And knowing all this with one look at Cecily who had a bitchy expression on her face like she was preparing to crush me and was looking forward to it, I was ready for Cecily.

Then again, this was where being an ex-Vegas showgirl came in handy. Even if I didn't know this about Cecily, I'd still be ready.

"Heard you were back," she stated, her girlfriend, who was weirdly avoiding looking at me, and her cart coming abreast of me.

"Yup," I stated the obvious.

She did a head to toe with sneer on her face that she didn't have it in her to commit to because she couldn't quite bite back the envy.

Her eyes came back to me. "Nice shoes," she drawled and I kicked back a foot and rounded an ankle.

"Thanks, my ex-lover bought them for me. I love them," I replied chirpily.

"Gray's not gonna be able to keep you stocked in eight hundred dollar shoes," she remarked, still sneering.

Yes. Envy. She knew exactly how much they cost and she didn't have anything like them because Buddy might be a bank VP but he was no millionaire like Lash.

I grinned. "That's okay. I have, like, a hundred pairs. I think that'll last me awhile."

Red started creeping up her cheeks and I glanced at her friend who was still strangely avoiding my eyes.

Weird.

My attention went back to Cecily when she crossed her arms on her chest.

I'd scored two points and, still, she was settling in.

Shit.

"Sure no one has told you but you should know, Gray's been busy while you've been gone. *Very* busy."

Bitch.

I knew what she meant, it couldn't be missed.

Gray had had women after me.

It sucked but I knew that Gray hadn't remained blindly devoted to the memory of me even while thinking I'd never be back. Cecily was right, no one had mentioned it, including Gray. And I was glad he didn't because I didn't want to go there. He was a man, all man and no way he would remain celibate, devoted to his hand like I was to my vibrator. I made the decision I made not to put myself out there again. Gray had needs, needs he'd see to and I didn't know if in quenching them he'd attempted to open his heart and make a go with someone else.

What I did know was that even if he did, he didn't succeed, so when I came back, he was available for me.

And that was all I needed to know.

"I find it fascinating that, twice, I've been in your company, and twice, you've felt it's your duty to inform me about Gray and the women in his life. All this while, back then and still now, you're with

Buddy. I mean, obviously, since he's giving it to me and I like it...*a lot*," I leaned in on those last two words to add meaningful and deserved emphasis, "I know how good he is. But you, a married lady, all this attention to my man? My guess is, you liked it a lot too and you miss it. What? Does Buddy not do it for you? Have you been pining for over seven years for Grayson Cody?"

More red drifted into her face and her friend shifted on her feet and there was my answer.

Buddy Sharp didn't do it for her and for over seven years she'd been pining for Grayson Cody.

She didn't speak so I did.

Saccharine sweet, I commiserated, "Oh honey, you know, I understand your pain. You..."

I trailed off as my eyes moved to the girlfriend who *still* wasn't looking at me.

And that was when I knew. It hit me like a rocket.

I knew that Cecily had helped Buddy separate Gray and me. I didn't know how but she either helped or he'd told her about it.

And she'd told her girlfriend, a woman who lived in Mustang. A woman who knew that everyone was gleeful we were back together. A woman who was uncomfortable that her friend had a hand in tearing us apart. A woman who might even be wondering why she had a friend who would do something that despicable. And even though she was friends with Cecily, she was a decent enough person not to like it.

My eyes went back to Cecily as everything I had went into stopping myself from launching a full-on bitch smackdown in the chiller cabinet aisle of Plack's.

Instead, locking eyes with her, I finished on a whisper, "*You* know."

The girlfriend shifted again, this time differently. Her discomfort had ratcheted up and there was fear wafting off her.

And the red was now draining with all the rest of the color in Cecily's face.

Yes, the bitch had a hand in it.

I kept speaking and doing it quietly.

"I don't think you're getting this but, even back then, when you strutted your ass right up to me happy to be a complete bitch, I wasn't a pushover. And I'm even less of one now. So I advise you to learn from then, from this and from what I did to foil your troll of a husband's plans to take down my man. We're impossible to defeat. That happens when you've got good and right at your back and not greed and envy. So I suggest you share that with your husband and you two stop focusing your energies on Gray and me and instead convincing yourself that his money and your big house make up for not having the care and respect of your neighbors."

"You bitch," she hissed.

"You would know," I replied and tossed the cheese into my cart before looking at her friend. "As for you, you should be careful the company you keep. Sometimes a stench shifts and it might be a kind that's impossible to wash away."

She didn't look at me as I spoke to her but she knew I was talking to her. I knew because she swallowed nervously.

And with that, I was done. I put my hands to the handle of the cart and rolled it down the aisle toward the meat without offering my fond farewells. I needed to get the rest of what was on the list, get it in my car and get home before I blew a gasket.

I did this and, wheeling our groceries packed in the canvas tote bags I bought at Hayes to my Lexus, I saw them moving to an SUV. I would do it anyway because that was me, but then I did it for different reasons. I put the top down, slid my fabulous shades on my nose and buzzed my expensive, flashy convertible behind their SUV.

Luckily, the uncontrollable urge didn't strike to reverse it and slam my bumper into theirs. My car was new but it was paid for, I loved it, and if Gray's truck was anything to go by, I'd need to keep it awhile.

I drove home fuming and as I was coming up the lane, Gray, in a tight, wine-colored tee, one of seven (yes *seven*, I'd investigated, all were equally battered like he inherited them from his father or something) of his tatty baseball caps on his head, leather workman gloves on his hands, came sauntering out of the stables as I did.

This was something I was discovering that I loved about Gray. Not only the fact that he was so hot he could look delicious wearing a ragged baseball cap. But also, when he knew I was going to the grocery store, I got back and he was around, he always stopped what he was doing to bring in the groceries for me. I might take in a couple of totes but I stayed in and put the groceries away while he went back and forth and lugged them in.

So I drove around his truck (thus closer to the back door to the kitchen) and parked. I got out. Then I slammed my door and planted my hands on my hips.

Gray stopped two feet away from the other side of the car and took me in.

Then he muttered, "Oh shit."

"Oh shit is right!" I snapped. "Guess who I ran into at the grocery store."

"Osama bin Laden?"

That was funny but I was not laughing.

"No, Gray, he's dead," I told him something he already knew then leaned in and hissed, "*Cecily.*"

His torso swayed back an inch as he crossed his arms on his chest. "You know she lives here, dollface, you knew it would happen eventually. What the fuck?"

Something about Gray then and now, he was rational and logical to a fault and mostly very easygoing. Unless it was Buddy Sharp, my brother (back then) or his uncles (then and now), he didn't get riled easily.

Which sometimes sucked and I discovered that at that very moment when I was in rant mode and I wanted someone to understand exactly why and commiserate with me.

So I explained why.

"She had a hand in the play Buddy made to get me out of Mustang."

And there it was. I got someone to commiserate with my rant.

The problem was, in my snit I had temporarily forgotten that when Gray wasn't being rational, logical and easygoing and he got pissed, he got *pissed.*

"Say again?" he whispered and he was across the car from me but I heard the menace in his tone.

"She had a hand in the play Buddy made to get me out of Mustang," I repeated a little less heatedly, studying him and wondering if I should have kept my mouth shut.

"She tell you that?"

I shook my head but said, "I know."

"How do you know?"

"A girl knows."

"Think, you say something as explosive as that, Ivey, you need more than 'a girl knows,'" Gray replied and it was then I realized the hole I'd dug with my fit of temper.

Because I didn't want to go there but now that I'd mentioned it, I had no other direction available to me.

I sucked in breath, walked to the car, put my hand on my door and said, "Remember when she came up to us at the VFW our first date?"

"Ivey, I think you know I remember everything about you, specifically everything about you when you were with me. Outside of our kiss and watchin' you bendin' over a pool table for an hour, that was the best part of the date."

He wasn't happily reminiscing, unfortunately. He was telling me to move it along.

Still, Gray impatient or not, I liked what he said.

I didn't share that.

"Well, our, um...conversation in the chiller cabinet aisle at Plack's was along the same vein."

"Again..." Gray started, clearly seeking patience, "*say again*?"

Damn.

Here we go.

"She walked right up to me and told me, essentially, that while I was gone, you'd been with other women."

At that point I learned something new about Gray and how to deal with him.

Because he had been pissed, alert and impatient.

Now he was enraged.

So I learned, belatedly, that I should tread cautiously even when I was justifiably in full rant.

"That bitch," Gray whispered infuriatedly.

"Gray, honey, it's not like I didn't know."

"That...*fuckin'*...*bitch*!" Gray clipped, this time loudly.

"Gray," I said softly, "it's okay."

"Right, I know, Ivey, fuck, I know," he returned, uncrossing his arms and throwing one out. "You aren't stupid and you know me, you knew about the girls before you. I know you know but that doesn't fucking mean," he leaned in, planted his hands on his hips and thundered, "*she had to tell you!*"

"Honey." I was still whispering.

"I was not gonna go there with you. Not ever. I knew you knew and I didn't need to make myself feel better and you feel like shit by goin' over it with you. I knew what I felt when I called you in Vegas and Lash answered the phone at twenty past seven, knowin' he was in bed with you, thinkin' what I thought he was to you. It burned through me but I was in my own fuckin' kitchen on my cell phone. That bitch threw that shit in your face while you were in fuckin' *Plack's* fuckin' *grocery shoppin'* and knowin' she gleefully set about makin' you feel that burn when you were *not* in a safe place or fuckin' doin' it *ever* pisses me right the fuck off."

"I can see that," I said soothingly.

Gray glared at me then bit out, "That fuckin' bitch."

"Gray, that isn't the part you need to know. What I mean is—"

"That fuckin' *bitch*."

I fell silent.

Gray deep breathed.

I waited.

Gray kept glaring at me and deep breathing.

Then he asked, "Anything frozen in the car?"

"Ice cream," I answered quietly.

"Right, toss me your key. Let's get this shit in."

I tossed him my keys, he nabbed them and bleeped the trunk open.

I headed to the kitchen. He brought in a load and I started putting it away. Then he brought in the second and last load, dumped it on the counter and I continued putting it away while he rested a hip to the counter, crossed his arms on his chest, watched me and ordered, "Right, now, give it to me."

I kept putting food away while I told him, "She has a thing for you."

"No shit," Gray replied.

Right. Gray wasn't stupid.

Moving on.

"She doesn't have a happy marriage with Buddy."

"Again, no shit."

I finished with all the stuff that needed fridge or freezer and turned to Gray.

"She was with a girlfriend who wouldn't look at me. Cecily bore down on me just like the last time, without hesitation, wanting to get a dig at you and crush me. She's Buddy's wife, she was seeing him then, and still, she went after both of us. The girlfriend knew, Gray, and being around me, especially with Cecily, made her uncomfortable. I alluded very vaguely to the fact she knew my pain at losing you and how she knew that and both of them reacted. She either knows what Buddy did, which, if he did it and now I feel certain he did, she would as his wife or she was involved. She wanted you then, she wants you now and she's one of those women who won't move on. And if she feels pain, she lets it turn bitter, so much, she can't help herself from spreading that around."

"What'd this friend look like?" Gray asked immediately.

"What?" I asked back, confused.

"Cecily's friend. What'd she look like?"

"Uh, dark hair, a bit plump but it looked good on her. Shorter than me. She didn't give me her eyes so I can't say the color. Cecily's age, I'd guess."

Gray's face grew ominously darker when he stated, "Prisc."

"Sorry?"

"Prisc. Priscilla. Tight with Cecily. Tight for a long time. All the way back to school. Her, Courtney and Cecily, cheerleaders, the mean girls. That said, you got Prisc away from Courtney and Cecily, she could be sweet. Those other two, born pure bitch."

"And?" I prompted when he didn't explain why he was sharing this information.

"And, Prisc and Courtney were the ones who told everyone they saw you takin' off with Casey."

I closed my eyes and rested my hand on the counter.

"Like I said," Gray kept speaking and I opened my eyes. "Remember everything about you including everything that happened after I lost you. Remember that shit. Remember giving time to chewin' on those two bein' the two who happened to see you stealin' away in the dead of night. It was a long time ago but when you took off with Casey, can you remember if you saw anyone?"

I shook my head. "It was a long time ago but I remember because he was freaked, saying he was being followed so I looked and I did it hard. I can feel eyes, see a tail. It had to be three, four in the morning. The square was deserted, the bar closed. No one saw us."

"So they made that shit up."

"Probably," I replied.

"Definitely," Gray returned. "You felt it, life taught you to read people, situations and, dollface, like everything, you're good at it. What I know is, from what you told me, Prisc is a decent person who found herself with shitty friends and she's weak. It's gone on so long, she'd rather stick with what she has than dip her toe in the pond. She couldn't look you in the eye, there was a reason and not just that she knows Buddy's a dick 'cause everyone knows Buddy's a dick. She couldn't look you in the eye because she was in on it."

"So she knows what they did," I whispered.

"Likely." Gray didn't whisper.

"So we should go talk to her." Now I wasn't whispering.

He shook his head.

"No?" I asked.

"No, darlin'. First, weak or not, that shit's whacked. That isn't about bein' a mean girl. She fucked with people's lives, their happiness. If she knew they were doin' that to us, she shouldn't have participated or sometime in the last seven years she shoulda opened her goddamned mouth and said something to me. I've known her since high school. She came clean, she knew I'd be pissed but, at least with her, I'd get over it. So, I talk to her, I might lose it and she's not worth the emotion. Second, you talk to her, you might lose it and ditto the emotion. Third, we'll find out what happened but that shit is not gonna get Buddy Sharp's ass hanging out there. Nobody likes him already. They know he did that to us, they'll just like him less and that's no skin off his nose. Trespassing, breaking and entering, destroying property and poisoning horses will get his ass hanging out there. I doubt any of that will carry a huge jail sentence but it's unlawful and that bank isn't gonna keep a VP with a rap sheet in a corner office. *That's* worth our energy, not Prisc."

He was back to rational and logical if not, from the burn in his eyes, easygoing.

"People suck" I declared, Gray stared at me a second then grinned.

There it was. The easygoing. Back quick as a flash.

So Gray.

"Yeah, they do," he agreed.

"Well, I didn't tell you the good news and that is that your hard as nails, ex-Vegas showgirl kicked her ass verbally."

His grin became a smile.

"Too bad I missed that."

"I was awesome," I bragged.

His smile became a chuckle through which he ordered, "Come here, Ivey."

I went there and he folded his arms around me as I curled mine around him.

He tipped his chin down and caught my eyes.

"Know somethin'?" he asked.

"I know a lot of things, Gray, though one of them is not what you're going to say."

Gray grinned again then his eyes got tender (he'd dispensed with the "near to" part of that about a week and a half ago, after I mourned for the loss of the Grandma Miriam I knew, and now he just always went straight to tender).

"My dad was right," he said softly.

"About what?"

"Good things come to those who wait."

My breath clean left me at the same time my nose started stinging.

"Gray," I whispered.

Gray wasn't in the mood to comfort a sobbing me and I knew this when he said, "Got work to do, baby, so say you love me."

I gave him that play.

"I love you."

He grinned again before he dipped his head, touched his mouth to mine, doing so without cracking me with the bill of his baseball cap. He lifted his head, gave me a squeeze, turned around and walked out the back door of the kitchen to go off to do macho man rancher cowboy things.

I sighed.

Then I moved through the kitchen to do rancher cowboy's stylish girlfriend things.

By the way, Gray had never had it but he *loved* bleu cheese crumbled on top of a broiled steak.

See? I totally had this rancher's girlfriend thing down.

Totally.

Chapter 31

Seven

F*our days later...*

"Come here," Gray growled.

I slid him out of my mouth but wrapped my hand around him and immediately started stroking as I turned my head, kissed the inside of his thigh before my eyes went to him and I whispered, "Not done, baby."

"You're done."

"Give me a little while longer."

"You get longer, Ivey, I'll come in your mouth. You know I come in you and by you I don't mean your mouth. Now *come here.*"

This was true. And at his words I suddenly wanted him in me.

Therefore I started crawling up his body.

The room was dark. I had no idea what time it was. Gray had woken me with his hands then added his mouth then I added my hands and mouth. Except for me and my fans and sequined panties, we'd never done this. I'd adjusted to Gray's sleeping schedule just as easily as I adjusted to Mustang. A couple of days, I was there.

But if this was an indication that Gray had sleepless nights, I wasn't going to complain if this was how he worked through them.

I made it up his body, he shifted his legs so they were between mine and I was straddling him. One of his arms curved around my waist, moving me down, the other hand drove into my hair, his hips bucked up, my mouth hit his, my tongue slid inside and he slid inside me.

Oh yeah.

He rolled us, mouths and bodies connected, and his hips started moving, fast, hard, driving deep.

Oh *yeah*.

He was nearly there and intent to take me with him. I loved it when he got this way, driven, on the edge of losing control and what I loved about it was that I made him that way.

Then, from far off in the silence of the night I heard what sounded like a shotgun blast.

Gray's head shot up and he stilled a half a second then slid out, rolled and angled off the bed, clipping, "*Fuck*."

"What was that?" I whispered but I knew. Gray had told me about the shotgun rigged in the barn.

"Dial nine-one-one, Ivey," Gray ordered, tugging his jeans on.

"What?"

"Dial nine-one-one," Gray repeated, bent over and snatched up his shirt. I saw his head turn toward me in the dark and he went on, "Now."

I jerked out of my surprised stupor, rolled to his nightstand and grabbed the phone.

Gray tagged his boots and sprinted out the door.

"Shit, shit, fuck," I whispered as I dialed in the dark. I jumped off the bed and started looking for my nightie and panties.

"Nine-one-one, what's your emergency?"

"This is Ivey Larue. I'm at Cody Ranch off of fifty-seven west of Mustang. We have an intruder."

I had the phone tucked between my ear and shoulder and I was shimmying on my panties then awkwardly pulling my little, red satin nightie over my head, answering the operator's questions when I saw it.

A weird light dancing through the opened window.

I blinked at it while it hit me what that hue and dance meant. I rushed to the window and saw the barn was on fire.

"Oh my God!" I cried, cutting off whatever the operator was saying and dashing back across the room to my jeans. "Notify the fire department. Our barn's on fire. We have twenty horses in there! Hurry!"

I didn't even bleep it off before I threw it on the bed, yanked up my jeans, zipped them and didn't bother with the button. I raced out of the room, down the stairs, through to the kitchen and to the back door where I pulled on my wellies without socks.

I dashed out the back door.

I didn't hesitate to dash across the back lawn to the burning fire even as I saw Gray leading out two horses, smacking one on its rump, and both galloped toward the opened paddock.

Gray saw me and, running back in, he shouted, "Get in the house!"

Then he disappeared *in our burning barn*!

Gray was in there.

Our horses were in there.

Horses I fed, horses I watered, some of them even nuzzled my neck with their nose.

And the man I loved, who for seven years had been taken from me, was in there too.

And again, I didn't hesitate.

I ran into the barn.

Flames licked everywhere, and if I gave them a chance, they would terrify me.

So I didn't.

And it was hot, hotter than anything I'd ever experienced. The smoke was thick. And just the sound of the blaze burning was petrifying. That burn could burn me, that smoke could choke me and just thinking about it could paralyze me.

So I didn't.

Gray, no longer leading horses out, just opening stalls, racing through them and shouting, "Heeyah!" saw me instantly.

"*Get outta here, Ivey!*" he roared.

I ignored him, rushed through the barn and did what he was doing. I opened an unopened stall and luckily the horse raced out toward safety without me having to prompt her. Then again to the next stall and again. The fourth stall the horse, one of the ones with foal, was backing against the wall, eyes wide and wheeling, front hooves making short, panicked hops. I remembered Gray telling me not to get behind a horse and there was no way I was getting in front of those hooves so I rushed cautiously to her side, put one hand to her ribs pressing in the direction of the exit, slapped her rump and shouted, "Heeyah!" like Gray.

It took three slaps then she heeyahed.

I got one more horse out before the horrifying sound of creaking wood and the petrified shrieks of penned horses penetrated my brain. Before I could locate Gray, he located me. His hand closed tight around mine and he dragged me toward the opened front doors.

We weren't out of the barn when the back collapsed and I couldn't swallow my terrified scream at hearing the booming crash and feeling the force of the wave of air and blast of heat that blew my hair forward.

But we weren't back there. We were fifteen feet from the doors…then ten…then five…then we were out. The much cooler summer air hit me like a slap and I sucked in its clean air as Gray kept racing us away from the barn.

He stopped me, yanked on my hand and I looked up at his soot-streaked face.

"We need to get the horses in the paddock. They're spooked. Be cautious. Don't approach unless you get a good feeling. Guide them in, herd them in, chase them in, clapping and shouting, whatever you gotta do, but stay away if they're spooked. Yeah?"

I nodded.

He let my hand go and took off. I looked right and left seeing horses all around. I approached one then saw Gray with another one. It was the one he rode often, his horse, a stallion, white with big brown splotches called Answer. Then I watched in astonishment as, bareback, he swung up then somehow wheeled Answer around and started to race through the area, herding horses.

I did my bit, dashing around and herding them toward him.

My work was done, all of the horses near the house were in the paddock and Gray was galloping off toward a couple that were further away when I heard the sirens.

But I didn't look to the sirens. I looked to the still burning barn, the flames dancing high, licking the air. Another section had collapsed.

I looked to the paddock and counted.

Ten horses.

Numbly, my head turned and I watched Gray driving the two other horses toward the paddock.

With his horse and those two, that made thirteen.

Thirteen.

Thirteen.

Listlessly, I turned back to the barn.

Seven horses were dying in there or already dead.

Seven.

The sirens got closer. I heard shouts, men working and the red, blue and white of emergency vehicle lights flashed through the dancing light of the flames.

"Ivey!" I heard my name shouted but I stared at Gray's barn burning, knowing which horses were in those back stalls, stalls Gray and I didn't have time to get to. I'd fed them. I'd moved them to the paddocks. I'd even ridden two of them.

Two hands clasped my arms and pulled me away ten feet but I didn't tear my eyes from the barn.

I was shaken and heard, "Talk to me, Ivey. Gray's seein' to business and I gotta know what went down."

I turned and looked up at Captain Lenny.

Then I told him everything he needed to know.

"Gray's shotgun blasted."

Lenny's entire face went hard in a way that, if I wasn't numb with shock and sadness, would have scared me.

Then his eyes shifted to the dancing flames.

ONE HOUR, forty-five minutes later…

"I KNOW WHAT I SAW, LEN," Gray rumbled and Lenny stared at him as uniformed officers shuffled around and, far away, in the smoldering remains of the decimated barn, firefighters cautiously circled, beat out, stomped out and sprayed their hoses to dampen the embers and keep any sparks from catching something else.

I knew this was happening but I only had eyes for Lenny and Gray.

And this was because Gray had seen something this time.

And what he'd seen was Lenny's nephew Pete running to his pickup and racing away.

"You saw him get in it?" Lenny asked quietly.

"Saw him runnin' to the lane and jumpin' in the truck," Gray confirmed.

"You sure it was Pete?"

"Went to grade school with him, Len. Shared first grade, fourth grade and I reckon two dozen classes all through high school with him. Seen him in that truck at least a hundred times in the three years he's had it." Gray's voice was low, rough and really, *really* pissed. "I know Pete when I see him, Lenny."

"Fuck," Lenny whispered.

"He burned down my barn and killed seven of my horses," Gray stated, his voice starting with the same qualities but degenerating with every word. "Ivey didn't help, twelve horses would have gone down. And, I'll add, my woman was in there helpin'."

Gray paused and a muscle jumped in Lenny's cheek.

"You bring his ass in," Gray whispered. "You get him in the tank, Len. You know what I'm sayin' to you."

Lenny stared at Gray and he knew what Gray was saying. The safest place for Pete to be was in jail.

Lenny turned his head to an officer and jerked up his chin.

That officer jogged to a cruiser.

Then Lenny avoided Gray's eyes and mine as his went to the smoldering destruction.

Then he whispered, "Christ, boy's got shit for brains. Always has."

"This isn't shit for brains," Gray ground out and Lenny flinched. "Ivey was in that barn with me and I got seven horses down. Me and my woman are breathin' but half the fuckin' thing collapsed *while we were in it.*" Lenny looked back at Gray. "This shit's gotta stop, Len. You got this one last chance to make it stop. You don't, I'm takin' measures."

"Keep calm, Gray," Lenny whispered.

"*Fuck calm!*" Gray suddenly exploded and I got closer to him as Lenny's officers got closer to Lenny. "Did you not fuckin' hear me?" Gray asked. "Half the goddamned barn collapsed with me and Ivey *in it!*"

"I hear you son, but let me do my work," Lenny replied.

"Yeah, you do your work," Gray shot back. "You got one last fuckin' chance to do your fuckin' work."

As he was saying this, headlights bounced up the drive and all eyes turned to look.

Earlier, even though they had motion sensors, I had run into the house to turn on all the outside lights. We were on a ranch in the middle of nowhere but Cody men weren't stupid. The middle of nowhere could still hold dangers, evidenced by a now destroyed barn. There were a lot of outside lights that shone all around the house so the space close to the house and then some was brightly illuminated. Therefore, as the shiny, long-cab pickup stopped close and the engine died, I saw it.

I also saw a man get out of it and I knew instantly he was a rancher seeing as it was the dead of night and he was still in a western-style shirt, Wranglers, cowboy boots with his own tattered baseball hat on his head.

"Fuck me," Lenny muttered, and the officers and him all moved fast as I belatedly felt the vibes rolling off Gray.

Really bad vibes had been rolling off him but now they burned so hot they scorched.

I got closer, took his hand and the minute I did his fingers closed around mine tight. It could be they did this because he was glad I had fingers to hold onto. It could be, from what I was getting from him, he did this because he needed to hold onto me so he didn't whale on the newcomer.

"Who's that?" I whispered, getting closer and pressing to his side.

"Jeb Sharp," Gray answered tersely, I sucked in breath and I saw Lenny get up close to Jeb Sharp as the remaining three officers staggered themselves between Sharp and Gray, preparing, should Gray lose it, to lock him down.

Lenny and Sharp had words I couldn't hear even if they weren't that far away. Lenny shook his head then moved his body as if to block Sharp but Sharp shook his head too and rounded Lenny.

"Not a good idea, Jeb," Lenny called after him as Sharp approached Gray and me.

Gray, already tense, went so solid I feared touching him would make him shatter. Still, I curled into him and put my other hand on his abs.

Sharp, astutely, stopped outside arm's reach.

He was like his son, good-looking. But he was that way in the way Gray was. He'd be that way until he died. There were lines on his face that came from hard work in the sun and hard laughing often in his life. There was a burn in his eyes that came from not a small amount of anger and a hint of shame he couldn't quite hide but he was trying. I knew he was Buddy's dad and, one look at him, I still couldn't help but like him.

Then he announced, "I'll deal with this, son."

"Time for that's passed, Jeb. Got seven dead horses and no barn," Gray returned.

"You're smart, you'll let me take care a' this," Jeb said quietly.

"He's been gunnin' for me since junior high and tonight he put my woman in danger. Not feelin' like bein' smart right about now," Gray replied.

Jeb's eyes came to me, his hand went to the bill of his baseball cap for a second before it dropped and he muttered, "Ma'am."

I lifted my chin to him but no more and he looked back at Gray.

"Ask you one more time, Grayson, let me deal with this."

"You do what you gotta do. Len'll do what he's gotta do. And I'll do what I gotta do," Gray stated.

Jeb Sharp held my man's eyes.

Then he whispered, "Fair enough." Then his eyes went to the barn and he kept whispering when he said, "Cryin' shame."

He was not wrong about that.

I pressed closer to Gray and Gray's hand squeezed mine tighter.

Sharp looked through me and back to Gray.

"You need help cleanin' up and buildin', you call on me. I'll send some boys," he offered.

When Gray made no reply, I had a mind to suggest he didn't hold his breath but I kept my tongue.

"Right," Sharp muttered, knowing exactly what Gray's nonresponse meant then he looked to me. "Mizz Larue, wish we'd met under more auspicious circumstances."

"Me too," I whispered.

He nodded. Then he looked at Gray. Then he sighed deeply. Finally he turned and walked away.

That was when I sighed.

Jeb Sharp got in his truck, turned it around and drove down the lane.

I felt some of the tension leave Gray's body and he turned us to face the destruction.

Wood barn, it went up like tinder, came down in no time flat.

"I'm gonna go make coffee for the firemen, honey," I whispered.

"Good idea, baby," Gray murmured, his eyes never leaving the barn.

I squeezed his hand. He squeezed mine back but he did it not looking away from his loss.

I let him go, took two steps away then turned and took two back.

Pressing again to his side, I lifted up until I was as close as I could get to his ear and whispered, "Say you love me, Gray."

I rolled back to the soles of my feet and watched as he closed his eyes then he opened them and turned to me.

His hand came up, he cupped my jaw and his eyes moved over my face.

Then he said, "I love you, Ivey."

I grinned a small, sad grin.

He gave me the same.

Then he bent and touched his mouth to mine, dropped his hand and I turned and went into the house to make coffee for firefighters.

Three hours later…

Dawn was hitting the sky, weak light beginning to glow through the window.

Gray and I had had showers but no sleep. We were in bed, Gray on his back, me pressed to his side, my head on his pectoral, hand flat and lightly trailing his chest and gut, his arm around me, hand in my panties cupping my ass.

We'd been there awhile, lying close, not speaking but also not sleeping.

Finally, I broke the silence by whispering, "You okay?"

"No."

I pulled in a breath. Then I slid my hand up his chest, lifted and turned my head and rested my chin on my hand under me.

He had four pillows bunched haphazardly behind his head and shoulders (this was his way, my man liked pillows) and his eyes dipped to me.

"Please don't kill Buddy," I said quietly. "Just got you back after seven years. I don't want to spend the next seven visiting you in the penitentiary."

His face softened but he didn't smile.

Still, he replied teasingly, "You're in the mountain plains of Colorado, dollface. No jury from these parts would convict me for killin' a man who killed seven horses."

His joke fell flat, I knew he saw it on my face just as I saw it on his but I suspected his was worse. He was a cowboy, horses were kind of important to cowboys.

I lifted up, pushed up closer, sliding more onto his chest, my hand moving to curl around the side of his neck all as I whispered, "Baby, I don't know what to do to help you."

That was when he grinned. It wasn't a big one and it didn't warm his beautiful eyes the usual way but it still warmed his eyes.

His hand left my panties so his arm could close tight around the middle of my back and he told me, "You're doin' it, Ivey."

I nodded and smiled.

Then I said gently, "I'm sorry, Gray."

"Me too."

"We'll be okay."

It was his turn to nod. "One thing I got is insurance. So, yeah, eventually, we'll be okay."

It was good to know he had insurance but that wasn't what I was talking about.

"That isn't what I meant, honey."

"I know that, darlin', and my response still stands. We'll be okay in all ways. Just that right about now, when we need to crash so we can get at least a little sleep so we can face whatever the day's gonna bring, you need to know that it's *all* gonna be okay."

He was right.

I tipped my face so I could kiss his chest. Then I repositioned and looked at him again.

"Do you get sleepless nights often?"

"Nope, work hard all day, sleep hard all night."

"So, you waking up is unusual?"

"Can't say it's never happened, can say it's so rare don't remember when it happened last."

"So what woke you?"

That got me a different kind of grin but he still wasn't committed to it.

"Thought it was my subconscious reminding me you'd gone to sleep without your panties on."

I grinned back then pressed gently, "But that wasn't it?"

"If you're askin' if I heard somethin', then no. I heard somethin', I'd look. I wouldn't start somethin' with you. If you're askin' if I got a sense of somethin', a vibe, who knows? What I do know is, awake or asleep, I'd hear that blast. I sleep hard but I don't sleep so deep I'd sleep through that and I know since I didn't the last time."

"Mm..." I muttered, my eyes sliding away.

"Ivey," he called and my eyes slid back. "We got a mess outside and a fight that was already pretty fuckin' ugly that just got a whole lot uglier. We need to sleep so we can be prepared to face the day."

He was right.

"Okay, honey," I agreed and started to move to settle back into him but stopped when his arm gave me a squeeze and I focused back on him.

"I'm not used to sleepless nights but that don't mean after what happened tonight, seein' you run around a burnin' barn, I won't start to have them."

I knew where this was going from my macho man rancher cowboy so I opened my mouth to cut him off.

He saw it and his arm gave me another squeeze.

"Let me finish, baby, yeah?"

I closed my mouth and nodded.

"You saved five horses," he whispered.

I did. I did do that.

Gray wasn't done.

"You runnin' into that barn like that, workin' to save those horses, this ranch, I didn't like it and pray to God nothin' like that'll happen again. But I gotta say, wherever you were born and whatever you did, pool hustler, showgirl, tonight, you were a rancher's woman and just like you, when you do somethin', you're the best there is."

That meant so much, was so beautiful, my nose instantly started stinging and his face got fuzzy as tears filled my eyes.

He pulled me up his chest, ignored my burgeoning tears and ordered, "Now, say you love me, Ivey, kiss me then settle and go to sleep."

I swallowed then whispered shakily, "I love you, Gray."

"Now, kiss me," he whispered back.

I touched my mouth to his and he pulled me back down his chest.

"Now, go to sleep."

I put my cheek to his chest nodding and deep breathing.

I didn't go right to sleep, it took me a while just as it took Gray but I eventually got to sleep and I did it before him.

Chapter 32

It Was Family

The morning after the fire, early, we got visits from Shim and Roan. Roan on his way to work, Shim with the flatbed of his pickup filled with horse feed and hay. This was kind since ours went up in smoke, something they both obviously knew (thus the visits) since news travels fast in a small town even through the night. It was also a testimony to the kind of man my cowboy rancher was that he accepted it considering Shim was still a ranch hand on Jeb Sharp's land. It was too early for the feed store to be open so it was likely this was given to us by Sharp, not Shim.

For reasons unknown to me, regardless of the fact I was exhausted and dragging, I started the day by tricking myself out. I didn't put on one of my fabulous dresses but did the hair, makeup, designer jeans, complicated but casual (and expensive) top routine. I didn't strap on high heels, however, instead I slipped on some fabulous flip-flops. But I went for the gusto with everything else. It could be I needed my armor for the day after a tragedy. It could be that was just me.

In the end with who came calling, I was glad I did.

The night before, after the fireman and cops left, they cordoned off the barn with police tape. One could say waking up and looking out your window to see part of your property lined with yellow police tape was not a sight you wanted to see in the morning.

Or ever.

After I fed my man and served coffee to him and his friends, I dug out the insurance papers. Then I called Gray's insurance company and left them a message stating that after the police and arson investigators released the scene, we needed an urgent visit because we had seven dead horse carcasses fifty yards away from our house and we needed to put those bodies in the ground so we could put those souls at peace.

The arson investigator showed shortly after Shim and Roan left and Gray asked, while he was dealing with things on the ranch, if I would go to the nursing home to break the news to Grandma Miriam. Seeing as our phone was ringing off the hook already and it was just eight o'clock, he was worried news would travel and she'd learn from someone else.

So I hightailed it into town and, in a futile effort to soften the blow, I bought her another book, some magazines and a shed load of candy bars. I figured a nursing home was kind of like prison, you had to have the proper currency to make your way and garner favors, and for oldies it wasn't cigarettes. So I bought enough candy bars to make Grandma Miriam the queen of the swanky retirement estate. I also got some for Gray since there was a reason there were so many candy bar wrappers in his truck. Gray did not reach for a Power Bar or a banana when he got peckish and considering his day was physical activity from dawn practically to dusk, he got the munchies often. Though I did make sure most of his had peanuts so he had protein.

I was dreading my task and once the news was delivered I felt little relief. Grandma Miriam was stunned, scared for Gray and me and heartbroken that the barn built by her husband's father, a barn she saw out the back window while she was doing the dishes every day for over fifty years, no longer existed not to mention how she reacted when I told her we lost seven horses. And I was right, she was happy for her book, magazines and candy bars but they did not do one thing to soften the blow.

Before I left, her hand clutched mine with a surprising strength borne of fear, her fading blue eyes locked to me and she whispered fervently, "You and Gray stay safe, child. Promise me, please, you two will stay safe."

I promised her yet again that Lenny was on it, Jeb Sharp was on it and that her grandson would never let anything happen to him or me. It was this last that got her hand to relax in mine. Then again, it would. She knew Gray so she knew this was the truth.

I drove home to see an SUV and pickup parked by the house and to find out from Gray that his morning had been busy. Half of Mustang had been by and I knew this was a fact when I hit the kitchen and found the farm table practically covered in dishes, pans and plates filled with casseroles, pies, cakes and brownies. Gray said his big shed where he kept tools, equipment and peach tree things was now filled near to overflowing with horse feed, hay and used bridles and saddles that folks had popped by to bring.

For the next hour, I would experience this same thing as folks brought food, pop, beer and equipment but I was surprised to see these folks were not lookee-loos. They came, they gave us their sentiments, they dropped off their generosity and they left. They knew Gray and I had things to do and other things to occupy our minds. They knew they'd be underfoot. They knew it was taxing to have unexpected company. So they shared their kindness then they got the hell out of there.

I'd never experienced anything like it.

It was like experiencing beauty.

It was early afternoon and Gray and I had just had huge plates filled with Ang's, the waitress (still!) at the diner, Mexican chicken, cheese and tortilla casserole. We were still at the table when his head came up and turned. Mine did too and we looked out the big window over the cabinet at the side of the kitchen.

There we saw coming down the lane another SUV followed by a

pickup and as they careened closer at what appeared to be high speed I saw they were followed by a sedan.

"No," Gray whispered then I tensed when he clipped, "*fuck no.*"

Then his chair scraped back and he was out of it like a shot, stalking to the back door.

I had no idea who owned those vehicles but I did know whoever it was *really* wasn't welcome so I shot to my feet and ran after Gray.

When I got down the back steps I saw he was striding, long legs eating the distance, across the side yard that was dotted with big, shady trees toward the now parked trucks and car. And it was then I saw who was in them.

The SUV held Gray's uncles Olly and Charlie, the two I'd met, in the pickup was a man I'd never seen but his looks were unmistakably Cody and in the car was Macy.

As they exited their vehicles I quickly took them in.

Back in the day during my first stay in Mustang, I noticed Charlie had gone soft and carried extra weight. I had met and been around Olly when he was home during my cooking lessons with Macy but (wisely) he avoided the kitchen during those times and I only shared greetings, farewells and a handful of words in between. Olly, then and now, and the man who had to be Frank had not gone soft. They were tall, their burnished, dark blond hair only sprinkled with gray and they were still lean, fit and handsome. They wore their age, definitely, but they wore it well.

"Get gone," I heard Gray growl dangerously, still striding toward them as they lined up a few feet in front of their vehicles.

It was Frank, eyes narrowed on the remains of the barn, his face carrying an easily read emotion of being extremely pissed off, who cut his gaze to Gray and asked weirdly, "What you doin' 'bout this shit, boy?" Then he gave an irate jerk of his chin toward the barn.

"I said, get gone," Gray semi-repeated, stopping four feet in front of them and I hustled to his side.

"And I said," Frank leaned in, "*what you doin' 'bout this shit, boy?*"

I did not have a good feeling about this.

"All right, guys, let's all calm down, go inside, open a beer and talk calmly," Macy, arriving at the pack, put in and I knew by her bossy yet soothing tone she trailed the brothers in her own car because she'd tried to talk them out of coming, failed but followed them in order to play peacemaker.

"Stay outta this, Macy," Olly rumbled, not taking his eyes off Gray.

"You haven't answered my question," Frank prompted ominously.

"And you haven't moved your ass off my goddamned land," Gray shot back. "Now get...the fuck...*gone*."

"Maybe you guys can come back in a day or two?" I suggested but none of them even looked at me.

"Bud Sharp needs to learn a lesson," Charlie told Gray and I tensed.

"My problem, not yours. Get gone," Gray returned.

"Sittin' here, sittin' on your hands when you got fucked?" Olly asked then went on to state, "That's not Cody."

"You wouldn't know what Cody is, you asshole. Now get *gone*," Gray clipped and all of them tensed and it was more than a little scary.

"Seems we know more 'bout bein' a Cody than you, boy. Fuck. Half a day's gone and there's no Sharp swingin' from no tree," Frank remarked and my tense went ultra tense.

Frank wasn't done.

"Your daddy, my daddy, my daddy's daddy would not get his goddamned barn burned down right under his fuckin' nose and then delay to seein' someone pays."

And at that, something clicked in me. I felt it. I could swear I even heard it.

And when it did, I lost it.

"How dare you?" I whispered but that whisper vibrated with a feeling so strong it shimmered in the air and everyone present felt it. I knew this when all eyes came to me. "How dare you?" I repeated then I shrieked, "*How fucking dare you?*"

I took three fast steps to the Brothers Cody and got a steel band-like arm wrapped around my belly, which hauled me back into Gray's body and cut off my advance but it didn't stop my tirade.

"Buddy Sharp's been playing with Gray for years and you didn't have his back then. I've been home for weeks and not a one of you," my eyes moved to Macy, "even *you*, came to see me. You live in this town. You know what happened to us. And you know Gray nearly lost this land, this house, that barn," I swung an arm out behind me, "because he was taking care of *your* mother," I jabbed a finger at them. "And you didn't do shit. His trees were poisoned, his horses were poisoned and where were you then? Now you have the balls to show up here when you left your *nephew* blowing in the *breeze* and try to tell him how to deal with a tragedy? How he should handle that sick, jealous piece of shit in town whose entire life focus is taking Grayson Cody down? You show up here after we spent a sleepless night after being in a barn that was *collapsing around us*, taking our lives in our hands to save *your legacy*, a legacy you have given nothing to for decades but still you have the nerve to drive up here and get in Gray's face about it? *How dare you?*"

"Ivey—" Macy started, her voice placating but my eyes sliced to her.

"No," I cut her off. "Actually, I don't give a fuck how you dare. What I give a fuck about is that you, all of you," I swung an arm out to indicate them all, "get out of my man's space right now. He's survived this. He's survived the hits he took in his past. He's bent over backward and twisted himself into knots making it so *your mother* survived and had as good a life as he could give her after her legs were taken and he's *still* doing that. And he's done all this without even a little help from you three." I stabbed a finger in turn at the brothers three. "You don't get this so I'll give it to you. You have nothing to say to Grayson Cody, not about what he does or this land. So get in your cars and," I strained against Gray's arm and screeched, "*go*."

"I see, little lady, that you don't get when your momma turns her back on you, that has consequences," Frank informed me more than a little arrogantly.

"No, what I see is that Momma was disappointed in the sons she carried, she birthed and she raised when they acted like greedy jackasses after she lost her legs and her son, and they didn't set about doing everything they could to win back her trust, respect and affection. That shit was a result of *your*," another finger jab, "actions and I find it laughable that you three would come here and demand Gray man up when not one of you has done that same thing for over a decade. Gray taking care of this land, that house and your mother while you lived your lives carrying your grudges makes him more man than the three of you combined and then some."

"Ivey," Gray murmured warningly with an arm squeeze.

I shook my head and didn't tear my eyes off the Codys.

"You've lost her," I said quietly. "The woman you know as mother is breathing but she's gone. With the strength in her body went her fire. She doesn't boss anymore. Doesn't tell you what to do, doesn't have an opinion about everything. You live just miles away from a mother who's fading fast and soon everything, and that means *everything* about her will be a memory. Are you sure that in twenty, thirty years when you'll be in the same place that she is now you'll be secure in the knowledge you did the right thing by your mother? Because if you are then there's something wrong with you and if you were real men, you'd take time to reflect on that and then you'd use the time you have left to mend bridges with your mother and give her what you've got to give in the time she's got left."

Although I was talking quietly and standing still, I ended my rant breathing heavily. And when I ended my rant, I had three Codys just staring at me.

When no one said anything for a while, I noted, "You aren't leaving."

Frank tore his eyes from me to look over my shoulder at Gray.

"Ma's not doin' good?"

Jeez.

Seriously?

"Frank, she was, she wouldn't be in that fuckin' home," Gray replied, sounding as exasperated as I felt and then some.

"You said she couldn't take care o' her personal business," Charlie put in.

"Yeah, I said that," Gray agreed. "I also said she was deteriorating quickly."

"How bad is it?" Olly asked.

"Bad," I bit out and got all three Codys looking at me again.

Then Frank looked back at Gray and asked softly, "How much time's she got?"

"Not much, God feels kind," Gray answered.

These words spoke volumes and there was a moment of silence then some Cody men shuffling their feet. Then there was a very long moment of silence while all three Codys looked anywhere but at each other or Gray.

Men!

"God!" I cried, impatient and on edge. "Seriously?"

Again they all looked at me.

And again it was Frank who lifted his eyes to Gray but this time their blue depths were twinkling with something familiar, something I saw often in Gray, something I used to see in Grandma Miriam and he remarked, "Heard word, now see it's true. Your girl's quite the spitfire."

I rolled my eyes to the nearly cloudless Colorado sky as Gray's arm gave me a squeeze.

"O' course," Charlie said and I rolled my eyes to him to see him grinning, "Gray's a Cody." He leaned a bit toward me and shared, "Cody men like fire and not a little bit of it."

"You're still here," I noted.

Olly ignored my comment and asked Gray, "Ang drop off her chicken Mexican thing?"

Charlie's back straightened as he shot to attention.

"Fuck, yeah, that casserole could win awards," Charlie muttered, breaking off from the pack and, to my utter disbelief, heading toward the house. "Tragedy strikes, Ang breaks out the tortillas."

"Does he really think he can go to *my* kitchen and eat the casserole Ang made for *you and me*?" I hissed but I should have saved my breath seeing as all the Codys, including the one by name only, started toward the house.

"Seems like it," Gray muttered, I started to twist my neck to look back at him then I felt his arm and body tense around me and I knew why.

Coming down the lane was a police cruiser.

By the time Captain Lenny parked, got out of the car and approached a Gray who had wrapped his arm around my neck pulling me in close, front to his side, I felt the Codys all standing at our backs.

It was long overdue.

But at least they were there.

Lenny took in Team Cody and continuing to do so muttered, "Good to see this shit's had some good come outta it, you all workin' out your crap."

"Save the commentary, Len, you got news?" Frank barked, Lenny studied him then his eyes came to me. I give him a wince-faced apologetic look and he sighed.

Then he looked at Gray. "Pete rolled over on Bud."

Gray and I both got tense but Gray definitely was tenser and a wave of emotion came from behind us.

Lenny went on.

"Spent the mornin' gettin' a judge to get us warrants. Once we got those, we moved in on Pete's place as well as Bud and Cecily's. Boys are still at both places. Buddy's been at the station since eight o'clock this mornin' when we brought him in. We been talkin' to him on and off since then and he denies any involvement. We pushed it, he's lawyered up. We're waitin' for his attorney to get there so we can have another chat. That said, the warrants we got included lookin' into his phone records and financials and we found he took a trip to Vegas not too long ago, stayed a single night, this corroborating a statement Ivey gave us about when he went there to have his chat with her. This is new evidence we just got about half an hour ago and we'll be usin' that when we sit down with him and his attorney."

"Right," Gray muttered, his voice tight and Lenny held his eyes but shifted his feet in a way that was very un-Lenny.

I would know why when he said softly, "You know, Pete's been outta work now for goin' on two years."

Oh God.

Gray's body went solid, my arms slid around him and another wave of emotion hit us from the back.

"Do not defend that piece a' shit," Olly growled and Lenny looked to him.

"I'm not. I'm tryin' to do the impossible and explain the unexplainable. Sometimes, folks get wronged, they like knowin' what motivated the ones who wronged 'em." Lenny's eyes came to me. "He's taken odd jobs but they weren't makin' ends meet. He was gettin' desperate, thinkin' he'd lose his place, his truck. He said Bud paid him. Unfortunately, this was with cash but we're hopin' we can string that line together." Lenny looked back at Gray. "He knew about the shotgun, Gray, set the fire and then tripped the shotgun to give you warnin'. Boy's never set a fire before, didn't know the barn would go up that fast. Thought you'd have plenty of time to get those horses safe."

"I think you can guess my response to that is, I don't give a fuck," Gray replied softly, his voice still tight with restrained impatience and controlled anger.

"Yep, I could guess that was your response," Lenny muttered.

"He cop to poisoning my trees?" Gray asked, Lenny held his eyes a moment then nodded. "And, knowin' about the shotgun, he did my horses," Gray went on, Lenny's jaw went hard and he nodded again. "All paid for by Buddy?" Gray finished and Lenny nodded again.

Gray held Lenny's eyes and Lenny let him then Gray, his jaw now hard, looked to his boots, I knew, seeking control and patience.

"So what now?" Macy asked from behind us and Lenny looked at her then to Gray and me.

"We hope Bud confesses but I wouldn't hold my breath. Had a number of boys take a shot at him and he's not givin' us anything. Which means we gotta hope we can find somethin' at his house that ties him to this shit or find a trail that leads to him." Lenny told Macy then his eyes went back to Gray. "You got my promise, Gray, swear on my momma, rest her soul, that me and all my boys at Mustang PD are doin' everything we can. They don't like a man and his woman woke in the middle of the night to take their lives in their hands savin' horses. They don't like dead horses. And they don't like Buddy Sharp. You got a lotta motivation working for you, Gray. Trust in that."

"The only thing I trust is that Bud's lackey and fall guy is in the tank and stayin' there awhile so my horses that have no barn to give them a minimal amount of safety won't go poisoned until Bud gathers the money to find someone else to fuck with me. And maybe I can trust that knowin' this shit, Bud doesn't have the balls to do his own dirty work so me and Ivey got a window of time to feel safe. That could be a day, a week or a month but we won't know how long that is so I think you can guess I won't be hangin' around waiting for whatever he plans next. I appreciate you're doin' what you gotta do how you gotta do it, and the way that is it takes time. But what I said last night stands, Len. You don't take care of this shit, I will."

"Not smart to make an open threat to a police captain." This warning from Lenny was gentle but it was still a warning.

"Probably not," Olly put in from behind us, "but I'll tell you too, you don't take care of this shit, Gray doesn't, I will."

"And I'll say," Frank added, "you, Gray or Olly don't do it or I get a wild hair up my ass waitin' for this shit to get done, I'll do it."

"I don't even need a wild hair. Bud Sharp's an asshat. I'm already thinkin' of doin' it," Charlie threw down.

"So there you go," Frank summed it up, "four Codys, four threats, four men in Mustang with fierce reason to carry them out. Somethin' happens to Bud Sharp, you got four directions to turn."

At that, Gray went solid again and I knew why.

By making open threats, they had Gray's back by casting suspicion four ways.

It was clever, it was kind (in its way) and it was family.

Feeling something I didn't think I'd ever feel, my heart warming to Gray's uncles, I pressed closer to my man's side.

"Though, sayin' all that, somethin' happened to Bud Sharp, you'd probably have to bring in most of Mustang for questioning," Olly muttered.

Lenny stared at them then he sighed.

Then his phone rang. He grabbed it, looked at it, moved his glance through all of us and lifted a one minute finger. Then he took the call and put the phone to his ear. He talked and listened and we all waited.

Then he said, "Right, with Gray now, be back in around ten."

Then he flipped his phone shut and looked at Gray.

"The station," he explained. "Jeb Sharp just came in and asked to speak to his son."

"About time Jeb had words with that boy," Macy mumbled.

Lenny ignored Macy and noted softly to Gray, "This could be good, Gray."

"We'll see," Gray replied and it was clear he felt Jeb Sharp had little sway over his son.

Lenny held his eyes. Then he nodded. Then he looked to the devastation his nephew wreaked, shook his head, his jaw got tight again then he looked back at Team Cody.

"Tape comes down, you need help cleanin' up, takin' care of those dead horses, you call me and Whit. We'll be here."

No hard feelings with my man, communicating what Pete did didn't reflect on Lenny, it reflected on Pete and he showed this by saying, "I'll call, Len."

Another nod from Lenny, a glance through us all, a lifted hand and he turned toward his cruiser.

And as he did I saw another car coming up the lane. More brownies or a casserole, undoubtedly.

Then I saw what kind of car was coming up the lane.

A shiny black Lincoln with shaded windows.

My body jerked then I smiled and tipped my head back to look at Gray who was staring with narrow eyes down the lane.

"Did you call him?" I asked excitedly and he dipped his chin to look down at me but shook his head. I looked back at the lane. "That has to be him." My eyes went back to Gray who also had looked back down the lane. "Do you know anyone in Mustang with that car?"

Gray again gave me his eyes and said, "No."

"Who's that?" Frank asked from behind us as the Lincoln came closer but Gray nor I answered, we just kept watching the Lincoln get closer.

Lenny couldn't drive down the lane with the Lincoln coming up so he was standing in the cruiser's opened door, watching the Lincoln approach.

Then it approached and I saw I was right.

Driver's side, Brutus. Passenger side, Lash.

"Oh my God!" I cried, jumping a small jump against Gray's body then I started to pull away to run toward my friends who were making a very well-timed surprise visit.

But I didn't get very far. Gray's arm locked around my shoulders and his other arm locked around my waist.

He also whispered, "No, baby."

I struggled, looking back and forth between Gray and the car, thinking he was playing with me, wondering why, pulling to get away at the same time still jumping excitedly and crying out, "Gray, let me go!"

His arms got tighter and his voice dipped lower when he locked me to him and whispered, "Fuck, baby."

At his tone, my head snapped back to the Lincoln to see Brutus had folded out, as had Lash. They were both wearing shades but I knew both their eyes were aimed at me and both their faces didn't look happy.

But it was the back door opening that caught my attention, made my breath clean leave me, my stomach hollow out and my heart stop beating.

Because out of that door came my brother Casey.

Chapter 33

Talk

I was in the kitchen, shaking.

Gray was standing in the doorway with Lash.

Macy was in the kitchen with me and she was crowding me.

"Tell me why you brought that motherfucker here?" Gray growled, keeping his distance from Lash and visibly keeping his body in check. They were close, the door not affording them much room and Gray was pissed beyond any kind of pissed I'd seen Gray be.

And I'd seen Gray be really, freaking pissed.

The Brothers Cody, Brutus and Lenny, who had wisely taken one look at Casey, undoubtedly remembered him and decided to stay, were all in the living room with Casey.

Casey!

Oh God.

"Because I know what he has to say, the Mustang police should know and hear it from him and, last, she deserves this, Cody, and you do too," Lash replied, he was alert but calm and holding Gray's eyes.

"Maybe but you could have called," Gray returned and this was true. So, so true. "You did, you'd know the barn burned down last night and we got seven horses dead. Ivey was in that barn with me savin' the thirteen we got left."

Lash's face got hard and his eyes sliced to me.

"Look at me, Caldiwell," Gray rumbled and Lash's eyes cut back to Gray. "Why didn't you call?"

"Because I thought if I did, you'd protect Ivey by not giving her what Casey has to give."

Gray's body straightened and seemed to expand, such was his increased anger but Lash shook his head.

"Calm, my man, that guy in there has not pulled one over on me. I'm not here to orchestrate a family reunion. What he's got to give is no good. It's just truth. Ugly truth. And I read from you right now and read it the same seein' you with her before that you'd protect her from that shit and that is not your call. It's not mine. It's Ivey's. I'm giving her that call."

"You don't know me enough to know I wouldn't give her the same," Gray clipped out.

"You're right but I also wasn't going to take any chances," Lash fired back, his eyes slid to me then back to Gray. "Timing sucks but better to get this shit over with and do with that guy whatever you decide you want done with him. Deal with him or cut him loose. One way or another, I want shot of him. Filth stinks and I'm really not fond of his smell."

Lash, a man I loved, a man who looked out for me, a man who took care of me, a man who out-and-out spoiled me was talking about my brother that way.

Pure Casey.

Obviously he hadn't changed.

"Ivey, you okay?" Macy asked softly, still crowding me.

No, I wasn't.

I didn't answer her.

I spoke to Lash.

"I know why," I said softly and both Gray and Lash's eyes came to me. When I got Lash's attention, I continued, "If you gave Gray the info and he chose not to tell me, you thought, if Casey made his way back to me whenever and for whatever reason, because being Casey, even though it's been years, he'd eventually need me, you thought I'd buckle."

Lash gave it to me straight with his prompt answer of, "Yes."

I studied him knowing he was right.

I loved my brother.

It was a failing.

I looked to Gray then to Macy then to my feet as they moved me through the kitchen and I muttered, "Let's get this done."

Gray and Lash separated so I could squeeze through them. I led and, with Macy, they followed.

Casey's eyes came to me the minute I hit the living room. I took two steps in and stopped, feeling Lash and Gray position themselves behind me.

Brutus was standing behind and beside the armchair in which Casey was lounging negligently, even belligerently. The Brothers Cody and Lenny were positioned around the room, all standing. Macy went to Olly.

Casey didn't tear his gaze from me.

"Looks like you landed on your feet, sis," he remarked and I felt the heavy atmosphere in the room get even heavier.

I took in my brother.

He'd lost weight. He had a scar I knew came from a deep cut on his cheek, another one from a shallow cut curving up from the collar of his tee by his collarbone. His hair was a mess and, even though he was only thirty-four, it had already started to go gray. There were lines around his eyes and mouth that didn't come from work in the sun or laughter but hard living and a lifetime of worry. His tee, jeans and boots weren't dirty or tatty but they weren't good quality and he'd had them awhile.

He looked ten years older than he was. He looked angry. And he looked beaten but even so, he was trying to hide it behind hostility.

When I made no response, his eyes moved over my shoulder to Gray then back to me.

"See you and your cowboy again aren't gonna offer me hospitality." His brows went up. "No cool, refreshing glass of homemade lemonade on the farm? Not an offer of a nice, cold bottle of brew?"

Jeez.

Casey.

Finally, I spoke. "Lash says you have something to say to me."

"Got a lotta things be happy to say to you," Casey replied and I heard Gray draw in breath.

"Casey, be smart, just tell me what happened, what you did seven years ago so you can be on your way to continue to do whatever you've been doing," I urged softly, hating this and wanting it done.

"Seven years ago, my sister upped, stole a wad of my cash, my car and took off on me," Casey returned.

"Cash you were given to take me away from Gray, from Mustang," I reminded him, it was a guess but I knew it was the right one when Casey's eyes flashed. But he didn't confirm this information.

Instead, he noted, "Car was mine, sis. You left me high and dry with no wheels."

It was my turn to remind my brother of something. "If I remember, I won the pinks to that car in a game of pool."

Casey's face got hard and he inched up a bit in his chair. "I primed that mark."

"We both know," I said quietly, "that I didn't need you to prime anything."

"Jesus, fuck, yeah," he spit, eyes narrowing. "You didn't need me, right? Fuck, Ivey, you got a selective memory."

Pain ripped through me.

He was very right at the same time being pitifully wrong.

At this point, Gray entered the conversation. "This is not why you're here. We're not goin' over the history of Casey and Ivey Bailey. You're gonna talk about what you did seven years ago."

Casey's eyebrows shot up and he asked sarcastically, "I am?"

"You are," Gray confirmed.

"I wanna talk about somethin' else, I can't. If I can't talk about what I wanna talk about, why would I talk about what *you* wanna talk about?" Casey asked.

"You owe it to your sister and you owe it to me," Gray replied.

Casey inched up even more, his body tensing, his face twisting and he hissed, "I don't owe *you* or that *bitch* shit."

Then it happened so quickly it was like I didn't see it. Gray was across the room, Casey out of his chair and Gray tore him out of it with such force, the chair, which was not light, tipped to its back and skidded a couple of feet. The end result was Casey, his back to the wall, and Gray, his body pressing into Casey, his hand wrapped around Casey's throat, squeezing.

Casey kicked out his feet but Gray positioned his body to Casey's side so he had no target at the same time the fingers on both Casey's hands curled around Gray's forearm to pull it away but Gray had such a fierce hold on him, he had no hope.

"*Talk!*" Gray barked in his face.

"Let me go!" Casey wheezed, still kicking, still pulling at Gray's hand and all the men in the room closed in on the two of them.

Gray either was so focused he didn't feel them or he didn't care. Instead, using Casey's neck, he pulled him away from the wall and slammed him into it so his had cracked against the drywall, sounding with a sickening thud.

Then he did it again.

Then he roared, "*Talk!*"

Clearly, he'd also put more pressure on Casey's throat because now Casey was gurgling in an attempt to get air in. He'd stopped kicking out with his feet because all his effort needed to be at Gray's arm, which still didn't budge.

When Casey formed no words, Gray again pulled Casey away from the wall and his head lurched forward like a ragdoll and smashed back against the wall when Gray slammed him there.

"*Talk!*" he again thundered.

I stood still and frozen and Frank got close to Gray.

He put his hand on Gray's shoulder and said quietly, "Son, man can't talk with you squeezin' the life outta him."

I deep breathed as I watched Gray's upper body moving in a way that I knew he was doing the same. He took a moment to consider his uncle's words then he yanked Casey away from the wall and threw him across the room. Casey flew over the turned chair, ass over head rolling and landed on his stomach on a skid that took him dangerously close to a table with thin, curved legs and an old-fashioned, glass-based lamp I particularly liked.

Once he stopped, Gray stalked to him and stood over him, repeating, "Now, talk."

Casey rolled to his side, clutching his throat with one hand, coming up to the other forearm, his eyes going to Gray. The belligerence was still there but significantly muted because now there was not a small amount of fear.

Yes, my brother Casey had not changed. Gray had shown him he could best him. It was a long time ago but everything about Gray showed he had matured and remained fit and healthy and everything about Casey showed the exact opposite, and still, Casey had underestimated Gray.

When he sucked in enough breath to function, he reminded Gray, "You got a cop here."

"I know," Gray returned immediately. "A breakdown of who's in this room is not what I want you to talk about. Now, talk."

This explained why Casey thought he had the upper hand and could be an asshole. He thought the presence of Lenny would be his shield.

Casey looked to Lenny as did I and seeing him leaning a shoulder nonchalantly against the wall opposite the drama, even someone as stupid as Casey couldn't miss that Captain Lenny was not here in an official capacity and had no intentions of stepping up for Casey.

When my eyes went back to my brother I saw he was making

movements like he was going to get up but Gray stepped closer to him, leaned over and whispered, "Stay down. You say what you gotta say from right there."

"Man, I gotta get up," Casey clipped.

"No, *man*, you gotta learn when you're beat and stay down. You're beat. Stay down and..." he bent further at the waist, "*talk*."

Casey glared at Gray then he put his hand at his throat to the floor, looked beyond Gray to me and finally got smart.

"That guy, name's Sharp, the one you beat at pool, he sent a tracker out to find me."

Gray straightened and took half a step back. Everyone else in the room also partially retreated.

I kept my eyes locked to my brother.

He kept talking.

"Tracker found me, brought me to him. He offered me ten K to get you outta this shithole and keep you out. No one knows, no one sees us leave. When I got you gone, no phone calls, no comin' back, nothin'. I made it so you ceased to exist for Cody for good and forever."

I guessed it, deep down I knew it but it still hurt like hell to *know* it.

Casey continued, "Five K up front, five more after I got you gone. They came up with the story I was gonna feed you and to convince you, him and his three friends took free shots at me."

My head started shaking at how stupid and greedy and just plain *stupid* my brother was but I didn't tear my eyes away from Casey.

"You take the note?" Gray asked and Casey looked up at him.

"No," he answered, showing he knew exactly what Gray was referring to. "But when I called to confirm we were gone, told him she wrote it. He told me it was seen to."

"The rest of her stuff, he tell you about that?" Gray kept questioning and Casey shook his head.

"He didn't tell me shit but I reckon he had someone go in and nab the note, they took the rest of her shit. Objective, she vanished. I did my part, he did his."

Everyone was silent.

"Ten thousand dollars," I whispered into the silence and Casey looked back to me.

That was when it leaked through. The real Casey. The one that faded through the years as he let life beat him down without fighting back.

The Casey who loved me.

And I saw it through the remorse that shone from his eyes.

And I didn't care.

"Ivey—" he started but I kept talking.

"Even if Gray wasn't here, in this town with these people, the way it is, I was happy here," I told him. "I'd found a home."

"Sis—" he tried to break in but I didn't let him.

"But Gray *was* here and so not only did I find a home, I found a family."

Casey closed his eyes.

I kept speaking.

"All I ever wanted, Casey," I reminded him and he opened his eyes. "I told you that, I don't know how many times. All I ever wanted and you, my own brother, all it took was ten thousand dollars and you took that away from me."

He pushed up to sitting but stayed down, eyes never leaving me and he opened his mouth to speak but I got there before him.

"Seven years. You stole seven years from me."

"I—" he tried again but I shook my head.

"There is absolutely *nothing*," I leaned in on the last word, feeling my blood racing through my veins, the rush of it in my brain, "you could say that would explain or make me understand why you would do that to me. Not one thing."

Casey swallowed.

"I loved him," I whispered, the surge of anger disintegrating, instant sorrow taking its place. "I loved him with everything I had, everything I was. He made me happy for the first time in...my...*life*. And you took him away from me."

Casey didn't speak.

I did.

"You're dead to me."

His face paled, pain slashed through his features and I didn't get that. I didn't get how he could sit there and think for one minute that my reaction would be anything but what it was.

Then again, for a long time I didn't get a lot about Casey.

"Dead to me," I whispered.

Then I turned on my flip-flop, walked out of the living room, up the stairs and to Gray and my room.

I was standing at the window looking at the burned remains of our barn when Gray's arms wrapped around me, one at my ribs, one at my chest and his lips came to my ear.

"Lash and Freddie need to know what you want done with him," he said softly.

"I don't care."

His arms gave me a quick squeeze and he kept speaking softly in my ear.

"I get you feel that way now, dollface, but you gotta power through that just for a second 'cause those two men are itchin' to teach your brother a lesson. You open that opportunity to them—"

"I don't care."

"Ivey—"

I turned in his arms, put my hands to his waist, looked into his deep blue eyes with their russet lashes, eyes that were the last thing I should have seen every night for seven years and eyes I should have woken up to every morning and I repeated slowly and firmly, "I... don't...*care*."

His beautiful eyes held mine before they moved over my face then his hand came up, fingers gliding along my cheek and back. He slid them into my hair, cupped my head and dropped his to touch his mouth to mine.

When he lifted his head, he whispered, “Okay, honey.”

“Okay.”

He bent his neck to touch his forehead to mine for a second before he gave me a squeeze and let me go.

I watched his ass in his jeans until he turned down the hall.

Then I turned back to the window and looked at the burned out barn.

Twenty-two years of hell. Seven years of happy limbo.

Now I was home.

I was *home.*

I focused on that.

Then I drew in a steadying breath and waited until I heard the car start. Then I heard another one. I also heard them going down the lane.

Only then did I walk out of our bedroom, but I turned away from the stairs and walked the few feet to the end of the hall where there was a window seat and a big, sashed window that looked out to the side of the house.

The cruiser gone. The Lincoln gone. The Cody cars remained.

And there it was. I had a house full of family, a kitchen table full of generosity, so I had to get my ass downstairs and provide hospitality.

So that was just what I did.

Chapter 34

That Kind of Sweet

Three weeks later…

I was in the kitchen doing the lunch dishes and smelling the cake I was baking in the oven for after dinner.

I looked out the window to the cleared out area where the barn was.

Gray with Shim, Roan, Danny, Barry, Gene, Sonny, Lenny and Lenny's son—a seriously good-looking man with an easy smile like Gray's and a quick wit who I put in his late twenties—Whit, helped him clear away the debris, pull out the dead horses and bury them.

Fortunately, the insurance company didn't mess around with their inspection or getting us a check. Now, there was a massive pile of wood covered in see-through plastic tarps wrapped with thick wire and weighed down with bricks next to the skeleton of the barn that soon would be. So soon, the roof was done and at the back they'd already put up the wall.

The insurance company paid for us to have builders see to it but Gray and his posse were doing it themselves. They knew what they were doing and it saved money. It surprised me but the work was going quickly even though Gray did it with mostly just him and

Sonny, who was retired so he had the time. All the rest of the men had jobs but a few always came at night to put in an hour or two. I fed them if they didn't have women at home to do it and then they'd leave. Weekends, usually the entire posse was there. Gray reckoned, with the progress, the barn would be up and our horses would have their new home in another two weeks, at the most three.

Gray told me I got to pick the color he'd paint it. The house was white with two different shades of gray adorning the woodwork intermingled with hints here and there of barn red. The old barn was painted gray.

I picked barn red. It *was* a barn and I liked the idea of living on a ranch-slash-orchard with a barn painted the stereotypical red. I might be a cowboy rancher's stylish girlfriend who often wore designer clothes and high heels but we lived the rancher life. Might as well go whole hog.

The quick raising of the barn was the good news.

The bad news was, Lenny's nephew Pete was going down for what he did but Buddy wasn't. He didn't confess, even after his father put pressure on him to do so. And he might be an asshole with a freaky, scary obsession with Grayson Cody but unfortunately, he wasn't a stupid one.

Pete bought the poison. Having once worked (and lost his job at) another orchard in the vicinity, Pete had the knowledge to procure the virus he injected in the trees. Cash withdrawals from Bud and Cecily's accounts could be traced as to what Pete told the cops Buddy paid him to do his nefarious deeds but Buddy contended he gave him the money, "to help out a friend."

Unfortunately, Ted and Jim, Buddy's other two sidekicks, stepped up to throw Pete right under the bus, corroborating that Buddy, being a good guy, just wanted to help Pete during a tough time and Pete was talking shit to get his ass out of hot water.

The fact that Pete had no motivation to do what he did to Gray and Buddy had publically carried on a one-sided, seriously whacked feud with Gray since junior high was unfortunately all Pete had. All the material evidence was found at Pete's house and he gave his confession. Outside of the payments made with timings that loosely coincided with the deeds done, nothing linked any of Pete's activities to Buddy. With only the word of a man caught and going down to connect Buddy to the crimes, they had nothing to go with so they couldn't charge him with anything.

Lenny gave us this information in our living room and he did it hesitantly and angrily. He didn't like that he'd failed Gray but his hands were tied.

Gray's were not.

Therefore, Gray had visited Buddy at his place of business. In his glass-walled office he explained exactly what would befall Buddy at the hands of Gray, as backed by the Brothers Cody, if anything else happened on his land, to Gray or to me. No one heard any of the words, they just saw the exchange and it was the talk of the town.

I didn't suspect this would stop Buddy.

What I did suspect would stop him was that the Mustang Police Department put our ranch on radar and they did this openly. Random but frequent drive-bys not only from cruisers of the Mustang PD but also the county sheriff during which, often, the cruiser would coast up the lane. They were visible and meant to be.

They weren't the only ones.

The Brothers Cody, Shim, Roan, Whit (the latter three when they weren't working on the barn) or one of Jeb Sharp's ranch hands were nearly always parked across from the mouth of our lane on the side of the road in front of our property, standing vigil. Also often, night or day, Shim, Roan or Whit would drive down the lane, saddle up one of our horses and take him or her for a wander through Gray's land. Further, Gene, who was an electrician, set up random and very bright lights in the orchard that had motion sensors and would light up like a beacon if someone tripped them in the night. They made no noise but they could be seen from our bedroom window and anyone out there doing something they shouldn't could wake up a rancher under fire who was not sleeping soundly (and, alas, this was true for my man) but also might make them visible to a passing cruiser or the vigilance of the Brothers Cody and Jeb Sharp.

It made me feel safer but I knew it didn't make Gray feel that way as evidenced by the aforementioned light sleeping.

My man was struggling.

And I knew why because he talked to me about it.

He had no plays open to him. He couldn't beat the shit out of Buddy to teach him a lesson because he'd not only done that before (several times) and got nowhere but also it was against the law and all eyes in Mustang were on him. He also was not the kind of man to play with him or get to him through making plays against Cecily or their children.

He had no options except the one he took, to warn Buddy off.

And he hated it.

But I also knew if Buddy did one more thing, Gray would lose it and then we'd both be screwed.

That said, Gray might not be the kind of man to play with Buddy but Janie, Chastity and Stacy had shared with me that others didn't feel the same way. Since our barn burned down, Buddy and Cecily had had a lot of bad luck.

A lot.

Buddy's car had had two flat tires then it quit working altogether and considering it was only a year old, this was suspicious. Their house had been vandalized, windows egged and the words "horse murderer" painted on the front in blood red. Their mailbox sitting on a post at the road had been targeted twice by drive-bys and baseball bats. And Whit had shared with Gray that his dad had shared with him that Buddy came into the station with a note Cecily found on their doorstep that was just one piece of paper in an envelope with four words computer printed on it, "Get out of Mustang."

Cecily wasn't showing her face in town and Janie told me she was doing what she needed to do in Elk but otherwise keeping a low profile. Rumor had it she was terrified.

I didn't have it in me to relish this. They had kids. This stuff was not nice and although they'd brought it on themselves and arguably deserved it, their daughters didn't.

I also didn't know who did it. It could be Gray's uncles but it also could be anybody. No one believed Buddy didn't back Pete, everybody respected Gray and the filling in of the blanks from Casey about what Buddy did to Gray and me was spread far and wide. This, I knew, was by the Brothers Cody. Unfortunately, this wasn't felonious so no charges could be lodged. But this also didn't sit well with Mustangians as a whole.

So it could be anyone.

Further, I didn't relish it because Buddy was not the kind of man to put his tail between his legs, sell his house and slink off to the next county, never to be seen again.

He was the kind of man who would want payback.

Considering what he'd already done, this could mean anything and after it was achieved, if Gray and I remained standing, Gray wouldn't be able to control his fury.

I did not see good things.

So now I was doing the dishes and baking a cake and my man was in town picking up nails or something to continue working on the barn. Sonny was out there and I heard a hammer pounding. I also knew one of Jeb Sharp's boys was at the mouth of the lane. I knew it because it was a long way, but I could see the pickup sitting there. I also knew it because Gray would not leave me alone unless he knew Sonny and that pickup were there with me.

So he left me alone.

Therefore with this backup, I was surprised to hear a vehicle approaching and when I turned my head to look out the side window I was further surprised to see the SUV heading down the lane without the pickup following it. An SUV heading down the lane wasn't a surprise, the fact I'd never seen that particular one, though, was.

I shoved the last dish in the dishwasher, closed the door, dried my hands and headed out of the kitchen, down the hall and out the front door. I was standing on the porch when the SUV stopped and parked. I noted Sonny coming into view, his eyes on the SUV but he didn't approach. I didn't know if that was strange or not.

Then I watched as a woman got out.

Her hair used to be blonde, you could still see traces of it, but now it was turning an attractive blend of white, silver with hints of light gray. It was wild and she, rightfully, regardless of her age, kept it long and left it free. Its waves and curls tumbled down her shoulders and back and, except for the fading color, it reminded me of mine.

She wore jeans, a blouse that was way cool, managing to be very feminine and attractive but still practical. She had a pair of scuffed, old cowboy boots on her feet. I placed her in her fifties, I'd say early fifties but I couldn't tell. She had great skin, lovely features, was fit but not slim, rounded and she was clearly lucky with genes. It could be she hid her age or it could be she always would naturally.

She looked at me, turned her head to take in Sonny then she looked back at me and started my way. She didn't come to the steps but instead approached the side of the porch where she stopped three feet away, her eyes, the entire way, never leaving me.

"You don't know me," she started, telling me something I knew before I could get out a greeting. "I'm Eleanor Cody."

My breath clean left me as I stared at Gray's mother.

I'd never seen her, never even seen a picture of her, she was wiped clean from Chez Cody. And I'd never seen this woman in town, I would have remembered her. This wasn't surprising because, regardless of all that happened, I'd spent approximately four whole months in Mustang. I'd seen and met a lot of people but I hadn't seen and met everybody.

I forced myself to breathe at the same time my mind ticked over ways to play this.

I started by introducing myself. "I'm Ivey Larue."

A small smile played at her mouth and her brown eyes twinkled briefly as she replied, "I know."

Of course, everyone did. Being who she was, she would too.

I looked at her then looked at Sonny who hadn't moved, didn't look like he intended to approach but also didn't look like he intended to retreat.

Keeping an eye on things.

My eyes went back to Eleanor Cody.

"Would you like to come in?" I offered and that got me another small smile, this one with no twinkle but a hint of sadness and a shake of the head.

"Don't see Gray's truck, reckon he's not here," she answered. "Reckon, he comes home, he won't want me in his house."

There was a reason for the sadness in her smile because this was definitely true.

"Yeah, but he's made it clear this is my home and I don't mind," I said quietly.

Her head tipped a bit and she studied me a moment.

Then she righted her head, took a step forward and suggested, "How about you swing for a while and I'll take a rest on the porch?"

A nice compromise.

I nodded, moved to the swing and sat down. She moved to the porch and sat on its edge, body turned toward the barn, her eyes again never leaving me.

"Like they're all sayin', you sure are a pretty little thing."

My heart clenched because her son felt the same way and told me, repeatedly.

"Thank you," I whispered then smiled. "You aren't so bad yourself."

She smiled back and rested her weight in a hand on the porch.

"Do you want a pop, some lemonade? A glass of water?" I asked.

"No, Ivey, but thanks."

"Okay."

Her eyes moved toward the barn and I leaned forward in the swing to see beyond the house. Sonny was moving back to do his work.

"Gray okay with all this?"

This was Eleanor and she was speaking softly and tentatively and I looked back at her to see her eyes still on the barn.

"No," I answered honestly and her gaze came back to me. "He's angry, feels threatened, feels I'm under threat and his options are so limited they're non-existent so he's frustrated. So, no, he's not okay."

She nodded then murmured, "Abel."

"Sorry?" I asked and she focused harder on me.

"Just like his father. Abel. Don't let those uncles of Gray's make you think differently. Knew Gray's granddad, knew Miriam, so don't know where Olly, Frank and Charlie got their brand of ornery. Miriam could be ornery but not like that. All the Codys could be wild but when they settled, they settled and that was it. Olly, Frank and Charlie are a mystery for the ages. Didn't know, down under the surface of what they show everyone, it wasn't all good and that no way would Miriam step out on her husband, I wouldn't believe they were Codys."

She was right about that.

"Abel, he was pure Cody," she went on. "Fair. Patient. Controlled. But you threaten something or someone he loved, it'd rile him, rile him enough to take action. But he would not mete out unjustifiable justice no matter how angry he could be. See my son grew up like his father."

"Yes," I agreed.

She drew in breath then her eyes slid from mine to my ear and she announced, "Talked to Prisc."

Oh God.

"What?" I asked.

Her eyes came back to mine and she repeated, "Talked to Prisc. Priscilla. She's a friend of Cecily Sharp."

"I know. I've kind of met her."

"Good girl," Eleanor said quietly but my back went straighter and I replied, "I disagree."

Eleanor held my eyes for a long time and it was like she was psyching herself up and I would know why when she again spoke.

"I understand that, Ivey, but sometimes folks do stupid things for equally stupid reasons. That doesn't mean they aren't good people."

Well I knew that was a fact. I'd had ten years of living it.

I fought against holding my breath but I did hold my tongue.

Eleanor didn't.

"Don't know you, what I do know of you, I know you're a good gal. Know my son loves you. But I don't know what he's told you about me so I don't know if you want to hear this and even if you're polite enough to let me have my say if, once you hear it, you'll care. Abel didn't. Miriam didn't. And Gray didn't. Then again, they didn't let me get close enough to share. Don't know you but I'll tell you what they never let me tell them."

And with this preamble, she launched right in.

"Abel wanted children, not just a son, a passel of them. Before we got engaged, all through when we were engaged and after we got married, he talked about it all the time, filling the house with Codys. His brothers might be hard to take but he loved them. They grew up close, had good times, family times, brothers being wild and getting into trouble times. Six people in this house, I used to love coming here. My parents both died when I was young, raised by my aunt who never married so I never experienced anything like that. Those men and Miriam, way she was. It was loud, always something going on. Someone in trouble. Someone telling a joke. Someone laughing or fighting or up to something. Abel, he wanted that, he wanted to fill this house again with that. And me, well..." she hesitated and looked to the barn, "I couldn't give it to him."

Shit.

There you go.

Shit.

"Eleanor—" I started and her head turned back to me.

"Norrie," she corrected me softly then continued. "Lost babies, again and again, lost them. You know that?"

I nodded.

She nodded after me.

Then she kept going.

"Each one, I felt it. I hope you never know, Ivey," she leaned in, "but *I felt it.*"

I kept my peace. It was hard, she felt it and I felt her words but I kept my peace. And I did this because I sensed that was what she needed from me.

She leaned back, drew breath and went on.

"Abel felt it more. Hurt worse, can't tell you how bad it hurt, right to my soul, to lose my babies then have to watch Abel trying to pretend he wasn't hurting worse than me. Each one I lost, feeling that, watching that, having it settle in me, I asked myself what do I do? What do I do?"

She looked to the barn again and told me what she did that I already knew.

"I left. I thought, if I did, he'd find someone who wouldn't give him that hurt but who *would* give him what he wanted most in this world." Her voice dropped to a whisper when she finished, "I had no idea what that was, was me."

Oh God.

I closed my eyes.

When she spoke again, I opened them to see hers on me.

"By the time I heard he hadn't moved on, by the time I figured out I was for him what he was for me and he didn't care he didn't have a house full of sons and daughters, just as long as that house had me, it was too late. I came back, I stayed and I tried, but it was too late. I knew, that hurt he was feeling when I lost my babies, it was losing those babies but what I didn't see was most of it was watching *me* lose them, knowing *my* hurt. I was too late understanding that too."

When she didn't speak for a while and I knew she was done, I said gently, "I'm sorry, Norrie."

"Me too, Ivey, me too."

Yes, she was sorry. Very sorry.

God.

I nodded.

She again spoke.

"I told you that because I want you to know. What you do with it," she shrugged, "up to you. I lost Gray with his father. I've come to terms with that. Wake up, every day, live with it and I don't like it much but I made a stupid decision based on stupid reasons that were emotional and I lost my boy with my man. I also tell you that because I reckon there are reasons Prisc did the stupid things she did. But now, what's gone down, she's not liking what she's feeling and she wants to do right. She couldn't go to Gray or you, definitely not Miriam and probably not anyone else in Mustang. So she came to me."

Here we go.

"And she told you?" I prompted.

Norrie didn't hesitate. "She told me she lied about seeing you go off with your brother, she didn't. She told me Cecily was the one who cleared out your stuff. She told me she, herself, had seen your note to Gray because Cecily showed it to her. And she told me that Cecily took all of it to Buddy and Cecily told her and Courtney that Buddy burned your note and tossed your stuff in the garbage."

I figured this and now all the blanks were filled but, just like with Casey, I hated to have it confirmed. I hated knowing that all the stuff I left behind, stuff I bought with money I earned, was thrown in the garbage. I hated that Cecily, Priscilla, the unknown Courtney and the despicable Buddy Sharp read the desperate and sad note I wrote to Gray where I told him why I was leaving, that I hoped I'd be back and just how much I loved him.

And I hated knowing it was long since discarded ash.

"She also told me she didn't like it then and tried to talk Cecily and Courtney out of it but Cecily is Cecily, Courtney is Courtney and she got nowhere. Before the plan was put into action, they froze her out. She learned her lesson, not the right one but the one they were teaching her, and she got on board. She's never liked it and now, Gray's barn going down, those horses going down with it, she can't live with it. So she's told me and she's also gone to the station and told Lenny. It's just information to him, he can't do anything about it, just closing the loops but she did that too. She's frozen out now from Cecily and Courtney but she no longer cares. Learned the hard way that no friendships are better than toxic ones."

I guessed that was right though I still didn't understand what motivated Priscilla. Then again, I hadn't had very many friends but I lucked out in the fact that the ones I had were the best kinds to have.

"I don't know what to do with this, Norrie," I told her, she tipped her head again and gave me another small smile.

"Nothing, something, whatever you want. But you deserve to know and you deserve to have the option to do something if you want. So now you have both. It's your choice."

I nodded.

She stood and I knew by her manner she was done, likely keen to get away before Gray came home so I stood with her.

"Best go," she muttered.

"Right," I muttered back.

She looked up at me. "Thanks for giving me time, Ivey."

"Thanks for taking the time to come and talk to me, Norrie."

She again studied me and the small smile came back. The sad one.

Then she whispered, "Glad Gray found a good, strong one."

Oh *God*.

She kept going.

"Hold on tight, Ivey."

"I will," I promised and I would, I knew that definitely.

She nodded and moved toward her car.

I called, "Norrie," and she stopped and turned back. "I'll tell Gray what you told me."

She shook her head. "Not why I told you that, sweetheart."

"I know, but I'll still tell Gray."

She held my eyes then she nodded again. "Okay, Ivey."

"Be well," I said softly.

"You too and stay safe."

It was my turn to nod.

She moved to her SUV, got in, started it up and drove away.

I watched the lane.

Then I went inside to check on my cakes.

They were out and on the wire rack cooling when the back door opened. I turned to it to see Sonny had swung his upper body in, hand still on the knob.

"You good?" he asked, his eyes sharp on me.

"Yeah, Sonny. I'm good," I answered quietly.

"Lived through Abel losin' her," Sonny announced and I blinked.

He wasn't done.

"Lived through him bein' stubborn and not taking her back."

I drew in breath. Then I nodded.

"Man's gotta do what a man's gotta do even if what he's gotta do is a fool thing to do."

"I guess that's right," I replied.

"Know it is," Sonny returned but he wasn't done. "When I thought history repeated, ticked me off. But it didn't. So what you learn from this, girl, all o' this shit, and where you find it in you to lead Gray, is that this shit is life. You got it worse than others but everyone has their crosses to bear. You bear 'em then you keep on keepin' on and you do it together. 'Cause shit always passes and you got enough sweet, it always sweeps away the bitter. You and Gray, this'll be done and you'll taste your sweet."

"Sonny," I smiled, "I've had enough bitter to last a lifetime. Now I'm baking cakes in a kitchen that when I first walked into it, I knew I wanted to walk into it dozens of times every day for the rest of my life and it's the kitchen of the man who I looked at once and I knew. I *knew*. And, honey, you know exactly what I knew. There's nothing that can take away that kind of sweet."

Sonny stared at me. Then he smiled.

Then he bitched, "I'm dyin' out here in this heat. I'm gettin' back to hittin' it and you're bringing me a glass of lemonade. Lotsa ice."

Then he disappeared behind the closed door.

And before I started on the frosting, I took out a glass of lemonade with lots of ice to Sonny.

Five hours later...

"Should I not have told you?" I asked quietly.

I was lounging mostly on Gray but partly on the couch and I'd just told him all about his mother's visit. The TV was on but I'd hit mute. I had Gray's undivided attention and he had mine.

I just couldn't catch hold of any of the expressions warring for prominence on his face.

Then he settled on one and that was mild annoyance.

"Why would you not tell me?" Gray asked back.

"Just that..." I paused, "you're dealing with a lot. You don't need more."

"Firstly, dollface, don't ever keep anything from me and especially not something important. Secondly, this is a small town, learn that, shit gets around. You keep something from me it's likely I'll find out about it. And lastly, yeah, *we're* dealing with a lot. But I'm not about to have a nervous breakdown."

"Right," I whispered.

He rolled us, switching positions so I was on my back and he was pressed the length of me. I could internally debate the merits of both positions, probably for years, but suddenly being in this one, I liked it better.

Gray took my mind off his long, hard body pressed into mine when he spoke.

"We figured it out about Prisc, suspected Cecily and we knew about Buddy. Don't care about that shit and I'll say, right now, better late than never doesn't wash with that shit Prisc let herself get sucked into. She wants to make amends, she can do it. But she'll feel no forgiveness from me. Twenty years from now, we'll see. Right now and for the future, I don't give a shit about what stupid reasons led to stupid actions. Yeah?"

I nodded. His call and it just so happened that, even though I didn't know her, it was the same one as mine.

Gray went on, "As for my mother, it was the right thing to do, it was a good thing to do and she has my gratitude. Whether I share that with her personally or not, I gotta chew on that awhile. You with me?"

I felt hope because I knew Gray and he might chew on it awhile but he'd do the right thing. And the right thing was sharing his gratitude personally then keeping that door open so she could walk through.

"Dollface," Gray called and I left those thoughts and focused on him. "I see what you're thinkin' and I know you're fired up to collect all the family you can get. But her stupid decision meant I didn't have a mother for twelve years. She left my dad but she also left me. One thing, as a wife, to have fucked up but understandable reasons to leave your husband. Another, as a mother, to have fucked up and not understandable reasons to leave behind your child. Maybe I got it in me to work with her to move past that, maybe I don't. But don't get your hopes up."

"Okay," I agreed because he was very right.

But I still had my hopes and Gray knew it because he grinned, giving me the dimple.

Then his eyes changed, my body responded to the change and they dropped to my mouth a second before they came back to mine and he pressed deeper into me as his face got closer.

"Now, you got a choice seein' as this is a rerun, I don't like this show anyway, you do. Still, I'm not watchin' it and that means neither are you. Instead, you got the choice of takin' my cock in your mouth then in you right here or doin' it in the bedroom. We move, when we get up there, I want you on your knees in front of me. Either way, you got a second to decide."

I didn't need a second.

I'd been on my knees in front of Gray once before and I'd liked it. It was *hot*.

"Upstairs," I whispered breathily.

He gave me the dimple again and I knew he knew what my answer would be. This was likely because, when he fucked my mouth when I was on my knees in front of him, it turned me on so much he barely got me to my back on the bed and thrust into me before I came. And when I came, I did it hard and I did it *long*.

Then I lost the dimple when he kissed me. And when he did, he did it hard and he did it *long*.

Then we went up to our room, lost our clothes and I gained my knees.

And I was pleased to find do-overs were no less hot.

Chapter 35

I Still Want You to Take Mine

Four months later…

"Honey! We're going to miss our reservation!" I called up the stairs to Gray who was changing into his suit.

Or at least I hoped he was. I heard the shower go off ten minutes ago and my man was not a man who primped.

"Be down in a minute, darlin'!" Gray shouted back, I sighed and walked on my high heels into the kitchen.

It was October and it was my birthday and we should have left the house in order to make our reservation at Jenkins five minutes ago.

Gray had gone into town and came back late. Now we were running late.

And I was hungry.

THE LAST FOUR MONTHS, things had settled on the land and in Mustang.

The barn was up, painted red with white trim and it was old-fashioned like the last one was. That one was old-fashioned because it was old. This one was because that was what Gray wanted it to be.

It was also enormous.

Seeing as horse breeding was the family business, the other one was too and had twenty-six stalls.

But this one had thirty, a big tack room, a big feed room and a hayloft complete with the pulley outside and double doors with criss-cross white boards on them that led to it.

I loved it because it looked awesome, because my man built it with his own hands, because I got to watch him do that and because, with it being there, it was easier to forget how the old one ceased to be.

And last, because Gray and I had broken in the hayloft by repeating history, kind of, as this time, he got his own treat.

It was awesome.

The peach crop came in, and Gray taught me to hire and I helped him manage the dozen workers who worked right alongside Gray and me. It was mindless work, hours of it, but with the smell of peaches all around, the summer sun kissing your skin at times, the shade of the trees offering relief at others and cheerful banter (though most of it was in Spanish, a language I didn't know, still it was cheerful), there were worse things to do. Gray had replanted the lost trees but it would be a while before they bore fruit and his new growth also wasn't there. Still, his crop earned a load, so much I was surprised. Then again, he had a huge orchard so I supposed I shouldn't be.

It was fun when it began but I was happy when it was over.

Gray contacted the Bureau of Land Management who manages the wild mustang herds and he adopted ten more mustangs.

Yes, *ten*, putting our number over twenty straight to twenty-three.

Shim, Roan and Whit went with him to go get them and they all worked to help him break them and train them. It was fascinating and slightly scary to sit on our porch swing, eyes pointed to the corral where the boys did this. But if I didn't know already, what with watching my man jump bareback on a horse and control the thing without any reins, this proved irrevocably he was all cowboy mostly because he got thrown often (the scary part), didn't seem to mind a bit and the best part, he wore chaps.

No joke.

Chaps.

It.

Was.

Hot.

Seriously.

Until I saw Gray wearing them, I would have told you I was not a girl to get turned on by a man in chaps.

Then I saw Gray wearing them.

Suffice it to say, after day one of watching Gray working the horses wearing chaps, I didn't care he'd spent hours being bucked off the backs of those beings. That night, I worked Gray and it was clear he didn't mind being ridden hard after a day of riding.

He didn't mind it a bit.

After the Brothers Cody got their shit together and got their asses to the retirement home, saw their mom, the state she was in but the care she was being given, Gray got a welcome surprise and that surprise was not prompted by me (directly, unless of course you counted my rant).

This started with Olly who was clearly driven to do it by Macy and I knew this because her eyes mentally whipped his ass straight into our kitchen where he presented Gray with a check for fifty thousand dollars. It wasn't what I thought he owed but it was something. Frank followed a week later with the same.

Charlie was still a holdout mainly because, in Frank's words, "He's a piss-ant. Always was, always will be." Though I knew Olly, Frank and Macy were working him to do the same or at least offer something.

Gray took them and paid them directly on the note, which more than halved what he owed. When my year was up on what I paid on the loan, we'd again face his hefty payment but it would take half as long to pay it off. Further, Frank informed Gray that if Grandma Miriam's stay went beyond what I'd paid, the Brothers Cody would be seeing to it from there on in.

So that was all good.

AND THE OTHER good was that there were no more fires, no more poisoned horses and no more diseased trees.

There was nothing, not from Buddy or Cecily.

Not just for Gray and me but for everyone in Mustang. Buddy and Cecily had their home outside Mustang but they lived their lives mostly in the next county and did their business in Elk. Gray and I had seen them and their daughters (who were very cute) at the cinema but other than that, I'd not seen them and others didn't either. They didn't go to Plack's, the diner, The Rambler, The Alibi, Jenkins, Hayes, the pharmacy, nothing.

Courtney, too, had disappeared and she'd one-upped the Sharps by moving to Denver. When it all went down with Gray's barn and then her participation was leaked by (my guess) Norrie, she'd been in the throes of a nasty divorce to a guy the town actually liked. He got the town. She, when everyone found out what a true bitch she was, got the hell out of it.

It would seem that having "horse murderer" painted on their

house and threatening notes left on their doorstep did the trick for Buddy and Cecily.

I was breathing easier but Gray was not. He'd had this since junior high and he didn't believe Buddy was going to go down at all. This didn't mean that, as the days passed into weeks then months, he didn't sleep easier but he was on the alert. He didn't mind me going to town or to visit Grandma Miriam at the home by myself but it was rare he left me at the house alone and, when he did, it was when whatever business he had didn't take him long. If it was going to, he took me.

I didn't mind.

If it gave him peace of mind, what did I care?

THAT MEANT, him being in town that day for a while was surprising, especially seeing as it was my birthday.

But it did give me the opportunity to take my time getting all done up.

Even though Jenkins was fancy for Mustang, it was not Vegas fancy. Still, I had on one of my dresses that I used to wear at Lash's club. It was red with a deep dip that exposed most of my back, short spaghetti straps that held it up near to the points of my shoulders and it was short and clingy. I was wearing Lash's rubies and a pair of strappy, red, high-heeled sandals with rhinestones (also from Lash). I had a lot of hair, a lot of makeup and several sprays of my favorite, and most expensive, perfume.

But regardless of Gray's late afternoon absence, the day had been great. First, I started it with Gray. Second, he made me breakfast (chocolate chip pancakes and my man was a master at pancakes). Third, a FedEx package came with a pair of exquisite, eight hundred dollar designer pumps (a gift from Lash) and a bottle of the aforementioned expensive perfume (a gift from Brutus), which was followed by me talking to them on the phone (Lash, for an hour, Brutus for five minutes, not unusual, either of them).

Apparently, I'd continue to be stocked up on the finer things in life even when that life was on a ranch. I talked to them often. Lash several times a week. Brutus, less frequently but I checked in and so did he. I should have known they'd be generous, it was who they were and they loved me, but still, it was a pleasant surprise.

Their gifts were nice. They were sweet. And they were pure Lash and Brutus.

Janie had also popped by to give me a present that was from her, Danny, Gene, Barry and even Peg (yes, Peg, where she got her money, I had no clue but she'd given some to the present for me). It was a pair of fawn suede, kickass cowboy boots, the first pair I'd owned since going the way of the Vegas showgirl and better than any I'd ever had even when they were nearly all I used to wear.

I loved them.

And now I had Gray and Jenkins and then we'd be home and I'd just have Gray.

It was the best birthday ever.

And I didn't know it, but it was about to get better.

I WAS SCREWING around in the kitchen, killing time waiting for Gray by getting the coffee ready so I could just flip the switch in the morning when I heard, "Told you, bears repeating, like that dress, dollface."

I turned and saw Gray leaning shoulder to doorjamb wearing his dark blue suit. He also had on a light blue shirt that did great things for a tan he still had seeing as, even in October, he spent most of his time outside.

He looked beautiful.

"Thanks, baby," I replied on a smile then I turned back and flipped the door to the coffeemaker closed.

Then I moved to approach him but stopped when Gray ordered, "Stay right there, Ivey."

I blinked then I stared and when I did I noticed his gaze was intent and not the kind of intent that said he really liked my dress.

A different kind of intent.

An intent that made my heart beat faster.

I would know why when he told me casually, "Went to see my mom today."

My hand moved out to hold onto the counter but otherwise I didn't move. It had been months since Norrie's visit. Months. I steered clear of her for Gray (even though I wanted to get to know her) and Gray had steered clear of her for his own reasons that I let be.

Now, he'd gone to see her.

Wow.

Gray kept talking.

"She had somethin' belongs to Codys, I wanted it back. We talked awhile. She's comin' to lunch on Sunday after church. That cool with you?"

Was that cool with me?

Was he crazy?

"Yes," I forced out on a wheeze, shocked, pleased and cautiously happy because I couldn't tell if Gray was or if he was doing this for me.

Gray said no more.

I didn't either nor did I move and I also found it hard to breathe.

Finally, he spoke and when he did, it was to whisper, "Prettiest thing I've ever seen."

Oh God.

My belly melted.

"Gray," I whispered back.

"In that getup, in your jeans and tees, in your bikini on the lawnmower, when I open my eyes in the morning and see you next to me, anytime I see you, that's what I think. First thing that comes to mind. Anytime. Every time."

I swallowed, held onto the counter and said nothing, just let his words rush warm and sweet through me.

Then he gave me, a woman who once had nothing but a bag full of stuff, not much of it good, but who, standing there in that kitchen thought she had everything, the world.

"I love you, Ivey, and you got a name you gave yourself that means somethin' to you but I still want you to take mine."

Oh God.

Oh God.

Oh God.

Tears filled my eyes.

"You want that, baby?" he whispered.

Instantly, unable to speak, I nodded.

And just as instantly, he walked across the kitchen and when he arrived at me, he took my left hand, lifted it and slid an old-fashioned diamond ring on my ring finger. It was large, a rounded off, wide rectangle surrounded by smaller diamonds all of this on a simple, thin white gold band.

It was old. It was Cody. It was beautiful. It was perfect.

"My mom wore that ring. My gran wore it too. And so did my great-gran. Took it to Lazar's in town, they cleaned it, said it's in good repair," he muttered, finishing, "and it fits."

It did. And thank God it did because I was never taking it off.

Not ever.

Except, of course, when he slid on the wedding band that would go under it.

His fingers folded around mine and he lifted my hand to his mouth, bending his neck and touching his lips to my finger above the ring while I watched, a tear sliding down my cheek.

Then he pulled my hand to his chest and flattened it there.

"It's old, darlin', not new, not fancy but there it is." His thumb tweaked my ring. "Happy birthday."

I ripped my hand from his and threw my arms around his shoulders. Then I went up on tiptoe as the fingers of one hand drove into his hair pulling his head down to me and I kissed him. It was wet and not just because my tongue danced with his but because my tears slid to our lips.

We made out in the kitchen for a long time before Gray finally raised his head but rested his forehead to mine and he whispered, "Say you love me, Ivey."

"I love you, Gray. I really, really love you, baby."

He grinned and his arm gave me a squeeze.

Then he let me go but grabbed my hand and, as he dragged me to the kitchen door, he ordered, "Now quit bawlin'. I'm hungry and we don't have time for you to fix your face."

Since I had no choice (but wouldn't choose differently), I hurried after him as he took his long-legged strides toward the front door, my free hand dashing at my face and deep breathing to control the tears. Gray stopped us at the hall tree and helped me put on my coat. I nabbed my purse. Then he grabbed my hand again and dragged me out the door to his pickup where he put me, in my expensive shoes and a dress that cost a small fortune, to take me into town for my birthday dinner.

And as we were underway, even though night had fallen, I noticed that the detritus scattering the floor of the old girl had accumulated again.

It was time to clean out Gray's truck.

And on this thought, my one hand in my other, my thumb moving over the hard diamond, I looked out the windshield and smiled.

Chapter 36

The Wait Was Over

Six thirty in the morning, Christmas Eve...

I WOKE to darkness with Gray's hands and mouth on me.

"Baby, it's Christmas Eve. On Christmas Eve can't we sleep in?" I asked drowsily.

Gray's hand made it to my breast and curled around as his lips made it to the base of my ear where he muttered, "No."

Then his thumb slid over my nipple and I decided I no longer wanted to sleep in.

Instead, I twisted my neck, Gray's head came up then it immediately came back down so he could kiss me.

SEVEN OH THREE in the morning, Christmas Eve…

"NEED YOU, BABY," I breathed my plea.

I was stroking him, so desperate for him it was part stroking, part pulling.

His hand was between my legs, two fingers buried, thumb working me. Our mouths were close and we were both breathing heavily.

"Not done," he muttered, pressing deeper and rolling.

Oh God.

"Baby, *I'm* gonna be done and I want to be done with you inside me," I begged, my hips jerking, my hand still stroking and I did this hard, hard enough for him to groan.

I liked that and I was hoping that meant he was ready to move us directly to the final phase.

He didn't.

Instead, he whispered, "Take you there again."

Oh yes.

My eyes held his, close up.

"Really?"

He stopped rolling and started finger fucking me.

My head arched back.

His mouth went to my throat. "Really."

Yes.

His fingers slid out, his hand cupped me and my head righted with a jerk, my eyes locking on his.

"Baby—" I started to protest.

"On your back, Ivey, spread your legs wide for me. I wanna watch you come while I fuck you with my fingers," he ordered.

Oh yeah, I wanted that too.

So I did what I was told. Then Gray did what he wanted. And when he did, it was so good, my back arched clean off the bed, my head dug into the pillows and my hips ground down on his hand.

"Fuck me," through the daze of my orgasm I heard him growl, "prettiest fuckin' thing I've ever seen."

Then he was between my spread legs, his hips drove into mine and he started fucking me.

Hard.

Then he did as promised and took me there again.

It was brilliant.

Eight thirteen in the morning, Christmas Eve...

Gray shoved his plate in the dishwasher I had open, sucked back the last of his coffee, upturned his mug and slid that in then his hand snaked out and tagged me behind the neck.

He pulled me in and up and dropped a light kiss on my lips.

When he lifted his head, he said, "Got shit to do in town. Then gonna go get Gran. You need anything?"

I shook my head.

"Got everything we need from Plack's?" he went on.

I nodded my head.

"I'm ready," I told him.

And I *was* ready, boy was I ready. I'd spent hours in Plack's, Hayes and on the internet, shopping. More in the guest bedroom wrapping. More creating menus and searching for recipes.

I was definitely ready for Christmas and I couldn't wait.

Gray read this in my eyes. I knew when he grinned, giving me the dimple.

Then he dropped another light kiss on my lips.

Then he let me go and I watched his ass as he sauntered out of the kitchen, muttering, "Later, dollface."

"Later, honey," I called to his back then turned to the sink to finish the breakfast dishes.

I did this smiling to myself mostly because my eyes were on my hands and I could see my ring there.

Gray would have a time of it, besting his birthday present.

But he was making the effort. I knew this because he was getting Grandma Miriam from the home and she was going to be with us until the day after Christmas. And we could do this because, early that evening, his mom was coming. She was a nurse, she was spending the next two nights in our guest room and she, with the help of Gray and me, could give Grandma Miriam what she needed. Then, tomorrow, after we had a small family Christmas in the morning, in the afternoon, all Gray's uncles, their wives and Audie and his girl were coming over for Christmas dinner.

I couldn't wait.

For any of it.

More than six months of peace from the machinations of Buddy Sharp and more than six months of going to bed and waking up with Grayson Cody, the last two and half with the Cody family heirloom ring on my finger.

Life was good and with Gran there, Norrie, who Gray was getting to know slowly and cautiously but he was doing it, then his uncles, aunts and cousin, I'd have a *real* family Christmas.

The first one ever.

Ever.

Thirty years and there it was.

Yeah, Gray was close to besting his birthday present.

Nothing would be better than the symbol that stated plainly I was soon going to take the name Cody.

But a family Christmas wasn't far off.

Nine thirty-eight in the morning, Christmas Eve…

. . .

I had Christmas music playing, a bay and rosemary candle burning and I was making Christmas cookies. It was my fifth batch of the season. This was because, with Christmas cookies in the house, Gray had foregone his candy bars and nabbed a cookie (or four) whenever he had the munchies. This was also because, now that there was peace amongst the Cody men, anytime his uncles were fighting with their wives, they were over at our house.

Which meant they were over a lot.

And they grew up in that house so they had no problem helping themselves.

I didn't mind.

Not at all.

I was standing at the kitchen counter, kneading the dough, Christmas all around but my mind was on flowers.

Not flowers for my wedding, planting them around the house.

During a visit with Grandma Miriam she told me, before she lost her legs, every year she planted a thick border of impatiens around the front and side of the house.

"Perfect for them, child, with the trees that shade the house, they get their bit of sun but they like their shade," she'd told me.

I had the ring she wore on my finger. I was making Christmas dinner in the kitchen where she'd prepared it for five decades.

So, come spring, the house would have Grandma Miriam's flowers.

I heard the approach of a car and my head turned to the window, surprised because I figured it was Gray. I had no idea what he had to do in town but going to get Grandma Miriam and dealing with packing her up and checking her out alone would take an hour and he'd been gone just over that.

But it wasn't Gray's pickup bumping down the lane. It was a silver car, an Audi, new and clean like it had a garage for its home.

I found this interesting. Audis weren't popular cars in Mustang.

I took my hands out of the dough rubbing off the lumps. I rinsed them quickly, dried them, headed out of the kitchen, down the hall and out the front door.

Then I stopped dead on the porch as I watched Bud Sharp get out of his Audi and out the passenger side was a man who Buddy would definitely not hang with. Not ever.

He was older, tall, beefy, with longish, wild hair that held its blonde but had more silver, and to say he was rough around the edges was an understatement.

I didn't hesitate to call to them, "Best get in your car, Buddy. I'll be saying these words to you then calling nine one one then calling Gray. If it was me, I wouldn't be here when Gray gets back."

Then I turned to the front door, walked three steps and stopped dead with my hand on the doorknob after Buddy called back, "Now, Ivey, is that any way to act the very first time you lay eyes on your daddy?"

It was stupid, I knew it. I should go in, call nine one one, call Gray, but instead my head turned and my eyes went to the man walking toward the porch with Buddy.

That hair was my hair.

That hair was *my hair*.

I stared.

They got close to the side of the porch and stopped.

Buddy, I noticed when I flicked my eyes to him, was grinning. Pleased with himself.

The man had his eyes glued to me. He looked curious. He also looked hesitant. And, even though he was tall, sturdy, weathered, worn and rough around the edges, I sensed a hint of fear.

"Hoot Booker, I'd like you to meet your daughter, the ex-pool hustling, ex-Vegas stripper, current cowboy piece, Ivey Larue," Buddy introduced, loving every minute of this but my eyes were on Hoot Booker...

Hoot Booker...

My father.

And at Buddy's words, Hoot Booker's eyes narrowed scarily and sliced to Buddy.

"Merry Christmas." Buddy smiled happily then leaned forward. "Oh, and just so you know, Hoot here, coupla years ago, got outta prison. Murder one. Now, I don't know much about these things but I think that's the bad kind."

"Think you're done, chief," Hoot Booker's deep, rumbling, pissed off voice stated and he looked from Buddy to me. "Don't know this guy. He found me, said he knew you, paid for me to get here. Swear, girl, until this very second where he turned dick, the man's been nothin' but cool with me. I see now you two got history but I do not have a place in that. I just wanted to meet my daughter."

His daughter.

Me.

I stared at him, immobile, hand still on the doorknob.

Buddy was glaring at Hoot Booker.

Hoot Booker was staring at me.

Then he shook his head, closed his eyes and looked away for a second, taking a moment for what I wouldn't know before he opened his eyes.

They came back to me and I saw his face was pained before he whispered, "Jesus, fuck, I look at you, can't believe my eyes, can't fuckin' take it in. *I* created somethin' as beautiful as *you*?"

Oh my God.

"I don't know," I whispered, only my lips moving.

"Sheila Bailey your momma?" he asked.

"She gave birth to me," I answered, still talking quietly.

He nodded his head, a small smile cracking his face, "Yeah, see Sheila never changed."

"No," I whispered.

The smile fled and he stared at me, reading me like he knew me my whole life either because I was too stunned at what was happening to hide it or because he had more practice than me.

I figured it was both.

"She didn't treat you good," he whispered.

"No," I repeated, that one, one syllable word weighty.

Hoot Booker read that too and emotions he didn't try to hide either rolled over his face, more pain, anger, despair.

"That brother a' yours?" he asked when he got control of his emotional roller coaster.

"Dead to me."

He knew what I was saying and I knew he knew when he whispered, "Fuck."

"This is all very touching," Buddy put in snidely and I finally moved, turning away from the door to face him and see his expression was even more spiteful than his tone. "Why am I not surprised that an ex-stripper doesn't mind havin' a murderer as a daddy?"

"Think I told you, you're done," Hoot Booker reminded him and Buddy turned to my father.

"I am? What are you gonna do, big man? Kill me in front of your long, lost daughter?"

"No, but, the way she said hi, not sure she'll mind I fuck you up a little bit," Hoot returned and I couldn't help it, a giggle escaped me.

Buddy's eyes cut to me and he hissed, "Shut your slut trap."

Then Buddy wasn't there because Buddy was on his back in the snow-covered yard, Hoot's knee in his gut, his calf in his arm immobilizing it, one hand at his throat, his other hand wrapped around Buddy's wrist pressing it into the snow.

Oh God.

I moved to the edge of the porch but could go no further because I didn't have any shoes on, just a pair of thick woolen socks so I cried, "Please, don't! He isn't worth the trouble. Honestly, he isn't worth the trouble."

But Hoot Booker didn't even look at me.

Nose an inch away from Buddy's, he whispered scarily, "You called my girl a slut right to her face and right in front of me." He paused a scary pause and finished, "I don't like that."

Buddy kicked out his legs and snapped, "Get off me!"

Hoot lifted his head and aimed his eyes at me before he ordered, "Go in the house. You call the cops then you call your man." When I hesitated, he clipped, "Now, girl. *Go*."

"I don't want you to get in trouble," I said softly, his head jerked and his face changed. It softened and under all that rough, weathered and worn I saw my father was handsome.

"Then keep me outta trouble by gettin' some folks here to deal with this assclown before I lose it and do it myself," he said gently.

I held his eyes then I nodded.

Then I ran into the house, dialed nine-one-one, told them what was happening then I called Gray.

He answered with, "Hey dollface. Remember something you need?

"Buddy's here," I replied. "He brought my father with him. He said a few things my father didn't like and now my father has him pinned in the snow in the front yard."

Silence then, "Say again?"

"Buddy's here," I started. "He brought my—"

Gray cut me off to rumble, "You are fuckin' shittin' me."

"No," I whispered.

"*You are fuckin' shittin' me!*" Gray roared.

Oh God!

"Honey, are you driving?" I asked carefully, reminding myself *again* to tread cautiously and not get lulled into stupidity by the usually easygoing Grayson Cody.

A moment while I suspected he deep breathed then, "Yeah, on the way to Gran. I'll be there in ten. You call the police?"

"Yes."

Then I got, "This man, is he really your father?"

"Well, I can't be sure but he's got my hair, he said I was beautiful, he knew my mom's name and when Buddy called me a slut, he took him down in, like, a nanosecond."

More silence and I didn't get the same seriously unhappy vibes traveling over the airwaves that I did when I first shared my news so I didn't know what this one meant.

Then I knew when Gray's voice came on a vibrating, "He called you a slut?"

Okay.

Again.

Tread cautiously, Ivey!

"Gray—"

He cut me off. "You feel danger from this man, your father?"

"No."

"Right. You get your fuckin' baseball bat, you lock all the fuckin' doors, not in that order, and you stay the fuck inside until I get there. Not the cops, *me*. Do you hear me?"

"Yes, Gray," I agreed as I moved to the front door.

"Do it now. I'll be there soon."

"Okay, baby."

"I'm done with this guy," he whispered.

Shit!

"Honey, please stay calm."

"I'm done," he was still whispering and he was also gone.

Shit!

I locked the door, then I ran to the back door and locked that, then I ran upstairs and got my baseball bat (well, it was Gray's, I didn't have one anymore), then I ran back downstairs to the living room where there was a window where I could see Buddy Sharp and Hoot Booker in the snow.

Their positions hadn't changed.

I twisted the window latch, crouched low, shoved the window up an inch and called out, "Uh...sorry if you heard the lock turn. No offense but my man isn't real comfortable with me being alone here with a man he doesn't know and Buddy."

Hoot Booker's head was up, he was looking at me through the window and he was smiling a huge, white, wild-ass smile.

"See you found yourself a decent man," he remarked, still casually holding Buddy in the snow.

"Uh...yeah. He's great." I was still calling out the crack of a window.

"Good news, girl," he replied.

"I, uh, also called the police. They know about Buddy so they'll probably be here really soon," I told him.

"More good news," he said.

"Fuckin' let me up!" Buddy shouted, still struggling against Hoot's hold, snow flying all around, but Hoot ignored him and kept his eyes on me.

"So, you live here long?" he asked conversationally and I again couldn't control the giggle.

When I controlled it, I answered.

"Just over six months but Gray and I've known each other for over seven years," I told him, decided, considering he seemed willing and able to dole out justice for me, I would leave out the history and Buddy's place in it and finished, "It's a long story."

"Gray?" he asked.

"Gray, uh...Grayson Cody. That's my man's name."

"Fuckin' hell, I get from the dude ranch I'm on he's a cowboy but, Christ. Grayson Cody? That's like the most cowboy a name can get."

I giggled again.

Yep, this was totally my dad.

"Let...me...*up*!" Buddy shrieked and Hoot looked back down at him.

"Your car, your clothes, your house, chief, I get you think you'll get whatever you want but, clue in, right now is not one of those times," he stated.

"Fuck you," Buddy spat.

"Lotsa money," Hoot Booker muttered, still looking down at Buddy, "no class."

My heart skipped a beat. Then it warmed.

That was when I heard sirens.

"Uh...um...Hoot?" I called and he looked at me.

"Yeah, darlin'," he replied softly and I felt my nose sting but I fought back the tears.

"Well, just so you know, Gray doesn't want me out there until he's home so the cops are gonna be here soon but I won't be out until he gets here. Just wanted you to know. Okay?"

"You give your man peace a' mind and do as he asks, Ivey. I'll be good until he gets here," my father assured me.

My father.

I smiled at him through the window and called, "Thanks."

"You're welcome, beautiful," he called back.

My father.

It seemed this *was* going to be a family Christmas.

And, again, I couldn't wait.

Nine fifty-seven in the morning, Christmas Eve...

I was ready by the time I saw Gray's pickup truck speeding down the lane.

There were two uniformed officers outside in my yard wearing their big, bulky winter uniform jackets.

Buddy was up, his back still caked in snow and he was shouting, complaining and threatening.

Hoot Booker was standing removed, beefy legs planted wide and beefy arms crossed on his chest straining his jeans jacket with its sheepskin collar. His eyes were on Buddy and there was an expression on his face like he'd never encountered anything quite like him and, to save anyone else from doing it, he was struggling with the idea of crushing him like a bug.

The cops were staring at Buddy, clearly unhappy that what

they'd hoped would be a laidback Christmas Eve shift involved a run-in with the town's most hated inhabitant.

As for me, to be ready for Gray's arrival, I'd run upstairs to yank on my cowboy boots then back downstairs to pull on my jacket, wrap a scarf around my neck and tug a fitted, knit cap on my head down to my ears.

What I couldn't do was wrap my mind around the fact that the man outside was my father but I also couldn't think about that just then.

I had to think about Gray.

So the minute his pickup turned in and stopped, I dashed through the living room and out the front door and I didn't stop. I jumped off the porch and raced through the snow toward Gray.

And I knew with one look at him that the time it took for him to make his drive did not cool his anger. He'd been pissed when Casey came to call, angrier than I'd ever seen him.

Now, he was beyond enraged. I knew his control had snapped. He had not lied with what he said to me on the phone.

He was done.

And I needed to stop him from doing something he'd regret and something that might take him away from me.

I made it to him just as he viciously slammed the door on the old girl, the door making the usual creak but also the entire truck rocked ominously.

His eyes were riveted to Buddy, his face set in stone.

I put my hand to his gut. "Gray, baby, don't. Take a minute. Calm down."

Not tearing his eyes from Buddy, he put a hand to my chest and firmly but gently shoved me back, growling to no one in particular but to everyone except Buddy, "Keep her away."

"Don't, Gray!" I cried frantically, following on a rush as his legs swiftly closed the distance between him and Buddy.

He ignored me and stayed on target.

"You called my woman a slut?" he asked Buddy on a low, rumbling mutter and no one, but no one, could mistake his fury.

Buddy straightened and faced him down, informing him of something he could not miss, "You got a police presence, Cody."

Gray's hand, which never left my chest, gave me another shove. It was not violent but it was forceful. Forceful enough for me to fall back three feet and then Gray moved.

Fast.

Before I could launch myself back at him, two iron arms clamped around me and I shouted, "*Gray!*"

But he was on Buddy, hands in his jacket powering him back through the snow. Buddy, for some insane reason, didn't read the threat and was not prepared. Then again, he likely never would be. Gray was fury unleashed and, except maybe Hoot Booker, no one there had experienced anything like it.

Two feet from the corner where the porch met the house, Gray shoved him off and Buddy staggered back and slammed in between the porch and the house.

Gray instantly took those two steps in.

"*You called my woman a slut?*" he roared in Buddy's face.

"*Gray!*" I shrieked, fighting the arms around me and I vaguely heard Hoot Booker whisper in my ear. "Still, beautiful, let your man do what he's gotta do."

I didn't calm. I strained as I watched Buddy try to slide out from in front of Gray but Gray's arm slashed out and shoved him savagely right back into the corner so Buddy's body thudded into the house. Buddy recovered and tried the other side but Gray moved fast, shoving him back in so hard Buddy almost went down to the porch. Buddy quickly righted himself, again tried the other side and again Gray kept him pinned with another body slam into the house.

Then Buddy aimed an upper-cut to Gray's jaw. I whimpered, but again, lightning fast but still almost casually, Gray lifted a forearm and deflected the blow before his fist even came close.

Then he stepped in, chest-to-chest, nose-to-nose and rumbled quietly and terrifyingly, "You came to my home on my land when my woman was alone and you called her slut?"

"Step back, Cody," Buddy demanded, tried to slide out from in front of Gray again but Gray just shoved him back.

"Fuckin' answer me," Gray ordered.

Buddy finally realized he was going nowhere so his eyes went beyond Gray to the two officers and he asked irritably, "Aren't you gonna do anything?"

My head turned toward them to see one had his hands to his hips, the other his arms crossed on his chest, both of their eyes were on Gray and Buddy and neither moved nor spoke.

They weren't going to do anything.

Buddy realized this too and went back to Gray.

"*Step back!*" he screeched.

"What is the matter with you?" Gray asked.

"Fuck you!" was Buddy's answer.

Gray kept his face in Buddy's and thundered, "*What is the matter with you?*"

"Get off!" Buddy shouted.

"What did I do?" Gray asked.

"*Get off!*"

"What the fuck did I do?" Gray repeated. "Fuckin' decades, Bud, decades you played this game. Then you took my fuckin' woman away from me. Seven years. Seven fuckin' years, Bud. In that time, you got two girls. What did you take from Ivey and me? I'm marryin' her next year but that house right behind you should have *my* kids in it by now and you took that away from her and me."

At Gray's words, Hoot Booker's arms flexed powerfully around me but I kept my eyes glued to Gray and Buddy.

"Step the fuck back," Buddy hissed.

"You diseased my trees, you poisoned my horses, you burned down my barn, you tried to take my land from me. Why? I don't get it. Why the fuck would you do this sick, crazy, whacked out shit? What's the matter with you? Give me one fuckin' thing in the miserable time I've known you and explain to me what the fuck I did to you."

"Just like you, the Great Grayson Cody, thinkin' everything is about you," Buddy sneered.

"You and I been livin' in the same town at the same time all our lives, but I don't know you and you sure as fuck don't know me so you don't know you can say that kinda shit about me," Gray shot back.

Buddy glared at him a second and then demanded, "Fuck off and let me pass."

Buddy misinterpreted Gray seemingly calming down (a bit) because at his demand, Gray put his hand in Buddy's chest and shoved him hard into the house. When Buddy's body swayed back out, Gray did it again and his head slammed against the side.

Then Gray got nose-to-nose with him again and barked, "*Explain this shit to me!*"

"It's not about you! It has not one fuckin' thing to do with you!" Buddy shouted back. "It's about the land!"

I stopped straining and stared in shock. Gray moved back three inches and did the same.

Buddy, though, now it was Buddy who was unleashed and he went wild.

Throwing his arms out then slapping his hand against the side of the house, he began.

"Since I could remember, all Granddaddy talked about was Cody land. Then my father went on and on and fuckin' *on* about it. 'Good neighbors but that sure is some damn pretty land.'" His last words, undoubtedly repeating his father, were sarcastic and biting. "And I took Granddaddy's shit, I took Dad's shit. Want me up on a horse. Want me muckin' fuckin' horseshit. Want me ridin' the fences with the ranch hands. Want me out herdin' the cattle. Want me in the pens wrestlin' fuckin', filthy, stinkin' calves. Fuck that. I got no interest in that. Do they care?" He shook his head. "No. 'You're a Sharp, Bud, quit pissin' around and be a fuckin' *Sharp*.'" More of Jeb Sharp's words to his son coming out snide with his face twisted. "So I decided, he wouldn't let me be me, he only would let me be what he wanted me to be, I'd be what *I* fuckin' wanted to be and I'd see about taking what he most wanted. I'd sit in this house on this land with *my* family. A Sharp would be here but he'd know it would be me, he'd know this was all mine, he'd know *I* got what *he* wanted, what his daddy wanted, what his daddy's daddy wanted, *I* got. And it would be *mine*, not his and fuck him. *Fuck him*."

"This shit is true, then why the fuck did you take Ivey from me?" Gray asked.

"You found a girl, got married, had children, you're a Cody. If you had a family I'd *never* get you off this land."

This was definitely true.

But Gray obviously didn't believe it.

"This shit, Bud. It's all bullshit. You targeted me."

"Bonus, Gray," he snarled. "Mr. Mustang, the Mighty Cody, everyone in town thinkin' you control the sun and moon, call the tides. Made me sick watchin' it, hearin' it," he leaned in, "*livin' that shit*. Made me sick."

"That's it?" Gray asked incredulously and I thought strangely. "Controlling lives, breaking hearts, destroying property, killing animals for that shit?"

Oh. Well. I could see his point.

"Yeah, *Gray*, that's it. You didn't live my life. *Your* daddy strutted through town makin' damn sure everyone in it knew he thought you could control the sun and moon, call the tides, talkin' you up so much, they believed it. *My* daddy didn't do that shit."

"And this?" Gray went on. "Your visit today. What the fuck is this all about?"

"I ate that shit all my life, *you* don't get to live free and easy. You don't get your happily ever after. And neither does she," Buddy answered on a sneer.

"So it *is* about me and it's also about Ivey," Gray stated.

Buddy glared at him and said nothing which meant yes.

"I don't believe this," Gray whispered.

"Believe it," Buddy clipped.

"I don't believe this shit," Gray kind of repeated.

"*Believe it!*" Buddy shouted and Gray stood there, staring him down, silent.

Then he broke his silence.

"You're pathetic," he stated and Buddy blinked.

Then his face twisted again.

"Fuck you. You think I care what you think?" he asked.

"Yeah," Gray answered. "I think you care too damned much about what *everybody* thinks."

And there it was. Gray had another excellent point.

He also wasn't done.

"I also think you're weak. You wanted to be your own man? Bud, all you had to do was be your own man. Fuck, you got a college degree. You found a job that paid a shitload. You found a pretty wife. You gave her beautiful daughters. You put a nice house over their heads. But you're so fuckin' pathetic you didn't see that you *already* showed your dad. Instead you hurt people, including your wife and kids, to perpetrate some sick-ass shit so you could show everybody..." He trailed off then asked, "What? To show everybody what?" He didn't wait for Buddy to answer, he just kept talking. "I don't know. It's so whacked I don't get it. The only thing I get is that you are sadder and less of a man than I already thought you were and, Bud, that's sayin' somethin' because me and the rest of Mustang thought you were lowest kind of person a person could be."

Buddy opened his mouth to reply but Gray took a step back and beat him to it.

"That's it, then that's it. You don't wake up and be a man, that's on you, not on me. You pile more shit on me and Ivey, it's fucked, but it reflects on you, not me. You are obviously not wakin' up but every time you fail to beat me, you...just...*fail* making you less and less the man you wanna be and more and more the man your daddy feared you'd be. So, do what you gotta do. Nothin' a pathetic excuse for a man like you could do could defeat me."

And with that, he was done and I knew that when my man turned and walked through the snow toward me and Hoot Booker. He didn't even glance at the cops and he didn't look over his shoulder and give Bud Sharp any more of his attention. He just stopped two feet away from my father and me.

His eyes did a scan of my face then they went over my shoulder to Hoot.

"You wouldn't mind, I'd like to have my woman."

"Sure, hoss," Hoot Booker muttered, letting me go and the second he did, Gray leaned in, grabbed my hand and pulled me to him.

Then he slid his arm around my shoulders, tucking me to his side, his eyes still on my father.

Then he lifted his hand. "Grayson Cody."

God.

God, but I loved Grayson Cody.

Hoot lifted his, took Gray's and gripped.

"Hoot Booker."

"Ivey tells me you're her daddy," Gray remarked, letting Hoot's hand go.

"Reckon so, she's got my hair, or, at least, hope it's so," Hoot replied.

Some tension left my body because that was sweet.

I heard movement and muttering around us and knew the officers were rounding up Buddy but, like Gray, I was done with him. He ceased to exist. So I ignored this.

Gray looked side to side then back at Hoot. "You got a car?"

"In town," Hoot answered.

"Stayin' at the hotel?" Gray went on.

"Yeah, paid for by that douchebag. Think that ride's ended though," Hoot noted and I swallowed a giggle but that didn't mean I didn't smile.

When I looked up at Gray I saw the dimple was out.

Then he said, "Right, how 'bout this? We go in, have a cup of coffee, warm up. Then I gotta go get my gran from the nursing home.

I'm thinkin' you can guess I don't want Ivey too far from me so I want her with me. That said, my woman's never had a family so I can guess, you're here, she'll not want to be too far from you."

He had that right.

Gray continued, "So, you follow in Ivey's Lexus, we get Gran, Ivey can ride with you on the way back and you two can get to know each other. Work for you?"

Hoot stared at him a beat not hiding his surprise. Then he looked to my car. Then back at Gray.

"You're lettin' me alone in a Lexus?" he asked softly.

"You gonna steal it?" Gray asked back.

"No," Hoot answered instantly.

"Then yeah," Gray replied and Hoot's brows shot together even as he moved his big body uncomfortably.

"Hoss, maybe you don't know, I—" he started.

"I know," Gray cut him off firmly and my body twitched.

"You know?" I asked him, my head tipped back and he looked down at me.

"Lash," he answered.

"Right," I whispered, not sure how I felt about this.

"Told you, dollface, he told me everything about you. You didn't know this because you'd had enough, he didn't want to give you more. I saw his play and made the same one."

Well, knowing my father was in prison for murder one would not have been joyful news, especially back then even if I was living happy limbo.

I supposed I could be pissed. Then again, the men in my life loved me and wanted to protect me so I decided not to be.

And anyway, it was Christmas. I had a father to get to know, a grandmother to pick up from the nursing home and cookies to bake.

I had other priorities.

"Whatever," I muttered and Gray grinned down at me then he looked to Hoot.

"So, you wanna come in for coffee?"

Hoot stared hard at Gray then he looked at me then he looked at Gray.

Then he smiled a huge, wild-ass smile and stated, "Fuck yeah."

Gray jerked up his chin then led me to the side of the porch. He disengaged from me to lift me up onto it even though I could, and had (often), jumped up on my own. He climbed up after me and led me to the house.

I glanced and saw the Audi and cruisers gone.

Gone.

Then I drew in a breath.

Then my man guided me and my newfound dad into our house where we had coffee while Gray called the nursing home and explained the delay and I chatted with Hoot Booker and got to know my dad.

Then we went to get Gran.

Then we brought her home.

Then I finished my cookies.

Then Gray, Grandma Miriam and Hoot Booker ate a bunch of them.

Then Norrie came over.

Then Gray and Hoot went into town so Hoot could check out of the hotel and get his car.

Then in a beautiful house on a big, beautiful patch of land, Grandma Miriam in her chair wrapped with her shawl, Norrie in the armchair, her hand wrapped around a mug of hot cocoa, my father sitting in another chair, his hand wrapped around a beer, and me curled into my man, I found myself surrounded by family.

The wait was over and I found Gray was right.

Good things come to those who wait.

But he'd left out one word.

Because those things were *really* good things.

TEN TWENTY-TWO AT NIGHT, Christmas Day...

GRAY and I were in bed, front-to-front, arms around each other, whispering in the dark about our day.

It had been a great day. So great it was hard to pick which part was the best.

But I was thinking it was the fact that Gray and I unintentionally settled on the same theme for each other for Christmas.

First, he unwrapped my gift which was a scarf. The minute he saw it, his eyes came to me. They were warm and soft with memories and when I tipped my head to the side and bit my lip, he looked at my mouth and burst out laughing. Then, right in front of everyone, he hooked me with a hand at the back of my neck and laid a hard, closed-mouthed kiss on me.

After that, I told him to look in the bottom of the box and muttered, "You preempted my instructions."

I said this because there was a note at the bottom of the box on which I wrote, "Your real gift comes after a kiss."

Even though he'd already earned his present, after reading the note, Gray gave me another kiss immediately.

That one was softer, shorter but no less sweet.

It also wasn't closed-mouthed.

Then I gave him his real present, a kickass, to-the-hip leather jacket with warm lining. He had the same one he'd had since I met him and I noticed the lining was ripped, worn and some of it had come out entirely.

He loved it.

Then he gave me my presents.

First, a beautiful, soft wool knit cap and scarf in gray with the barest hints of black, the scarf wide and long and gorgeous. Second, a pair of gray suede gloves with fantastic stitching and lined in soft fur. And last, a matching hip length, hide coat that was like no coat I'd ever seen. The sleeves were belled and both sleeves and hem were jagged following the natural lines of the hide. The lapels also fell in the natural lines of the hide but they fell wide and deep exposing the thick, super-soft fur that was mostly gray with an undercoat of cream and wisps of black hairs that was the inside of the coat. It tied closed with a hide belt.

It was unusual, it was sophisticated, it was classy, it was cool, it was stylish and it was Colorado.

It was the perfect coat for a macho man rancher cowboy's stylish soon-to-be wife.

I opened it, put it on, felt that soft fur against my skin, loved it instantly and my eyes drifted to Gray.

Then I burst into tears.

In turn, Gray burst out laughing. Then he held me as I cried and multitasked by ignoring it and continuing to hand out presents.

"Let's see, dollface," he muttered, breaking into my thoughts. "Got me an ex-con whose smile scares me a little and whose also my woman's long lost daddy snorin' on my couch. Got my gran in a rented hospital bed, also snorin'. Got my estranged mom lyin' in the guest bedroom, luckily not snorin'. And got no beer left in the house because my uncles drank it all."

"I know," I whispered, "isn't it *awesome*?"

I saw his grin in the moonlight but he said, "Not fond of a house without beer."

"I'll go to Plack's tomorrow," I promised.

"Know you will, my woman takes care of me," he whispered and I sighed happily.

I did, I took care of him. And I loved doing it. But I also loved knowing he noticed and liked it.

Then his arms gave me a gentle squeeze.

"You have a good Christmas, baby?"

I pressed closer to him. "Yeah, honey."

"Good," he murmured.

"You?" I asked.

"Best ever," Gray answered.

Oh yes.

Yes.

I loved Grayson Cody.

"Good," I said softly.

Then I dipped my chin, moved in and kissed his chest.

There, my lips against his skin, I whispered, "It's been a wild ride and I can't say over the years that I didn't wish I'd made a different decision. But right now, in this bed with you, our family in this house, your ring on my finger, I'm glad that when I was on the sidewalk on the square in town with you and Casey all those years ago, I decided for the first time in my life not to play it safe."

Gray's arms gave me another squeeze, this one so tight I was forced to take my face out of his chest, tip my head back and look at him.

"I'm glad too, Ivey, seriously fuckin' glad you took a chance on me."

Yeah, I loved Grayson Cody.

He dropped his head and touched his mouth to mine, giving me a light kiss then ordering against my lips.

"Say you love me, Ivey."

My lips smiled against his. "I love you, Gray."

His lips smiled back.

Epilogue

Him and Me. Mr. and Mrs. Cody

F*ive and a half months later…*

"THANKS JEB," I said quietly into the phone, my eyes looking out the window over the sink to the barn.

"Thought you and Gray'd wanna know, Ivey," Jeb said quietly back.

I pulled in breath then asked, "You okay?"

"My wife misses her grandbabies," he answered meaning he did too. "But she doesn't miss the headaches." This meaning he didn't either. Then he stated, "Right," in a tone that said the conversation was imminently over. "Candace told me to tell you to talk to Gray about you and him comin' over for dinner again. She liked that. You talk to Gray, give her a call, let her know."

I'd talk to Gray but he didn't overly enjoy our last dinner with Candace and Jeb Sharp. He got what they were trying to do, apologize for the behavior of their son, and he was trying to be a good guy. He didn't blame them. Still, he didn't enjoy it.

"Will do. Take care, Jeb." I gave my farewell.

"You too, Ivey," he replied then he was gone.

I bleeped the phone off and looked back out the window.

Then I smiled.

Then I walked to the back door and pulled on my cowboy boots even though I was wearing a tight tank, a pair of cutoff jeans shorts and no socks. I also nabbed one of Gray's raggedy baseball caps off the hook and tugged it on my head, tucking my hair behind my ears.

It was a crazy, cowgirl look but I knew I worked it seeing as the first time I pulled on one of Gray's hats and my boots with shorts rather than ran upstairs to find some flip-flops in order to go out and talk to Gray, my message wasn't received for a half an hour. This was because that half an hour was spent mostly naked in our hayloft.

And during that half hour, Gray didn't take off my boots.

I loved those boots. But after our time in the hayloft, I loved them more.

I went through the back door and my eyes slid through the space. There were three dozen, wooden picnic tables sprinkled across the vast area beside the house, in front of the barn and beyond. In two days, these would be covered in white tablecloths with a bucket of daisies and black-eyed Susans in the middle of each one. All the trees were already strung with Christmas lights and there was an enormous kettle grill set up on a stand of bricks. And, in two days, seven dozen white and yellow balloons and a wooden dance floor were being delivered.

This was because in two days Gray and I were getting married at the church and having the reception, a big barbeque, here.

I couldn't wait.

Still smiling, I strode to the huge, open, double doors of the barn and walked right through.

In the middle of the aisle between the stalls, Gray had one of the horses tethered. He had on his own hat, a tight, white tee, jeans, boots and work gloves and he was currying the horse.

His gloved hand with the brush strapped on kept moving on the horse's coat but his head turned to me.

He looked me top-to-toe and when his eyes came back to mine, he grinned.

God, that dimple.

Loved it then, loved it the day before, loved it the first time I saw it and would love it for eternity.

I grinned back and wandered to Answer's stall. Answer wandered to me and shoved his head over the door. I wrapped an arm around his jaw and with my other hand stroked his nose.

He snorted.

Gray's horse loved me. Then again, I bribed him with apples.

"So," I drew out the word, "you want an early wedding present?"

Gray's hand kept moving on the horse but his eyes had strayed to my legs.

When I spoke, they came back to me.

"Yeah," he answered.

"It's a big day for Buddy Sharp," I announced, Gray's hand stopped but he kept the brush to the horse.

"Yeah?"

"Yeah. Cecily's all settled in Durango. Don't know, maybe she's planning a celebration for tonight since her divorce is final today. Maybe she's planning to dive into a gallon of ice cream. Doesn't matter, she's there and we're here. They also closed on their house today. Oh, and," I kept going, "Bud has taken a job in New Hampshire. He's packed up and he left this morning."

I didn't know if after Gray's crushing set down, Buddy got smart. I did know we didn't have any more trouble with him. This might have been because of what Gray said to him. But it was also because his hands were full.

Apparently, Cecily was done being the town pariah and she was done with Buddy doing more things to make her stay that way. She knew Buddy's play with my father and while he was making it, she took her already packed bags and her daughters and she drove straight to Durango.

On Christmas Eve.

She'd never been back.

And she'd filed for divorce, the timing being that Bud received the papers the day after Christmas. With all his machinations and her knowing about it, not to mention she knew he'd cheated on her repeatedly but, until then, turned a blind eye, he didn't have a prayer in the world of getting custody of his daughters. So he didn't fight it. Apparently she got a huge settlement and an even bigger child support payment and, word was, she was already seeing somebody.

So maybe no ice cream for her.

As for Buddy, Jeb Sharp heard about his son's Christmas Eve play and he was as done as Gray.

So he started to talk to his cronies. Then his cronies took his back.

So the day after New Year's, Bud Sharp went to work and was told immediately that he was required to attend an emergency board meeting. At this board meeting, Buddy was informed that a variety of ranchers, orchard owners, farmers and businessmen who held their money in Buddy's bank were threatening to pull it if the board didn't do something about Buddy. So they did. They told him they'd give him some money to go away quietly and asked for his voluntary resignation. Then they told him if he didn't resign, he was fired and they'd give him no severance.

Finally, in all his years, Bud Sharp did something smart.

He resigned.

He had been out of work for five months. This was because no one in seven counties would hire Buddy Sharp.

And the settlement with Cecily wiped him out.

Now he'd found the only job he could find.

In New Hampshire.

Which was a long, long way away.

Thankfully.

Gray grinned. "That's a great fuckin' wedding present."

"Yeah," I said softly.

He took his hand from the horse and turned fully to me.

"Come here, Ivey."

I didn't hesitate.

I gave Answer one last stroke and went there.

Gray watched me move.

When I got there, his arm with hand not holding the brush wrapped around me and he pulled me close. Then his head slanted and dropped, mine tilted the other way and, since we had a lot of practice, we didn't crash the bills of our hats when he laid a long, wet one on me.

And also with lots of practice, he was able to shove his gloved hand down my shorts and in my panties to cup my ass.

As usual, it was tremendous.

When he lifted his head, I asked quietly, "Want some lunch, honey?"

"Yeah, dollface," he answered and I smiled.

He smiled back.

Then he slid his hand out of my pants and turned back to the horse.

I turned to the doors but I felt his eyes on me as I walked so I stopped and turned back.

Yep, I was right. My man's eyes were on me.

"Okay, you walk away from me, I watch your ass," I told him. "What do you watch when I walk away from you?"

"The prettiest thing I've ever seen."

My heart jumped, my belly warmed and my lips smiled.

That was a really good answer.

So, still smiling, I turned and walked out of the barn to go to the house to make my man some lunch.

Two days later...

I had my hand in the bend of Lash's arm, my other hand wrapped around a huge bouquet of little baby daisies mixed with big, beautiful white roses and my eyes were on the doors in front of us that led to the church sanctuary.

"Nervous, babe?" I heard Lash ask and I looked up at his handsome head on top of his fabulous tuxedo.

"No," I told him honestly.

He grinned.

I leaned into his side.

His grin faded and his eyes grew warm.

"Love you, Ivey soon-to-be Cody."

"Love you too, Lash, my awesome ex-fake-boyfriend."

He burst out laughing.

I did too.

My music started playing then Stacy, Chastity, Macy and finally Janie strutted down the aisle in their gorgeous yellow dresses in front of Lash and me.

The wedding march sounded.

Still smiling, I walked on my high-heeled, fabulous designer shoes in my unbelievably expensive, exquisite wedding gown on the arm of my ex-fake-boyfriend who paid for both and I did this straight to my waiting, seriously gorgeous, macho man rancher cowboy.

Three hours later...

My feet moved on the wood boards set out on the grass to act as the dance floor, the song a slow one. One of my arms was wrapped around a pair of broad shoulders, one of my hands held in a hand that pressed mine to the chest of a beautiful man.

He swayed, I followed his lead and we danced cheek-to-cheek.

We didn't talk.

We didn't need to say anything.

This was because I knew Brutus loved me.

And this was because Brutus knew I felt the same.

SEVEN HOURS *later in The Brown Palace, Denver…*

I FELT Gray's breathing turn to normal against my neck as mine did the same against his.

He didn't move.

I didn't either.

We lay connected, my legs wrapped tight around his hips, his fingers laced in mine held over my head and pressed into the pillows.

We stayed that way a long time, him and me.

Mr. and Mrs. Cody.

SIX AND A HALF MONTHS LATER…

CHRISTMAS MUSIC PLAYING, a bay and rosemary candle burning, my hands kneading cookie dough, I heard my father muttering beside me, "Fuck me, I can squirt out a fuckuva Christmas tree."

I looked to the half a tray of perfectly formed, green-tinted, Christmas tree-shaped butter cookies he was pressing from the cookie press then I tipped my head back and looked at my dad.

"You're a master," I told him.

He looked at me and smiled his huge, wild-ass smile.

"Fifty-seven years on this earth, I learn my calling is cookie making."

"Worse callings to have," I told him.

"That's the damn truth," he told me then went back to pressing out Christmas trees.

Hoot Booker stayed in Mustang and worked the late shift at The Rambler so Janie could give that up after doing it for years. He lived in the room over the bar where I used to live. He didn't make a mint, he didn't live in a palace and he didn't care.

He didn't need much seeing as he was right where he wanted to be.

See? Totally my dad.

He was just like me.

He'd shared his story with Gray and me and there were no protestations of the wronged man. He had lived hard, played rough, did what he could to earn a living, not all of that legal and eventually found himself in a blood feud. A blood feud he ended.

But he did his time, a lot of it, and took that time to reflect.

And those reflections led to some decisions.

When he got out, he'd spent half his life in prison.

He wasn't going to waste another second on stupidity.

Lucky me.

"Right," I heard Gray say and I looked over my shoulder to see him on his cell walking into the kitchen eyes to his boots. "Right," he repeated, stopping on the other side of the table and lifting a hand to wrap it around the back of his bent neck and taking in his posture made something stutter uncomfortably in me. "Right," he whispered. "Yeah, thanks, man. Later."

He studiously stared at his phone as he disconnected, kept his eyes downcast as he shoved it in his back pocket and then, slowly, he lifted his head and his eyes came to me.

One look at his face, that something in me stuttered to a halt, stalling all my systems.

"Wash your hands, Ivey," Gray ordered gently.

Oh God.

Oh *God.*

Not today, not three days from Christmas.

"Mrs. Cody?" I whispered and Gray shook his head.

"No, baby. Now wash your hands, yeah?"

When I didn't move, stood frozen to the spot, Hoot's hand wrapped around my forearm and he murmured, "Wash your hands, beautiful."

I looked to him then to the dough. Then I rubbed my hands clean of lumps, walked to the sink and washed them.

I was drying them, turning and nearly bumped into Gray when I did. I had barely got my body to facing him fully when both his hands settled on either side of my neck, he bowed his back and his face was in mine.

"Fast, right? I tell you fast."

Oh God.

"Gray—" I whispered.

"That was Lash. He got word. Casey's body was found a week ago in Oakland. He'd been shot in the head. Cops don't know why. They're investigating."

I stared at him.

"Ivey."

I kept staring at him.

"Baby," he whispered, his hands giving me a squeeze.

Casey.

I closed my eyes, twisted my head and shoved my face in his neck as the sob tore through me.

His hands left my neck and his arms wrapped around me tight.

My arms did the same.

My brother.

My Casey.

Now really dead to me.

My body bucked with another sob and I felt my hair shift to the side then I felt my father's big, warm hand curl around the back of my neck.

And I stood in a warm kitchen with Christmas music playing, bay and rosemary scent all around me, safe in the attentions of two men who loved me as I cried for another one who used to love me, who used to be everything to me.

Until he wasn't.

Eleven months later...

The noise came on the monitor, my eyes opened to darkness and Gray's arm tightened around me.

"Your turn," I muttered into the dark.

"Yeah," Gray muttered back, shifted, kissed my shoulder and exited the bed.

I pretended to fall back asleep.

But I didn't.

I did what I did every time it was his turn.

I gave it time then slid out of bed silently, tiptoed out of the room and went one room over, a room that became Gray's office when the den was taken up by Grandma Miriam.

Now it was a nursery.

The light glowed through the opened door and I approached it, with practice, without a sound.

Then I peered around to see my man in his light blue, drawstring pajama bottoms, his glorious chest bare, sitting and rocking in the rocking chair with our baby son, Holt, cradled in his arm, Gray holding the bottle to his little baby lips.

Holt was my idea. Holt Cody was the only name I could come up with that was more cowboy than Grayson Cody.

I loved it.

Gray thought I was crazy but he didn't fight me.

I watched for a while thinking pretty much everything Gray did, walking, talking, working, sleeping, breathing, was hot.

But nothing was hotter than watching him feeding our baby.

Once I got my fill, I tiptoed back to our bed.

And, as usual, I was dead asleep when my husband came back to me.

Four months later...

A buzz of low noise filled the house as I walked down the hall in my tight, black skirt, my exquisite little blouse doing so on my fabulous, high-heeled designer pumps.

I moved to the sink and dealt with the dishes I carried, dumping the remains of food, rinsing them and shoving them into the dishwasher.

I noted it was full.

This was because there were a lot of people there.

I put in a tablet, shut it, locked it and turned it on.

Listening to the motor start, the water gushing, I stood with my hands light on the edge of the sink and my eyes slid out the window to the barn.

It was March. Next month, I'd need to plant my impatiens.

"Ivey, honey?"

I turned my head, surprised to see Macy standing right beside me.

"Hey, sorry, I was..." I trailed off then finished, "Sorry."

She smiled and it didn't reach her eyes.

Then she moved and I looked down to see she had an envelope in her hand.

I looked back at her.

"What—?" I started.

"She wanted you to have this," she whispered and tears stung my nose but I held them back, lifted my hand and took the envelope.

She wrapped an arm around me sideways, gave me a brief hug, kissed the side of my head then moved out of the kitchen.

My head dropped and I turned the note over.

My name was written in slightly wobbly, cursive writing.

I closed my eyes.

Then I opened them, used my finger to slit the envelope open then I pulled out the papers inside.

There were three sheets covered front-to-back in that same wobbly, cursive writing.

At the top of the first sheet, it read:

Ivey, child,

Gray told me you liked my preserves. I never got the chance to teach you how to make them and since Gray's great-grandma taught me and his great-great-grandma taught her, I best get on with teaching you...

Then for the next six pages she gave me step by step by step *by step* instructions on how to make strawberry jam.

All of them bossy.

My eyes went back to the barn as I clutched the papers to my chest but I didn't see it, it was way too blurry.

We'd put Grandma Miriam in the ground that day and I thought I'd lost her forever.

Now, I realized, standing in her kitchen, wearing her ring, married to her grandson, planning to plant her impatiens and holding her bossy letter to me, I'd never lose her.

Not ever.

"Dollface?" I heard and I turned my blurry eyes to the door, blinking and (kind of) seeing Gray carrying Holt and coming at me.

Then they got to me.

"Baby," Gray whispered and I kept hold of my piece of Grandma Miriam as I took hold of another piece of her by taking my son from his daddy. "You okay?" Gray asked gently.

"Mm-hmm," I mumbled instead of lied, curling Holt close to me.

My beautiful baby with his deep blue eyes with their dark, russet tipped lashes grabbed my hair and yanked.

I smiled a shaky smile at him.

Gray's arm curved around my waist.

"What's the letter?" he asked quietly.

I shook my head to get control of myself and lifted my eyes to him.

"Nothing, just Mrs. Cody being bossy."

His brows drew slightly together then his deep blue eyes with their dark, russet tipped lashes moved over my face. Then his brows relaxed and he gave me his tender look.

Then he leaned in, pulling me and his son closer with his arm going tight around me and he kissed my forehead.

Then he kissed Holt's.

Then his eyes caught mine and he whispered, "Say you love me, Ivey."

I leaned into him.

Then, through my sadness, I happily did as ordered and whispered back, "I love you, Gray."

And then I turned my neck, leaned deeper and rested my head on my husband's shoulder. Gray pulled us both closer and I aimed my eyes out the window where I could see our barn, part of our orchard and, in the distance, the purple ridge of Colorado mountains.

Holt fidgeted and gurgled in my arms.

My husband stayed silent with his arm wrapped around his family.

I sighed.

Four months later...

My preserves turned out *great*.

Two years, one month later...

I sat on the porch swing and watched.

Gray was standing with Norrie beside her SUV. He'd dipped his head as she lifted up to her toes in her cowboy boots and kissed his cheek. His hand was at her waist and from my place I couldn't see but I knew in my heart it gave her a squeeze.

They moved away from each other and she turned and waved at me.

I waved back.

She moved to the driver's side door and Gray bent to look into her backseat where I could see the thick, burnished blond-haired head of Holt who was strapped in a child's seat and I could also see Abel's near-identical hair where he was secured in his baby seat.

Norrie started up the truck and waved again as Gray backed away, not waving but jerking up his chin.

Then she reversed out as he turned and made his way to me.

He had to go to the stairs because there was a lush, thick, wide border of white, pink and red impatiens all around the house including the porch. He could leap it, I had no doubt, but he never did.

Norrie drove down the lane as I watched my husband move. And as he made his way to me, he lifted his hand, doing what men do for whatever reason they did it. He grabbed the bill of his baseball cap, pulled it off, flipped it back on, pulled it off again then settled it back on his head.

I didn't know why men did that and I didn't ask because I didn't care. Like everything Gray, when he did it, I thought it was hot. I didn't want to bring his attention to it because if I did, he might stop.

He walked up the steps and came right to me, bending low to grab his beer bottle that he left on the porch floor when Norrie came to get the kids.

She did this often and she did it to give Gray and me a break. But she mostly did it because she was a grandma who loved her grandkids and she was a mother who missed her son growing up. Therefore, if she could help it, she was not going to miss any more of her family.

This sentiment was shared by Hoot who came regularly, stayed long and, not as often, but it happened, took the boys off on some adventure with their granddaddy.

I grew up with very little.

Therefore I loved it that my boys had everything.

Gray settled on the swing at my side, immediately hooked an arm around my chest and pulled me into him, forcing my hips to twist in the seat as he pulled my back to the side of his front.

With ease borne of practice since we sat here often just like that, I lifted my bare feet and tanned legs, cocked my knees, set my feet in the seat and I settled my weight into Gray.

When I settled, my eyes aimed themselves toward the paddock where the horses were standing or wandering lazily. The sky was blue. It was late afternoon but the sun was still bright and warm. There was no sound except the whispered rush of a breeze in the leaves of the trees.

I sighed.

Then I smoothed my hand over the stylish (I thought) but still countrified, cowgirl sundress I was wearing, my hand moving over the growing baby bump that was my belly.

For a while, Gray and I sat in silence as we often did.

Then I broke the silence.

"What do you think about the name Booker?"

I named our first boy Holt Grayson Cody. Gray named our second boy Abel Lash Cody.

Yes, Lash.

Seriously, I loved Grayson Cody.

Now, we'd found out the baby growing in my belly was another boy.

I didn't mind another boy. The two I had were awesome.

But it was my turn to name our child.

"Booker?" Gray asked.

"Booker Frederick," I answered.

I felt him take a sip of beer.

Then he muttered, "Works for me."

Easy as that.

Works for me.

I grinned at the horses.

We fell silent again and the swing swayed gently.

Then it hit me I was in a swing when I first met Gray.

And now we were in a swing together on the porch on his house on his land.

Him and me.

"Baby?" I called.

"Yeah, dollface," he answered.

"Paid in full," I whispered and his arm gave me a squeeze.

"Say again?" he asked.

"You promised me by the time I left this earth, you'd pay me back. You should know, you paid that debt early," I answered softly then slid my hand again over my belly and finished quietly, "*Way* early and *way* paid in full."

Gray was silent and still a moment then he shifted and I felt his lips on my hair.

He shifted back and muttered, "Good."

I grinned again.

Then we fell silent again and swayed.

We did this awhile.

Then Gray asked, "Feel like headin' into town for a pulled pork sandwich and a coupla games of pool at The Rambler?"

I turned toward him and shifted up then looked into his beautiful eyes.

Then my gaze drifted up to the short, barely visible scar over his eyebrow.

I lifted my hand and, with a finger, I touched it gently.

Then I dropped my hand to his chest and my eyes back to his.

His were tender.

Yeah, oh yeah, I loved Grayson Cody.

Then I replied, "Works for me."

Gray lifted a hand and tucked my hair behind my ear.

Then he grinned, giving me the dimple.

I grinned back.

The End

Keep Reading for More Kristen Ashley Standalones

Heaven and Hell

After making a bad decision when she was very young, Kia Clementine finds herself in hell. Then, suddenly, within the time it takes for a shotgun to blast, her hell changes.

Completely.

Out of the blue she sees Sampson Cooper, her celebrity crush. A man the whole world knows is decent. A man the world knows is loyal. A man the world knows is good. All of these very unlike her now dead husband.

He's sitting at a table right next to hers. And she catches his eye.

Terrified of the interest Sam shows in her, Kia still finds the courage to go out with him. Not long after, she shares her dark secrets and Sam shares that he'll stop at nothing to gain her trust.

As Sam leads Kia to heaven, Kia realizes that Sam is living his own hell. But although he gives her beauty and she gives him everything, he withholds his trust.

Even with all the beauty Sam shows her, Kia wants it all.

But Sam forces Kia to make a heartbreaking decision and only she can decide: It's all or nothing.

Continue on to read an excerpt of *Heaven and Hell.*

Heaven and Hell

Prologue

Hell

The television was on and I heard him. Like his voice was a magnet, even though I wanted to avoid that room, would do anything to avoid it unless ordered otherwise, my body floated from the kitchen to the living room.

Cooter was in his easy chair watching it, and automatically, my body stopped nowhere near his chair.

My gaze was riveted to the television screen, watching the gorgeous man, with his white smile and intelligent eyes, talking to the sports commentators.

They were probably talking about football, something I had absolutely no interest in whatsoever. But I knew a lot about it. This was because Cooter lived and breathed football during football season. He was the quarterback at our high school, popular, hot—God, I'd wanted him. So young, so fit, so talented, so cool, so beautiful.

And, dream of dreams, when I was a junior and he was a senior, he'd picked me.

I was in heaven.

Three years later, that heaven turned to hell.

I heard a yapping but ignored it. This was Cooter's dog, Memphis, saying hello to me.

When Cooter got Memphis, everyone in town was shocked. Cooter was definitely a pit bull or Rottweiler type of guy, and not because both those types of dogs were really cute but for other reasons. So when he came home with a brown and white King Charles spaniel, I was stunned. When he proceeded to dote on that dog like it was his child, I was freaked. I didn't think Cooter had an ounce of affection in him available to give to anyone, no human and certainly no dog.

But there you go. He did. He adored Memphis. Completely.

He'd named her Memphis with the declaration, "Fuck the redcoats," like the English were still our enemies and him naming a spaniel after an American city would offend them in some way that would cause nationwide distress.

Then again, Cooter had a full supply of animosity for a lot of people, places, and things, and he kept it stocked up.

Not to mention, Cooter was the quarterback of a winning team in a small town that lived football, and therefore, he hadn't had to worry too much about books. And not knowing this then, but definitely knowing it now, he was scary lazy; if he didn't have to do it, he didn't.

So he didn't. I wasn't certain he cracked open a book throughout high school. But I *was* certain he didn't do it in his very short tenure in college.

Therefore, Cooter was not the brightest bulb in the box.

"*And there he is, folks, Sampson Cooper. Thanks for stoppin' in, Coop,*" the commentator said, and I watched Sampson Cooper smile.

My heart fluttered.

Sampson Cooper. Very tall. Very dark. Very beautiful.

I adored him. When Cooter was out of the house, I Internet-stalked Sampson Cooper. I knew everything about him.

Everything.

Well, everything you could learn on the Internet.

I knew his stats when he played college ball. I knew his stats when he played pro ball.

I knew the exact day he requested to be released from his contract playing for the Indianapolis Colts so he could join the Army. I knew he did this in memory of his brother, who had died in Iraq and he'd died a hero. I knew this upset Sampson Cooper greatly. I knew not long after he joined the Army, he'd disappeared "off the grid" for four years. I also knew when he came back.

And lastly, I, and everyone probably in the world, knew what he'd done when he was "off the grid," considering a tell-all (but anonymous) book was written about it and a big investigation was launched when it was. Therefore, I knew what he'd done was dangerous in a way people like me couldn't comprehend the level of danger. I knew it was also heroic. And lastly, I knew that he tried to keep a low profile, but when he found this impossible, he'd come out into the limelight and stayed there. I guessed he did this because, at least if it was his choice, he had some slim chance of controlling it.

"*Anytime, Frank,*" Sampson Cooper replied, his voice deep and weirdly rough—not rough like sandpaper, rough like velvet.

My stomach melted.

"*Babe!*" Cooter snapped. I jumped and my eyes shot to him.

Oh no.

He was getting out of his chair, and now, ten years later, he was no longer fit (in fact, he had a serious beer belly, which was only partly due to his copious consumption of beer; the other part was food, and the last part was being seriously lazy). I'd discovered he was not talented at all. He was definitely not cool. And he was anything but beautiful.

At the look on his face, my mind became consumed with what my next move would be. I knew one thing: I had a fifty-fifty shot at success. I could take a step back and piss him off more (for whatever reason he was pissed off), which would make it worse (but conversely, it could serve as a deterrent, snapping him out of whatever mood had hold of him), or I could stand my ground, which also led to both options.

Like often happened, I chose wrongly and my choice was to take a step back.

He advanced quickly, and no matter how much of a beer belly he had, my husband could move.

I didn't have a prayer to avoid it—I'd learned that—but still, I tried.

As usual, I wasn't fast enough.

He got close and backhanded me hard. With some experience, it was at the upper end of the scale of how hard he could hit me. I knew this because it hurt like a bitch and also because I flew to the side and landed hard on a hand and hip. I lost focus on the pain in my cheek when the pain radiating up my arm from my wrist took precedence.

Then he kicked me in the back. I bit back my cry at this new pain focus and thanked God he was only wearing a sock. When he kicked me, he did it no matter what footwear he was wearing, and since his job meant he had to wear steel-toed boots, I'd learned a sock was far, far better.

"I said," he snarled, and I sucked in a breath and stared at the carpet, "get me a fuckin' *beer*."

A beer.

I'd been watching Sampson Cooper, mesmerized by a beautiful man, a good man, a strong man, a loyal man, a loving man, and I'd missed my husband, who was none of those things, asking for a beer.

And he hit and kicked me because I hadn't jumped at his command.

God, *God*, I hated my fucking husband.

I stayed prone and kept my eyes from him. Again, it was a crapshoot how he would react to this.

Luckily, his presence retreated.

When it did, the beautiful Sampson Cooper was the last thing on my mind.

Heaven and Hell is available everywhere now.

About the Author

Kristen Ashley is the *New York Times* bestselling author of over eighty romance novels including the *Rock Chick, Colorado Mountain, Dream Man, Chaos, Unfinished Heroes, The 'Burg, Magdalene, Fantasyland, The Three, Ghost and Reincarnation, The Rising, Dream Team, Moonlight and Motor Oil, River Rain, Wild West MC, Misted Pines* and *Honey* series along with several standalone novels. She's a hybrid author, publishing titles both independently and traditionally, her books have been translated in fourteen languages and she's sold over five million books.

Kristen's novel, *Law Man*, won the *RT Book Reviews* Reviewer's Choice Award for best Romantic Suspense, her independently published title *Hold On* was nominated for *RT Book Reviews* best Independent Contemporary Romance and her traditionally published title *Breathe* was nominated for best Contemporary Romance. Kristen's titles *Motorcycle Man*, *The Will*, and *Ride Steady* (which won the Reader's Choice award from *Romance Reviews*) all made the final rounds for Goodreads Choice Awards in the Romance category.

Kristen, born in Gary and raised in Brownsburg, Indiana, is a fourth-generation graduate of Purdue University. Since, she's lived in Denver, the West Country of England, and she now resides in Phoenix. She worked as a charity executive for eighteen years prior to beginning her independent publishing career. She now writes full-time.

Although romance is her genre, the prevailing themes running through all of Kristen's novels are friendship, family and a strong sisterhood. To this end, and as a way to thank her readers for their support, Kristen has created the Rock Chick Nation, a series of programs that are designed to give back to her readers and promote a strong female community.

The mission of the Rock Chick Nation is to live your best life, be true to your true self, recognize your beauty, and take your sister's back whether they're at your side as friends and family or if they're thousands of miles away and you don't know who they are.

The programs of the RC Nation include Rock Chick Rendezvous, weekends Kristen organizes full of parties and get-togethers to bring the sisterhood together, Rock Chick Recharges, evenings Kristen arranges for women who have been nominated to receive a special night, and Rock Chick Rewards, an ongoing program that raises funds for nonprofit women's organizations Kristen's readers nominate. Kristen's Rock Chick Rewards have donated hundreds of thousands of dollars to charity and this number continues to rise.

You can read more about Kristen, her titles and the Rock Chick Nation at KristenAshley.net.

facebook.com/kristenashleybooks
instagram.com/kristenashleybooks
pinterest.com/KristenAshleyBooks
goodreads.com/kristenashleybooks
bookbub.com/authors/kristen-ashley
tiktok.com/@kristenashleybooks

Also by Kristen Ashley

Rock Chick Series:

Rock Chick

Rock Chick Rescue

Rock Chick Redemption

Rock Chick Renegade

Rock Chick Revenge

Rock Chick Reckoning

Rock Chick Regret

Rock Chick Revolution

Rock Chick Reawakening

Rock Chick Reborn

The 'Burg Series:

For You

At Peace

Golden Trail

Games of the Heart

The Promise

Hold On

The Chaos Series:

Own the Wind

Fire Inside

Ride Steady

Walk Through Fire

A Christmas to Remember

Rough Ride

Wild Like the Wind

Free

Wild Fire

Wild Wind

The Colorado Mountain Series:

The Gamble

Sweet Dreams

Lady Luck

Breathe

Jagged

Kaleidoscope

Bounty

Dream Man Series:

Mystery Man

Wild Man

Law Man

Motorcycle Man

Quiet Man

Dream Team Series:

Dream Maker

Dream Chaser

Dream Bites Cookbook

Dream Spinner

Dream Keeper

The Fantasyland Series:

Wildest Dreams

The Golden Dynasty

Fantastical

Broken Dove

Midnight Soul

Gossamer in the Darkness

Ghosts and Reincarnation Series:

Sommersgate House

Lacybourne Manor

Penmort Castle

Fairytale Come Alive

Lucky Stars

The Honey Series:

The Deep End

The Farthest Edge

The Greatest Risk

The Magdalene Series:

The Will

Soaring

The Time in Between

Mathilda, SuperWitch:

Mathilda's Book of Shadows

Mathilda The Rise of the Dark Lord

Misted Pines Series

The Girl in the Mist

The Girl in the Woods

Moonlight and Motor Oil Series:

The Hookup

The Slow Burn

The Rising Series:

The Beginning of Everything

The Plan Commences

The Dawn of the End

The Rising

The River Rain Series:

After the Climb

After the Climb Special Edition

Chasing Serenity

Taking the Leap

Making the Match

Fighting the Pull

The Three Series:

Until the Sun Falls from the Sky

With Everything I Am

Wild and Free

The Unfinished Hero Series:

Knight

Creed

Raid

Deacon

Sebring

Wild West MC Series:

Still Standing

Smoke and Steel

Other Titles by Kristen Ashley:

Heaven and Hell

Play It Safe

Three Wishes

Complicated

Loose Ends

Fast Lane

Perfect Together

Too Good To Be True

Milton Keynes UK
Ingram Content Group UK Ltd.
UKHW040756300124
436963UK00001B/105